A naked woman s\
in the West Palm Beac
the longest day of the
know who killed your \

Jimmy awakens from his beer-induced stupor and starts on a journey that will take him fifty years into the past to discover who he really is and who his wife really was.

A lifetime of deceit, misdirection, and lies of omission unfold before him as he examines his childhood from a new perspective, while his days as a hopeless dreamer threaten everything he holds dear, including his own life.

From Florida's Cocaine Cowboy-crazed 1980s comes an emotional roller coaster ride that takes the reader from the exotic mansions of Palm Beach to the shanties of Florida's back roads and deep inside the tormented mind of a long-dead, long-forgotten, literary visionary.

ensueño

(en-SWAYN-yo)
[Spanish] illusion, dream

A story driven by compulsion,
scandal, greed, lust.....and murder.

Set in Palm Beach......

Told in the noir tradition.

PALM BEACH.....
Balmy breezes, sunny days,
tropical nights, exotic women,
pristine beaches,
riches beyond belief.

A world so far removed from the
realities of life,
it's almost like...
...a dream.

ensueño

a novel by

FRANK EBERLING

*"The genesis of all art is the pursuit
of the irrecoverable"*
John Fowles

ensueño

a novel by
Frank Eberling

AUTHOR'S NOTE:

This is a work of fiction, however, it incorporates many real historical figures, events, and geographical locations. Great liberties have been taken with the above items in terms of historical accuracy and geography. Any resemblance of the characters to others, living or dead, is purely coincidental.

Ensueño ©1983, 1989, 1995, 1999, 2002, 2006, 2013, 2014, by Frank Eberling. All rights reserved. No part of this publication may be reproduced, stored in a retrieval system, or transmitted by any means – electronic, mechanical, photographic (photocopying), recording, or otherwise – without prior permission in writing from the author.

PALM BEACH FILM GROUP, Inc.
palmbeachfilmgrp@aol.com
(051913)

Printed in the United States of America
ISBN-10: 1500751766
ISBN-13: 978-1500751760

Learn more information at:
www.frankeberling.com

ACKNOWLEDGMENTS

Historical Florida photographs courtesy of
STATE ARCHIVES OF FLORIDA
FLORIDA MEMORY PROJECT
www.floridamemory.com

Additional thanks to Stetson Kennedy and Charles Foster of
THE FLORIDA WRITERS' PROJECT for sharing their time and
their memories with me.

THE FLORIDA WRITERS' PROJECT was a division of the
FEDERAL WRITERS' PROJECT from Franklin D. Roosevelt's
WORKS PROGRESS ADMINISTRATION, 1932-1943.

Two hundred men and women, including Zora Neale Hurston,
Veronica Huss, and John and Alan Lomax, roamed the State of
Florida collecting folklore, recording oral histories, and preserv-
ing for our collective memories a forgotten Florida of long ago.

I wish I could have been there with you all during those days,
but this is the next best thing.

As Stetson Kennedy told me, "We were on a great treasure
hunt, in search of nuggets of historical lore."

We are all following in your footsteps.

We are all heirs to your fortunes.

Frank Eberling

PROLOGUE

Where were you on the night of June 20, 1986?

You probably don't remember. If you're like most people, you may not even remember 1986. But I remember what I was doing on the shortest night, before the longest day of that year. I remember because I was kidnapped.

Kidnapping can take on many forms. Usually, it implies that a child has been stolen from parents. In my case it takes on an entirely different meaning.

Even though I was over thirty years old, you might say I was still a "kid." And I was definitely "napping."

As far as being stolen from my parents, I prefer to think they were stolen from me.

And what I was doing the night that I was kidnapped and what happened as a result?

I remember it quite vividly, because that night was the flash-point that ignited changes in my life that had been in the making for quite some time, without my knowledge.

Now, when I think of my "kidnapping," it's almost like it was......a dream.

CHAPTER 1

I sit, typing, filling up a canary yellow second-sheet with my story. The words flow from me and spill onto the page as effortlessly as if I had taken a razor and sliced the veins in my wrists and allowed the blood to flow onto the keys.

As I type in the darkened room, I feel his hand fall upon my shoulder. It is a touch of comfort, approval, love perhaps. He keeps his hand on my shoulder for a moment, then taps his cupped fingers twice, slowly, and walks away.

I finish the sentence on the page before I turn. But, by then he is gone. I walk to the door and as I step over the threshold he disappears into the darkness before I can call his name. I am too late. I am too late.

Then like a drowning victim filled with gasses, I ever-so-slowly rise to the surface and awaken from my dream.

JUNE 20, 1986:

The full moon in June cast a long shadow on Lake Worth as it rose over the Flagler Museum on the Island of Palm Beach. From across the water on the West Palm Beach side of the Intracoastal, I lay aboard my forty-foot Morgan sailboat, half dozing from my dream. There was not a breeze in the air, and as I stared dreamily over the water toward that mysterious, palm-laden island paradise, I kept waiting for the familiar lapping sound of the water against my boat's wooden hull. But the sound wasn't there. The water was as flat and still as a table top. As black and motionless as death.

I had been thinking a lot about death lately. How it comes so unexpectedly and leaves you with such mixed feelings: sorrow, regret, an empty longing than can never be filled; pain, and sometimes, even relief. At least those were the feelings I had felt about my late wife, Nikki: dead at the age of thirty.

I was trying not to think of the events of the last two months: all the changes I had gone through; the emotional turmoil, the "going through the motions" of work at school; ignoring my students and waiting for the school day to end.

Trying to forget about those Spring days was not possible, even now that it was early Summer and school was out and I had nothing to do but sit on my sailboat in the almost empty downtown marina and decide what to do with my life.

Suddenly coming into a lot of money is not all it's cracked up to be. Not when you were as confused as I had been lately.

So I just sat there in my sling chair on the shortest night of the year and stared out at Flagler's "Whitehall" and wondered what life had been like for the railroad tycoon eighty years before in the big white palace across my watery front yard. And still, there was no lapping sound against my hull. Not so much as a ripple.

Half asleep, I climbed down into the hold and pulled another beer from the box and rolled the icy bottle against my forehead. The cold felt good against my sunburned skin. One more beer in this heat and I would be asleep again before I knew it. Another chance to dream.

A yacht sounding its horn went by out in the Intracoastal as it motored north toward the Palm Beach Inlet. The bell on the draw-bridge rang, announcing its intent before the red lights started blinking and the black and white gates swung down and the steel roadway cracked open and pointed toward the black sky like a trap door. In a moment, the passing boat's wake would reach me and I would feel the lapping of waves I had been waiting for all night.

As I climbed up the gangway, the gentle rocking began, and I had to grab onto the rail to steady myself as I pulled up the ladder. And then it stopped and I was once again alone on the hot, motionless water.

There were only a handful of boats roped to the three T-docks in the Downtown Marina. Four months earlier, at the height of the tourist season in February, over one hundred boats had been moored, and the make-shift city afloat, made up of the finest boats from the North, had been a bustling winter community of its own. But now, the boats were all in their home berths in Newport, Providence, Baltimore, Annapolis and Martha's Vineyard, and I was here to sweat out the summer with the few remaining permanent residents.

I don't know how long I had been dozing when the rippling sound began somewhere out in the channel. I was so used to hearing the water break in my sleep I didn't think much about it until I remembered there was no breeze and no boat to cause it.

And then I could hear the coarse breathing, of what could only be a person, swimming closer to the end of the dock where I was moored. I sat up in my sling chair and squinted my eyes into the moonlit darkness. Behind me, no one was about on the few boats nearby. Whoever was swimming toward me was coming from out in the channel. Unusual. No one swims in the fouled Intracoastal, at least not on purpose, especially at night.

And then I saw it wasn't a *whoever,* it was a woman. She had dark hair and a dark tan to match, but even in the bright moonlight I had trouble making out her features until she was holding onto the rope attached to my dive platform. As she pulled herself up hand-over-hand over the transom, gasping for air, I could see what looked like a pure white, two-piece bikini. But then as she walked over to where I was sitting, spellbound in my chair, I could see it wasn't a bathing suit after all, just pure white skin with dark tan lines. I glanced down to the glistening black patch between her legs and then up to her white breasts and dark nipples and then to her face. When she opened her mouth to speak, her teeth were so beautifully white, I almost didn't hear what she said in a breathless, urgent whisper.

"I know who killed your wife."

CHAPTER 2

My wife, Nikki, had died two months earlier from what the Coroner's office said was heart failure caused by a cocaine overdose. Not too unusual an occurrence for 1986. And certainly not too unusual for a place like Palm Beach.

Someone once said that cocaine was God's way of telling you that you have too much money. That expression could have been written for Nikki. She had too much money and too much of anything money could buy. Not that she always had to use much of her own money for the blow.

But she had so much money that she did a lot of stupid things with it. One of them was to spend it on me the entire three years we were married. Another was to buy me The *ARIEL* for my divorce present. When she left me and filed for divorce, she was filled with such remorse for about ten minutes, that she also gave me a settlement. I guess it was to assuage her guilt. Some people say she bought me out. Others told me her real intent was to piss-off her father. She seemed to revel in annoying him. But I haven't yet found a label for what she did. Maybe when it comes time for me to spend some of the money I'll think of a label.

By a lot of folks' standards, it wasn't much. But for me it was a windfall. The settlement was designed to double my teaching salary for a period of five years. Theoretically, I could have quit

teaching then and still lived the same lifestyle I had lived before
we had met, plus pay for what I needed to dock and maintain the
ARIEL. What would've been left over would then translate to just
slightly above poverty level; perfect for a sailboat bum in South
Florida.

The real surprise had come later during the reading of Nikki's
will, when I was named the recipient of the trust fund her grandfather had set up for her: interest on the principle was three hundred
thousand dollars a year, for life, assignable to my own heirs. I
have serious reservations about Nikki "being of sound mind and
body" when she made out the will. In her last year, she was rarely
either sound of mind or body.

When you're a poor kid who grew up in West Palm Beach
and worked his way through school to become a low-paid schoolteacher, that kind of money can make you stop and think about a
lot of things.

Which was exactly what I had been doing in the two months
since she had died: I had stopped. I was thinking.

Mostly about Nikki, the poor miserable woman who had
dragged me around town for a few weeks, before we decided that
it was time we got married even though her father didn't like me.
I figured I would be a stabilizing influence on her. And I was, to
an extent. The extent that a shower curtain can hold back a tidal
wave.

We had met at *BEFORE THE MAST,* a local yacht club on
the West Palm waterfront where I had been tending bar at night to
supplement my teaching income. We spent that first night and the
next few nights together, talking, before anyone could warn me
about her and before I realized who she really was.

Her father, Hamilton Fletcher III, had been heir to his family's
lumber fortune which had started in the Florida Panhandle during
the Civil War. Her father had taken his grandfather's millions and
quadrupled them in his lifetime. Along the way he had helped
his younger brother, Nikki's uncle Danforth Fletcher, to become a

State Senator. Nikki could have spent a carefree life of leisure at poolside sipping mint juleps, or she could have become a corporate executive in the family business, whatever she chose. Instead, she chose to be a fuck-up of the first magnitude, and marry some poor slob of a school teacher from the wrong side of the Lake that her family despised for his poverty. I was not her type, they said. They were right about that.

For the three years that we were married I was able to spend money as easily as some people can breathe air. Life was a whirlwind of unmarked school papers, repeated empty excuses to my students, spending sprees, long weekend jaunts to the islands and lots of wasted time. "Idle time," I believe the rich and famous call it.

Then, after three years, Nikki kicked me out. Banished me to the *ARIEL* and to my textbooks and to my students who couldn't even read the books I was trying to interest them in.

I was too boring, she said. I was too studious. My "Little Professor," was what she had called me, whenever she wanted to ridicule me or whenever I made her feel guilty for not loving me like I wanted her to. Like I loved her.

All the while she snorted a line of coke up her nose the size of a pencil stub. "Just go read your goddam books. I want to party."

And party she did those last few months, from what I've heard. To death, apparently. At least that's what everyone thought. When the police found her, she was on a urine and vomit-stained mattress in some flea-bag, "ma-and-pa" flop house up in Conchtown, north of West Palm Beach, surrounded by a lot of cheap Fifties' formica furniture, free-basing and crack paraphernalia, and enough cocaine in her bloodstream to kill the first string of a pro-basketball team.

Not to mention the traces of semen found in and on her from at least three different men.

I hadn't been surprised by any of this when I had heard it during the coroner's inquest. After we split up, or who knows, probably before, she had started fucking anything that moved. The story goes she started with all her Daddy's rich friends. And then their sons. And then their wives. And then when they got tired of her and didn't want her around anymore because she had become an embarrassment, she came over to my side of the Lake and worked her way up the Lakefront to Conchtown.

And all of this time I sat exiled to life aboard my "going away present," trying to figure out where I had gone wrong......Where had I failed her? I finally found out the answer to both questions. I went wrong the first night I ever spoke to her and fell in love with her. Then, having made that irrevocable error, I failed her by never saying "No." By letting her push my face in the dirt at every confrontation, thinking it would help her. When you've been a schoolteacher as long as I have, trying to "help" others is part of the stupid, naive nature you develop. You get to the point where you are convinced you can help people like some of the students I have. Even people like the kind of person Nikki was.

But after ten years of teaching and three years of marriage to a hopelessly moral and emotional derelict, the "Little Professor" finally came to a brilliant conclusion: There's only one person in the whole world you ever have even a *tiny, little* chance of ever really helping: yourself.

Even then, that's only sometimes.

CHAPTER 3

I don't know how long I stood staring at the wet, dark-haired beauty who now stood before me dripping on my deck and developing goose bumps despite the heat. The only thing I could think of to say was, "Can I get you a towel?"

She nodded, and as I disappeared into the hold, she followed me. I moved tentatively, as if it were moments after taking a blow to the head, when you're not quite sure where, or how you are, so you do a lot of talking to yourself for reassurance. That's what I was doing as I walked to the V-berth in the bow where I kept my towels. What was this person talking about? My wife had killed herself. Oh, sure, she had probably been with a bunch of people partying when she died. People had probably run out the door, wiping their noses and pulling up their pants when they realized the party was over and it was time to leave before the cops came. But there was no doubt in *my* mind at least, that she had simply overindulged. Any drug worth taking was worth taking to excess, right Nikki?

And so who was this woman who had boarded my boat at nine o'clock at night by swimming across the channel from Palm Beach?

And why was she naked?

When I extended the towel toward her she made no effort

to cover herself. Her shoulders were held square and there was no self-conscious lowering of her eyes or crossing of the legs to cover her pubis.

But there was something in the way she looked, something remote that I couldn't quite yet identify.

Partly to keep from staring and partly because I was still speechless, I turned and cranked up the Mr. Coffee. Something told me it was going to be a long night, and with three beers in me fighting to put me to sleep, it was time to start the counter-attack.

CHAPTER 4

I'm sure what few neighbors I had at the marina were wondering what was happening when I started my diesel engine and left the mooring at nine o'clock. In retrospect, I wonder what made me leave that way too. It was not exactly what you would call the prudent thing to do. But then, I've not always been known to choose the most prudent, wisest path.

What prompted me to leave in the first place was that I was a sucker for the woman's story. I don't know whether looking at her standing there naked in front of me made me more susceptible to her story, but I bought it, hook, line, and sinker.

She had stood there before me, dripping onto my interior deck, looking helpless, pitiful, and beautiful as I got the coffee ready. Her naked beauty was humbling, and it stirred something in me I hadn't felt since months before Nikki left me; a primal urge most guys don't like to talk about.

And when at first I didn't react the way the woman wanted me to with her first headline, she repeated herself, but this time with a little more feeling, a little more emotion, and with what sounded like a little more fear. And so this time I listened.

"I know who killed your wife," she said again.

I was still stunned from when she had said it the first time, but I didn't flinch. I tried to sound nonchalant.

"What's your name, anyway?"

"Adrianne."

"I'm listening, Adrianne."

The chill was beginning to catch up with her from having been in the water, and she rubbed her arms across her chest as she spoke.

"There's these two guys, they wanted her dead because they thought she screwed them on a drug deal, and now they're after you because they think before she died she told you where the stuff was hidden. They think that you were in on the scam from the beginning."

I started listening real hard then. The woman began shaking again, but I wasn't sure it was from the cold anymore. She looked more strung out than cold from the water.

"What kind of drugs?"

"Coke. Lots of it. She was supposed to deliver it to them, and they think she changed her mind at the last minute and decided to keep it for herself. They started talking about it tonight when I was on their boat at a party, and then they said they were going to come and get you. They think the stuff is on this boat."

"Wait a minute. Who are these guys?

She hesitated a bit before answering, and that should have been my first tip-off.

"They're two guys from Coconut Grove. They sailed up here this afternoon to have some fun. They're over at the marina just south of the Royal Poinciana Bridge. The Brazilian Docks. I've partied with them in the past and I'm getting sick of it. I think they were the ones with Nikki the night she died. I heard them talking about it. When I heard them say they were going to kill you if you didn't tell them where the coke was, I decided it was time to leave. So I got up while we were all in the cabin fucking some stupid chicks and jumped ship. They probably think I passed out, or drowned in the head, that is if they've even noticed that I'm gone. When those guys fuck on coke they can go all night long without stopping. I had to swim because if they saw that I was getting dressed to go somewhere they would have stopped me.

"I know this sounds crazy, but I knew Nikki for a long time. We used to run around together a lot and she told me all about you. I felt kind of sorry for you sitting at home every night while she was out fucking her ass off. I just had to tell you. And now they're probably going to kill me too, for telling you. We've got to get out of here."

"You swam all the way from the middle bridge?"

"Shit, man, I got so much coke in me I could swim to Greenland and leave a wake. Come on, let's get out of here."

"Why do that? I can call the police and they'll be here in five minutes. Headquarters is just down the street from here. I've got a friend on the force..."

"NO! Don't do that please. Get me out of here first. I'm too fucked up. You've got to hide me. When those guys find out that I'm gone they'll know I've come to see you. They were going to come over here later tonight anyway. I got into an argument with them about it before and I stood up for you, I told them I didn't think you knew where the stuff was. Do you?"

I searched her face. She was biting down hard on her gums and sniffing constantly through her nose. I didn't think it was from her salt water swim. She looked as if she had taken a real blast before she had jumped ship.

"Why shouldn't I just call my friend? He can have half the force down here in a minute."

"NO!" Please, please! Just get me out of here. I don't want to have anything to do with the police. You gotta trust me on this. You gotta help me. It's the least you can do for me. They were going to rough you up tonight and I warned you. Just get us out of here. That's the least you can do to return the favor. They know where you are and they could be here any minute."

She was pleading now, heading toward that panic stricken state, that paranoia that some folks get after trying to snort half of

South America up their noses. I hesitated before turning to the Mr. Coffee to pick up my first of many cups that night. She stood there before me, pathetic. I thought about the view from my sling chair above us; a view down the length of the dock to the lighted phone booth. And then I thought about my own portable cell phone. Access to two phones. Five steps was all it would take. Just five short steps and everything would have turned out differently.

Maybe it was the two months of almost complete inactivity I had just passed through that made me do what I did. Maybe I was just trying to save a beautiful naked damsel in distress. What better ulterior motive? Or maybe it was just from watching too much television. They say it rots your brain cells. From observing my students' behavior in the classroom and judging from what I did next, I'm beginning to believe it's true. I put the cup of coffee down. "Okay, where to?"

"Out of here. Out of the inlet. Go out into the ocean someplace where they can't find us. Just get me out of here and then you can drop me off somewhere and do what you want to do; go to the cops, anything, just leave me out of it."

"I might have to buy you some clothes first."

She didn't laugh. She sat on the bed and continued to rub her shoulders. Her breathing was somewhat erratic, either from the long swim or the fact that her pulse rate was probably somewhere up around 400 beats a minute from all the rocket fuel in her system.

And so, much to my surprise and to the chagrin of my sleeping neighbors, I cranked up my diesel inboard and prepared to leave port. Outside on the deck I threw off the lines and then backed slowly out of the berth. This time of night during this time of year, I didn't have to worry about too much marina traffic. What few neighbors I had, up until the time I started my engine, were enjoying their stoned, semi-somnambulant state, dreaming about past or future sails, set to the tunes of Jimmy Buffett's greatest hits, content to spend this summer night in port.

I took the *ARIEL* out to the channel and glanced up to the

bridge attendant's perch. Then it was my turn to wait for the red lights and the clanging bell to signal the raising of the bridge. Ten minutes later we were passing Peanut Island and the Coast Guard Station and were heading into an outbound tide that would carry us out into the Gulf Stream. A fisherman stood on the jetty and cast his line toward the boat as we passed. I waved, but he turned away. I looked out into the moonlit horizon and made out an occasional whitecap.

An hour later we had reached the edge of the Gulf Stream a mile off Palm Beach. We started to pick up some wind as we came out of the inlet and I had to work fast to put up the sails. For ten-thirty it was still warm and as I ran around in the gathering breeze from out of the southeast, I began sweating out the beers I had consumed. The first few coffees would be over ice. Today had been the second longest day of the year, and there was still a line of orange sky on the western horizon at this hour.

The breeze and the sound of the lapping water I had been waiting to hear earlier had finally arrived. With the southeasterly that was blowing through my hair at that point, the best choice was to catch the winds and head north. That was fine with me, since I knew the perfect place to hide.

Of all the places near Florida, The Gulf Stream passes closest off the coast of Palm Beach. With its massive flow and strength, it can push any craft northward at an amazing speed at times. When the sea is rough and the sky is clear during the day, you can stand on the beach and see the swells. The natives have dubbed it "elephants walking," since from the viewer's perspective on shore, it looks like the swaying backs of a herd of elephants walking rhythmically across the distant horizon. The northbound current is so swift, so strong, that it carries all the way to Great Britain, warming the air above it, bringing a temperate climate to the island nation that would otherwise be blanketed in snow during the winter.

Ships heading south travel to the inside of the Gulf Stream, to avoid the strong northbound current. But off Palm Beach, where it comes so close to the land, it creates a bottleneck. During the Second World War, southbound cargo vessels became sitting ducks for the German U-boats which preyed these waters. A dozen freighters were torpedoed and sunk during a two month period at the peak of the German's success. The glow of the explosions could be seen from the balconies of the mansions on the Palm Beach shore.

A half-hour later we were heading across that Gulf Stream bottleneck in the *ARIEL*, me hoisting the sails, my visitor below, trying to overcome her case of the shakes. I set course with the wheel, studied the horizon for the lights of other vessels and went below to see how she was faring. Here eyes were red-rimmed, but she was still beautiful, and she appeared to have a troubled look about her.

"Can I get you some coffee?"

"Oh, no, man, I don't want to stay awake. I want to sleep. You got any 'Ludes?"

Her question took be by surprise, but I had to admit that I did, in fact, have some Quaaludes. They weren't mine, they were Nikki's. From her times aboard the *ARIEL*, before we said our final good-byes, she had stashed a travel kit. Or should I say a portable drugstore. It was a tiny canvas flight bag from some South American airline. Inside was the remains of some dope; a plastic bag with some twiggy stems and some seeds; a packet of Zig-Zag rolling papers; a large mirrored compact-like container with a razor blade and straw inside; and several bottles of assorted pills. I should have thrown it out when I first found it, but I hadn't. It's just one of those things you know you should do, but for some unknown reason you never get around to doing. Like cleaning out the garage or attic of stuff you know you'll never, ever use again in your lifetime. But there it sits. Bad memories can sometimes be like that, too.

And so I pulled the flight bag out from under the pantry

drawer where I had stashed it and opened up the brown prescription bottle of bootleg Quaaludes.

The woman's eyes lit up. "Wow, man. I thought Nikki told me you were a straight-arrow."

"I am. This shit was hers. Help yourself."

She took the bottle and opened it up. Before I knew it she had swallowed two Quaaludes whole, and was lying back down on the bed. This time a little more relaxed in anticipation of what was to come.

"Geez, thanks. These will make me feel a lot better." She started giggling. "They also make me hornier than shit."

"Thanks, I'll remember that in a little while when one of your good friends has his MAC-10 poked in my cheek."

She laughed softly again "You're nice. Nikki told me you were nice." She extended her hand toward me and I dismissed it with a brotherly pat. I tried not to think about what she had looked like without the towel.

I was starting to have an uneasy feeling about her. Maybe because it was just starting to sink in that someone might actually be out to kill me for information I knew nothing about. Or maybe it was because I just don't like women who are fucked-up on drugs. I'd had my fill with Nikki. There was just something about trying to relate to another person who is drunk or stoned or speeded out or whatever. Trying to tell them anything or listen to anything they say is a waste of your time. I'm not the type who likes to talk to drunks in bars or get into any deep philosophical discussions with anyone who is stoned. It's especially true with drunk or stoned women. I don't want to talk to them and I don't want to fuck them. Better an inflatable rubber doll for all my efforts at conversation, or whatever. Nothing like intelligent, coherent conversation to turn me on, that's what I always say.

It was even true of the lovely specimen before me now who was on her way to sleepy-town, judging from the smile on her face and the way she was cooing softly and snuggling in. She relaxed her grasp a little on the towel I had given her, and it slipped off her shoulder to reveal her white breast. I was tempted to reach over and pull the towel down even more, but instead I reached under the berth and pulled out a blanket and tucked her in like the good little boy that every daughter's mom knew I was. She was still biting down on her jaw, but she managed a semi-comatose smile of thanks.

I poured some more coffee over ice and hurried back on deck before the wind had a chance to change.

We were making good time, sailing on a surprisingly strong southeasterly breeze by the time midnight rolled around. If there were someone after us, they would now have to be in a power boat to catch up, even if they knew where we were going. But I had already decided, if there was someone after us, after *me*, the safest place to be was not out on the open sea where anything can and does happen on a daily basis around here. I didn't want to end up as some shark chum out where there were no witnesses.

CHAPTER 5

The *ARIEL* is a forty-foot, one-ton, with a solid lead keel that makes it slide through the water like a knife through butter. I'd had it for almost three months now, and was getting to know it well; all the ropes, pulleys, hardware that manipulate the wind that runs through her 350 square-feet of sails and transforms the energy to the mast and down to the hull. I had often marveled at the fine craftsmanship and the design engineering that could harness the wind so effortlessly.

A month after we had divorced, Nikki had shown up on my mother's doorstep down in the Flamingo Park section of old West Palm Beach where I was staying during my transition period. I had been grading compositions. She was tan and lovely, as usual, and relatively straight, given the late afternoon hour when she arrived. My mother had discreetly excused herself and left us alone. Nikki smiled and pulled out a set of keys on a tiny foam buoy and extended them to me.

"Come on, professor. I bought a going away present for you."

Going away present? I remember thinking. Who's going away?

And as usual, she led me like puppy dog to wherever it was she wanted to take me. This time it was to the City Marina.

My feelings about her were mixed at the time. I still loved her in my own stupid way, and even missed her. I had been surprised at the settlement I had received without soliciting. When I protested at the divorce proceedings, she had laughed and explained it all away with a shrug of her head and a "You deserve it, shithead, for putting up with me for so long. So just get out of here and leave me alone."

She had been laughing the day she had said it, but she was serious. I shouldn't really complain. She could have been her old malicious self. So I had been really surprised when she had shown up on my doorstep, back from her travels, with still another going away surprise for me. I can remember thinking at the time, "Is she subconsciously asking me to come back to her?"

So she had yanked my arm down the dock to the end berth, and presented me with a little trinket she had picked up on one of her foreign shopping sprees: The sailboat I was now navigating northward, forty miles up the coast.

At first I though she had been kidding.

"I picked it up at a distress sale in Columbia. Been sailing it back here ever since. Stopped off for a day or two in Puerto Rico and the Exumas for a little 'R. & R.' I didn't think you would mind having something like this."

I'd stood there, dumbfounded, not knowing what to say.

"Don't look like such a schmuck. It's all yours. All you have to do is sign the title. Come on, you always said you wanted a sailboat like this."

Instead of being deliriously happy, it saddened me. All of it. The fact that she bought it for me, the fact that she felt that she had to do something; give me something, to make up for all the misery she had caused during the past three years of my life. And the more I thought about it, the more miserable I became. In her month-long absence since we had split up, I had run through the usual gamut of emotions from shock, to remorse, to rejection, to guilt. I must have done something wrong. I must have failed her.

It was all my fault.

But finally I had reached a point where I had traumatized myself enough. I had tormented myself to the point of distraction, and was then entering the acceptance phase of the break-up. It had taken me thirty years of living and three years in a marriage cast in hell to make me realize one very simple fact of life. Here I was, a teacher, trying to prepare the nation's youth for life as adults, and I hadn't even figured out the easy stuff yet: Just because you love someone, doesn't mean you can live with them.

Whatever it was that had caused me to fall in love with Nikki had been eating at me from the inside out for over three years, and now that I had this sickly, hollow feeling inside of me, now that I was trying to recover from the weeks of anguish and growing bitterness, she had popped back into my life, smiling and tan.

I groveled at her feet; back for more abuse.

I had stood there at the dock and decided at that instant that I was going to accept Nikki's gift, no matter how crazy and exorbitant it seemed to be at the time. So what if I was taking advantage of a woman who might have been, probably should have been, judged incompetent at that stage of her life. Hadn't she taken advantage of me, humiliated me enough in the past three years to make me deserve whatever she wanted to give me to assuage her guilt? She *was* guilty, why *shouldn't* I rub it in her nose? It wasn't as if she couldn't afford it.

And so I accepted the boat. I tried to tell myself that I was not accepting it in and of itself, but as a symbol of a new beginning to my life. That night, at the dinner table, I told my mother it was time that I moved out and started living on my own again. I had only moved in for a short time as a transition; to help me get back on my sea legs again after my split up from Nikki. My mother had just smiled across the table and placed her cool dry hand on top of mine and repeated her favorite line from her play on her own stage of life. "Whatever you think is best, Jimmy."

Who knows what's best in this world? Not me. So I moved

out of my mother's small white stucco house on Mango Promenade, from the room where I had spent my boyhood nights listening to the planes from the airport take off over my head, and tried to begin my life over again for a third time. I saw myself as a swashbuckling boat captain, sailing off to the Bahamas or Caicos for extended weekends or summer-long cruises. Since then, I had taken The *ARIEL* out a few times, but nothing of the exotic nature of which I had always dreamed.

Then, a week after Nikki gave me the boat, she was dead. She didn't even bother to call and say "Goodbye, Jimmy. I'm taking an accidental drug overdose tonight, so I thought I'd call and let you know I won't be seeing you ever again."

So instead, I did nothing except exist. I went to school and went through the motions until the school year ended and then I just sat and vegetated on my new home in the Marina and tried to shake off my post-marital depression. Only an accident of time had made me a divorcee instead of a widower. For as much misery as I had been through, as much as Nikki was a truly disturbed person, as much as I had grown to hate her and her self-centered lifestyle full of debauchery and lack of self-discipline, I still loved her. I still missed her and every time I thought about her it felt as if my stomach was being ripped out of my body. I just *knew* I could make her change. If only she had listened to reason, we could have lived happily ever after.

CHAPTER 6

And so when a beautiful naked-mermaid-come-to-life, who claims to have known your beloved wife, approaches you and says she knows who murdered her, you listen. Even though something inside tells you that it's all bullshit, you still listen because we all believe what we want to believe in this life, no matter how stupid it may sound in retrospect. It was just a little something like this that took me from a beer-induced semi-stupor at nine o'clock, to a caffeine buzz in the middle of the Gulf Stream two hours later. All I wanted to do was sail out until I could get some straight answers from this woman.

In some insane way, I thought it might bring back just a little piece of Nikki for a moment.

By 1:00 in the morning it started to get a little cool. We had passed the Jupiter Lighthouse two hours earlier, its beacon slicing through the night sky above us as it had been doing for over a hundred and twenty years. Its vigil had been interrupted only twice in all that time: once by some overzealous Seminoles who were naive enough to think they were going to stop the flow of white men into their land by capturing their lighthouse, and once because the keeper had imbibed too much moonshine to make it to the top of the stairs. As you pass by, the Jupiter beacon is now deflected by several condominiums on the beach that were built

before the height ordinance went into effect, their proximity to the
light's source interrupting its sweep at angles, creating pie-wedges
of darkness that widen the farther out to sea the light is seen.

In another two hours we were approaching the St. Lucie Inlet,
and anyone searching for us would not likely think we would be
headed where we were. I checked on the naked lady below again
when I went down for another refill of iced coffee, and she was
snoring softly, oblivious to the gentle roll of the boat as we cut
through the sea.

The white and yellow lights of the beach condos twinkled as
we turned into the channel of the inlet, and once again we were
lucky. It was between tides and I didn't have to fight the treacherous currents that mark the inlet. I scrambled to lower the sails
and tuck them away as the *ARIEL* drifted slowly in the current.
I started up the diesel again, hoping the sleeper below would be
lulled by its monotonous throbbing instead of being jolted awake.
She was beyond all that. The Quaaludes had taken care of her.

She slept through it all; the trip upriver past Sewall's Point and
Stuart. Past the savannas and the grasslands and the sleeping cattle. And farther west, underneath the Thomas B. Manuel Turnpike
Bridge with its middle of the night hum of truck traffic high overhead. Even the clanging and gushing of the St. Lucie locks didn't
wake her as we made our way up the navigable canal toward Lake
Okeechobee. In the daytime the landscape is baked white, with
dull brown and green splotches. In the middle of the night it was
silent and black, the stillness broken only by the engine of the
ARIEL and the moo-ing from the residents of a canal-side cattle
ranch.

CHAPTER 7

By daybreak we had navigated through the underpass at Port Mayacca and were heading deep into the middle of Lake Okeechobee, toward Canal Point, Sand Cut, and Pahokee to the South. There, miles away from anyone except some bass and cat-fishermen, we would be safe until my mind cleared and I could determine what we should do. I could always put up my passenger at the J&J Fish Camp in one of the little bungalows. Then I could get a hitch back into town and go see Bobby about this whole thing. It was probably what I should have done in the first place, instead of stealing off into the night, disregarding my own well-being, for the sake of some stranger who didn't want to get involved with the police. Bobby would know what to do in a situation like this. He always seemed to have all the answers.

As the sun rose over my shoulder I was able to turn off the motor and hoist up the sails once again, with the breeze picking up as soon as we were out into the open water. By eight o'clock that morning, were out of sight of land, out in the middle of the largest inland freshwater lake in the southeastern United States.

Lake Okeechobee sits fifty miles due west of the West Palm Beach Marina where we had started. But I'd had to sail thirty five miles north to the only deep-water access, and then back thirty five miles southwest to get to where we were. I lowered the sails and dropped anchor. It was time for some fresh coffee, and it may have been the aroma that woke my passenger. She drifted up from her sleep slowly, like a log, long submerged in the bottom of a lake, suddenly freed and drifting eerily toward the surface, like I, myself, had done earlier that evening. Had she, too, been dreaming?

"God, what time is it?"

"A little after eight."

Her nose was still irritating her and she sniffled as she spoke. "Jesus, my head."

She stretched, and once again the cover slipped to reveal her nakedness, which she made no attempt to cover. I wasn't about to complain. She was up and out of the berth and up on the deck before I could say anything else. I followed, two cups of coffee in hand. I wanted to talk to her some more, to straighten out in my mind exactly what was going on, pump her for information, so I could make a decision as to what to do. I figured the coffee would help. That and hiding the rest of the pills. Maybe if I could get her straight, she would be more coherent, less confused as to what was going on. She might even consent to going back to town and talking to Bobby about this whole thing once she settled down.

On deck she stood looking off into the early morning sun. Then she spun around in every direction, as if looking for something on the horizon or in the water. "This is beautiful out here. I've never seen the ocean so flat. But it's hotter than hell. I'm going in to cool off. I hope there aren't any sharks around here."

"Wait!" Before I could stop her, she leapt off the deck, feet first, holding her nose like a little kid. She surfaced screaming, less than three seconds later, a look of panic on her face.

"Oh, my God! I hit something with my feet. Something soft and mushy. Get me out of here!" She was so panic-stricken she was choking, taking in water and spitting it out as I pulled her over the transom. She didn't realize that what her feet had hit was the bottom of the lake. She lay face down on the deck, catching her breath and then she turned around and lashed out at me.

"Where in the hell are we? This isn't salt water! What's going on here?" She wiped her mouth and licked her forearm, tasting the water again as if to reassure herself that it was, indeed, fresh water. She looked to the horizon in four directions and squinted.

I was quite taken by surprise by her sudden mood change. One moment she is fearful of sharks, thinking she is in the ocean, the next she is angry to find out she isn't in the ocean.

She looked up from where she lay, still naked on the deck, furious with me for some reason I still could not figure out.

"What's the matter?"

"Where the hell are we?"

"No place where you're going to have to worry about sharks."

"Very funny, shit-head. Where in the hell are we?"

Moments ago I had been an innocent bystander, simply trying to save my own life and a woman who had come to save mine. Now I was a "shit-head."

This woman, whoever she was, was beginning to sound like Nikki. I put the coffee cups down. "Why the hell don't you tell me what's going on around here?"

"What do you mean?"

"What I mean is, last night you told me we should get out of the Marina as soon as possible because two guys wanted to kill us. Correction: kill me. Now you're upset because I found a safe place to hide."

She digested what I had to say and decided I was right for the moment. I looked her in the eye. "You *are* trying to *hide* us from those guys, right?"

"Where are we?" she said again, ignoring me, looking around for a landmark. But there were none. No land, no landmarks. She could have been in the middle of Lake Michigan for all she could tell.

"You're in the middle of Lake Okeechobee. The safest place I could think of. Isn't that what you wanted for us?"

She turned, contrite as the realization of where she was came over her. "Yeah, I guess so. It just kind of surprised me. I thought you were going to take us out into the ocean. How far are we from town?"

"Far enough to be safe from anyone who might be looking for us out in the Gulf Stream. I thought that's what you wanted." I kept looking at her reactions, and it suddenly dawned on me that maybe that wasn't what she wanted, after all. Now what was I going to do? "Why don't you tell me what's going on here, anyway? Last night you said someone was going to kill us, and we needed to escape. Now you seem to be mad that we didn't escape to the right place."

"I guess now that I'm awake and I realize the seriousness of the situation, I'm kind of jumpy."

I kept searching her face for a clue to what the hell was going on, but I couldn't find a thing. "Why don't we just turn around and head back to town to talk to my friend at the police station?"

She jumped. "No! No, don't do that. I told you, I don't want anything to do with the police. You gotta to keep me away from them."

"I don't 'gotta' to do anything. What about me? I don't have anything to hide from them."

Again, she started to panic. "No, no, wait a minute. Let's think of something."

"Why should I wait a minute? I don't have anything to gain by not going to the police. If my life is in danger, I want to be protected. I want the police after whoever is trying to get me."

I could see she was thinking quickly, calculating, trying to figure out a way to do something. What it was, I didn't know.

"Look. Why don't we go back out into the ocean. Wouldn't it be safer there?"

"Not really. Not if someone is looking for us out there, or trying to hurt us."

She stood up, confused about the situation confronting her.

It was as if something had gone awry, some plan of hers had not worked out as she had expected it to, and now she couldn't figure out what to do. There was no contingency plan. She spoke as if in a daze. "Do you have some clothes I can wear?"

Concerned, I went below, and she followed. She had obviously lied to me about something, but what was it? I pulled a pair of khaki safari shorts from the closet. They were bleached out by the sun and were rotting through in spots, but they would suit her. From the closet I pulled a large white T-shirt with Jimmy Buffet's face on the front. I threw them to her. "You want me to turn my head?" She stepped into the shorts and I said a silent goodbye to her shiny black muff as she pulled up the zipper. She held her arms aloft and her white breasts, highlighted by dark tan lines, disappeared behind Buffet's head. She tied a knot at her midriff, scrunching up his chin.

"I think...I think you better take me to another place. I don't like it here. I ...I think I'd like to do some snorkeling or something while we hide out for a few days."

I stared at her in disbelief. "Someone wants to kill us, and you want to go snorkeling?"

"Sure, why not? As long as we're hiding out, the least we can do is have a little fun for a few days. Where's that bag of dope I saw last night?"

"I think it's time to go back to town."

She jumped again. "Wait a minute. Do we have to go through this again? I don't want to go to the cops. Let's just leave them out of it. We'll hang out and have some fun for a few days and then when the heat is off you can drop me off somewhere and then you can go to the cops. Maybe those guys aren't after us. Maybe I was just being paranoid. Come on. Relax."

She started moving toward me, seductively. She reached out with her fingertips and slowly pinched my left nipple. "I can help you relax."

I brushed her hand away. I was too confused by what was

going on to be even remotely interested. Someone was trying to kill me and all she wanted to do was make believe she was at Club Med. Something was wrong here.

"Let's review, class. Someone wants to kill you, or I should say 'me,' and all you can think about is having fun, getting stoned and getting laid."

She stopped and looked at me, angry her approach hadn't worked. "Nikki was right. You are a jerk." She turned and started pulling out all the drawers, looking for the tiny flight bag with the dope in it. I let her go until she got close to the drawer underneath my bunk, and then I moved in.

"Hold it right there. What do you think you're doing?"

"Relax, will you? I just want a couple of hits. What do you care, anyway? You don't smoke the stuff." She pulled out the drawer but reacted too slowly. I reached in with my right hand and grabbed her wrist and pulled out the .45 with my left. Her eyes widened.

"Jesus! What are you doing with a gun?"

I just nodded. I wasn't too terribly proud to have one on board. My purchase had been an emotionless, pragmatic move. This was the late 1980's and I lived in South Florida. To not have one on board would have been an unforgivable breach of responsibility to any passenger I might take out on the open sea. An assault rifle would probably have been more practical these days, but I had to draw the line somewhere. I didn't even want the gun I had. "I think you just better take it easy and go back out on deck."

I didn't point the gun at her but she went up anyway with me right behind her. "Sit over by the mast." She sat, looking about her nervously, as if waiting for some boat to appear over the horizon and rescue her.

"This is fucking great! I try to save your life and now you've got me at gunpoint. That's the thanks I get for feeling sorry for you and trying to help you out."

"You're not at gunpoint. You're free to up and leave any time you want."

"Very funny." Again she looked out over the horizon.

I sat and thought about what to do. "Why don't you tell me what the hell is going on around here? I'm beginning to think everything you told me last night is bullshit."

"It's not bullshit, I swear. Two guys want their shit or they're going to kill you. I just wanted out from under them and I came and told you as a favor, that's all."

"You swear?"

"What is this, Sunday School? I'm telling you the truth."

"Then why do you object if I go to the police."

"You don't listen very well, do you? I said..."

But I cut her off before she could finish. "You're the one who is not listening. I said I was going to the police. I'll keep you out of it if that's what you want, but I don't want anybody after my ass for something I don't know anything about."

"So what does that mean? We're going back out into the ocean and heading back?"

I didn't like the way she was asking the questions, so I thought about it a moment. "No."

"So what are you going to do, swim back?"

"No." No, I had already decided what I was going to do. I picked up my cell phone and made a call.

"What are you doing?" She leaned forward from the mast anxiously. "Who are you calling?"

"Sit back down." I waved the gun toward her, not at her, and she jumped back.

"Who are you calling?"

"Never mind. You want to stay away from the police, that's your business. But I want protection."

Joachim answered the phone on the third ring. My hunch was right. He was at home icing down the beer in preparation for the afternoon's Braves' game. Joachim was a big Braves' fan, showing up at Spring Training sessions at the West Palm Beach

Stadium whenever he could, and spending his summer vacation afternoons watching them play on Turner's television station.

"Hey, Jimmy, what do you say, man? What are you up to?"

"I'm okay. You feel like doing some bass fishing?"

"Sure, Jimmy, but it's gonna have to wait. The Braves are playing the Dodgers at home this afternoon, and I got a reservation in my Barca-Lounger to watch it."

I had been afraid of that. I lowered my voice so he knew I meant business. "Hey, Joachim, I hate to pull you away, but I need to ask you a favor."

"Sure, man, what is it? You got a problem?" He said it as if he were ready to drop anything to protect me.

"It'll take too long to explain. Can you meet me on my boat? I'm eight miles due west of the J&J Fish Camp in Port Myacca. Why don't you hook up your bass boat and meet me out here as soon as you can?"

"I didn't think you were a fresh water sailor, Jimmy. Hey, man, are you positive you're all right?"

"Yeah. Why don't you tell Maria you might be gone overnight? Kinda like the old days."

"Sure, Jimmy, I get you. But Maria's gone to Philly for two weeks. Her sister's gonna have a baby any minute. I'll call her and tell her I'll be gone for a few days."

What he didn't know at the time was that it wasn't going to be that simple.

"Hey Jimmy?" I could hear the concern in his voice.

"Yeah?"

"You want me to bring, 'Uncle Frank'?"

I had to laugh when he said that. 'Uncle Frank' was a code word we had heard in a movie one time. A character in "ALOHA, BOBBY AND ROSE," had called his handgun, "Uncle Frank," and ever since, Joachim and I had incorporated it into our vocabulary. I hadn't heard him use the code word in a long time.

"Uncle Frank? Sure, It might not be a bad idea to bring him

along, Joachim."

"You got it, Jimmy."

I hung up and turned to the young woman. She had been listening closely to everything I had said. "Who are these two guys meeting us? What's going on?"

I smiled to myself at her misunderstanding. "Oh, you'll like them. Especially 'Uncle Frank'."

It was to be over two hours before Joachim's bass boat appeared on the horizon. While we waited, I had tucked my own 'Uncle Frank' into my waistband uncomfortably. I didn't feel very secure doing it. With my luck I would stumble and shoot my dick off. But what really annoyed me was the preposterousness of the whole situation. Yesterday I was a depressed schoolteacher sitting on my sailboat in the marina trying to get over my divorce and the death of my ex-wife. Today, I was out in the middle of Lake Okeechobee with a handgun, trying to protect myself from some probably-crazed cocaine cowboys from Miami who would squash me like a bug because they thought I was hiding their cocaine. How the hell was I supposed to know where their shit was? Nikki never told me anything, let alone her drug bulletins. Welcome to South Florida.

I didn't like the gun or what it represented, but I knew I didn't want to be a victim in a drug war. So I tried to ignore its cold oily feel against my stomach and went below to get something to eat. It was hot in the cabin and I went forward to set up my wind scoop on the front hatch. I opened it slowly, thinking only of what was going on. As I opened it, I saw my passenger, her back to me, deck chair held aloft over the aft hatch, waiting for me to make my exit from below so she could bring it crashing down over my head. I pulled the gun from my waistband and aimed it at her. "What the hell do you think you're doing?"

She jumped so fast, she lost her footing and I thought she was going to fall back into the water. She put the chair down and hung her head. I waved the gun toward her. "Into the water."

"What?"

"Into the water until I can get out of here."

She sagged her shoulders in despair and took off her T-shirt and shorts. "In! Hang onto the anchor line until I finish making lunch, and then you're going to tell me just what the hell is going on. And no bullshit!" She disappeared over the edge.

"Are there any snakes in here?"

"Just water moccasins."

I made four tuna fish sandwiches with chips and pickles and brought the plates on deck with some iced tea. Joachim would be here soon, I hoped, and he was always hungry.

"All right. You can come on board again."

I watched her even more closely now, as I pulled her up out of the water. PLAYBOY Magazine should be so lucky. I couldn't figure out why someone with attributes like hers would want to get wrapped up with the two jerks she had described. Just another South Florida nose-whore, I figured. She came aboard wet and angry and reached for the paper plate like a stubborn child in mid-temper tantrum. So much for maturity.

"You wanna tell me now what this is all about? What were you planning to do after you clobbered me over the head, sail out of here?"

You could've hung potted plants from her bottom lip, she had it out so far. But her pouting didn't stop her from wolfing down the sandwich.

"I just want to get out of here before the cops come."

"Didn't you hear me on the phone? They aren't coming here. I'm gonna leave you here with Joachim and go to them. This cop, Bobby, is a friend of mine. We grew up together and I can trust him. I'll just tell him you don't want to get involved and he'll be cool about it."

"I don't want to talk to no cops. You can't trust them."

" You mean 'I don't want to talk to *any* cops' ."

She looked at me before she caught on to what I had said. She threw the remainder of her tuna sandwich into the water. "Fuck you, asshole. Nikki was right about you. Grammar lessons in the middle of Lake Okeechobee. Jesus."

Two hours passed before we heard Joachim's boat, and we both turned to the east.

"I thought you said 'guys' were coming."

"Just one. 'Uncle Frank' is that thing around his waistband. In the holster."

She didn't say anything, but watched his approach, as if sizing up her new opponent.

Joachim pulled alongside before he spoke. "You okay, Jimmy?"

"No sweat, Joachim. Thanks for coming."

And then he saw that she was naked. "Jesus, Jimmy, what did you invite me out here to, a gang-bang or something?"

Adrianne snarled at him. "Hey, you wish, fat-boy. In your wet-dreams."

Joachim stood erect and stared her right in the eyes for a full five seconds before he spoke. "Listen, lady, shaking your titties in this guy's face may be as effective as hell. He's recently single, and I'm sure it's like shooting fish in a barrel. But don't think it's gonna work with me. I'm a happily married man. So mind your manners or I'll snap your skinny neck like it was a pencil."

"Take it easy, Joachim."

"Okay, Jimmy. What the hell are you doing out here with the likes of her, anyway?"

I told him while he ate the tuna fish sandwiches. It took about twenty minutes in all, with him interrupting me between bites to ask me questions I still didn't know the answers to. When I was finished, I stood and put on my Topsiders. "Give me the keys to your Scout. I'm gonna go back to town and see if Bobby can do anything to help me out. You watch her and I should be back in a couple of hours. Watch the game on my portable TV."

"Okay, Jimmy. Tell Bobby I said 'Hey'."

"I will."

"Take your time and I'll watch the little lady here for you provided she gets back into her clothes. By the way, you got anything to drink besides that English piss you call beer?"

"I got a couple of six packs of Bud left over from your last trip out. You'll have to drink it over ice, though. It's under the sink.

"That's the way I like it, Jimmy. Show me how to work this TV. That game is gonna start before you get back."

I left them there.

CHAPTER 8

It took me an hour to ride the bass boat back to the fish camp and another hour to drive Joachim's Scout back into West Palm. The back seat was filled with his three kids' toys, scattered haphazardly like it was a giant toy box. An infant seat was for his youngest.

Joachim had been right about his being happily married. For that matter, so was Bobby. The three of us had been friends ever since elementary school when Joachim's parents had escaped from Castro and arrived in West Palm Beach with little more than the clothes on their backs and ambition enough to put anyone else's parents to shame.

Baldwin "Bobby" Starke and I had befriended the dark, curly-haired boy from the get-go, Bobby sticking up for him whenever necessary and me teaching him English and helping him with his schoolwork. None of us had any brothers and so we became surrogate brothers for one another.

We were just three lonely boys trying to make it through our childhood with the help of the other guys. Our parents were shadow characters for the most part. Joachim's parents were typical hard-working immigrants, trying to make it in their adopted country. Bobby's parents were struggling through the middle class. My mother worked as a chambermaid part-time, living off a widow's pension, my father having died when I was three. My father had earned his primary income as a hotel maintenance man and golf course greens-keeper. He had spent most of his life dreaming of becoming a famous writer.

Our boyhood days were spent fulfilling the South Florida rituals of those who had come before us. In our elementary school years we fished incessantly; from bridges, canal banks, and the small boats we were allowed to navigate on our own. In junior high school we got the surfing bug and spent summers in our jams, waxing our boards, bleaching our hair with lemon juice, hanging ten, and jumping from the Palm Beach Inlet Pump House roof on Singer Island. Older, we became mates on drift fishing boats that were filled with obnoxious tourists.

One night in the summer before ninth grade, we boated out to Peanut Island to camp overnight. There, on the east side of the island, on the bank that looks straight out the Palm Beach Inlet toward the ocean, in the spell cast by our firelight and a thick cloud of no-see-ums, we formed a pact, vowing to always remain loyal friends. We called it "The Secret Society of Coconuts." It was a watershed moment in our young lives. We knew in some abstract way that part of being an adult was to honor a commitment, and this pact of loyalty, of friendship, was as serious as we had ever been with one another. Ceremoniously, we looked out toward the darkness of the Gulf Stream, our arms awkwardly around each other's shoulders, and knew that our pact would be different than any made by a group of friends that had gone before us. This one really meant something now, and would remain that way until death do us part. The silence lingered for a moment before adolescent embarrassment caught up with us and we went to our separate corners around the campfire.

Things were different then, as different from today as my father's boyhood in West Palm Beach was different from mine. More than anywhere else, Florida changes. Once-empty beaches look more like Coney Island on a hot Fourth of July weekend. The site of a fifty-year old dairy farm in my youth now serves as home to twenty-thousand first generation Americans who roamed the boroughs of New York as children and whose own parents were born in the ghettos of Europe.

We stood by and watched it happen.

Later, the Secret Society of Coconuts became inseparable in high school, playing on the football team, scuba diving off the Breakers' Reef, hanging out at the Lake Worth Pier, cruising "Double Roads" in Juno Beach and bringing our dates out on the beach or the golf course to make out. Walking on an empty beach on a bright moonlit night in the middle of winter, sneaking onto the ocean-side Seminole Golf Course, and then lying down on Bermuda grass to make love with a hesitant but eager high school girl, is an experience you cannot really relate to unless you have tried it. Not really knowing what you are doing or if she will say "stop," yields a frantic desperation. As soft and endless as a plush living room carpet, the grass yields, rolls with your naked motions, while the stars look down from above, and the salty breeze off the ocean fuels your lust. It beats the hell out of a stuffy sofa in a freezing, knotty-pine basement family room in a Northeastern city, on a late January midnight. The vastness of the open sky arena excites, liberates and inhibits simultaneously, until the urgency of your motions takes you to places you can never visit in the back seat of a car. The first time it happened like that on the Seminole Golf Course, the girl I was with laughed out loud in a long, liberating moment of passionate freedom; giddiness. I was moved to tears by the beauty of it all as she doubled her rocking efforts above me. She was giggling with a happiness beyond control. Do women even laugh like that anymore?

You could say empty golf courses on cold, moonlit nights are among the things I really like the most about Florida winters. Odd they are never mentioned in the travel brochures.

When it came time for us to go off to college in the Fall of 1970, Bobby and I decided to follow Joachim to the University of Florida in Gainesville, where he had won a football scholarship for being the meanest mother-fucking center in the state. I've seen him knock two people unconscious in a blocking assignment during the course of one single play.

Bobby and I, being of slighter build, to put it mildly, ended our football careers after the high school game that closed the season. That last night, we stood in the empty locker room and reluctantly, as if performing a ceremony of passage, hung up our shoulder pads after that final game and let Joachim live out our football dreams for us.

We all went to Gainesville that fall with our own separate goals. Joachim was going to play pro football. Bobby was going to become a politician. I had some vague notion, not quite yet clearly articulated, that I was going to become a writer. It was a dream based on what little I knew of then of what my long-dead father had attempted.

Four years later, our dreams seemingly on permanent deferment, we all got teaching jobs back at our alma mater, Palm Beach High. I taught English, Joachim taught Drivers' Ed. and coached the football team to victory. Bobby taught Civics and went to night school at Palm Beach Junior College to study law enforcement. We all seemed to have compromised our dreams and settled for second best. Another part of getting old, I guess.

And where had another dozen years taken us? At thirty-three, Joachim was still teaching and held the state record for coaching winning high school football seasons. He had three kids I loved like my own and a wife, Maria, who I loved like a sister. *Viva Las Latinas.*

As for Bobby, he got out of the teaching game after two years and drove Road Patrol for the West Palm Beach Police Department for three years before being promoted first to Sergeant and then to Detective. With his ambition and street smarts and a few lucky breaks on cases, he had worked himself up to one of the hottest homicide investigators around. He had a wife and two kids. They didn't seem to care for our friendship, and so I ignored them as they did me.

Time marches on.

Baldwin "Bobby" Starke became remote, detached. Joachim Gutierrez got bald and fat. Another year of comb-over technique and he would just have to accept his looks or join that club of people who hopelessly link scalp hair to self-esteem. As for me, Jimmy Phipps, through no fault of my own, I got rich and lazy. My two amigos were happy with their lives and with good reason. In the last years of my own marriage to Nikki I had given serious thought to the benefits of ending it all.

Now, almost twenty years later, after the original pact between the members of the Secret Society of Coconuts, Joachim and I were still ready to honor those early promises. Bobby thought the whole thing was just an embarrassing boyhood memory.

Nowadays, members of the Secret Society of Coconuts who grew up together and promised to be inseparable, had little time for one another. Joachim tried to discourage me from marrying Nikki when the time came. Bobby was even more adamant. He had apparently heard stories about her for years. Both friends showed up at my wedding, tied for first place in the role of my best man, and both spent the day as if at a funeral.

Love is blind.

When you stay in a town you grew up in, one of your old-time buddies is bound to be around in just about every job imaginable: the insurance racket or the cops or politics. Bobby was a cop with political ambitions. He was a poor kid like me, from humble beginnings, living in a town where the only important value system is measured in dollar signs.

I had been to Bobby's office at the Police Department dozens of times in the past. Most of the earlier visits were happy times;

stopping by to pick him up on a Friday afternoon on the way out
of town for a fishing trip or a trip to Gainesville for a Gators'
football game.

My past five visits to his office, in reference to Nikki's death,
had been unhappy. It was a wretched time for me; the anguish
and guilt I felt over her death, the relentless barrage of the local
press. Bobby had been suitably mournful, but I could sense a feeling almost of relief when we talked about it in the days during
the investigation; relieved that I had been able to extricate myself
without getting hurt anymore than I had been. He had tried to help
all he could, as much as his position would allow; making sure his
associates went easy on me; keeping the reporters away the best
he could. But there was only so much he could do.

The Police Department in Downtown West Palm Beach is
across the street from the Courthouse. On the same site for over
seventy years, it was a dingy collection of patchwork architecture
as each generation demanded more office space.....more jail space.

Inside was the overwhelming smell of cigarette smoke, mil-
dew, and the desperate sweat of men and women in trouble.

There was a familiar face in the hall outside Bobby's office
as I approached, and the sight turned my stomach. He was forty-
ish with sandy hair and pockmarked face. His hair looked dirty
and he wore a wrinkled cotton sport coat even though it was
ninety degrees outside. Hal Burns, a newspaper reporter from the
Palm Beach Tribune, was auditioning for this year's Woodward
and Bernstein award. It was the reporter I had cold-cocked two
months earlier.

It happened the night they found Nikki dead and I had to identify the body. I had stopped off at my mother's house to say goodnight before returning to the *ARIEL* to handle my grief.

I had heard voices when I walked up the sidewalk, and wondered who would be visiting my mother at that time of night. Hal

Burns was in the living room when I walked through the screen door. He was drinking a cup of coffee and taking notes as he spoke to my mother.

"What are you doing here?"

"Your mother invited me in for coffee."

"My mother would invite mass murderers in for coffee. That's her nature. I want you out of here."

"Can I ask you a few questions, first?"

"Out."

"Where you aware of the activities Nikki Fletcher was engaged in just prior to her death?"

"You're asking me this garbage in front of my mother? Get out."

"There are rumors she left you with a sizable fortune. Having lived on a teacher's salary for ten years, how does it feel to be suddenly wealthy?"

"My wife is dead, you asshole."

"Technically, wasn't she your ex-wife? Weren't you divorced?

I crooked my right arm and swung my elbow, throwing all my weight in a round-house that was aimed for his face. He turned his head at the last split second before my elbow connected with the side of his temple. He dropped to the floor, unconscious. Blood ran from his nose and ears while my mother knelt on the floor, wiping it up with a dishtowel. The ambulance was there in three minutes.

Twenty minutes later, Bobby showed up. "Didn't I tell you I'd take care of the press?"

"He was in my mother's house, pumping her for dirt."

"That guy could die from the way you hit him."

"From the things he was saying to her, he deserves to die."

"And you wanted to protect her delicate sensibilities."

"Right."

"Who the fuck are you, 'The Catcher in the Rye'?"

"You said you'd keep the press away."

"Shit. Now I've got to fix up this mess, too. Jesus, Jimmy."

"You want to fix things up? Go down to the hospital and pull the plug on that asshole."

"You're a real funny guy, Jimmy."

"Yeah, I know. Having your wife die makes you aware of the humor in everyday situations."

"Shit, I'm sorry, Jimmy. Look, I've known this creep for a long time. Someone was going to clean his clock sooner or later. His boss even told me so. I'll fix it so no charges are filed. He was trespassing, you thought he was an intruder, right?"

"Whatever you say, Bobby. You're the fixer."

Now, when Bobby saw me through the glass partition he waved me through. Bobby greeted me with a surprised half-smile that quickly disappeared. "Hey, Jimmy, it's good to see you, man. I haven't seen you in quite awhile. How are you?"

"I was all right until last night."

"What's the problem?"

Bobby was trying to keep his professional demeanor and distance as long as possible with Burns just outside the glass partition. It was an easy role for him. In recent years his short temper seemed to have a shorter fuse, and even though we had been like brothers for thirty years, I treaded lightly in his presence. He had been fighting a losing battle with his weight until recently, when he had started an all-out exercise program to trim down in preparation to run for an as yet unnamed public office. His white shirt appeared to be tailored, and his wardrobe, formerly an off-the-rack job from JC Penney's, looked like brand new, expensive designer stuff.

I looked around the office where we were sitting, surrounded by the two other detectives on duty. I didn't want anyone else to hear what I had to say. I wasn't sure what I wanted to happen at that moment. I didn't even know what to tell him about the woman

Joachim was babysitting, back on the *ARIEL*. Would Bobby be able to protect me? I wanted him to use his authority, his power to make everything all right for me as he had during Nikki's investigation. Then, Bobby had risked reprimand by hand-holding me through the ordeal. His shielding me from the usual stresses under circumstances like those which surrounded Nikki's death, and his literally hiding me from the press, were the only things that had allowed me to keep my sanity during those days.

I told him what had happened in the past fifteen hours.

Bobby sat there as if in a trance listening to my story. He didn't so much as tap his pencil eraser against his desk top, a habit he had picked up in elementary school that I watched develop all through high school and college into his professional career. It was almost as if he already knew the story, or had, at least, figured out the ending of a movie long before anyone else in a theater, and was now merely waiting for the reels to unwind.

When I was finished he didn't speak for a moment. He hung his head and put his face in his hands. He was not ordinarily inclined to such dramatic gestures. Of the three boyhood friends, he is the one who showed the strain of his job the most. Besides the quickly receding hairline, there were bags under his eyes that were dark; evidence of too much booze, too much caffeine, too many years of sleepless nights. When he finally looked up to me to speak I saw something in his eyes I hadn't seen in almost thirty years of friendship; there was something else there, something I didn't recognize at all. I had known this man since we were both four years old. It might have been anger. He had never been angry with me, but now, it looked as if that was all going to change, like he might lash out at me for something I had done that was unforgivable. What had I done to anger my friend?

"Look, go back out to the Lake and bring the woman and the boat in. Tow Joachim's boat behind you. If she puts up a fuss, just tie her up to the mast and stuff a rag in her mouth. I don't care if she wants to 'see cops' or not. What some little 'shit's' wishes are in this deal are of no concern to me. Just bring her in. I'll straighten her ass out when you bring her back, ask her a few questions, throw a scare into her. I'll find out who those guys are. We'll try to 'get in/get out' before anyone knows what's going on."

He made a gesture toward Hal Burns that could not be seen from the hallway. "In the meantime, if you want this out of the newspapers, we're going to have to do this alone. That guy out there has been like stink-on-shit lately. Otherwise you're going to have to go through all the stuff you went through two months ago, all over again. When you get your boat back to the marina, call me up and I'll come down. I'll see that Joachim gets a ride back to the Lake to pick up his car. If you run into a problem on the way back in, page me from your cellular phone and we'll have a helicopter there in a few minutes.

What Bobby said made sense. There was no reason to blow this all out of proportion. If we could make it back to the marina without getting shot, I figured Bobby could work it all out from there.

"And Jimmy, tell that 'Lard Ass' buddy of ours to lose weight, or he's gonna have a heart attack out on the football field next season."

He said it with the conviction of the newly converted. I tried a laugh. On my way out the door, the reporter looked at me again, trying to act nonchalant. I avoided his look and walked away. I'd had enough press coverage to last a lifetime. My mother had been hurt by it all. My students had asked too many questions. I didn't want to go through it all again.

CHAPTER 9

I drove back to the Lake. If my timing was right, the Braves would be in the middle of the game by now and Joachim could watch the last innings as I navigated us down river. With a strong wind, we could make it back to the Marina by nine that night.

Joachim's bass boat chugged past the rim-canal and into the lake and out toward the *ARIEL*. Joachim and Bobby and I had spent a lot of time on his little bass boat at one point in our lives. Before responsibilities, before kids, before Nikki. It was a relic of our enduring friendship.

A long line of heavy black clouds was forming on the western horizon as they do every afternoon in June. They come out of the southwest, from over the Everglades, and force their way east with a deluge of summer rain before disappearing over the Bahamas. I would have to be real lucky to miss the thunderstorm.

There was no one on the deck of the *ARIEL* as I approached. I slowed and cut the outboard and still there was no movement aboard, although I could hear the screaming fans at Atlanta Stadium coming across the silent water from the television set on the deck. I could only think they had both gone below for a nap. With Joachim, that would have been the extent of it, and even then, highly unlikely at best. He was true to Maria to the bitter end, no matter who was there to distract him.

"Hey Joachim! Wake up!" I drew alongside and tied up the smaller boat. There was no movement from within. I sat there in the silent stillness.

On deck I could see the remains from the sandwiches we had eaten earlier and six empty Budweiser cans folded over and mashed from a 'Joachim crunch.' I got a sick feeling in my stomach like I was about to throw up, and then fear ran through me and I felt faint in the heat. I picked up the gun from the bottom of the bass boat where I had left it, and held it aloft. The sheer idiocy of my motions occurred to me, but I had seen enough television shows to at least allow me to go through the movements. But I was sure there was no one on board. I peered down into the foreword hatch to the new V-berth I had just built-in. Nothing there. I opened up the aft hatch doors and peered down the staircase. Still nothing. I reached over and turned off the television before lowering myself into the cabin.

Below deck, the boat had been pulled apart and clothes and equipment were strewn all over. Drawers and cabinets were pulled open and shelves dislodged. There were soup cans and empty ice trays at my feet. The woodwork had big chips gouged out of it. There was dead silence all around, and suddenly, at that moment, I knew my friend was dead. I leaned against the wall to steady myself and regain my composure. The still, hot air was suffocating me.

The thousands of things we had done together as kids and then as young adults crossed my mind and I was sickened. I thought of his three kids' toys in the back of his Scout, and Maria, in Philadelphia, helping her sister give birth. I lowered myself to the stairs and hung my head. What had I done? I looked up to the open refrigerator door and shut it and it was then I saw the note for the first time.

PHIPPS:
> *You get the stuff for us,*
> *we give you back your friend.*
> *That easy and that simple.*
> *Call the cops and Fatso is*
> *dead meat.*
> *Don't fuck up.*

My head started to swim. The heat in the cabin was stifling and I went above for some air. What I saw on the deck made me feel even worse. There were a half-dozen drops of blood on the starboard rails and side that I hadn't noticed earlier. They were dry to my touch except for a tiny spot of wetness inside a circle of brown crust. Good old Joachim. He hadn't been taken without a struggle.

I had to sit down again and think about what I was going to do. How would I be able to tell Maria what happened? How would I be able to face Joachim's kids?

I was sweating profusely, the perspiration running off me like a fountain and I got down on my hands and knees to try to ease the breathing in the heat. I looked down at the drops of blood as they led to a trail off the boat and into the water. My mind reeled with the possibilities of what could have happened. Could the woman have overpowered Joachim and somehow knocked him out? Maybe she called her friends and they somehow, came out here to the boat? Now they were getting to me through one of my best friends. Remembering what Bobby had said about a helicopter, I looked up to the sky. It was empty except for some turkey buzzards circling lazily overhead. I gazed down into the water, searching for an answer of what to do. If I called in the police, I was convinced Joachim would be killed, just as the note threatened.

The sun beat down on my head making me dizzy and sending a shimmering slash of light down through the water. On the bottom of the lake, beneath ten feet of water, I could see the reflection of a fisherman's discarded beer can.

I lay, staring at it, my cheek against the warm teak, watching the shiny metal below flash me signals as the waves above bent the shafts of light reaching it. I don't know how long I looked at it before I realized it was not a beer can, but something smaller.

I was back on the deck in seconds, having sifted through the debris below for my mask and flippers. I hopped in the tepid water and hung onto the anchor line, adjusting the snorkel one last time. The water was murky, yet clear enough to see the object below. I sucked in some lungs-full of air and dove. It was embedded in the rotting vegetation and sand, waiting for deepwater currents to cover it up forever. I reached down and pulled it toward me. It was Joachim's wristwatch.

Back on deck I looked at it carefully, scrutinizing the back plate.

COACH JOACHIM GUTIERREZ
From the Class of 1985
"That Championship Season"

The Twist-o-flex band was broken at the connection, as if ripped off in a struggle. Joachim wasn't about to take any shit from anyone, guns or no guns. I tried to picture what had happened. Somehow a boat had found them, taken Joachim and the woman in a struggle? Now what?

How could they possibly think I knew anything about any cocaine deal? I had only seen Nikki that one afternoon when she had presented me with the boat. That was only for a few hours. That day she was the straightest I had seen her in months. Before that I hadn't even seen her for at least a month, except in court. She had never told me anything. So who told them, two months after she was dead, that I knew something about hidden cocaine?

I tried to think of all the things she had said to me the last few times I had seen her, reviewing our dialogue over and over, searching for a clue to some hidden message. Most of the time she was so fucked up from partying, she didn't know what she was saying. It all sounded cryptic. At the divorce she had been with her attorneys, and had been friendly, but abrupt, as if she had other, more important things on her mind. I tried to think of what she had said to me when she took me to see the *ARIEL* that first and only time. Were there any hidden messages in her foolish, lighthearted talk?

And then I was hit with another wave of fear and recognition. Maybe she had told me something. What had she said? She had picked up the boat at a distress sale somewhere on the South American coast. Then sailed to Puerto Rico and the Bahamas. All I had to do was sign the title and it was mine. I tried to remember the name of the boat when I first saw it. *"Mañana,"* that was it. Was there anything in what she said to me? *A going away present,* she had called it.

I pulled a warm soda from the litter on the floor and drank from it. It was still somewhat cool from having been in the refrigerator. My mind was racing. How much cocaine were these guys talking about, anyway? A couple of ounces? Would they kill anyone for a couple of ounces? What in the hell did a couple of ounces look like? What was it worth? Could it still be somewhere on the boat? Would long exposure to heat and the elements render it worthless?

I stayed below, straightening out the wreckage they had made of my closet and berth space. Nothing was permanently damaged, except the scars where some interior shelves had been thrown against the teak woodwork, or chipped with a knifepoint. As I put everything back in order I double-checked every possible corner of the boat. Up in the fore cabin I checked every strut and panel. There was nothing loose, nothing hollow-sounding. The month before I had had to pull off some of the paneling in order to anchor the supports for the V-berth I had built in there. Each one had been attached solidly; no hollow noises or loose planks. I moved as if in a dream through the boat, trying to picture any hidden corner large enough to store contraband. I pulled the cover off the engine compartment and searched thoroughly. There was nothing. No space available unless it was beneath the planking on the side of the ship. I decided to take a look.

I checked first along the waterline and underneath the deck seam. There was nothing out of the ordinary. Taking deep breaths I felt my way along the keel in the water, a minute at a time, my lungs burning for air. I was exhausted from holding my breath. Three more dives would do it. The first breath took me down to where the prop was attached to the keel. There was nothing. Simply the fittings and the brass prop on the solid lead keel. Or was it solid lead? My next dive brought me along both sides of the keel looking for seams or cracks, anything that would indicate an opening to the center of the counterweight.

I rose to the top of the water and prepared for my last descent. I wanted to check out the bottom of the keel, which now hung hovering only two feet off the sand and muck lake bottom. I would have to swim down underneath the boat and look straight up. I floated on the surface, my flippers undulating in the water, my lungs sucking in fresh air to oxygenate my blood before my last dive.

I took one last gulp of air and dove, trying to forget for the moment about Joachim's probable, present condition. If it meant finding some cocaine for the return of my friend, I would find their goddam cocaine; they could have it.

Below, I grabbed the bottom of the keel and pulled myself forward and down. I lay on my back directly under the boat, only inches above the muck, the keel bisecting my sternum, my face to the sky. A sudden shift in the boat could have pinned me to the bottom.

And then as my lungs began to scream for air, I found it. In the bottom spine of the keel there was a five-inch diameter cylindrical opening in the lead. Inset in the lead surface, I could see what looked like a larger version of threaded brass floor-plate, the kind that cover electrical outlets embedded in the floors of school libraries. Bisecting its center was a slash for a broad-bladed screwdriver.

I rose to the top and almost blacked out. I hung suspended from the anchor line for five minutes, gasping for air before I had the strength to climb aboard. Underneath the V-berth was the scuba tank I had just stored away. Still out of breath I dragged it up on deck and checked out the regulator. The tank was full. The regulator worked. Back in the water I headed for the bottom again, this time with plenty of air. I was on the bottom before I realized I had forgotten a screwdriver. It was on my next trip that I decided to slow down. That kind of breathing underwater could be dangerous, and I didn't want any stupid mistakes to screw up my plans or put Joachim in any more danger than he already was in.

I descended slowly this time, but when I tried to slide under I realized I wouldn't be able to with my tank on. I knelt alongside the keel and unstrapped the tank. With the regulator in my mouth and the tank alongside me, I looked up into the shaft. The screw-driver blade was broad enough, but the plate itself was so deep in the keel I had trouble getting a strong enough grip on the handle. I had to go back up again for a pair of vice-grips.

Haste makes waste.

I had to slow down. I wasn't thinking clearly. This was my fourth trip below with the tanks, as a result. I was sick with anxiety and the events of the past eighteen hours. I sat on the deck for a moment to calm myself before descending for the final time that day. I couldn't let the events of the past eighteen hours effect me. Joachim's disappearance was taking its toll.

This time it worked. By clamping the vice-grips onto the end of the screwdriver, I was able to get enough leverage to turn the brass plate. I turned it three complete revolutions before the weight of what was inside forced it down and over my wrist, gashing the heel of my hand. I looked down to see the open white flesh before the blood came. It seeped out from the cut in a meandering crimson fan wave. But what was more important was what had forced the plate down. It was a four-inch diameter PVC pipe, sealed at the end with a cap, that had slid down from inside a larger diameter PVC pipe that held it like a sheath. The interior pipe's end was now embedded six inches into the muck below. The brass retaining plate was next to it, a chunk of my flesh from the heel of my hand still attached to the sharp, threaded edge.

I tried to lift the pipe straight up, but only by shoving my back against the bottom was I able to get enough leverage. It was that heavy. So this was it. Joachim's ransom packed into a long skinny white tube that probably ran straight up through the keel and who knew how far into the mast.

It took me another ten minutes with my bum bleeding hand to force the tube back into its sheath and force the plate back into position so I could screw it into place. By the time I reached the surface I was almost out of air and my hand was bleeding badly. My fingers were raw and numb from pain.

On board I wrapped a towel around my hand and hoisted the sail and pulled up the anchor. The black clouds of the thunderstorm were noticeably closer and the temperature was beginning to drop.

The diesel cranked over on the first try and I headed north, helped by the still strong southwesterly breeze that blew me to the St. Lucie locks in less than an hour. The southbound trip back, staying east of the Gulf Stream, took longer than I expected and I didn't make it back to the marina until almost ten o'clock that night.

CHAPTER 10

As with most childhood pals, in addition to the countless thousands of hours that bond the friendship for life, there is often a watershed event after which nothing can separate them in spirit, no matter how far their lives later diverge; no matter how deep a subsequent betrayal might occur. An event of this magnitude in some way chains you together for life. No matter how far you stray from that proverbial tree trunk during your life, there are still the spiritual shackles that will allow you to travel only so far before you have to turn your head and look back to the others tethered to the same originating spot. There is never an escape.

And so it was with Joachim and Bobby and me. We were by no means alone during our such event, but it served to cement what was already a lifetime familial commitment.

It happened in 1969, during the autumn of our Junior year in high school. It started out like any other year, with football practice starting ten days before school began in the unrelenting jungle heat.

As we expected, Joachim, although a Junior, would be on our starting Varsity line-up as the star center. His size and abilities had won the respect of even the largest, hardened teammates in the Senior class. Bobby and I starred on the Junior Varsity, chalking up win after win while awaiting our turn the following year when we would be Seniors playing on the first-string Varsity.

As that summer waned, we routinely stashed our surfboards, shelved that other obsession temporarily, and concentrated on football. We temporarily transformed our images from beach rats to jocks and lived and breathed the game those autumn days, as far out of the mainstream of regular school activities as we could be. As the weeks wore on, our Varsity racked up victory after victory. So immersed were we in the practices, it was difficult to put our winning streak into perspective. It all seemed like such a natural progression. First Seacrest, then Palm Beach Gardens, Boca Raton, Clewiston, Bishop Spellman, even the powerhouse, Lake Worth, fell in the wake of Palm Beach High's onslaught.

Our games were played on Friday nights under the lights to standing room only crowds. Being in the old downtown section, many of our players were third generation at Palm Beach High, and the loyalties ran deep. On each successive Friday night, the crowds grew larger and more demonstrative. Bobby and I spent each game dressed-out, yet warming the bench, watching Joachim chew up our opponents on both offense and defense. We were still part of the team.

Thursday nights we would all eat dinner at Coach Morrow's house and watch scouting films of the opponents that we would face the following night. Schools in Florida had just gone through the painful throes of desegregation the year before, and it was one of the first seasons in history when blacks and whites played on the same teams together, or even in the same games, for that matter. Unlike many other aspects of that painful transition, the guys saw beyond race and we accepted one another for what we were. We had all come to worship at the same altar: football. Our teammates reflected the ethnic diversity of our entire community as we sat down to share dinner. At least in this tiny microcosm, during this brief moment in history, the social experiment known as school desegregation and busing seemed to be working.

The last Friday night of the season, we were scheduled to play our final game against the feared Belle Glade Central. Twenty-five of the largest, meanest, dirtiest players in the State. If we won, we would finish the season 10-0, undefeated for the first time in Palm Beach High's history. The chance of that happening was "between slim and none," since they were a formidable powerhouse.

As usual on that Thursday night before the game, we took part in a long-time ritual. Coaches' wives prepared a gigantic fried chicken dinner for the entire team. Then, after an inspiring pep-talk from Coach Morrow, we were sent home at eight-thirty. He was a gifted coach, enabling us to reach down inside ourselves and pull out something we never knew existed. He brought out whatever was best in us. We wanted to win for ourselves, but we also wanted to win for him. Thirty minutes later, we knew, Coach would be personally calling each parent to ensure we made it home by our nine o'clock curfew.

An uncharacteristic November rain had been falling all day and when we all pulled out of his driveway, it had picked up with surprising intensity. We'd resigned ourselves to playing in the mud the following night, had even made adjustments for it in our game strategy.

But on this night, the night before the biggest game of the season, something went terribly awry. The first five calls Coach Morrow made to the homes of the quarterback, the three starting back-fielders and our high scoring wide-receiver resulted first in confusion, then dismay. None of the five boys had made it home by curfew.

Coach Morrow knew instinctively it wasn't in defiance of his orders. There was too much at stake for them to risk his wrath by missing curfew. He knew his "sons," as he called us all, would never disobey his orders. Leaving his assistant coaches behind to continue the frantic calls, Coach Morrow drove off in his car in a blinding rain to find his missing boys.

Thinking back, I remember the five star players laughing and bragging as they crammed into Charlie Tate's GTO convertible and drove off into the storm.

Coach Morrow arrived at the accident scene not long after the first troopers to arrive were setting flares along the big bend on Belvedere Road out by the airport. Another trooper sat on the ground covered with canal mud. He was bootless and stripped to his skivvies, and his face was buried in his hands, sobbing uncontrollably. Coach ran out into the driving rain to the small group of witnesses who had gathered at the canal bank.

"What happened?" he choked out.

A dazed eyewitness answered. "Carload of kids. Started skidding on the wet road. Lost control. Slammed off that concrete power pole before rolling over into the water."

Coach Morrow had to be restrained by the troopers from jumping into the canal. It was far too late anyway. In those days no one wore seatbelts. Tossed around by the spinning car and then careening off the pole, their scalps were filled with tiny shards of glass from their skulls smashing out all the windows like bellclappers. The car's impact with the water had knocked them all unconscious. All five died in a twisted tangled, muddy embrace, hearts filled with the hope of impending victory.

Mickey Perez, halfback;
Darville Roberts, quarterback;
Roland Pinder, halfback;
Calvin Jones, fullback;
Charlie Tate, wide receiver.

One Cuban, two Conchs, a black kid and a white kid; all newfound friends. All with locked-in football scholarships starting the following fall. All dead at the age of seventeen.

Word spread quickly through town, and by the time the bodies were pulled from the wreckage an hour later, over four hundred people were standing on the canal bank in the pouring rain, including the remainder of the team, all of our parents and the students who had heard about what happened.

Friday night's game with Belle Glade Central was postponed one week. We buried them all on Monday.

Tuesday, Wednesday, Thursday and Friday of that week the team was excused from regular classes and we met in a basement classroom behind locked doors.

The first meeting began Tuesday morning in stunned silence while awaiting Coach Morrow's arrival. He walked in carrying a cardboard box and stood before us, a man who had aged a hundred years over the past weekend. He paced quietly, fighting desperately to maintain his composure before starting. A deep-nosed sniffle broke the silence and he looked up to address the boy in the rear corner of the room who fought to hold back his tears.

"Willie…..You other boys…..I loved our lost friends like they were my own sons. But I'm going to ask you today to hold back on your tears until after Friday night. I know I don't have to tell you why we have to win that game. What I do have to tell you is *how* we're going to do it."

With that, Coach Morrow passed out copies of a sixty-page folder to the twenty-five players in the room. It had materialized over the weekend.

"What goes on here in this room over these next few days, never leaves this room. Never. I need your promise on that, boys."

As he began, Joachim and Bobby and I exchanged glances.

That Coach Morrow was a fine football coach we had never once doubted. What we didn't know was that he was a brilliant strategist in more than just football.

All day, every day that week, we remained locked behind closed doors in that classroom in the school basement. Parents brought clean clothing and sleeping bags for us so we could sleep on the gym floor. Each evening they cooked our meals in the cafeteria, and when they left, we ran plays in our socks and gym shorts until midnight. I can still hear the muffled thumping of our feet on the varnished wood; the hoarse snorting of heavy breathing and the padded pounding of our choreography.

Each morning at six a.m. we showered again in the locker room before spending another twelve hours behind locked doors in the basement classroom. Then it was dinner and back to running plays on the gym floor.

Friday afternoon school let out early for a mandatory pep rally in the gymnasium. The Thursday afternoon a week earlier, in anticipation of the Belle Glade game, there had been another pep rally, with wild cheering accompanied by a raucous cacophony of marching band music to celebrate the last game of the season that had been postponed. But that past Monday, that same gym had been packed once again for the memorial service for our fallen warriors.

Now, the packed gym held a confused, eerie silence as the students waited for the rally to begin. At the coach's request, the cheerleaders remained seated at the bleachers' edge. At the far end of the gym, on the stage, a microphone had been set up. Hanging above, suspended from the proscenium arch with black thread as to be invisible, were the five jerseys of our fallen comrades. The team walked from the wings and stood at parade rest wearing sneakers, jeans and our jerseys. Coach Morrow walked up to the microphone and looked out over the crowd. A week's worth of sleepless nights had taken its toll on him. He looked up at the fifteen hundred faces. He cleared his throat once, twice.

"Tonight at eight o'clock, the finest football team I have ever had the honor of coaching, is going to defeat Belle Glade Central on their own field. We would all be honored if each and every one of you and all your parents were there to support them."

With that, he turned abruptly and looked at his team before his footsteps echoed through the silent gym and he walked out the side door. The pep rally ended in less than sixty seconds.

An hour later we boarded the bus in another November downpour. The drive to Belle Glade on the narrow, two-lane State Road 80 back then was treacherous even on a good day. Built during the Thirties on soft sand and shell-rock, and traveled heavily by sugar cane trucks all day, the surface was like corduroy. It was lined on both sides by canals and on the north shoulder a straight line of Australian Pines stretched for twenty miles, towering over the road. On this late afternoon, the driver never got beyond third gear the whole trip. Not a word passed between anyone during the drive west. As we drove over the bridge at Twenty Mile Bend, the storm intensified and if there had been a place to pull over on the narrow road without falling into the canal, the driver would have. But there wasn't and we hydroplaned through the afternoon darkness.

When we arrived almost two hours later, the rain had stopped, but the field was soaked. A backhoe was digging a trench from along the sidelines and over to a nearby drainage canal to help siphon the water off the field. Even if it didn't rain again this evening, the field we would be playing on would truly be a swamp.

At 7:45 when we emerged from the locker room, we looked up to see the entire Visiting Team side of the bleachers filled to capacity with fans who had driven from West Palm Beach through the torrents to show their support. Upon seeing us emerge, the crowd stood on its feet and stared in rapt attention. But unlike every other game, we didn't race onto the field screaming our heads off. We walked sedately, businesslike, to the bench and sat down. Our opponents looked at us with confused faces and jeered. Was our fear evident?

There was no pre-game banter and ass-slapping on our team. We had come with a job to do, and now it was time to deliver. We stood shoulder to shoulder in silence. During our stay in the locker room the temperature had dropped twenty degrees. We were used to playing in the stifling heat.

At the coin toss Belle Glade won and elected to kick-off, just as Coach Morrow had told us they would. If we had won, we would have elected to receive.

As we faced our opponents, it was obvious they outsized us and outweighed us. Belle Glade's sons were sweet-corn-fed farm boys who were born huge and grew bigger. No one watching at that point would have given our team a chance. Anyone outside our school who was unaware of what had transpired that week in the basement, would just assume that we were there to receive our inevitable trouncing as a matter of duty.

Ronnie Sistrunk caught the kick-off and ran the ball straight down the middle for twenty yards before he was stopped by a brutal double tackle that had our opponents high-fiving it. They cavalierly congratulated themselves and laughed with condescension, taking their time to line up at the scrimmage line. Then, almost immediately, the laughter from the Belle Glade team stopped.

Without a huddle and without even signals being called, we took our stances on the scrimmage line and ran the ball three plays in immediate succession down to Belle Glade's fifteen yard line. In frustration their head coach ran onto the field screaming for a time out. The players were dumbfounded and looked to their coach as if to say, "they can't do that."

Coach Morrow walked onto the field with a copy of the rule book. The referee read a highlighted portion and related the news to Belle Glade's coach. "It is not required to have a huddle or for the quarterback to call signals to start a play." Livid, Belle Glade's coach screamed for his boys to "pay attention," and play continued.

The next three plays were long counts and defensive off-sides penalties brought us down to the three-yard line. Belle Glade's defense scrambled for a goal-line stand, but it was too late. Before Baldwin Bobby Starke even got close to Joachim's backside and bent over, he stood still for the required split-second and Joachim hiked the ball to him. Bobby took two steps back and lobbed a pass to me as I cut in toward the goalpost. We had scored in the first two-minute drive of the game. The Palm Beach fans went wild, perhaps more out of surprise than anything else, but our offense marched silently to the bench as our defense walked to their kick-off positions.

After that, there was no stopping our offense. It unnerved their defense not to have us huddle and not to hear Bobby's count on the line. Every short count still had their defense scrambling in confusion to be ready at the scrimmage line and on every long count we picked up five yards for off-sides penalties.

Again the Belle Glade coach called a time out and gestured wildly to an unswerving referee. "Unorthodox, yes," the referee conceded, "but it was legal and it was fair."

In their frustration, Belle Glade started playing dirty, and with their penalty yardage tacked on, we were picking up fifteen yards in addition to what each play ran.

I've since seen the scouting films of that game and to watch the choreography of our offense is to watch a never-ending ballet. Their exasperated defense kept shrugging their shoulders and looking to their coach for advice. But he could offer none. He had never seen anything like it. In all, during the first half, we ran 75 offensive plays without a huddle and with no signals being called by the quarterback from the line of scrimmage.

The most frustrating aspect of our offensive effort was that neither Belle Glade's coach, his team nor fans from either side could figure out how we were doing it. To our opponents, it was as if each of us were telepathic. Even the referees made Bobby and the backfield players remove their helmets to look for radio receivers.

Our defense was not as lucky. For every touchdown we scored, Belle Glade mowed over our defense. Between the disparity of their offense and our defense and the conditions of the field, we were leading at the end of the first quarter 28-27. With the ball hiked from Joachim to Bobby and then passed to me, I scored the first three touchdowns of my Varsity career in just twelve minutes.

By half-time we were leading 60-59. It appeared that fighting was about to break out in the stands. The dirty players' fans thought our tactics were dirty, maybe even communist, or at least un-American. But the arrival of twenty state troopers and sheriff's deputies and a light drizzle seemed to quiet them down.

In the locker room at half-time we looked like drowned mud-rats. We sat panting, too exhausted to speak. We had taken Coach's plan on faith, and now we had been bathed in the river. Coach Morrow walked in and paced. "It's working, boys. Stay with me and think.....Think."

The rest of the fifteen minutes passed in another palpable silence before we walked out onto the field.

The rain was now a steady drizzle as we kicked-off to them. Joachim hammered the star receiver and took him out of the game. It was a clean hit.

On the next play, he took out the quarterback. Another clean hit that managed to break the quarterback's arm. The second-string quarterback was brought in. He was good, but he telegraphed his plays and other times he was so rattled, he left the center before taking possession of the hike. A fumble recovery by us led another non-stop assault downfield. A series of ten running plays executed without huddles or audible calls from the quarterback brought us another six points.

And on it went. We moved as if automatons. I had a sense of separation, as if I were standing on the sidelines watching myself play. By the end of the fourth quarter, we were simply wearing down their morale. They couldn't cope with a team that played in total silence, never huddled, never called signals. When the jeering and playing dirty didn't work and with their off-sides penalties mounting, they gave up. When the final buzzer went off, we were ahead 98–86, one of the highest scoring games in Florida high school football history. The Joachim-to-Bobby-to-me combination had enabled me to score twelve touchdowns in my first

Varsity game.

As we walked off the field in silence, three thousand supporters who had driven through the torrential downpour from West Palm Beach to watch us pay tribute to our fallen friends, stood to honor us. I scanned the crowd and caught a glimpse of my mother staring down at me, flanked by Joachim's parents on one side and Bobby's parents on the other. I could tell she was proud, but I also knew she was thinking something else.

With our job now over, the ride home on the bus brought us back to our own private memories of our dead friends. We had accomplished the impossible through Coach Morrow's strategies, his faith in us, and the faith we had found in ourselves that we had dredged up from the pain in our guts that week.

It wasn't until months later that we all came to the realization that Coach's plan, however brilliant, was really devised as a defense mechanism for us to cope with the pain of losing so many friends at once. Instead of allowing us to drown in our sorrows that first week of loss, he had immersed us in the task that lie ahead. Outlined on the pages he had passed out that first day of the secret practice sessions had been two hundred random plays that we had memorized, verbatim, including the precise signal count that accompanied each one. So intent had we been on learning the game plan that we had no time to mourn. So focused had been our concentration that we never missed a call, never missed a block, never confused a play or fumbled the wet ball. Every hand-off, every lateral, every pass, every pull, every fake, every reverse, every screen pass had been perfectly executed, and all from memory.

To a boy, we've all honored his request that no further details ever leave that basement classroom. But now that it was over we knew the mourning was about to begin.

To this day, if you asked any of the surviving members of that team of twenty-five to recite the plays in order with the counts, I have no doubt that any of them could still do it after all these years.

At midnight that Friday night after the game, the three of us drove up to Double Roads and parked along the sea grape overlooking the ocean. The rain had stopped on the bus trip back home as we had crossed east over the Range Line, and now the stars were peeking through the clouds and there was a chill in the air. A hundred feet below us the surf roared lazily. There is something about that sound that is soothing, comforting. In many ways, that familiar roar is what makes this my home. We had parked here a million days and nights before and listened to the hypnotic whispers of the surf.

The ocean had always drawn us to it whenever an important event transpired. It seemed that every one of our short life's milestones up to that evening had ended at one beach or another. When we were kids we rode our bikes across the bridge to Palm Beach and sat on the seawall to discuss whatever incident had drawn us there. When we were old enough to drive, we always came to Double Roads in Juno Beach. Whatever power the surf had that drew us to it every day of our lives was intensified when visiting at night. Somehow, the sound, the breezes and the sharp smell of brine had a way of allowing the three of us to step back and look at things in perspective and discuss them openly. We knew we could say anything to one another at the water's edge. And so through our youth we had come to the sea to mark the important passages: the first day of junior high school; first girlfriends and first kisses; breaking up; after every football game; every basketball game; every dance with or without our dates; every family argument and every triumph and adolescent trauma we all shared. Atypical of so many adolescent boys, we three, who thought of one another as brothers, opened up our hearts and minds to each other and the sea worked its magic.

Tonight was no different. We sat on the hood of the car looking out into the Gulf Stream. We knew we had somehow accomplished a form of perfection earlier that evening in Belle Glade, but in the manner common to teenage boys, no matter how much we discussed it, we were at a loss to express what it all meant in the big picture of life. Somehow we had crossed a threshold and closed the door on our childhood that night, and everything we ever did for the rest of our lives, no matter whatever greatness we might achieve, it would be measured against those forty-eight minutes on that Belle Glade football field. In the days and years ahead, the twenty-five who had played on our team that night would never discuss the game with others or even amongst ourselves. It was an unspoken, private, personal victory won against incredible odds, but a game whose bragging rights were voluntarily forfeited for all time. No high-fives or "remember the Belle Glade game," during nights of drunken reminiscence have ever been uttered. It was a perfect moment in history come and gone; born of sorrow; forever reflected upon in silence but never spoken about aloud. If someone not on the team tried to broach the subject, they would be met with lowered eyes or a faraway look accompanied by a polite nod and a quick changing of the subject.

Occasionally, out in a crowd, I will see a former teammate, a veteran of that game. Despite the passing of the years, the first thing that will pass through our minds after the initial recognition and before the first nod, is the Belle Glade game. No words need to be spoken, but I can see it in their eyes; the memory of those two rainy nights in November that changed our lives forever.

Coach Morrow never coached another game. He quit teaching the following Monday and went to work at his brother's paint store delivering cans of paint to construction sites. After what had happened, he sought the mind-numbing routine of the manual labor. The next time I saw him was sixteen years later at my wife, Nikki's, funeral. He came up to me and shook my hand, and it was only then that I realized that some people just never recover from things that happen. We were, all of us, his sons. He blamed himself for the death of our teammates; for having them out for dinner on such a rainy night. He had never been able to pick himself up off the mat. Of the two hundred people who had attended Nikki's funeral, his presence had surprised me the most, and I was touched by his caring and thoughtfulness in coming to pay his respects. The look was in his eyes; a look that said I was still one of his boys.

As for Joachim and Bobby and me, from that game night on, like it or not, we would be joined at the hip for life, regardless of where our future paths would take us. Even though we had been assisted in our win by two dozen teammates, it was generally accepted that the three of us had done it in an unstoppable, precise choreography.

The following year, when we were all Seniors playing on Varsity together, we finished the season 7-2-1, not a bad year, but nothing like the previous year. After what we had experienced in Belle Glade, all other games seemed anticlimactic. For the three boys in the Secret Society of Coconuts, the Belle Glade game began as a slow turning point, and ended in the closing of a certain chapter in our lives.

That night after the Belle Glade game, after fifteen minutes of mute staring toward the Gulf Stream horizon, Bobby broke the silence. The enormity of what we had accomplished had still not sunk in, but somehow we were beginning to understand that now we would be moving on to something else. "What's out there?" he pondered. We knew he was speaking rhetorically. We all sensed the frightening uncertainty of impending adulthood. We knew we couldn't answer his question, but all three of us knew we were afraid.

CHAPTER 11

After I arrived at the Marina and secured the *ARIEL*, I beeped Bobby and he called from his home. I told him about Joachim and the note. "SHIT!" was his first reaction. "Meet me at the station as soon as you can."

I got there and got the same dip shit smile from the same dip-shit reporter I had slugged two months earlier. Don't those guys ever go home? I ignored his questioning face. Just a social call, I wanted him to think. Say a word to me and I'll have you up for violating your restraining order, I wanted to tell him.

I had decided what I was going to tell Bobby and what I wasn't. On the way back south that afternoon I had decided to tell him everything that had happened except for the exploration I had done after finding Joachim's watch, and the discovery of what I was sure was the cocaine. I didn't want to take any chance on my bargaining power. If Bobby was not in a position to help, or didn't have his priorities straight, I still wanted to be in the ballgame and be able to ransom Joachim.

The first thing he said when he walked into his office surprised me. "Are you sure you don't know anything about the missing cocaine? You're gonna have to tell me sooner or later, whether you want to or not. So you might as well come clean now."

"I swear, Nikki never said anything about it to me at all." That was no lie. "If it was on the boat, they would have found it when they tore my boat apart. They didn't miss a trick. Go see for yourself. What about Joachim? Aren't you worried about him?"

He rubbed his face a full minute before speaking again. "We're just gonna have to go slowly on this. If they think you told me, they're gonna kill Joachim. So we're just going to have to play a waiting game."

"A waiting game? That's easy for you to say. This isn't just some guy off the street they kidnapped. This is Joachim! You remember our childhood pal, don't you?"

He exploded in my face, screaming. "They're just *bluffing!*"

Again, his face went to his hands. I had the strong feeling he didn't want to have anything to do with the case. It was like we were complete strangers all of a sudden and he didn't want to have to deal with it. I looked across the desk and tried to determine what he was thinking behind his empty words.

"Jimmy." He spoke slowly, searching for the right words. And then I could see it wasn't anger in his eyes. It was sadness. "Jimmy, I'm sorry. Why didn't you listen to me?"

I looked at him a moment before I was able to figure out what he meant.

"Why didn't you listen to me when I told you not to hang around that trash, Nikki? You remember what I said that first night you told me? You could have done so much better than her. You were always the best of us."

The emotion and the content of what he said surprised me. It was as if his words were taken out of some crazy context where they didn't apply. What did that have to do with my life being in danger? With Joachim's situation? What did he mean by me being the best of us? It is not a subject I had ever contemplated; who among us was the best. In what context? By what set of standards, what criteria could he possibly come to that conclusion? I didn't have time to think about it for very long.

"I knew something like this would eventually happen to you. I'll tell you, Jimmy, God forgive me, I was glad when Nikki died. It was a relief in a lot of ways. She wouldn't be able to fuck up your life and hurt you anymore. I know that's a horrible thing to say about a best friend's wife, but I was glad. Good riddance to bad rubbish."

Bobby's attitude surprised me. I knew he had disliked Nikki, but I had never realized the degree. I was angry.

"I thought after she was gone that you would be better off, but all her shit is finally catching up with us."

"Us?"

He shook his head again and looked down to his desk top. For some reason he seemed to be holding back, as if he wanted to tell me something else but was not going to.

"Look, Jimmy, if we're lucky, we can work this out between ourselves and everything will be okay. Just a couple of friends trying to save another friend. No cops....no press. Isn't that what you want?"

"What I want is to get my friend back."

Bobby was silent, so I continued. "Is there any chance Nikki *was* murdered?"

Bobby looked away from me to the wall. I wasn't making it easy for him, but I wanted to know more.

"Jesus, I just wish this whole thing would blow over. Jimmy, there are a lot of things about Nikki's death that were never fully explained to you. I wanted to.....protect you, I guess."

"Things like what?"

"Jimmy, you know she had been with three guys before she died?"

I'd been trying to force that image out of my mind ever since I found out about it. "I'd heard those stories, yeah. And?......"

"Any one of them could have killed her...given her an unusually strong dose, forced her to O.D. That's not uncommon. And from what we have been able to tell, they probably didn't have to force her to take anything. No offense. We just don't really know what kind of people we were dealing with. There's no way of proving they were even there when she did it."

"So who would be the suspects?"

"Anyone. An angry drug dealer. Somebody into kinky sex.

"Why do you say that?"

"Trust me on that one, Jimmy. She had been with three guys, okay? I'll spare you the details."

"Where would I go....how would I find out who deals drugs on that level locally....who's interested in that kind of sex stuff?"

"What do you wanna go and do that for? It's been my experience that lots of people are interested in that kind of stuff around here. Not everyone has whatever it takes to actually 'act it out'.

"So what have you got in mind?"

Bobby seemed almost distraught. Was it just for my benefit?

"Look, Jimmy, while you've been daydreaming your life away, lost in the past somewhere, this town, the whole world, has grown up and left you behind. I've seen shit these last couple of years we wouldn't have dreamt about when we were kids and it would break your heart to hear about it all. So many senseless murders. Life has no value in this town, *no value at all,* anymore. Especially when you're dealing with these types of people."

He was right, of course. I loved this town, even though it wasn't the sleepy little place we knew as boys twenty years earlier. I used to think of it as a Southern version of Hannibal, Missouri; a Mark Twain river town. With the water traffic and activity along the lakefront, this must have been quite the place before highways made their way through the swamps. All the merchandise, trade and traffic came by water: freighters on the open seas or steamboats on the inland waterways carried goods, tourists, pioneers. And then later, Flagler's railroad.

Most of the land people live on today would still be underwater if the canals hadn't been dredged during one of the largest, state-sanctioned land swindles in history. "Ditch and Drain," they called it, as if it was doing us a favor to let the lifeblood of the swamp hemorrhage into the ocean so they could build on the land and alter the eco-system, at-will. They knew you have to reap what you sow. They just didn't care. They knew they wouldn't be around for the harvest.

"Flood Control," they called it, a euphemism that fooled most of the people most of the time. What we had witnessed as boys growing up was the end-product of a century of unbridled destructive growth that will remain unchecked into the Twenty-First Century, when all of South Florida will become uninhabitable; a morass of irresponsible whiners and cry-babies from the frozen Northeast, demanding their rights as retirees, as they clog the roads to a standstill, and turn this once beautiful paradise into a mall parking lot.

And as the tourists come, they squeeze out the second, third, fourth generation Floridians and fill them with resentment. With all the angry poor and the transients and losers looking for the solution to their problems, the rate of crime and atrocities has risen to the point where it is now commonplace.

A Green Mountain Yankee retiree recently arrived from a tiny rural town in Vermont moves to Palm Beach County with his life savings, and while stopping for a quart of milk at a convenience store is shot in cold blood in the parking lot by a French-speaking illegal alien from the Caribbean Basin, who is fucked up on drugs from Bogota and is carrying a MAC-10 made in Miami. He *"just felt like doing it,"* he told police.

Some kind of Paradise.

Bobby finally spoke. "Gimme twenty-four hours...and stay away from that reporter outside, or I'll arrest you both."

"You don't have to worry about that."

I wanted to know more about what Bobby felt, but I was just

going to have to be satisfied for now. I kept to my decision not to tell him that I'd found the cocaine. I had a gut feeling I was going to need that edge as ammunition in the future.

"Go back to your boat and wait. I'll have a uniform guy hang around down there. Whoever has Joachim will have to get in touch with you sometime to arrange a swap. I guess you're both safe as long as they think you've got what they want. I don't think they're going to bother you while you're berthed at the marina. There are too many people around. It's too public. In the meantime, I'll try to keep this between the two of us until I can figure out what to do. I'm going to have to find a way to bait them. I could take some coke out of the evidence locker and you can offer it as ransom. We get Joachim, they get a possession charge. Let me see if there is any word out on the street."

"You mean an informer? You really have those things?"

"We wouldn't be able to break a lot of cases without them. It's easy to be a 'master sleuth' in a town full of tattle-tales."

Bobby stood as a signal it was time to leave. He avoided eye contact during his whole exit maneuver. "And don't worry about Joachim. This could just be a routine business transaction if we play it right. They won't hurt him. They just want their stuff. If he's dead, they can't bargain. They know we'd come down hard. Anyway, he should be able to hold his own."

I couldn't tell if Bobby was trying to convince me or himself.

CHAPTER 12

Back on my boat I picked up my phone and put in a call to Joachim's home telephone. As it rang I looked around to see if I could tell if anyone was watching me.

I thought of the countless times Joachim answered the phone in the years we had known each other. I half expected to hear his voice, but I knew no one would answer now.

On the fourth ring I heard the message machine pick up and then Joachim's voice request a message; first in English and then Spanish. Where was he now?

I knew his wife would be calling from Philadelphia at midnight as she did every night when she was away, and when he didn't answer she would punch in her touch-tone code to retrieve the message from Joachim that would usually be waiting for her. I listened to Joachim finish the Spanish version of the request and then there was a beep. I almost hung up, but I went ahead with the well-rehearsed lie, my cheery voice almost cracking with self-hatred and fear.

"Hey Maria! Buenos Noches. This is Jimmy calling from Lake Okeechobee, once home to the best catfish and bass fishing in the world, that is, until they heard we were coming out here for a few days. Anyway, Joachim's fighting a two-ounce bass at the moment so he asked me to call and tell you why he's not at home."

As part of the act, I called out over my shoulder, "Hey Joachim, say hello to your bride!"

Back in the mouthpiece I wound up my award winning performance. "He says he doesn't wanna lose the only fish he'll have on the line all week. He'll call you in a couple of days and he hopes your sister's doing okay. My love to the kids. Talk to you later."

I hung up the phone and wiped the sweat off my forehead. I hated to lie. It's my Achilles' Heel, I suppose.

On deck it was a lot cooler and I took a swig of beer and looked around the skyline. They could have been watching me from any one of two hundred windows; The Helen Wilkes Hotel? The Marina Tower? The black, plastic-looking Darth Vader Building? Was there anyone staring at me now through binoculars from above? Would they see my planned morning swim? Had Bobby's protection shown up to watch over me from the shadows? I couldn't see anyone.

I had called Maria because no matter what happened, whether Bobby stepped in and saved the day, or whether Joachim managed to escape, I didn't want her to worry about him. I didn't want her sister to be concerned, hours away from the start of her labor. Whatever happened, I knew it would take a couple of days to clear up anyway. What would Joachim be doing? How much suffering would there be? Was I too selfish, accepting so readily Bobby's intent to keep this whole thing low profile? To keep me out of the press again? I didn't know. But I had a pretty strong idea what I was going to be doing. I lay back in my sling chair and stared straight up at the stars and planned it all out. Overhead was a magical sky, with stars popping in and out of clouds back-lighted by moonlight. It had been a while since I had seen the sky without the ambient light of big cities confusing my view. I wanted to sail out into the Gulf Stream again, away from landfall and see the sky in all its rich blackness.

This is not a detective story. There is no real "*whodunit?*" There are no shootouts, no high-speed car chases on slick city streets, no using my fists and years of martial arts training to overcome insurmountable odds and surprise the tough guys when they show up on my doorstep in a third act turnaround. There is no snappy bedside repartee with a femme fatale.

You don't have that question nagging at the back of your mind, "Why didn't he just pick up a phone and call the police?" I like the cops. I trust the cops and there was no doubt in my mind whatsoever at this point, that Bobby would do everything in his power to get it all straightened out, no matter how odd his behavior this evening. But I have no real belief in justice, so I didn't really expect, or want, to find any other justice than to get my friend back safely.

There are no superheroes in this story. I was just a bicycle-riding, ineffectual English Teacher of bored, semi-literate, self-indulged adolescents. On summer hiatus, I was simply trying to find out what happened to my ex-wife; tired of the routine of the last ten years and desperate for a change. A change had just been dropped in my lap. Maybe it would shake me from my endless torpor.

So if this is not a mystery, what is it? Here are some clues:

It's a love story. It's three love stories. A love story between a man and a woman; a love story between two people who hardly ever knew one another; and a love story that should never have happened.

Sure, there is theft and murder, more than its share of unhappiness and broken lives, but it's really no mystery. More than anything else, this is a love story.

The stars above led me to the rest of my decision on this moonlit night: Life is so short. So sudden. So taken for granted. To live it vicariously is to live an unfulfilled existence. We live through soap operas, television, movies, even fiction, while all

around us are the real characters, the real mysteries of life, in the
flesh. Some lie hidden, disappearing deeper with the passing of
time, forgotten by all but a few, who no one listens to anyway. I
know that for a fact.

The mysteries of my own life had kept me a prisoner of my
own remorse–paralyzing me. Does everyone feel this way?

So, maybe for that, or for whatever reason, I decided to step
across that line and free myself from whatever restraints we tie
ourselves down with; that hold us back from whatever it is we
really want to do. I wanted to find out whatever there was available to find out about my wife's murder, Joachim's disappearance,
the missing cocaine and the mysterious two men who were after
me. I would do it without Bobby's help, if necessary. That was all
right, too. I was used to working on my own.

Maybe it was decision based on hopelessness. I just thought I
really didn't have a reason for living anymore. I was tired of it all;
nothing really to lose.

The ordeal of never having a father around when I was growing up had deprived me of one of life's great pleasures. Not only
had I never had a real conversation with him while he was alive,
but until I was out of high school, I really knew nothing about
him; who he was; what he was like.

But even though I had never grown up under his guidance,
never had the benefit of him putting his arm around my shoulder
during a lesson on "good judgement," after a bad adolescent decision, I knew exactly what he would have done in a case like this.
I even knew *how* he would have gone about it.

Now dead for over thirty years, my father would lead the way.
How is that possible, you might ask?

"The grave is never silent
for those who plan ahead."

So I got up out of my sling chair and went below to plan my
own future. It was destined to be a long week.

CHAPTER 13

The next morning it was over eighty degrees at daybreak. Summer mornings, the humidity is high, as the early sun cooks the dampness and dew that has accumulated overnight. Steam rises off the ground, and any activity is rewarded with sweat-drenched clothes.

I took the *ARIEL* out of the berth convinced I was being watched by the police and probably by at least one other person. I didn't go far. A few hundred feet out near the channel where the water was deeper. There was no boat traffic around me and I bobbed on a flat surface.

I dropped anchor just outside the channel and looked around the bay as if nothing were going on. To the east was Flagler's Whitehall, back-lighted by morning sun. To the west, the West Palm Beach skyline was yellow with morning sunlight. Below deck, I gathered my scuba gear and tools in a dive bag. Topside, I tied a rope around it and dropped it overboard on the Palm Beach side in a nonchalant move, as if it were a bag of garbage kicked overboard by accident.

I took a deep breath of the humid June morning air and jumped overboard into the cool water. If any innocent bystander were watching, they would be less surprised that there was a treasure in cocaine on board my boat and more surprised that I was swimming in the Intracoastal.

Below, the water was just over thirty feet deep. The channel had been dredged out as part of the waterway system almost one hundred years ago.

Still holding my breath, I cleared my mouthpiece with the last gasp of air from my lungs, slipped into the scuba tank backpack, and went to work. My sore, injured hand reminded me of the weight of the inner PVC pipe, so I unthreaded the brass plate with caution this time. I watched the gold disk reflect the morning sun as it shimmered in slow-motion toward the white sandy bottom.

Again, it was followed by the PVC pipe, but this time there was no mucky bottom two feet away to stop its descent. Instead, it fell straight into the sand like a twenty-foot arrow. I had to arc the far end out over the sand and away from the hull to pull out the last eight inches. I was hoping it would not snap from the stress of being bent. Had it been another eight inches, I would have had to moor in deeper water. As it was, the arced pipe sprang from its casing. The freed end fell to the sand bottom, kicking up a silent, silty cloud.

I replaced the brass plate, and tied a fifty-foot length of nylon rope to the end of the pipe, cinching it tightly against the PVC cap. At the end of the rope I knotted a one hundred foot length of eighty-pound test mono-filament line. I swam to within fifty feet of my berth underwater, the long white pipe almost weightless in my hand as I kicked against the current. I felt like an underwater pole-vaulter, swimming my way toward the vaulting pit, the long pole arcing at each end as I swam toward my dock. There, within that same fifty feet from where I would re-berth my boat, I scooped a long narrow trench in the sand and buried the PVC and the rope. I tied one end of the mono-filament to the buried rope and the other end to the piling closest to where my transom would be, about two feet below the low tide mark. I snaked it around the piling, making it all but invisible from above.

Later, from on deck or on the dock, I could use a gaffing hook and snag the mono-filament. Then, hand over hand, I could pull on it until the stronger nylon rope was in my hands. The long white tube I was sure was filled with the missing cocaine would now be within arms' reach. Hidden beneath the sand, it was easily accessible, without me having to get wet.

As I dried off moments later in the cabin, I calculated. Four inches in diameter times twenty feet long. What was the formula for determining the volume of a cylinder? Pi times the radius-squared, times the height. (P x r2 x h) or 3.1415x 2 inches squared x 240 inches equals 3,015.84 cubic inches or almost two cubic feet of what was surely uncut cocaine. What could that be worth?

Not Joachim's life.

CHAPTER 14

To begin the next step in my plan, I dressed and rode my ten-speed across the bridge and then north on the bicycle path toward Alligator Island. The heat was so oppressive I almost started to laugh. How could laborers work in this? The smell of boiling tar filled the air, and I half expected my bicycle tires to sink into the soft macadam.

I pedaled over the Royal Poinciana Bridge and turned left on Bradley Place, and past The Biltmore Hotel. Before it went Condo, I had worked there one winter season as a convention busboy, making about thirty-five cents an hour because the Bus Captain was stealing most of the tips.

As I made my way over to the bike path, I could see Alligator Island looming in the distance. It was the tiny island made from what was once a mangrove cluster a mile or so north of the Bridge. In another in a long line of early Florida's corrupt land deals, developers had been allowed to fill in the mangroves with channel spoil at the turn of the century.

In their entrepreneurial zeal, they turned the resulting twenty acres into a jungle-like Alligator Farm, complete with tropical foliage, wild monkeys, and a population of cockatiels, wild parrots and parakeets. A Florida land rip-off became one of Palm Beach's first tourist rip-offs.

After WWI it had been converted into a residential island, subdivided into four residential lots. Now, four mansions sat in the dense jungle setting, the monkey families long since removed but the descendents of the bird colony still filling the island trees with their brilliant plumage and constant chatter. These days, a different kind of reptile inhabited the island and kept the birds company.

Alligator Island was at the end of a narrow causeway across the one hundred feet of water that separated it from the main Island of Palm Beach. A guard house blocked entry onto the island, and each of the four houses controlled its own perimeter security system around each individual five-acre lot. A triggered alarm from Alligator Island had been known to bring the entire Palm Beach police force in response. This was where the heavy-weights lived, those who controlled most of what occurred, on the Island of Palm Beach. They did it with little resistance and little concern for the tenets of democracy. They considered the entire island town their own private domain, and any who disagreed, were ignored. None but the hopelessly naive and the newspapers believed the decisions were actually made by the Town Council.

I pulled off the bike path and swung in toward the guardhouse. The guard looked at me with recognition, but couldn't seem to make the connection. I gave him my name and he called the Fletcher household for clearance. As I had hoped, Consuelo answered the phone and authorized my entry.

The home of my ex-father-in-law sat on the prime, five-acre lot on the southwest side of the island. Across the broad Intracoastal was the Coast Guard House on Peanut Island. The Fletcher mansion had been built right after World War I as a typical Mizner house. It was one of the last homes designed and built by the architect, scoundrel, and raconteur, Addison Mizner. Not long after, thirty miles south, his Boca Raton project disintegrated during the Florida land bust, just as the Great Depression and winds of a killer hurricane were looming on the horizon.

This house Nikki had grown up in had all the distinguishing features of a true Mizner, ideas he borrowed or stole from Moorish Architecture in Spain and Central America, and updated to Palm Beach's Island lifestyle; a terracotta, barrel-tile roof made by artisans Mizner had imported to West Palm Beach to work in his factory; pecky cypress beam ceilings, hand painted with floral designs; Moorish windows filigreed with leaded glass, and window exposure into the prevailing winds to assure cross-ventilation; external circular staircases, almost as if they had been built on as an afterthought. It was all typical Mizner, a culmination of a style he almost seemed to make up as he went along. It is the only Mizner still in the hands of its original owners, or at least the blood heirs of its original owners.

The front and rear lawns were covered with coconut palms, accented by clusters of bright yellow coconuts hanging overhead. The Chattahoochee gravel in the driveway gave way under my tires and my bicycle skittered out from under me. I walked the bike the rest of the way down the long drive to the portico.

Consuelo answered the door, surprised and happy to see the familiar face of a former household ally. A Cuban refugee, she had worked in the Fletcher home since she was a teenager in the early Sixties. Now, close to fifty, she was a stabilizing influence on the household. After Nikki's mother had been shipped to a rest home in North Carolina in a Thorazine haze, Consuelo had been Nikki's big sister until Nikki went nuts and decided she didn't like Consuelo's silly, Old-World notions of right and wrong.

Consuelo had been a beautiful woman once, but time had taken its toll. Now there was extra weight on her hips, and her once jet-black hair was prematurely streaked with silver. She wore a gray housekeeper's dress, trimmed in a white apron.

She held out both hands to grasp mine. "Jimmy." She was genuinely glad to see me, but hung her head shyly.

It was strange being in the house so many months after the

divorce; after Nikki's death. While we were married, she and I had lived in the cabana in the back yard, the only concession to non-Mizner architecture on the entire island. It was a two story, Bahamian-style, poolside house strangled in chartreuse bougain-villea. Blazing white louvered Bahama-shutters jutted out from the tall windows like outrigger sails, keeping the interior of the cabana naturally cool and dark. Now, standing in the entryway by the main house, I could see our cabana through the rear windows.

"Hello Consuelo. It's good to see you again." She wanted to speak, but was fearful of being put in her place by the master of the household, a common pattern for Hamilton Fletcher III. I gave her a sympathetic smile as if to say, "I know. It's all right."

"Is Mr. Fletcher here?"

Before she could answer, Hamilton came storming into view. He was making an effort to restrain himself. He was tall, thin, with a ruddy complexion from long years of struggle on the golf course. He was in remarkable shape for a man in his early six-ties. His silver-white hair offset the tan and made him even more handsome. Dark, muscular arms hung from the sleeves of a bright yellow Polo shirt. Ordinarily, he had the look of someone used to getting his own way. Now, his look was one of surprise, anger, disbelief.

"What are you doing here?" He turned to Consuelo. "Did you let him in here?"

Before she could answer, I continued. "We need to talk."

"We have nothing to discuss, unless it's the robbery you're perpetrating on my daughter's estate. I still can't believe that someone like you would be able to get their grubby hands on my family's money."

Someone like me, I thought? "It was her money. That's what she wanted."

"She never knew what she wanted! That's why she married someone like you."

I had been in the main house a million times, but this day was different. Overhead, the pecky-cypress crossbeams, painted by local artists long dead, spread across the ceiling. At my feet were clay tiles baked by Mizner craftsmen a few blocks west of where I had grown up.

I looked Hamilton Fletcher III in the eye. "Somebody murdered Nikki."

He didn't hesitate to even consider my remark. There was no emotion or feeling for Nikki in his face. "That's preposterous. Is that what you came here to tell me? Talk to the coroner. Talk to your policeman buddy, Starke. She killed herself with drugs. End of story. Now I want you out of here!"

"Who was she hanging around with when she died?"

"How should I know? Low-lifes, just like you."

"Why are you fighting me on this? Don't you want to know what really happened to your daughter?"

"Who's fighting you? It's over. Do you think this is going to bring her back? Make me forgive you, take you under my wing as if you were family, or *like* you because you think someone killed her?"

"I talked to someone who knows for sure."

"Who? That's bullshit. They're lying. Let it go."

"And now the same people want to kill me."

"Why do you say that?"

"I thought you might know something that could help me figure that all out."

"Let it go, Phipps, or I'll drag your ass in and out of court for the rest of your life and bleed you dry in lawyer's fees. You think I can't do that? You think I wouldn't do that, just on principle? It would give me pleasure to see you not be able to spend a penny of my family's money, no matter how much it cost me." Hamilton paced, fuming. "Where's Nikki's boat?"

His sudden concern was uncharacteristic. "You mean my boat? Where it always is, why?"

"In case I need to have you served with papers, I don't want to have to track you all over the goddam Caribbean."

Consuelo appeared in the doorway and announced with lowered eyes that Hamilton was wanted on the phone.

"Who is it?"

"It's your brother sir, calling from Tallahassee.

He turned back to me. "Get out of here. And do what I said. Just drop it."

Hamilton left the room addressing Consuelo over his shoulder. "Call the guard house and make sure he's never allowed on this island again." He raised his voice to me. "I'll have you arrested for trespassing."

Consuelo's eyes met mine for a long moment and something passed between us. I couldn't tell if it were anger, fear, sympathy. Finally she turned. "I'll show you to the door, Jimmy."

As I passed through the hall I could hear Hamilton in the study. His voice echoed down the hallway and filled the interior of the concrete circular staircase as I passed. "I'll see you tonight. Yes, I'm sure. Don't we always? I'll send the limo for your jet."

I glanced up at an oil painting, commissioned fifty years ago, that dominated the foyer wall. It showed the happy Fletcher family when Hamilton III, my ex-father-in-law, was in his early teens. His own father, Hamilton Fletcher II, is seated on a mahogany throne, his blonde wife standing behind him, her hand on his shoulder. Their son, Hamilton III stands on the other side, and a cherubic faced, ten-year old Danforth is kneeling, petting a Golden Retriever. A typical Palm Beach family in 1938.

CHAPTER 15

Yes, it was a happy, Palm Beach Family Unit who had gathered for their portraits that winter day in 1938. A family of privilege and untold monies, living off the interest of a vast accumulation of wealth earned by a twenty-five year old former lumber jack during the Civil War; the very first Hamilton Fletcher.

Originally a kid from the streets of Manhattan, my wife Nikki's great-grandfather, Hamilton Fletcher I, had sailed a steamship to Jacksonville, then rode a stagecoach to Tallahassee, and finally overland on horseback to the Panhandle, drifting into lumberjacking and turpentining. After losing his right arm in tree fall, they transferred him inside, where he worked his way up to office clerk. Along the way, he developed a touch of good natured larceny.

Hamilton Fletcher I, in the spirit of American ingenuity, began his vast accumulation of wealth by pilfering lumber scraps. He took the white pine strips home at night from off the floor of the mill and fashioned them into Adirondack chairs; twenty-four pieces per chair. It was a craft he had learned as a child on a trip to Schroon Lake in upstate New York. He sold the chairs made from stolen lumber to tourists at a handsome profit.

Later, by altering the company books, he was able to steal lumber from the old man who owned the mill, without ever touching the wood. It wasn't long before his talents grew into another American tradition. Stealing from the government in the name of patriotism and defense. By falsifying the counts on the railroad cars that poured from the sawmills during the Civil War, Hamilton was making The Confederacy stronger by stealing from it during its time of need.

At the end of the Civil War, the twenty-nine year old former lumberjack with one arm had become a millionaire with an expertise in lumbering. By 1900, at the age of sixty, he owned vast tracts of pine and cypress in North Florida. On those tracts he didn't own, he leased the lumbering rights. The pine was tapped for creosote and cut for railroad ties. His crews cut hundreds of one-thousand year-old bald cypress trees, forty feet in circumference from Florida's interior for months on end. What once resembled a pristine, prehistoric jungle with Spanish Moss covered limbs hundreds of feet above the enriched animal habitat, became a clear-cut, low-lying swampy morass of worthless palmetto palms and tree stumps as big as house foundations. There are pictures of the lumberjacks standing on a felled cypress almost as big in circumference as a Sequoia. For leveling the state and clear-cutting almost every one of its ancient trees, Hamilton Fletcher I received citations from Tallahassee, and rewards beyond belief. By the turn of the century, his fortune was only overshadowed by the barons Rockefeller, Carnegie, Morgan and Henry Morrison Flagler.

Hamilton Fletcher moved to Palm Beach in 1900 with his wife and twenty year old son, Hamilton Fletcher II. They were tired of the cold winters in the Panhandle.

Hamilton Fletcher II, my wife's grandfather, was an early pioneer of what has become a Palm Beach tradition. Surrounded by wealth beyond imagination, he became a spoiled, indulged, privileged child, who was both a tyrant and a financial genius. He himself fathered two boys who stood at his side in the oil painting before me, next to the beautiful, intriguing blonde woman in the painting.

Hamilton Fletcher III, Nikki's father, took over the management of the family fortune. He was the older of the two boys in
the hallway oil painting. The younger boy, Danforth, two years
younger and not nearly as intelligent, was reduced to becoming a
politician and running for State office. When Danforth turned the
qualifying age, his father, Hamilton II and his brother, bought him
a seat in the Florida Senate. Every April for the thirty-three years
since then, during the annual two month legislative session, Danforth Fletcher went to Tallahassee, accompanied by the arrival
of the dogwood blossoms and the azaleas, to earn as much influence money from special interests groups as he could, and vote in
favor of laws detrimental to the best interests of the environment
and people of the State of Florida. The rest of the year he spent
trying to correct his slice at Seminole Golf Course and picking up
flight attendants thirty years younger than he was at trendy bars in
Palm Beach. Uncle Danforth Fletcher became an institution in the
Florida Legislature, and a renowned lecher at home.

Hamilton Fletcher II died in 1960, leaving the bulk of the fortune his father made to these two sons. The rest of his substantial
fortune was placed in trust for the twin grandchildren. Hamilton
III had sired Nikki and her twin brother, Victor, in 1956, four years
before Hamilton II's death. The two grandchildren intrigued him,
so similar as they were. It was due to a lifelong fascination for
twins, he told everyone. His fascination for them served as the
catalyst for him to place some highly irregular codicils in his will.

It's the old man in the family portrait, Nikki's grandfather,
Hamilton Fletcher II, who I have to thank for the lifestyle I live
today. Partly because of the money Nikki made available to me
in her will and those controversial codicils. Her grandfather made
sure no one could take the trust from her and made sure she could
will it to whomever she wanted. Yes, it's Hamilton II, I have to
thank for my life being the way it is today. A man I'd never met–
who probably never even knew I existed–who died when I was
seven years old, had inadvertently provided that I would never

really need money again in my life. Isn't money everything?

Meanwhile, my dead wife's twin brother, Victor, the other grandchild and trust fund recipient, chose to live another lifestyle.

CHAPTER 16

Georgia Avenue bisects the industrial South end of West Palm Beach. Starting at Okeechobee Boulevard and running two miles south, Quonset huts and squat concrete block buildings serve as home for auto mechanics, wheel alignment shops, aluminum window and awning contractors, cabinet makers and junk yards. Just north of Forest Hill Boulevard, I pulled my bicycle through the gate of a chain-link fence onto a shell rock driveway stained black by years of automotive oil and grime. A windowed showroom offering used motorcycles dominated the front of the property, and the backyard was filled with a motorcycle graveyard, a tiny house trailer from the Fifties sitting on its axles, and a plywood lean-to offering the resident motorcycle repairman some relief from the sun. It stood in absurd contrast to the home where I had just been.

It was here, in the putrid, grease-filled tangle of motorcycle frames, chrome-spoked wheels, crushed and punctured pin-striped gas tanks and the wild, lost dreams of bikers, that the vast Fletcher Lumber dynasty, started over a century ago by a drifting larcenous, one-armed lumberjack, had seemingly reached the end of its lineage.

Victor Fletcher looked so much like his late twin sister, my dead wife, that when I had first met him four years earlier, I just stared at him in disbelief. He could've passed for Nikki in men's garb. Seeing him now, after my wife was dead, gave me a feeling of unsettling eeriness. It was as if Nikki had been reincarnated as a motorcycle mechanic.

His delicate facial features, now covered by a week of stubble, were unable to hide the anger and bitterness he felt for his family. Three years before I met Nikki, Victor and his father had apparently had a violent argument that no one in the family would talk about. Victor moved out, and with a small part of his trust fund, he bought the two acre industrial site and dedicated his life to his two passions: fixing motorcycles and hating his father. He spent his days crouched over broken down, derelict motorcycles in his grease-soaked clothing, dipping his blackened fingertips into hubcaps filled with gasoline-soaked motorcycle parts. His nights he spent on a mattress on the floor of the dilapidated house trailer that sat on the same lot, with no furniture, no air conditioning, no running water, no cover for his pillow or mattress ticking. It was a lifestyle his grandfather had tried to prevent him from ever having to live.

Victor rarely left his compound except to take his restored, classic 1948 *Indian* motorcycle for a spin across the Southern Boulevard Bridge and down AIA to the Lake Worth Pier. There, on Thursday nights, he would talk with other antique motorcycle enthusiasts who congregated there in a clash of chrome and black leather and Fifties' nostalgia, and invite them to bring their repair work to his shop. I saw him there one night. He didn't know who I was then. It was the only time I ever saw him smile or appear at ease with himself.

When I rounded the corner and Victor saw me, I thought for a moment he was going to cry. The sight of his dead twin sister's ex-husband coming to visit him was more than he could take. But instead of crying, he stood, and shook my hand humbly and turned back to his work, averting his eyes.

When Nikki was alive and the two of us still lived together in her cabana, she would fix Victor a hot meal in the main house and put it in a picnic basket and we would drive down here to visit him. She would lie to her father about where we were going and then smuggle the food out of the kitchen with Consuelo's help. In Victor's tiny trailer, Nikki and I would join him on the floor and watch him eat the only home cooked meals he ate during those days. He would eat absently, without pleasure, the crumbs sticking to his chin in the heat.

Victor wore his sadness heavily on those nights, looking at Nikki as if pleading for her to somehow save him from whatever demons possessed his thoughts, yet resenting her suggestions that he move back in the house or accept any help from their father. Any mention of their father, Hamilton III, and Victor would turn sullen, refuse to answer, brooding over some unknown or untold slight or from the years of ridicule and derision from his insufferable bully of a father. Whatever it was that Hamilton had done to drive Victor from his home and family was never to be discussed; never to be forgiven.

Victor and Nikki would take long walks together while I, the ever-dutiful husband, stayed behind and straightened up the mess inside the trailer; washed the dishes outside with hose-water, swept the filth off the floor. He might as well have been living in a cardboard box on the streets of New York, for all his household amenities.

On those walks they rarely spoke, but something passed between them in the silent way things do between close siblings. It was as if she were trying to comfort him; help him cope with an overwhelming sadness that had engulfed him that he couldn't shake. Her looks were pleading, as if begging him for something I could never understand. They would sit on a bench, the glow from a streetlight outlining their silhouettes, while an audience of rusting, crippled, Harley-Davidsons cuddled around them protectively. They shared a closeness, a bond Nikki and I never seemed to achieve.

Later, on the way home, Nikki would shake off Victor's mood, saying, "You know, it was just one of those typical father-son conflicts that every boy seems to go through."

No, I didn't know, as a matter of fact. I would give anything to know about a father-son conflict first-hand. My heart had ached for one my entire life. Perpetual conflict would have been better than my perpetual sense of emptiness.

At Nikki's funeral, it was the first time Victor and his father had been in one another's presence in over six years. Neither made any attempt at a reconciliation. Of the few people who had truly mourned the death of my wife, I could take only second place in the "most hurt" category. That day at the gravesite, as we stood in a drizzle from the early Spring rainy season, I saw a man seeming to suffer far greater pain than I ever thought imaginable. He stayed off to the side, alone in a stand of Australian Pines, his shoulders rocking with his silent sobs. I expected at any moment that he would cry out in anguish and collapse to his knees, such was his heartbreak. And yet there was no one there to comfort him, least of all his own father and uncle. I, myself, was struggling, trying to cope with my own grief that day to be of any help. But later, I remembered his grief, and tried, as a child without a sibling, to understand the depth and nature of their bond. What could the loss of a twin sister mean to the remaining brother?

Now, Victor stood before me, not wanting to be reminded once again that his twin sister was dead. For what other reason would I possibly be there, but to talk about Nikki? What else linked us together, a poor boy from West Palm Beach and this heir, living in a hovel, with year-old black grease under his fingernails? Only the connection of a beautiful woman who was a beloved, dead, ex-wife to one, and a beloved, dead sister to the other.

I watched him work in silence, knowing if I started to talk to him while he was still working on the bike he would continue to keep his attention focused there. So instead I knelt beside him and just looked over his shoulder as the hot fumes of past oil spills filtered up to my nose from the hard-packed shell-rock beneath my feet. A carburetor, torn apart, lay stretched out on a piece of oily canvas. Tiny, grease-drenched parts lay frying in the afternoon heat. A stack of newspapers stood at the ready to absorb any spills. At least he was keeping in touch with the world outside his own compound exile.

Finally, he dropped his box wrench and turned to me as if to say, let's get it over with.

I started slowly. "Victor, I need to talk to you."

His sad eyes met mine for only a moment. He finished my sentence. "About Nikki..." It was as if he had been waiting months for this conversation, wondering what had taken me so long to arrive, and now it was finally beginning.

"Yes, about Nikki."

Victor stood, wiped his hands on an oily rag and reached into a cooler in the nearby lean-to and pulled out a small Gatorade. It was a delaying tactic. If he had been a pipe smoker he would have cleaned, filled and tamped his pipe. He offered me a hit. I took a swig.

"Victor, I know this is difficult for you."

He looked away, staring to the spot under the streetlight where he used to sit with Nikki for hours. It was as if he expected to see her there, beckoning him to their spot.

"Go ahead," he said returning the bottle to the cooler in slow motion.

"Victor. I think....I have reason to believe Nikki's death was not accidental."

His eyes locked on mine. He was firm in his convictions. "Death by drug overdose is never accidental. It just takes a little longer than normal suicides. She understood completely the eventual consequences of the life she was living. She had stopped living long before that. The actual overdose was just a housekeeping gesture."

"That's not what I mean. I mean I think someone killed her intentionally."

Victor's eyes remained on mine for the longest they'd ever had in the whole time that I knew him. There was pain in those eyes. And defeat. But not surprise. "You're not surprised?"

"No. I would only be surprised to learn that my father had nothing to do with it."

His remark caught me off guard and I had to think about what it all meant. There was too much there for now. "What do you mean?"

"I mean she became an embarrassment to him and my world-famous uncle. The horrible things she was doing. The type of people she was hanging around with. The things she was saying about them."

"You mean her drug thing?"

Victor picked up the box wrench and absently stroked its oily surface back and forth with his thumb. "Yeah, sure, her drug thing."

"So you don't know anything else that could help me?"

"No." I could tell he was lying. What secrets was he hiding?

What did he think about all day, hunched over his machines, baking in the sun, cracking his fingernails and cutting his palms as he fine-tuned these motorcycles to perfection? How could he live with such an all-consuming hate and sorrow, spending his nights in the stifling, moldy trailer, wrapped up in a filthy, sweat-stained sheet? Across the Intracoastal Waterway in a pastel colored bank, his trust fund grew fatter, into the millions, untouched since the day he'd bought this property six years before. Nikki had once told me that when Victor had first left his family's house in a breathless rage, that there were weeks that went by when he never left his bed in the tiny, fetid trailer. He'd become paralyzed by whatever was devouring his emotional stability. Now, with his sister's death, I'm not quite sure he would ever be whole again. He could live another sixty years, but for him, his life had already ended. However long he lasted, he was just doing time. Why do people become inert with a self-inflicted paralysis? It was a question I would do well to ask myself.

I left him there, this multi-millionaire motorcycle mechanic, his legs spread under the bike, staring down at his motionless hands, unable or unwilling to enjoy the fruits of his family's fortune.

CHAPTER 17

How different Nikki's family was from my own. But her wealth was only a small part of that difference.

My mother had raised me all by herself, making up beds in hotel rooms as she had done when she first arrived in Florida. She cared for me, loved me, sacrificed her time, her life for me.

For years, we lived meagerly, struggling to make ends meet on her modest salary and a small pension from my father. Now sixty-five, she received Social Security and her own tiny pension from The Breakers. More recently, her hard times had been relieved from what I gave her of my newfound inheritance. She was always a warm and giving mother, with enough love to go around even if I'd been blessed with twenty brothers and sisters. As it was, she was devoted to me and she never let me forget that I was the only thing that kept her alive, the only thing in her life worth living for.

More recently, her mind seemed to be deteriorating, and she sat quietly for long periods, dwelling in the past.

When my mother was twenty-one in the winter of 1942, her name was Jeanette Summers. Her parents put her on board a train in Elmira, New York, which took her to Penn Station in New York City. There she transferred to the Seaboard Coast Line train, "The

Silver Meteor," to spend the winter days with her Aunt Eleanor in West Palm Beach. The train was packed with Servicemen in a variety of uniforms, and they each looked at her face with a condemned man's desperate longing she tried to comprehend. Some were headed off to Camp Murphy in Hobe Sound. Some were headed to Miami Beach to train along with 80,000 others in the Army Air Corps at their new facilities. All were going off to war.

She sat up all night, playing cards and joking with the boys in the club car. They had all watched this young woman who reminded them of the girls they had left behind: in the noisy assembly lines of factories; baking rhubarb pies in wood-burning stoves; beneath hand-hewn ladders in apple orchards, and on the merry-go-rounds and tire swings in playgrounds of the Northeast.

The new recruits with sad faces sang songs through the night to cover their fear, while she wondered what life would be like if she married one of these rosy-cheeked boys who smiled at her. One soldier, her exact age, a private from Fort Dix, stared at her for a long while, making her feel self-conscious, awkward, until tears formed in his eyes and rolled down his cheeks. He'd meant her no harm. The realization he was subconsciously fighting had just won out: he was never coming home to someone like her; he was never going to come home at all.

As the sun came up the following morning they were passing through Waldo, Florida, and she could smell the distinctive pine-swamp air of a North Florida winter mixed with the hot diesel of the train.

Her Aunt Eleanor met her at the station at the end of Clematis Street and drove her to a Spanish cottage down in the El Cid area of West Palm Beach. The morning was warm and sunny, and as she sat on the patio of her Aunt's home, surrounded by elephant ears and the shade of a grapefruit tree, she knew she would never go back home to the dark northern town that always looked dirty. Here, everything was bright, clean, and warm.

A week later, she bicycled across the Flagler Memorial Bridge, just as I had done earlier this day, and there, she was hired as a chambermaid at the Breakers Hotel in Palm Beach. That spring when the tourist season ended and the weather up north turned warm, instead of going back home, she fell in love and stayed forever.

All the boys her age were taking trains out of town, fighting the war in Europe and the Pacific; so when a forty-two year old maintenance man at the hotel asked her to sit on the seawall after hours and listen to the orchestra inside the ballroom play for the rich guests down from New York, she accepted. Was this older man merely being friendly, or was this considered a date?

My mother spent that first night with this man on the seawall in the balmy air, listening to the big band sounds and the whispering, papery bristle of the palm fronds overhead.

The man who would eventually become my father told her he was too old for the war, even if he hadn't had his knee crushed in a labor riot in a turpentine camp during his stint as a WPA/Florida Writer's Project writer back in the Thirties. As she listened, he unraveled stories from those days in his slow, mellifluous, articulate drawl that kept my mother spellbound for hours. He liked to tell her he wove Southern tales with a New York sensibility, an unusual combination that apparently swept my mother off her feet, despite the fact he was twenty-one years older than she was.

The fact that he had gone to the University near where she had grown up in Western New York on The Finger Lakes, made her feel comfortable with the man, as if they shared a common bond; a territory they could both visit in their daydreams. One night, years after my father had died, she told me she had dreamt of meeting him while strolling around the tree-shaded college campus on the shores of Seneca Lake. The meeting had never taken place, despite their ostensible proximity for a time. She hadn't even been born when he went to college near her home town. She told me in the dream they had walked and talked of nature until the sun went down. They were standing in a lakefront gazebo, about to kiss, when she awoke.

When they were dating in that winter of 1942, he told her he was a struggling novelist and then he let her read a few of his short stories, and later, when he grew to trust her, she read the novels he had written. By that time she had decided their twenty-one year age difference would never matter. This was the man with whom she wanted to spend eternity.

They were married at Bethesda-by-the-Sea Church when the War ended and they built a small, Spanish stucco house on Mango Promenade between South Dixie Highway and South Olive Avenue in West Palm Beach. My mother mixed the stucco with a hoe in a wheel-barrow and my father caressed it onto the wire-meshed wooden framework in gentle sweeping motions with his hand-hewn trowel. The wet scrape of the wheelbarrow bed and the rasping slap of the stucco as he smoothed it over the screen were rhythmic sounds that were etched into their collective memories. That and the nightly clack of his typewriter keys denting the hard rubber platen as he typed out the handwritten notes of his novels that went largely unread by the public.

Later, she helped him roof the bungalow. After a twelve-hour workday in the hotel rooms of the "wealthy," she climbed a ladder and lifted every single one of those terra cotta barrel-tiles that now sit on the roof. She climbed that ladder over and over again in the failing light, carrying as many as she could, passing them gingerly to her man. He first sat perched on the roof edge, then limped to the roof peak, carrying each one, to tack them into place to protect them from the beating sun and tropical rains. What did they talk about?

I was born eight years later in the summer of 1953. While I was growing up I never knew much about their lives together before I was born, and I've often wondered what passed between them; what they thought, what they dreamed, what they planned. Why had they waited almost eight years for a child? Were they happy lovers on an endless honeymoon, or had they descended into the angry silence that often passes for marriage? She rarely spoke to me of their lives together before I came along. It appeared to be too painful. Growing up, I knew little of my father, other than that he had been a struggling writer earning his money primarily as a greens-keeper on the Breakers Golf Course, and later, for a short time, a hotel maintenance man and nightwatchman, until he died in 1956.

My father was fifty-three when I was born, and he died, committed suicide, before I turned three. I wish I had known him better. I wish I had known him at all.

There was a picture of him I remembered seeing as a child. It was on a shelf in that near-empty workroom of his in that little stucco bungalow on Mango Promenade. He is sitting on the bumper of a 1929 Whippet, a typewriter temporarily, precariously perched on an orange-crate at his knees. He holds forth a Speed Graphic press camera and gestures to the typewriter *as if* to show off the tools of his trade. (It would be years before I saw another, truer meaning in this photograph).

In the photograph he could pass for Tom Joad as I imagined him in THE GRAPES OF WRATH: His thin, angular face, his round tortoise-shell frame glasses, a cigarette stuck between his nicotine-stained fingertips, his straw fedora writing hat tilted back on his head. His eyes in the photograph look *through* me. I spent hours as a boy growing up, trying to imagine all those eyes had seen; what they had seen that would cause him to think the way he did; cause him to end it all the way he did. What made him do it? What sights could have caused him so much pain? Was it the agonized looks of the migrant workers he met who lived in lean-to's made of branches and rags? Was it the looks of hopelessness and despair in the eyes of the old black men who had been born into slavery and had never seen their lot in life improve? Was it the memory of the Rosewood riots and the smell of burning flesh etched into his memory? Was there just too much dead, dying and decay on Florida's back-country roads? Or maybe he just longed

to hop a northbound freight to the Panhandle and work the turpentine forests once again, free of the burden of a wife and a child.

I was to conclude it's almost as if I had two fathers: one, the
writer, who felt compelled to tell the rest of the world everything
he knew or could remember or could make up about Florida. The
other father didn't stick around long enough to say anything to his
own son about what he had seen.

Nowadays, my mother wanders aimlessly around a house
she knows will be torn down to make way for the new Uptown/
Downtown development, as if trying to commit to memory every
inch of the house she created with her long-gone husband before
it is bulldozed into rubble: to re-create movements of so long ago
that resulted in their collaboration. She runs her fingertips along
each stretch of wall, touching the wainscoting, each casement. I
have found her on her knees, tracing the floor moulding with her
fingertips. Does her touch serve to help jar her memory, or does
it serve to record old memories re-awakened? Did she hold the
nails as he tacked down the Dade County Pine tongue-and-groove
planks on the floor? Did she help pull the chalk-line taut on the
roof to align the tar-paper? Were her fingertips pinched and stained
red as he snapped the line? Did she realize the taut tugging of the
line, then sudden, snapping release, was a symbol of their love for
one another? Every mitered joint; every strip of moulding; every
puttied glass panel in the kitchen cupboard doors. "Measured
twice–cut once." Everything plumb; level; square, because they
loved one another. In another few months, the fruit of their love
would be leveled by anonymous machinery. Their modest house
on Mango Promenade, conceived in the long silences of their love
long before I was born, is the closest thing I have to a brother or
sister.

CHAPTER 18

From my deck I watched the sun disappear behind the new profile skyline of West Palm Beach. The tall buildings' shadows crept across the Intracoastal, sneaking up on Palm Beach. Before long, the bright white facade of Whitehall turned a deep yellow and then faded.

Downtown traffic had thinned and the marina had turned into a still life. I was waiting for some word from Bobby, hoping he had some news about Joachim. I hadn't heard a thing, and the sick feeling I had about his disappearance wouldn't go away. I wanted the thugs to call so I could tell them what I had decided. "Here, come get your stuff, give me back my friend." But that call didn't come.

Instead, when the phone rang, it was Consuelo. She sounded nervous, frightened, as if someone might be listening in on the line.

"Can you stop by my house tonight? I want to talk to you about something."

"Sure. I can come over right now. Is everything all right?"

There was a hesitancy on her part, but she finally answered. "Yes. I would just like to discuss something with you."

I hung up and wondered what it was she wanted.

Consuelo and her husband, Hector, lived in a little cottage off Belvedere Road in Flamingo Park. It was in a section of town that had become increasingly Hispanic in the last few years. Members of the Latin Community from Miami, tired of the crime and congestion in Dade County, had started the new phase of their immigration a decade ago, and small groceries, bodegas, bakeries and gift shops opened in what had been a working, middle-class Anglo neighborhood. In an irony that really escaped no one, Latin families were moving into Spanish-style homes that had been originally built for New England tourists seventy years before.

I drove past the tiny, freshly painted homes and immaculate yards. Some of the houses boasted ironwork filigree security bars around the windows, looking as if they had been removed, intact, from the Dade County windows and packed along with other household items to adorn their new homes.

Consuelo and Hector's house was one of the many real estate holdings of Hamilton Fletcher III that he rented out to people who worked for him. In the case of Consuelo and Hector, it reminded me of indentured servitude. They earned just enough money to live there. As I pulled into the tiny gravel driveway, I couldn't help but marvel over the perfect condition of her house and yard. Hector had been a member of *Brigada 1066* during the Bay of Pigs invasion, and served two years in a Castro jail. His diabetes aggravated the injuries and kept him confined to a wheelchair for the past two years. He wasn't able to do any yard work or housework.

That left it all up to Consuelo to do after a demanding twelve hour day at the Fletcher mansion. And yet the condition of both the house and the yard looked like the work of a full time staff.

Like my own mother, Consuelo had spent her entire life cleaning up after others. Hector spent his days angry and resentful over his fate and the hand that life had dealt him. In recent days he was particularly bitter over Hamilton's treatment of Consuelo. She would come home in tears, after a day of verbal abuse by her lord, and have to face her own husband's anger over how she was being abused. His real anger was over himself being trapped, power-less, in a wheelchair. What other choices did they have? If she left her job, they would have to move out of their house, as well.

Consuelo met me at the door, concern washed over her face. She had been crying. Hector sat at the kitchen table, his wheel-chair nearby. Consuelo offered me a Cafe Cubano and I couldn't refuse. So much for sleeping this night. The air in the house was still, but for a small breeze kicked up by the paddle fan. No air conditioning: too expensive.

They seemed hesitant to start, so I made it easy on them. "Is everything okay?"

Hector was ready and on my cue he was off and running. "No, everything is definitely not okay. I am sick of that man and the way he treats my wife. He is abusive to her. She told me you came by today and after you left he screamed at her for an hour! For what? What did she do?"

I looked over to Consuelo. Her head was hanging low. She lifted her eyes to meet mine.

"I'm sorry, Consuelo. I didn't know he would take it out on you."

"Almost thirty years of loyal service and this is what she has to put up with. No one's blaming you, Jimmy, but why should she have to put up with his treatment?"

I wasn't sure where all this was leading. There was really nothing I could do. If I tried to intercede on her behalf with my ex-father-in-law, it would only make things worse. I knew Fletcher would take it out on her.

"And for what? For slave wages and so we can live in this cracker-box! And what did I get for my loyalty to him for twenty years? Two months severance pay and no disability, no retire-ment. He wouldn't pay the insurance premiums, so now we have to live like this. Do you know how hard this woman works for him? And what does she get for it besides his belittling attitude? Not even three hundred dollars a week! It makes me sick." Hector paused, looking toward Consuelo. She did not look up.

"He packs more up his nose every night at those sick parties of his than she makes in fifty hours of working."

I looked from Hector to Consuelo, confused by what he'd just said. He knew he had struck a chord with me. Consuelo refused to meet my look. "What do you mean?"

Hector was reaching his stride now. It was as if he was uncorking a bottle that had been ready to explode. "What I mean is that Hamilton and his brother, our trusted public servant, snort at least that amount of cocaine up their noses at those sex parties they have."

I sat back in my chair and looked at Hector in disbelief. Consuelo was motionless, but she didn't have to confirm what Hector was saying. I could tell it was true by the look in her eyes.

"You wouldn't believe what goes on over there. Those two old men and young girls. I mean *young* girls. It's disgusting what they are doing, these rich men. This Senator and his brother. They're both over sixty! They're animals. If the public only knew. And they subject my poor wife to all of this…this. Do you know how many times she has accidentally walked in on something like that? They'll even call her into the room while those things are going on without a thought as to whether or not she'd object. It's like they don't even consider her human. My wife is a very religious woman."

I looked over at Consuelo. Her face was red with embarrassment. "What kind of things?"

Hector looked to his wife as if he was going to ask her to leave the room. "Honey…."

Consuelo looked up first to me and then to Hector. "No. I want to stay. I'll tell him." She turned back to me. "They have young girls there a few nights a week. Usually around the weekends. They sit around the pool and the cabana and don't put any clothes on for the whole weekend. They do cocaine all night and sleep all day. Hamilton and his brother walk around…"

Consuelo stopped, embarrassed, but she was determined to go on.

"They walk around and feel up these girls any way they want, as if they were petting a dog. And they give them cocaine, lots of cocaine and have their way with them. And on weekends, in the cabana, sometimes they have these young men there and they have these sex parties with everyone together in a big pile....... doing things..."

Hector interrupted her. "That's enough. He gets the idea."

"Who are these people?"

She looked to Hector for approval before going on. "The men are usually the same every week. I've seen them around before. One is Mr. Fletcher's helicopter pilot."

"What about the girls? Who are they?"

"They're different all the time. Sometimes new ones from Friday to Saturday night. They're very young, fifteen, sixteen. He gives them all the cocaine they want as long as they do what he says."

"Where does he get them from?"

"I'm not sure about that. Runaways, I think, maybe. There is another woman who is always there. She shows up with them and they stay for a day or so and then she takes them away and brings in a couple more. I don't know where she gets them."

"Who is this woman? Do you know her? Have you ever seen her before?"

Consuelo stopped and looked at Hector once again. Hector nodded. "Tell him."

She shrugged, as if unsure of herself. "Her name is Adrianne. I remember seeing her before.....I think she might have been a friend of Nikki's. I think I remember Nikki bringing her around just before......"

"What does she look like?"

"She's about thirty. Dark hair. Very beautiful. She....leads the way."

"What do you mean?"

Hector put his hand on her arm. "She means this woman shows these young girls what to do, she demonstrates what's expected of them. She keeps them in line, and if they don't do what's expected right away, she gets them out of there."

"Do the girls do what she wants?"

Consuelo lowered her eyes. "Some hesitate.. ...But as soon as they see the cocaine......"

I sat back in my chair and drained the remaining *Cafe Cubano* from my cup. I looked to Hector, shrunken in anger. "Why are you telling me all this?"

"Because I'm sick of the way these men treat my wife! There is no reason why she should have to put up with it! She has spent her whole life, working her fingers to the bone to make an honest living and what thanks does she get? She is a religious woman, a moral woman, and they subject her to this decadence. Why should she have to see things like that? They have no respect for her. We thought we were leaving behind oppression and tyrants like them when we escaped from Cuba."

"What can I do?

Hector struggled to his feet and pulled the wheelchair to his side. His anger forced him to move and he fell back into it, trying to regain his composure or retain some shred of dignity.

"Because I tell you right now and before God that if those men are rude or disrespectful to my Consuelo again or abuse her in any way, I am going to make sure they suffer." Hector was nearly screaming, in his frustration. He was trembling and his voice was cracking as he tried to keep under control. "If I have to die in my attempt to make them suffer I am willing to die. What have I got to lose?" He gestured to his legs, his wheelchair, his surroundings, breathing heavily, defeated. "They have taken our dignity. No one should be allowed to do that to my wife. I am a *freedom fighter*. I have shown my willingness to die for what I believe in. And I will do so in the future if that is necessary."

I tried to think of something to comfort him, make him feel less ineffectual. How could I possibly understand the horror of what this man had seen in his lifetime. And here I was, giving him advice. "Hector, wait a minute. Please don't do anything just yet. Let me try to think of what I can do. If you do something right now, you'll be out on the street and you can't do that."

"Being out on the street is better than my wife having to work in the sewer with those people."

"Let me see what I can do. Give me a few days to think about this. Maybe I can do something. Consuelo, has Hamilton ever given you a retirement program, anything at all that you could live on until you can find another job if you leave there?"

"No, nothing. He doesn't even take Social Security out of my check. We....we have nothing for the future. We can hardly even keep up with Hector's medical bills."

"Let me see what I can do." The hollowness of my words made me angry with myself. I left them there, hopeless. I had tried to comfort them, but aside from trying to help Consuelo find another job, I couldn't think of how I could do anything just yet.

A thunderstorm was rumbling lazily overhead as I drove back to the Marina on Flagler Drive. The streets were empty, rare for a Friday night. I loved the streets empty and wet like that. Driving along the lakefront with no one else in sight made it seem as if this were my own private domain. No traffic made it look like it must have years ago, when my parents bicycled down the waterway and across the bridge to work. All this beauty and no crowds. Never to be that way again. A Paradise Lost, forever.

What Hector and Consuelo had told me distracted me from my concern about Joachim. I wanted to help them, but it would have to wait until I got the other problems in my life straightened out. But still, I couldn't get out of my mind what was going on at the Fletcher cabana, *our* cabana, since after my marriage had broken up and I had moved out. It was as if our private space were being violated.

Nikki had taken me to the cabana on our third date, and it was there, under the intoxicating slow breeze being stirred up by the paddle fans fifteen feet above us, that we made love for the first time. But I had already fallen hopelessly in love with her by then.

CHAPTER 19

That first night when I met Nikki, almost four years before, I was bartending at *BEFORE THE MAST*. It seems so long ago. She'd come in and had sat down at a table with some friends and from that very first moment, I couldn't take my eyes from her face. She was deeply tanned and she wore her shiny, streaked blonde hair in an intricate French braid. With her dark blue eyes, she was the perfect Palm Beach Aryan dream-child. She was the type of woman who wore her wealthy breeding subtly, despite her otherwise classy look. A simple glance should have told me the entire story: old money, private schools, concerns different than everyone else's. She was with another beautiful woman and two guys in blazers who looked as if they had stepped out of a *LAND'S END* catalog. I felt like one of my nerdy high school students in the school cafeteria, watching the in-crowd pass by with their trays, while I sat with the steerage class, wondering how to fit in. I was definitely out of her league.

They drank for an hour and then the other three left, while Nikki remained behind. She moved from the table to the end bar stool and took out a cigarette. With a typical bartender flourish, I lit her cigarette and she smiled and then turned back to the picture window that overlooked the Intracoastal, Alligator Island, and the Old Biltmore Hotel on the other side of the Waterway.

I started to walk away, when, to my surprise she started talking. I heard her voice behind me, and since the bar was empty, I knew she had to be talking to me.

"Nice view. Not a bad work environment."

I looked out the window. A sixty-five foot Rybovich was cruising by, its lights aglow.

"It's beautiful, all right. Takes my mind off my day job." For some reason I felt compelled to let this stranger know I was more than just a bartender.

"What do you do during the day?" She seemed genuinely curious. Another surprise.

"I teach High School English over at Palm Beach High."

"The Hill."

She was right. "The Hill." A dilapidated old building on a bluff on the south edge of West Palm Beach's ghetto, filled daily with students who didn't care a whit about its rich history.

"Only the natives know it by that name."

"I am a native."

"Really? Where did you go to High School?" The question has always been a litmus test around here. Like a lot of small communities, you could tell a lot about a native by where they went to High School.

"Graham-Eckes Academy."

I was surprised at the mention of the exclusive Palm Beach private school. "I went to Palm Beach High."

"So you went back to your Alma Mater to teach."

"Yeah, living out some idealistic adolescent dream."

"Why are you working here?"

"So I can afford to teach."

She laughed at that. "The old 'school-teacher's-salary-syndrome?'"

"You got it. How about you?"

"I help out in my father's business. Building supplies."

She answered so quickly, so naturally, in so off-hand a manner, I didn't realize it was a gross understatement. I wouldn't find out until three dates later, when it was already too late for my heart, that her father owned the largest lumber conglomerate in the country and that she was an heiress.

We talked for another hour, until closing, and she was so beautiful, so friendly, so down-to-earth and level-headed that I wouldn't have guessed who she was or what she really was about. As I was checking out the cash register, she surprised me again.

"You have time for a cup of coffee?"

"Sure."

"How about Denny's?"

"A personal favorite of mine."

"Great...."

"I have to start teaching in eight hours."

"We'll make it half a cup."

Outside, the night was clear. She looked toward me.

"Shall we go in two cars?"

"I rode my bike."

She pointed to a navy, 450-SL Mecedes convertible. I pretended not to notice, but suddenly I was self- conscious over my beat up Bug parked back home in my mother's driveway. I almost laughed out loud at myself and the irony.

We drove her car, top down, west on Okeechobee Road. First over coffee, and then two hours later, Western omelets, we spent the rest of that night in a chilled restaurant booth, talking. We talked about our common interests, my teaching, growing up in Florida, even American Literature. We discovered our mutual fascination with Florida History.

We talked about everything, everything that is, except who she was and what she was. But by that time, in those few short hours, I had fallen for her. It was all so easy. She seemed so aware, so alert, with a confident, easy sense of humor that told me she felt comfortable with herself and with me. She told me her favorite books, her favorite authors, and I was surprised and secretly thrilled by our common interests and her wealth of knowledge. It was one of those moments that I was tempted to say, "Where have you been all my life?"

I was so swept up off my feet, I didn't realize that by daybreak we had been talking for over six hours. She drove us back to *BEFORE THE MAST* as the Eastern sky was turning blue and pink.

As I was building up my courage to ask what I figured would be a preposterous question, she beat me to it. "This was fun. Why don't we get together again sometime?"

I tried to act nonchalant. "Sure. Maybe we can catch a movie. When would be a good time?"

"How about tomorrow night? Or I guess I mean 'tonight,' since it's already 'today'. Does that make sense?"

We both laughed, and she radiated such warmth, such friendliness, I wanted to take her smiling face in my hands and bury my face in hers.

That night was my night off as bartender, but I would have said yes anyway.

"Why don't we meet here around seven? You bought breakfast, so I'll buy you a drink before the movie starts."

It seemed too good to be true. "Sure," was all I could say.

She extended her hand for me to shake. "It was nice meeting you. I had a great time. I like surprises like this."

And what a surprise. Yes, it certainly was a surprise. Nikki was full of them. I shook her hand and nodded and she got back in her car. Something told me that this was going to be the start of something. I didn't know what. I didn't know how. But I had almost a premonition that this was not just another casual date. This was going to be something different. I only wish whatever spirit it was that spoke to me that night had finished the story.

She started to drive away, but stopped. "Hey Jimmy."

"Yeah?"

"Don't fall asleep in front of your kids today." She laughed and drove off before I could react. I watched her car cross over the Flagler Memorial Bridge and into the Palm Beach sunrise.

I went through the motions at school that day, unable to concentrate on what I was doing; a bad sign.

That night we met in the parking lot of *BEFORE THE MAST*, as arranged, had a drink inside and then drove over to the Carefree Theater to see a foreign film. Usually films carry me off, much like fiction, and for two hours I am distracted from my everyday life. But on that night I was distracted by Nikki. I hardly paid attention to the film, except as it related to Nikki's reactions. Instead, I sat and paid attention to how she reacted, what made her laugh. During a rather explicit lovemaking scene, we both sat motionless, as if afraid to react, and the silence between us became awkward. What was she thinking about while the two on-screen lovers built toward a climax? Was she wondering what I was thinking? Was she thinking of me? What the movements we were watching on-screen would be like between the two of us?

Later, near the end of the film, she reached over and put her hand on top of mine, then turned it over and held it softly. She held it until the film had ended and we reached the car. We drove aimlessly down South Dixie Highway and at Lake Worth Road she suggested we drive over the bridge to the Lake Worth Pier. Another surprise.

We passed a group of men admiring restored antique motorcycles, swapping maintenance tips, travel yarns, and lore. I asked her if she wanted to stop and look at the cycles, but she pulled me forward quickly, after pausing first, almost as if in a pose, in front of the men.

We bought spectator tickets at the Bait & Tackle shop and Nikki ordered two tall cans of Bud. We walked down the long wooden planks to where two silent fishermen watched us sit down on the bench. At their feet was a pool of blood and fish scales from where they had cut bait, and the smell of the fish mixed with the brine in the breeze brought back a flood of memories of my own fishing trips.

The pier had originally been built in 1957 as a tourist attraction to compete with the Palm Beach "Rainbow" pier five miles up the coast. It had been rebuilt, undergoing extensive repairs after Hurricane David in 1978.

I'd landed an eighty pound shark off this pier on New Year's Eve during twelfth grade. Bobby and Joachim had been at my side, cheering me on. We welcomed in the 1970's grilling huge chunks of shark steaks on the beach at daybreak. Who could have known I would make a triumphant return to this very same pier a dozen years later with the most beautiful woman on earth? I sat there with Nikki, sipping from a can of beer, and she was smiling at me.

"I guess you've been here before."

"I used to practically live here."

"I'm surprised I never saw you here. I used to come all the time with my girlfriends and watch the surfers."

"Well, then you probably have seen me before. We used to surf here a lot, too." Only a thousand days on the endless vacation that made up my early teen years. The hardest part of those days was trying to decide whether to surf here or the Pump House on Singer Island in Riviera Beach. Different crowd; different girls; different surf; different breaks; different exhilaration; different payoff; different sense of triumph.

I looked toward Palm Beach. The lights of the condominiums twinkled. To the South was more of the same. That far from shore, it was almost as if we were at sea, looking toward landfall.

We sat there for two hours, exchanging reminiscences, wondering about how many times the paths of our lives might have crossed, yet, somehow, we'd never met before. After awhile the two fishermen left and we were alone in the moonlight. Looking toward Africa, the ocean was as smooth as a table top, and you probably could've water-skied to West End, Bahamas, in a couple of hours. It's been done before.

Then there was an awkward pause in our conversation as we sat there looking toward the bright, moonlit horizon, and we both knew it was the time. That moment, just seconds before a first kiss, when you change from unsure to positive, and then.....

I almost didn't want to kiss her right then. There would never be a moment of anticipation like this again. Holding back could make the inevitable moment even sweeter.

She turned to me and held my hand again. "I hope you don't think I'm too forward for holding hands on the first date?" The way she smiled when she said that, I had to kiss her. I couldn't wait any longer. I looked at her and smiled back and cupped my hand under her cheek and our eyes met and held. I didn't want to hurry. It was the moment. I didn't want to rush and have the moment end so quickly. So I caressed her cheek and pulled her toward me on the bench to hold her closely. Only then, after her reassurance, her silent approval, did I kiss her, and the moment I did, I knew somehow I would never kiss another woman that way for as long as I lived. From that first kiss, I knew we would never be apart, that we would spend the rest of our lives together, have children, grow old together. It was another premonition, so strong, I knew it had to be true. Somehow, I would make it happen despite what seemed like overwhelming odds against it.

After our kiss she smiled at me and leaned her head on my shoulder and stared into the night. A June breeze blew her hair into my face. There was something about this woman I was with that I had never experienced before. She seemed so open, so honest, so down to earth and level headed. Her intelligence was enticing. Everything about her excited me. But there were two questions that bothered me so, that I wanted immediate answers to them, and I thought then I would never know the answers:

What was a woman like her doing with a guy like me?

How could I keep her forever?

Since that Spring night in the balmy, fish-scented air on the

Lake Worth pier, three hundred feet closer to the African coastline than the rest of the world at that moment, I've found out the
answers to both of those questions.

I have found out "what" a woman like her was doing with a
guy like me.

I have found out that I couldn't "keep her forever."

We walked back to my car and drove back to where she had
left hers in the parking lot at *BEFORE THE MAST*. Along the
way, I tried to start a frantic, desperate strategy. How could I seem
interested in her without being overly so? I didn't want to scare
her off. I didn't have to worry about that.

At her car she smiled her smile again, and I knew I was in
way over my head. And then another surprise. "Would you like to
go on a picnic tomorrow night?" Somehow, a picnic was the last
thing I thought she would suggest.

"A picnic?"

"Sure. I'll make up a basket and we can build a fire on Blowing Rocks Beach."

"A picnic? I have to work the bar, here, Friday and Saturday
night. How about Sunday night?"

She nodded.

So Sunday night it was. But for the next two days and nights I
was obsessed with my new friend. I was so distracted, the waitress
even kidded me about it at work Saturday night. "You must be in
love."

Sunday night at sunset we drove north over the Martin County
Line and pulled into a grove of Australian Pines. The wind passing through the long branches whispered softly above us as we
walked on a soft blanket of fallen pine needles three feet thick. We
shared the picnic basket handle between us. Nikki reached down
to remove her shoes.

"Don't, I said. "Monkey balls," referring to the tiny round pine cones from the Australian Pines with dozens of razor sharp edges. "Wow, you call them that, too?" She laughed, replacing her shoe.

Another litmus test of a native. "Why not? That's what they are." Another laugh.

On the beach, the jagged limestone outcroppings stretched before us, separating us from the water. During the winter, when the rough seas pound against the rock, the wave action burrows underneath and creates a shelf-like overhang. Finally, the limestone wears thin, undermined by the taunting of a million winter waves, and first a tiny hole, then a larger one is created, the size of a saucer. The waves crash in with such impact, the rounded-out cavities act like blow holes, and the pounding surf is forced forty feet into the air in a *whooshing* explosion of salt water froth.

But now, this spring night, the sea was calm, and we staked a claim on the empty beach with our towel and basket and picked up dried driftwood for a fire. There, alone on that beach that night, I knew I had found the woman of my dreams. We cuddled in each other's arms like high school kids and she nuzzled my face. I explored her hair, pulled it back over her ears as I ran my hands down the curve of her neck, slowly, down her collar line to her shoulder. Finally, in the glow of the last embers, she stood and pulled me to my feet. I thought she wanted us to leave. But before I knew what was happening, she was dragging me toward the water.

In a cut in the rocky outcropping, we splashed in, unafraid, fully clothed but for the shoes we'd left behind. With only our heads above water, we embraced and kissed deeply. I was overcome by excitement, but even more overwhelmed with happiness, a happiness I hadn't felt for years. The combination made me want to tear our clothes off and devour her.

The buoyancy of the water helped her lift her legs up and straddle my waist. When she squeezed my hips gently with her thighs I lost my breath in anticipation of what this might feel like later. The hugs with her thighs meant she wasn't just inviting me in, she was accepting me, and it was the acceptance, more than the invitation, that drove me to madness. It was more than lust I felt for her. I was in love after three dates and didn't want this feeling to ever stop.

We went as far as we could in the water with our clothes on, caressing one another so slowly, exploring so gently, hesitantly, and then she pulled away, never taking her eyes from mine, never letting go of her innocent half-smile.

"I want to leave now."

I tried not to look disappointed, but apparently failed. She waited, as if taunting a reaction from me, then she spoke, choosing her words carefully. She smiled again. "I want to take you home with me," she whispered in my ear. Her breath in my ear made me shudder. The world was slowing to a stop as it approached its ascendancy.

Again, she led the way.

We drove back along US Route #1, our soaked, salty clothing sticking to us and my vinyl car seats. It was so exhilarating, I could hardly drive. She kneaded my right hand in her own the whole trip as we rode in silent anticipation. I didn't dare say anything for fear she would change her mind.

This time we didn't stop in the parking lot to pick up her car. We drove straight across the Flagler Memorial Bridge and headed north on Bradley Place toward North County Road. As we drove past the Biltmore Hotel, I stopped thinking about what was surely about to happen, long enough to remember, however briefly, about my tenure as a busboy there, then long enough to wonder about where we were heading. And then to my astonishment, she told me to turn left onto Alligator Island Road.

I had never been on Alligator Island before that night. I just knew about it and the four exclusive homes and property from an earlier era that now occupied the twenty-acre island. I could see it from the lounge window where I worked at night if I craned my neck far enough to the North. I could see how the other half lived.

The guard at the guardhouse recognized Nikki and waved us through, but not without first giving my Beetle a look of displeasure. We disappeared down a jungle road of hardwoods wrapped in strangler fig until we came to a cul-de-sac with four gateways in view. From her pocketbook, Nikki pulled out a remote-controller and opened the steel gate that blocked her driveway. The wide stone path ran to the property on the southwest corner of the island. On either side of the gate, hedges twenty feet high hid the property from view.

To say I was surprised the first time I drove around that bend in the jungle-like driveway and came upon her home would be understatement. It was something out of a Roaring Twenties' storybook. A real Mizner mansion, maintained to absolute perfection in a jungle clearing. I had seen most of the homes on Palm Beach, at least as much as you can see when you drive by, or walk past carrying a surfboard. But this was more. This transcended magnificence.

"That's where my father and uncle live. My place is around back."

She directed me to the rear of the house, and I parked my car on the edge of the Chattahoochee gravel. A white clapboard cabana with a high-peaked roof sat in a grove of Coconut Palms. A broad front porch held wicker chairs and two of the pillars supported a woven hammock. The floor-to-ceiling windows were covered with Bahama shutters.

Inside, it looked as if I were on the set of a 1930's tropical island movie mystery. Pecky cypress, pickled white, surrounded us on four sides in the huge, open, high-ceilinged room. Beneath our feet, thick, foot-square terra cotta tiles covered the floor; and above, suspended from the cathedral ceiling, two huge paddle fans hummed softly as the blades twirled in lazy circles. A single lamp burned on an end table next to a heavy, muslin-covered sofa, its amber light illuminating a hundred framed black and white photographs on the wall. I glanced at one, a family picture, people unknown to me at the moment, but soon to become my in-laws: A fifteen year old Nikki, seated on her father's knee; her mother, standing behind them with Uncle Danforth; and her brother, Victor, somber even at fifteen, staring straight ahead. It was an innocent enough looking photograph, I thought when I looked at it that night for the first time. But the look in their eyes couldn't disguise the fact they held secrets not very far below the surface.

In the back of the room, on the Intracoastal Waterway side, I could see a low platform bed in front of a set of French doors. Nikki walked quickly to the back, folded aside a row of louvered shutters and opened the outer doors. A breeze drifted in and filled the room with fresh, briny air.

She came to me, her sticky wet hair speckled with beach sand, and held me tightly.

I had been in love before. Once or twice in high school, and again, briefly, with a graduate student at the University of Florida who was two years older than me and who had an IQ up around 400. She had been way out there, intellectually speaking, and I couldn't keep up my end of the conversation. But nothing before had felt like this night. Nothing matched the intensity of my passion, the uninhibited flow of my emotions for this woman I had met less than a week earlier. I just let myself go; an endless, tumbling, free-fall backwards into the pitch dark void that surrounded my life.

It was almost as if I didn't want the inevitable to happen right then, because I knew I would not be able to abide it when the night was over. But there was not a thing I could have done to stop it, even if I had wanted to.

She took my hand and led me to the table lamp and turned it off. Moonlight spilled into the room, and after a moment, when my eyes adjusted to the darkness, I could see her eyes staring straight up into mine.

"I know we've only known each other for a few days," she whispered. "But I know for sure this is right."

So innocent and pure and sincere. I knew for sure it was right, too. I never thought to stop and ask any questions. No answers that night would have stopped me.

She led me to the edge of the bed and unbuttoned my damp shirt. I began to tremble. It was from the paddle fan breeze cooling my wet clothes, I told myself.

We moved as if in a dream. I wanted to rush, take her, not hold back, come inside her as quickly as I could. But I forced myself to move slowly, to savor each touch of her skin.

I rubbed my face all over her. I didn't want to just kiss her or lick her. I wanted to absorb her being, her essence, through my face. And so I traveled over her, sopping up every inch of her, exploring, deeply inhaling her private scents, tasting, until neither of us could stand it any longer.

She reached under my arms and slowly pulled my face up over her waist and breasts and neck until our eyelashes brushed against one another. Deliberately, she reached down, and with her fingertips she took me and gently put me inside of her, her eyes never leaving mine, as if wanting to see my reaction to the very moment I entered her slowly and experienced her wetness for the first time. I didn't disappoint her.

"There," she said. "There, now." As if comforting a deeply troubled soul before a deep, peaceful sleep.

I was too distracted to tell whether the look in her eyes matched mine: They pierced through me and I was hypnotized. I wanted to know exactly what she was thinking.

After we had made love for a second time she stood; looked out the French doors. She was in remote concentration, but it was impossible to tell whether with regret or joy or accomplishment. She turned and pulled me out of bed. Grabbing a towel, she led me toward the door. She was suddenly serious, as if having just offered herself to me, she was now allowing me to savor a special privilege.

Decisively, as if after long deliberation, she said, "I want to show you a very special place."

As if she hadn't already done just that.

She threw open the door and led me, naked, onto the lawn beside the cabana. I looked toward the darkened house and wondered who lived inside. What would their reaction be if they wakened in the middle of the night and glanced out the window to see two people prancing across the lawn, naked in the moonlight? They would call the police, and I would surely lose my teaching job.

Nikki held my cock in her hands as she led me, pulled me into a thick grove of coconut palms to what, in the darkness, appeared to be a tall hedge or solid wall of foliage. The sound of falling water, as if from a fountain in the distance, confused me. Getting closer, I could see it was not a tall hedge so typical in Palm Beach. It was a large berm, shaped into a small mountain, as tall as the house, and completely covered by exotic broadleaf foliage and jungle orchids. A pathway disappeared around the bend in the dark.

"What is this?"

"It's my grandfather's idea of a jungle-gym. Before he died he had it made for my brother and me to play on. It has over four thousand orchid plants and thousands of ferns and twenty varieties of palm trees. There's a Strap Fern that stands over twelve feet tall. It's almost prehistoric looking. He took a lot of the exotic plants from an old cypress hammock. The whole thing covers over an acre and at one time it was the highest land elevation in the Town of Palm Beach."

"I bet the town zoning and building people loved this."

"He made them love it. You can be very convincing when you

own someone."

She led me down her grandfather's garden path as it circled the man-made mountain. Walking up the incline toward the top I completely forgot we were unclothed. It was all so natural. I was Adam, Nikki was my Eve in this lush Garden of Eden.

On the opposite side of the mountain from where the path had begun, facing the West Palm Beach skyline to the south, was a wooden deck. A small coquina stone pool, the size of a large hot tub, was off the deck, and on the far side, water spilled over the coquina rock ledge creating an artificial waterfall.

"Come here, look at this."

As she stepped in front of me, I looked down at the length of her. The fluid we had just brewed between us was gushing out of her, running down the insides of her thighs in thick rivulets, and I was almost overcome with a primordial, animalistic urge.

Nikki led me down three steps and across the pool, the muscles in her thighs tightening like smooth brown ropes as they fought against the water resistance. The water was as warm as a bath. We leaned across the rocky lip, water slopping over the edge from our movement. Thirty feet below was another small pool, surrounded by dense tropical foliage. I felt as if I had stepped into a postcard from Jamaica.

"When we turn on the pumps all the way it's like a regular waterfall. You can slide down this chute to the bottom."

I hung over the edge, staring down at this rich man's version of a backyard playhouse. I looked up across the Intracoastal to the skyline I had watched change throughout my life. I was seeing it all now, for the very first time, from a new perspective.

"The best part of it all, is that from over there you can't even tell what this is. It blends in with all the rest of the high foliage on the island. People in West Palm just think it's another hedge. My grandfather planted it that way."

Nikki leaned back in the pool, her legs spread wide, inviting me to join her. I glided toward her, the look on her face wishing me instantly erect.

"It's my own secret garden," she whispered, grasping my hips with her ankles, pulling me inside her.

"And mine now, too," I wanted to moan, losing myself to her forever. *Forever.*

In just a few short hours' time, I had come to understand the feeling of the complete and utter powerlessness and hopelessness of an addiction.

Afterward, breathless, we lay in the moonlight, the breeze washing over the moistness of our skin, and murmured to one another until daylight. I had talked to her more in three long dates than I had ever spoken to another woman in my life, or so it seemed. Here was a very beautiful, super intelligent, obviously very rich woman, with a body that could serve as the definition of physical perfection, lying next to me in a private paradise. Now I knew how the "other half" lived. If it was, I wanted to be a part of the other half; a part of her.

Yet with all of these obvious trappings of her wealth, it was our conversations that left me with no other choice but to fall in love with her. It was the intercourse of our minds that I thirsted for most; that filled and nourished me. She was the only person I've ever met who has read more books than I have, and who was able to recall even far more details; recognize subtle allusions; analyze stylistic nuance and linguistic flourishes. Her grasp of the language and her recitation of specific passages amazed me. She would quote long passages from memory of Wordsworth, Frost, even Robert Penn Warren. That night she recited from memory, for over twenty minutes, the first person narration of Jack Burden, as he describes his falling in love with Anne Stanton in *ALL THE KING'S MEN*. Perhaps one of the most beautifully composed passages of fiction in all of American Literature, and she recalled it spontaneously, at will, to entertain and astound me. The music poured from her lips as she sang her song to me. It was as if someone had told her it was one of my favorite passages.

How could this be so?

I wanted to talk to her forever, walk through libraries of our collective pasts, pointing out favorite passages, dialogue, character sketches of friends created in the imaginations of Fowles, Styron, Oates, and Updike. I wanted to escape from the realities of teaching bored students in dreary classrooms and somehow live the literary lifestyles of the creators with my newfound *enamorata*.

As we watched the West Palm Beach skyline become brighter with the morning sun rising to the East of Eden, we had been talking almost non-stop for over eight hours. We had poured out our souls to one another that night, taking out time periodically to explore one another's bodies in a slow motion, liquid embrace.

I have never been happier in my life than I was that one night in that cabana and atop the hidden jungle mountain paradise on Alligator Island in Palm Beach. It was all too good to be true.

It was all too good to be true.

CHAPTER 20

I've never really given much thought to the meaning of true love. My experience in college was fleeting, and when it was over, I didn't have the time to dwell on it. The girl in question decided she didn't want to be involved with what she labeled a "scholar," even though she was one herself. So she moved on down the highway; drove off the jock-strap-party-animal-exit-ramp, and the last I'd heard, was having a hell of a time. I was in the final throes of finishing my Master's thesis after seventeen straight semesters in college, including summers, and didn't have time to get philosophical or morose.

Maybe that's why when I met Nikki and I fell in love with her, I didn't know what to expect or how to deal with it. I thought we would make slow, steady progress, keep seeing one another, and let nature take its course. If it worked out, fine. If it didn't, I would learn to deal with that, somehow, too.

That's not the way it happened. After our first night of love-making on her magic mountain, my life fell apart in any practical sense. I gave up caring about anything; my mother, my jobs, my life. If I hadn't already taught the same classes for ten years before, I would have been unprepared everyday. As it was, I was distracted, and the students sensed it. I put in the motions, went to the classes, assigned lots of classroom reading and spent hours gazing out the window waiting for the day to end so I could see Nikki again. All the love-song lyricists have the emotions pegged already: *spellbound; addicted to love; too weak to fight; just a prisoner of love.*

If it had been a normal dating situation, feeling our way along, things might have been different. But from the very first meeting, and especially after our first night of intimacy, she was in charge of the direction and trajectory of the relationship. We started out in the fast track and accelerated from there. I had never experienced anything like it. It was all just too easy. It was as if she spent her days researching, then planning something to take us to the next step that evening. Never had I met a woman whose sole ambition, however non-chalant, seemed to be to make me fall deeper in love with her. It was as if she had spent months researching my life; my likes and dislikes; my hopes and dreams. And every night, the knowledge that she had gained was put into practice until she had pushed every proverbial button on my somewhat limited emotional hit-list.

She really needn't bothered to have gone to all the trouble. After the first night I was so far gone, so far out of control, there was no going back. Any self-analysis or comparing my feelings to an obsession or a hopeless addiction was moot by that point. I was not in control of my feelings or my life, and I really didn't care. She was leading me around effortlessly. And little ol' me, so hopelessly naïve, was going along for the ride.

Was it her amazing beauty? Her unquestioning devotion to me? Her far superior intelligence? She was far more intelligent than I had ever hoped to be, as evidenced by her deeper and far more analytical understanding of all the literature I had read, studied, and taught; her command of languages, including Spanish, French and Russian; her comments on everything around her, expressed in an almost poetic way without hesitation. After many an astute observation on her part, I found myself asking "Why didn't I think of that?" Added to that was her almost uncanny ability to second guess what I was thinking. Was it her position in the Palm Beach Society that she was introducing me to? Her enormous wealth? The intensity of her devoted lovemaking? Her early commitment to allow me to lead my life while being absorbed into hers?

It was all of the above, combined with her decisiveness to take charge of the relationship from the beginning; to hold on to me and not let go. Not in any overt, obnoxious, or contrived way. There were no obstacles we couldn't overcome; that she couldn't overcome. I was just swept along by the tide, powerless to resist even if I had wanted to.

For two weeks we spent every minute together that I wasn't working my two jobs. We spent most of that time in her cabana, in bed, in some glorious, otherworldly marathon of lustful satiation that always began with delicate and sensitive love-filled passion and invariably ended in common animalistic rutting. Her sexual appetites astounded me, intrigued me, enveloped me, frightened me.

In between bouts she would lead me around town from one of the best of Palm Beach Society's watering holes to another.

After two weeks I quit my job at *BEFORE THE MAST*. It was a sign of my old life ending, and the beginning of my new life. After another two weeks, when she was sure I wasn't going to wander off out of boredom or burn-out or whatever other reason, she surprised me one Saturday afternoon.

"I want you to meet my family."

It was time. We had been traipsing across the back lawn of her family's home for a month, not exactly sneaking, but waiting until darkness to come and go, avoiding any contact other than the gatekeeper at the guardhouse. I had looked up at the huge Mizner home each time we walked toward the cabana or to her Garden of Eden. It always stared back at me silently. I was never able to understand why a house, albeit this was a mansion, could be so imposing,

By family she meant her father, Hamilton Fletcher III, her

uncle, Senator Danforth Fletcher, her twin brother, Victor, and
the housekeeper, Consuelo. Her mother had been institutional-
ized in North Carolina several years earlier and remained in constant care. After Nikki's first brief discussion of her Mom several
weeks prior, there had been no further mention. It was something
the family didn't talk about. I just assumed it was some sort of
embarrassing nervous breakdown, perhaps an alcohol problem,
and left it at that.

"All right," I said, curious about the urgency in her voice.

We had slipped into the cabana the night before and had spent
the next hours in our usual routine. Being intimate as I had never
experienced before, walking hand in hand to the waterfall and
gazing across Lake Worth to the West Palm Beach skyline. At
dawn, we had walked back to the cabana and slept until noon.
As I stepped from the shower, aching with exhaustion, she had
surprised me with the question

"I think it's time, don't you?"

"Sure, whatever you say." That was my problem. Whatever
she said was fine with me.

"Aren't you going to ask why?"

I laughed. "Okay, 'why?'"

Instead of answering, she stepped forward and embraced
me."I want us to be together. Forever. I want us to get married."

Overcome with emotion, all I could do was say over and over,
"Yes, yes. I want that too." In fact, I had thought of nothing else
since our first meeting.

I put on my standard-issue khakis, boat shoes and blue golf
shirt and we walked across the broad back lawn toward the house.

Entering through the rear kitchen door, she first introduced me
to Consuelo. Nikki had already told me her story, and I liked and
trusted her immediately.

We worked our way through the kitchen to the dining room
and then into the hallway that ran the length of the house to the
circular stairway at the opposite end of the mansion. It was like

walking through a museum. The family portrait of the father and mother and two young sons, who were now the two now-adult sons I was about to meet, commanded the hallway.

We stopped to admire the painting. "That's my father and brother when they were kids. Are you ready to meet them?"

"Sure."

At the end of the hall was the entrance to a study and she lead me in, unannounced, hand in hand.

Her father and Uncle Danforth, the Florida Senator, were huddled over a large mahogany desk at the far corner of the room. A bay window overlooked Lake Worth.

"Dad, Uncle Danforth?"

They looked up smiling. Their accommodating smiles were obviously the inspiration for Nikki's own. Their manner suggested they were used to this sort of interruption, being introduced to a friend of Nikki's.

Her father spoke first. "Morning, or should I say 'Good Afternoon,' Nikki." He stepped forward and extended his hand. It was a practiced gesture, one he probably used in business a hundred times a day. This was going to be easy, I thought.

"Dad, Uncle Danforth, I'd like you to meet my fiancé."

Her father and uncle exchanged looks. Curious smiles crossed their faces; surprised smiles; concerned smiles.

Hamilton looked from his daughter back to me for an awkward moment, hand still extended, smile still pasted on. "Well, I guess congratulations are in order," he said, attempting to disguise the coldness in his voice.

"Thank you, sir," I said, shaking his hand. He tried hard not to make his appraisal of me blatant, but he was sizing me up, trying to tell from my bearing, my boat shoes and khakis what side of the tracks I was from, whether I was acceptable breeding stock for his daughter. I half expected him to whip an application form out of his top drawer and ask me to fill it out. I tried not to take it personally. I was committed to doing my best for her at that point, even if it was only with a schoolteacher's salary. Nikki had warned me about their reaction to any prospective suitors, but I hadn't expected quite this reception.

Uncle Danforth stepped forward, his hand now extended as he completed his own split second evaluation.

"Congratulations, son. I'm sorry, I didn't get your name."

"Dad, Uncle Danforth, I'd like you meet Jimmy Phipps."

It's difficult to describe the progression of their facial expressions over the next few seconds. It happened so fast, so unexpectedly, that for months I ran it over and over again in my memory. Simultaneously, as if choreographed, the smiles on the brothers' faces faded as they turned from Nikki to me and then back to her. Their shoulders started to slump before they caught themselves. Then, there was a silence that engulfed the room for an interminable amount of time. Was it seconds? It seemed like minutes as they stared at Nikki as if trying to think of some appropriate response.

I couldn't figure out what it was, and was left to believe the worst. I had somehow failed their visual inspection, and was now resigned to the junk-heap of West Palm Beach riff-raff, who was simply unacceptable for their daughter to date, let alone marry. I hadn't realized that contempt and condescension could be so tangible. I was embarrassed more for their bad manners than for myself. Their immediate dismissal of me as unsuitable for their daughter didn't really bother me at the time. I was a big boy, I thought, well aware of how this Palm Beach crowd thought. I could deal with it. When they got to know the real me, they wouldn't be so judgmental, I was convinced in the split seconds that unfurled.

The silence went on. Nikki returned their stares in a display that was surely for my benefit. Her face was so innocent, so full of hope for the future; our future. Her silent expression seemed to ask, "What's wrong?"

Finally, her Uncle broke the awkward silence. He spoke

slowly, calculatingly, with a cold, even manner that would later become so familiar. "Have you lost your mind?"

Hamilton answered for her. "Yes. She has lost her mind."

Nikki turned and ran out the door and down the hall.

I turned back to her father who was exchanging stares with his brother. I was determined to prove my mettle to them. In the awkwardness of the moment I was able to stumble out, "I'll be a good husband for her, sir."

Hamilton sat in the leather chair behind his desk and turned to the lake view. Danforth busied himself shuffling papers on the desk, ignoring my presence.

"It was nice meeting you both. Mr. Fletcher, Senator, I've read a lot about you both. I'll do my best to prove that I am worthy of Nikki."

When neither responded, I excused myself and left.

Nikki was in the kitchen with Consuelo. She was seated in a ladderback chair, her head in her hands. Consuelo stood behind her, comforting her. It was the first time in our brief relationship where she was not in complete control of the situation.

I walked to them and put my hand on Nikki's shoulder. "I guess they don't like the idea of you getting married. Afraid that I'm some fortune hunter, right?" I tried to make light of it.

Nikki reached for my hand and gave it a squeeze. "I don't care what they think. We're getting married."

Two weeks later we flew to Las Vegas and were married in a quickie ceremony in a chapel on Decatur Street. No maid of honor or best man. No Elvis impersonators. No wedding party and limousine or gluttonous reception at Flagler's Whitehall. No society photographer and no society page coverage. Just us. Her family was unaware of what we were doing. My mother wished us the best when we stopped by to announce our plans and say goodbye on our way to PBIA.

And, oh, yes; there was no prenuptial agreement. Nikki had insisted on that.

When we got back to Palm Beach we moved into our little love shack by The Magic Mountain full-time. And so began our, or should I say *my*, "lost days."

After a month of marriage and lengthy closed-door negotiations between Nikki and her father, I was allowed into the main house. The interaction between her father, her uncle, and me was cold, distant, perfunctory, at best. I continued to chalk it up as "fear-of-fortune-hunter-son-in-law" syndrome.

The next three years were a whirlwind of ignoring my students and society parties. Seven nights a week of partying. Money being spent on a disgraceful level, the balmy tropical air heady with pretension. It was a difficult adjustment, trying to convince myself that I was really a part of all this. I tried to fit right in with Nikki's crowd, absorbing the new culture and taking on its airs, its special language and attitude. The harder I tried, the more successful I became and the more I hated myself for being a poseur. I might as well have been wearing clodhoppers and high-water pants. It would take much more than my new tuxedo to hide what I was to them. No matter how much money I might have acquired in the marriage I would never be anything more than some poor kid who grew up in a modest little home-made bungalow on the wrong side of town, whose annual schoolteacher's salary was less than what was spent on the party I happened to be attending that night.

And so I became "The Great Pretender;" *pretending that I was doing well; pretending to be, what I'm not, you see?* But one thing I didn't pretend to be was, in love with Nikki. Or is the type of love I'm having so much trouble describing more like some form of mental illness? Guilty as charged, your honor.

Did I really love her? Yes, I did. Yes, I do. I've never felt such extremes of happiness, of anguish, of desire, of hope, of fear, and I know I never will again. I loved her, *love* her, no matter what happened, no matter what she did to me and to our marriage, no matter how she turned out. If I had to list the ten *thousand* things I would require in a perfect woman for me, Nikki would have fulfilled every criterion and more. She was so much more than I could ever hope for. She was so much more than what she turned out to be, and that is the greatest tragedy. How does a person develop their character, their persona, their emotional and intellectual resources to the point of perfection, yet at the same time possess the wherewithal to achieve the opposite? Does this dichotomy exist in everyone? Did Sister Teresa possess the ability for pure evil? Could she murder hundreds of people with premeditated, malicious intent, simply on a whim?

Nikki had it all and she gave it all to me. My fault was in not realizing, not having the level of sophistication to realize, that in this package deal I was getting far more than what appeared on the surface. It would not, in fact, begin to appear even near the surface, until our marriage started dissembling at the end of three years.

CHAPTER 21

I decided to re-visit that cabana where Nikki and I had made love for the first time, just over three short years ago. I wanted to see for myself one of these parties Consuelo had just told me about. Had Nikki herself been involved with a similar party the night she'd died up in Conchtown in Riviera Beach?

Getting to the cabana on the heavily secured Alligator Island would not be easy. Going in the front way was out of the question. As far as the back way, all the properties were secured by electronic perimeter security systems.

But I knew there was a way. I had used it legitimately many times before.

I pulled my inflatable Zodiac over to the stern and loaded my dive gear into it. The battery powered 4-hp motor on the rubber raft started with a soft whirr and I was off. I hugged the shoreline going north, passing within a few feet of the lakefront television station and the same window of *BEFORE THE MAST* I had been looking out that first night I'd met Nikki three years earlier. When you grow up in a small town like West Palm Beach, you can't avoid passing where all your ghosts live. They are always around to haunt you no matter what streets you navigate. Through the picture window of the bar I could see the bartender inside mixing drinks. What fate awaited him? Would a Palm Beach heiress walk into the bar one night and sweep him off his feet?

I chugged past Good Samaritan Hospital and the radio tower.

Across the water to the East, the Biltmore Towers lit up the night sky. A mile north I pulled into the Currie Park Marina and tied up. As a child my mother had brought me here to slide down the giant slide that used to dominate the playground. Now, no one was around as I slipped into my wetsuit and pulled the double tank harness over my arms. I checked my wrist timer and compass and the small waterproof flashlight. I anchored the Zodiac about fifty feet from shore and disappeared over the side.

Underwater it was inky blackness ahead of me, but the moon cast a muted light off the white sand bottom. I checked my compass again and headed due Northeast to Alligator Island. Swimming at a depth of twenty feet, in a state of near-suspended animation, it was like floating in outer space; no sound except for my own breathing. Is this what a sensory deprivation tank is like, I wondered?

As I crossed the channel underwater, a yacht rumbled just a few feet overhead, oblivious to my presence beneath it. I stopped to watch it pass, the prop churning throatily. At that moment, did anyone on board suddenly have a sense that someone was swimming twenty feet below their hull? Did they look up to the skies then down to the water with a strange, eerie sensation? No, it can't be possible, they would have concluded.

On the east side of the channel I surfaced to get my bearings and made out the lights of the main Fletcher house rising above the grove of palm trees that surrounded it. Nikki's magic mountain was off to my left; the boathouse to the right.

I submerged and swam again until I was in shallow water. There, twenty feet from the island's shore, I turned off my air and looked around silently, cautiously, before treading water toward the gaping black entrance to the wood-frame and cedar-shake covered boathouse. The boathouse jutted out into the water from a concrete perimeter security wall, acting like a back porch to the property. I swam through the channel cut into the shoreline to harbor boat access and storage, and then coasted under the open archway. At this hour of darkness, the boathouse stood empty.

In the near darkness, I could see the ladder that led up the side of the pilings to the U-shaped dock. I pulled off my flippers and let them sink silently to the sandy bottom. It was low tide. The ladder descended below the water and I pulled myself up the rungs and stretched out quietly on the floor, catching my breath.

I removed my weight belt, tanks and vest. As I did, I thought of James Bond in "Dr. No," except there was no tuxedo underneath my wetsuit. Just a swimsuit and tee shirt. I checked the underwater flashlight that hung from my belt, twisting the end. The beam landed on the cypress plank doorway and the security box on the wall.

I stood, facing the moment of truth. I knew the code which would open the door. I had seen the maintenance men use it hundreds of times, and had used it myself every weekend. I knew that if a defeat code were not punched into the nearby security box just inside the wall within forty-five seconds, it would send out a silent alarm to the Palm Beach Police. I could only hope that Hamilton had not changed the six digit override code on the system. Whether or not the number was still the same, I would have no way of knowing unless, and until, the police arrived.

The security system was typical of many found on the island. There was even one at the front door of the house which would indicate "disarmed" on an L.E.D. read-out when the right code number was punched in. But that same "disarmed" indicator could also be triggered when a "hostage" or "kidnap" code number was punched in, tricking a would-be kidnapper into believing all was well until it was too late.

I took a breath and punched in the code. The deadbolt snapped open. I stepped through the boathouse door into the walled-in surroundings and raced to the metal box mounted knee-high, twenty feet inside, hidden at the base of a palm tree. There, I punched in the six digit entry number from memory. I waited silently for five minutes; more than enough time for the entire Palm Beach Police force to have arrived. But they didn't come. I've often wondered what would have happened if they had come that night. How it would have changed everything.

I followed the path northeast toward the cabana, passing through the foothills of the jungle garden. The Bermuda grass was soft on my bare feet as it had been that first night with Nikki. But this time, no one was leading me around by my cock.

Ahead, across fifty feet of open lawn and palm trees was the cabana. I knelt, waiting for any sign, any sound. The night was still. Through the Bahama shutters I could see a faint golden light from inside. I crawled across the lawn perimeter on my hands and knees, hoping to slide under the awning-like Bahama shutter. There, my view of the inside would be unobstructed.

Overhead, a hundred palm trees blocked the moonlight, their yellow clusters of coconuts appearing white. Their tall stately beauty, rising high above me on spindly trunks that looked like white concrete, had always amazed me. Apparently they had intrigued early settlers as well. Most people thought they were indigenous to South Florida, but like many things associated with South Florida, including the Seminole Indians, the namesake trees were relative newcomers. *La PROVEDENCIA* had wrecked off the coast during a storm in 1878 and a hold-full of wine and the African coconuts, on board as a food supply, had washed ashore. Early settlers considered them a novelty and had carried them inland and planted them. Within a few years, they had proliferated all over the island in thick clusters, creating groves and a town's namesake. Each June for the 108 years since the wreck, the coconut clusters hung heavy in the trees, until, one by one, their weight pulled them off and they tumbled down the chute created by the palm fronds; pointed projectiles building speed and momentum during the thirty foot drop; then landing like a cannonball, point down in the sandy soil or sod. Nature's own method of seed dispersal, not unlike the spreading of seed anywhere, but like most everything in Palm Beach, on a grand scale.

A decade ago the trees started dying off from a disease known as lethal yellowing. That fact and the ever-eroding beachfront could have added up to a cruel irony someday: "Palm Beach–no more palms, no more beaches." But through dredging and pumping and artificial reef programs and preventative tetracycline injections for the trees, the name Palm Beach would remain a fitting one, however artificially maintained now, at least for awhile.

So the Coconut Palm trees were holding their own, and as I slid silently underneath the Bahama shutter, a nearby tree followed Nature's master plan instructions. A coconut had chosen that precise moment to weigh more than its drying tendrils could support, and it came crashing down a palm frond and landed in the sod nearby with a thump loud enough to be comical in other circumstances.

At first I thought the crashing sound overhead was someone racing toward me through the bushes and I froze, petrified. I thought my chest would explode. Then I saw the coconut stuck two inches into the recently watered Bermuda grass sod, right out in front of the cabana porch steps, and I stifled a gasp. From inside came the startled murmur of a man's voice.

"What was that?"

"I don't know," answered another man's voice. I recognized the voices of my ex-father-in-law and his brother, the Senator.

There was a shuffling inside and then the door slowly opened, not ten feet from where I lay. The barrel of a .45 automatic came through the door first, followed by the Honorable Senator Danforth Fletcher, known throughout the political world as a powerful legislator and a force to be reckoned with; pro-handgun, anti-choice, and anti-pornography.

He was naked and his huge white belly hung down toward

his dick in an obscene flap of flesh. From where I was lying
motionless, I could only watch him, hoping he would not see me.
I thought of closing my eyes, thinking like a small child, that if
I can't see him, then he can't see me. But instead I kept my eyes
open as he looked around and headed toward my position.

Suddenly, *La PROVEDENCIA* was on my side and there was
another loud rustle above. Danforth looked up and jerked his gun
toward the sky. Another coconut landed at his feet and startled, he
laughed out loud. 'Tis the season. It was then that the first coconut
to land caught his attention and he stepped toward me to pick it
up. His face was inches from mine.

Carrying both coconuts inside, I heard him say, "Couple of
unexpected visitors. A coupla *nuts*." The soft laughter of four or
five others joined his. The laughter of men and women. Young
women.

"We've already got enough nuts here," a voice I didn't recognize said. More low laughter.

Slowly, I maneuvered myself under the Bahama shutter to
where I could see clearly into the room. There, in the same dim
amber light that had illuminated us that first night Nikki had taken
me inside, were five naked people sitting on the rattan sofa and
easy chairs. Senator Fletcher made it an even six. He walked in
and put the coconuts and the .45 on the end table by the lamp.
Hamilton stood up and took the hands of two thin women and
walked toward me and sat on the edge of the bed. They weren't
women, they were girls, probably no older than about fifteen. Both
may just as well have had "street urchin" tattooed on their fore-
heads. One had a dark complexion, with long, thick, curly hair. A
second one had mouse-brown hair and still had the remnants of a
baby face.

A third young girl, short, with an athletic build, stood and
walked to Senator Fletcher and led him to the coffee table. The
man remaining on the sofa I had seen before too. It was Hamilton's helicopter pilot, Lucky.

Hamilton pulled a saucer from the floor and with a razor blade chopped a few lines of cocaine from a white mound. The three girls took turns with a sterling silver spoon, snorting up the coke. The portions were huge. "Heartbreakers" Nikki used to call them, because she said it felt as if her heart would explode out of her chest whenever she did a line that big. (Did that mean she died of heartbreak? Not over me. Had she been doing lines that big the night she died? Probably).

Hamilton played with the stringy hair of the two girls on either side of him, and when they were finished snorting, he guided their heads toward his lap. "Shall we continue, girls?"

The two girls smiled and one of them rubbed her gums with some mirror residue. "Uhmmmm." Bending over from either side of Hamilton, they passed his cock back and forth, each taking turns sucking on it. The first of the girls was on all fours, less than five feet from where I lay, her knees wide apart, the soles of her feet facing me. Hamilton leaned back and smiled to his brother, who grabbed the third girl roughly and pulled her face down to his own cock. Lucky walked to the bed with a hard-on, smeared up some coke with a wet fingertip, rubbed his gums with it and entered the third girl from behind. She moaned in surprise and let out a small laugh. She let go of Hamilton's cock and slid around to bury her face between the first girl's legs.

Outside, just out of arms' length, I stifled a gasp to catch my breath. The blood racing through me was making both my heart and my head pound. The sight before me took on a surreal quality. A certain calming numbness came over me, like the characters in a film I had once seen set in an opium den. Did this kind of thing really go on in 1986 when not staged for pornographic movies? Suddenly I felt very naive. What an apparently sheltered life I had lived. I wanted to leave, but somehow couldn't pull myself away, as if the longer I stayed, the stronger the confirmation that this was actually happening. I watched for a full hour, filled with both curiosity and with disgust for myself for becoming hard. It was the first time I'd had an erection since my wife left me three months earlier, and I was selfishly savoring the moment. My cock was aching for relief. I thought about the religious Consuelo, walking in on such a scene by accident. How must she have reacted the first time? Surely a test of faith.

I thought about my first night there in the cabana with Nikki, and every night we had spent there during our three year marriage. I stole back to my diving gear silently in the night, with a racing mix of emotions; stimulated, peaceful, heartsick. I felt as if I had lost something, left some indefinable thing back there at the cabana window sill, but I couldn't articulate what it was.

On my way back home, swimming west in the darkness, I wasn't even thinking about the implications of what I had witnessed; of the Fletcher Brothers. Oddly enough, I was thinking of my parents.

Back on *The Ariel*, I lay on the deck, exhausted. A summer lightning storm moved up the coast, with a low rumble, lighting up the sky, bright enough to take a photograph. I looked at my skyline, grown up so much since I was a boy, and watched the light explode into the corners of the buildings. The wind blew through my hair with warm drafts as I watched. I stayed that way a long time, as the stroboscopic mass drifted northward. The rains would come soon. I wanted to call my mother and remind her to shut all the windows. It was a tradition we had, a ritual that had started when I was a young boy and she would call me from work when there was an impending storm to remind me to shut the windows. It started me thinking about my parents again.

How different they were, what different lives they led, what different values guided them.

Here I was thirty-three years old and I thought I had seen just about everything; knew human nature; could read people.

Just when you think you know it all.

CHAPTER 22

Just when you think you know it all........

I almost flunked out of college my first semester at the University of Florida. It wasn't because I attended too many football games or got drunk or idled away my hours or skipped classes or chronically overslept. It wasn't because I drank too many beers at the Rathskeller or took too many tubes down the Ichetucknee River. It wasn't because I had come from a sleepy West Palm Beach high school with a graduating class of 300, to the University of Florida campus of 30,000 and felt helplessly overwhelmed–distracted by this sprawling campus with a Southern beauty I never knew existed–or the sudden wealth of Southern beauties sitting next to me in class. (Where had *they* been all of my life?)

It wasn't because I wasn't a good student or didn't know how to do research or had bad study habits or wasn't motivated or didn't have an unquenchable thirst for knowledge.

Quite the contrary.

But something happened my first week at The University of Florida that would change my life forever and send me on a journey of discovery that continues to this day and will unquestionably last my entire life. It was a discovery so unexpected, so unsettling, so vast in scope, that I have never really recovered from the initial shock. With one simple step, I was to begin a new life, leaving behind forever a childhood filled with unasked and unanswered questions and the consequent adaptive behavior. You never miss what you never really had. Can you? Do you?

That Freshman year of college I was to meet my father, really get to know him for the first time, since his death fifteen years earlier, when I had been just three years old. How is that possible, you ask?

Like most college students in their Freshman year, in the fall of 1971, I thought I knew it all; everything about the opposite sex; everything about socializing; everything about my chosen field of studies; everything about life and the future that lay ahead of me.

Bumper sticker: *Hire a college freshman while they still know everything.*

The discovery and subsequent quest began, without my even knowing it had started, with a simple trip to the main University Library. That first trip was made, one night after dinner in early September of 1971, to check out a book of suggested Freshmen reading. During the walk from Hume Hall, on the other side of campus, I was as unsuspecting and naive as any Freshman can be. I had been enjoying the differences in the terrain, a contrast to what I was used to seeing, living in South Florida; rolling hills with deciduous trees instead of monotonous, table-top flatness from horizon to horizon. Everything about the flora was different as well. Huge pine trees and Live Oaks formed a canopy over the Plaza of the Americas, and I was distracted from my impending night of studying by the beauty of the campus. The smell of the air told me I wasn't at home.

Instead of balmy ocean breezes tinged with the smell of salt and rotten fish, this air carried the smell of damp baked earth, not sand, with a hint of pine and burned oak. It is just one of the many fragrances that I will forever associate with that first night.

Walking through the front doors of the library, I felt an air of excitement. How many other college freshman had passed through these doors before, with the exact same feelings of nervous elation during their first few days on this gorgeous campus built into the side of a rolling pine bluff? I looked up at the Southern Gothic architecture and wondered if I could ever feel that I was more than just another anonymous college freshman, a third of whom would never even make it through their first year. Would one of the three friends from West Palm Beach become a flunk-out statistic? Would it be me?

At the main desk, I pulled out my student identification card. The librarian, an elderly woman who had the face of someone who had spent her life checking out books and writing numbers on their spines in white ink in a shaky hand, looked down at the name on my ID card and then looked at me with a peculiar, wrinkled smile. It was such an unusual, searching look that it unnerved me. It was almost as if she had seen an angel. She excused herself and came back a moment later with a white haired gentlemen who could have been her brother. He looked at the picture on my Freshman identification card, then at me, as if to confirm that the face in the picture matched my own. Or perhaps he was looking for something else in my face.

I was baffled. "Is there something wrong?" There were so many new rules; so much unfamiliar protocol those first few days in Gainesville. Surely I had done something in violation of some code of which I was unaware. I decided I would plead ignorance to whatever charge I faced.

The elderly gentlemen looked down at the photo I.D. and then, kindly, up at me. "Jimmy Phipps?"

"Yes," I answered.

My heart started pounding. There was a long pause. Could there be another Jimmy Phipps on campus who had committed some unpardonable breach of ethics and with whom I was now being confused? And then I was blindsided.

"Are you Elliott Phipps' son?

The question was from so far out in left field, it sent a shock wave through me. Adrenaline surged. How could two librarians almost three hundred miles from my hometown, possibly know my long-dead father? "Yes," I answered, and waited for what, I couldn't imagine.

The two exchanged glances as if they had come upon some buried treasure, some important literary find. But, as I was to soon find out, it was me who had stumbled across a priceless buried treasure.

"You know, of course, we have your father's papers here."

I did, in fact, know my mother had donated some papers and effects to the University after they had requested them in 1957, a year after his suicide. My mother had mentioned it in a casual, off-hand manner one day as I stood in the doorway of his tiny study. As a high school senior, I had just been accepted at the University of Florida, and she was telling me how proud my father would have been, as I stood looking into the room where he had worked. My father's study had been nearly empty for as long as I could remember. Only a few reference books and pictures remained, and a musty armchair and reading lamp.

Two photographs hung on the wall, glimpses of my father on the road during the years he traveled for the Florida Writer's Project of Roosevelt's Works Progress Administration. He had traveled, contributing to the Florida version of the WPA Road Guide Series. One of the pictures, probably taken around 1939, was the one that showed him sitting on the running board of a 1929 Whippet, trademark straw fedora hat tipped back on his head, cigarette dangling from his lips. He's wearing a white shirt and tie. Suspenders hold up his worn khaki pants. He is seated behind an orange crate with a small Royal typewriter and a piece of paper rolled into it. Another photograph, taken immediately before or after, shows my father extending his hand toward the typewriter, and a Speed Graphic camera in the other, as if he is saying to the photographer, "Look what I do." Growing up, I remember staring at those pictures in awe.

What could my mother's donation to the University library have been? A small shuffle of papers turning yellow and brittle with age, stuffed into some forgotten corner of a library attic somewhere? How much material could there possibly be? I remember as my mother and I stood in the doorway to his study that I had dismissed her comment about my father's papers as insignificant. Surely nothing important. And anyway, I was still too excited about being accepted, about my impending move to Gainesville in the fall with my two friends, to have given her remark much further thought.

That night during my first watershed week at Gainesville, I looked at the two white-haired librarians. "Yes," I said confidently. "My mother told me that she had donated his papers."

"Have you ever seen them? I mean were you old enough..... before..."

I anticipated the rest of their question. "No, I was just three years old when he died."

They exchanged glances cautiously before proceeding further. Finally, the woman spoke. "Would you like to see his collection?"

They led me to the elevator and we rode it to the top floor. At the end of the hallway was a locked door, which the gentlemen opened with a key. He reached into the room and turned on a ceiling light, which revealed a circular staircase disappearing around a corner. The old couple led the way, and even though the room was temperature controlled, there was a smell of must in the air, unlike the surrounding Gainesville air, as I followed behind them. There was something foreign, yet familiar about this smell.

On the top floor of the library, in the far corner beyond several green steel shelves stacked with books, and adjoining a large dormer window, was a tidy corner where two, floor-to-ceiling book shelves came together. In one glance I took it all in.

A small writing desk with my father's typewriter that I recognized from the old photos:

Hundreds of magazines, some with obscure titles;

Fifty manuscript boxes stacked neatly and labeled meticulously;

A bulletin board above the desk with hundreds of scraps of paper in my father's handwriting tacked haphazardly.

In all, thousands of pages, millions of words.

The two librarians looked at me as if waiting for a response.

My heart was racing with a sudden denial. I asked the question I knew the answer to the moment I had rounded the corner only seconds ago.

"What is all this?"

The two librarians looked at one another yet another time, not quite understanding that I didn't seem to comprehend the obvious.

"Why, this is your father's work."

It was all there before me. The missing elements of my family history: Pictures of my mother and father; fifteen years of travel journals and articles; his entire written and photographic work from his W.P.A./Florida Writers' Project years; two hundred essays, boxes of standardized interview forms and over three thousand black-and-white negatives.

There were contemporary magazine articles by and about him from COLLIERS, PALM BEACH LIFE, FLORIDA ILLUSTRATED; over one hundred articles in all.

There were the monthly mystery magazines, over sixty of them, with his name on the cover as a contributor.

And then there were dozens of copies of his over forty published novels in hardback editions, including many duplicates, wearing colorful Thirties' and Forties'-style dust jackets;

Almost one hundred paperback books in various stages of

wear, and again many duplicates.

An immense burning filled my chest, I lost my breath and spontaneously, I started to cry, partly out of sorrow, partly from anger, outrage. Here it all was, the remains of the voice of the father I had never known, whom I never remember ever speaking to me, sitting before me on a bookshelf, waiting to be read; waiting to be heard. Hundreds of thousands–millions– of missing words, never uttered, waiting for *me* to read them; to hear them. More words than most fathers speak to their sons in a lifetime. Would they answer the questions I had? Would these words fill in the missing years? Could they make up for what a young boy needed?

My whimpering reaction frightened the two old librarians and they took a step forward to comfort me. I was breathing heavily, trying to hold back my tears. "He wrote *all* of this?"

"You didn't know?"

I shook my head "no." I stepped forward to touch a book, to somehow make a long-lost connection, and a corner of the dried dust jacket cracked off in a brittle triangle in my fingertips. I could hardly speak. Tears flooded my eyes, my chest heaved, struggling for breath, but I managed to choke out, "May I come here and read these?"

The absurdity of my question left them speechless as well, and finally, they just nodded, yes.

Every morning that first trimester at Gainesville I went to class and took notes distractedly, mechanically. Every afternoon I studied frantically, trying to absorb all the new knowledge. Supermotivated, I knew if I didn't do well, I couldn't stay in school, couldn't pursue the new, true objective in my life.

Every night I walked across the quiet campus at the University of Florida, the only sounds the dry rustle of fallen Live Oak leaves on the lawn where I walked, and the sudden, faraway laughter of a young girl falling in love. Past the stadium, past the

Bell Tower, past the Alligator pit, past the lovers stretched out on the Plaza of the Americas under the Live Oaks and the Spanish Moss. Each night it became darker a little bit earlier. On my first trip that August, it was bright daylight when I arrived after dinner. By the end of the semester in December, it was pitch black before I even left Hume Hall on the other side of campus.

On the attic floor of the library, in that back room next to a large dormer window, I spent my nights and weekends, relentlessly researching my father and his work. I can't walk into a musty room today without thinking of him. During September, when the humidity is oppressive; on October weekend afternoons, with the cheering of sixty thousand football fans at Florida Field echoing across the campus in my ears; in November, as the sun sank low in the crystal blue skies when the Live Oak turned brown and the air turned chill and filled with the scent of burning leaves; during Thanksgiving vacation when the campus emptied and I could walk from Hume Hall all the way to the Library and not see another student.

After almost four month's worth of reading, my reactions were many, but the strongest was an overwhelming, suffocating, gagging, paralyzing sense of remorse. I wanted to cry out, wail in a primal scream, until I became hoarse, and collapsed from exhaustion at this great tragedy.

Why had I never known about this collection? Why couldn't I be like normal boys growing up, swapping yarns with my father, playing catch, going fishing? Why wasn't I able to share all of his stories? What was it that happened to his mind that would make him want to commit suicide at the age of 56 and leave a loving, devoted wife and three year-old son behind? I cannot count the hours I spent in that small stifling upstairs library room, sobbing uncontrollably, as his written voice spoke to me from across the decades; tales from Florida's dusty back-roads; voices of his colleagues in the Florida Writer's Project; so many things I recognized from my home; my knowledge about the history of Palm Beach; the street where I grew up; even thinly disguised stories of my mother.

I longed to hear him read me the words aloud in a voice strong and clear—while I, as a young boy, would be seated on his knee after an evening of homework; as a teenager while bass fishing on Lake Okeechobee; as an adult while meeting me for lunch between classes. I wanted to hear him laugh, hear the timbre of the melodious voice my mother often described, as he told me the tales that fed his need to write the stories. His voice, I would eventually learn, was once recorded by WPA folklorists Alan Lomax and Stetson Kennedy as they wandered through Florida recording snippets of a vanishing era.

But he didn't want to go fishing with me. He didn't want to toss a baseball high enough into the twilight so it disappeared before returning to my mitt with a leathery slap.

Why did he leave us behind? Surely he knew what it would do to any son; to me. Didn't he care? Was he that selfish? Would I find an answer somewhere in his words?

Once, during one of my crying jags, the white haired librarian, who I knew now as Mrs. Todd, stepped from behind me and put a comforting hand on my sobbing shoulders. No words passed between us, and after a moment she turned and walked out, closing the door softly behind her, leaving me alone in my grief.

That Freshman fall at The University of Florida, I drifted away from the two friends of my childhood. At least part of it was due to what happens to all old friends during their first semester at college. The three amigos who had vowed to stay "friends forever" in the Secret Society of Coconuts, had come to a crossroads, an intersection in their lives, and they were now headed off in different directions. But I had no time for any other grieving than what I was already going through. Joachim was tied up with football practice. Bobby got involved in student politics. Our separate roads would converge again, later, when as University graduates without direction, we all came back to teach at our Alma Mater, Palm Beach High. But for a time, the distance between us continued to grow, separated by more than just interests.

Joachim and Bobby lived in the present and dreamed of their futures.

Sorting out the lost dreams of my childhood, in an attempt to discover where I had come from, I became lost forever in the past.

For many years after that first semester, I divided my life into two, distinct, segments. The first segment, I was like my friends: oblivious of the past, living day-to-day as life unfolded before me. The second segment began after that first night in the library. I spent the next ten years gazing into the past, suffering from what in earlier times might have been diagnosed as acute melancholia.

Much later, at age thirty, when I met Nikki, my life would once again careen out of control in yet another direction in the third chapter of my life.

Arriving home in West Palm Beach from Gainesville that Freshman Christmas, I confronted my mother. "I found the books." I didn't have to explain which ones. She just looked at me.

Angry, I asked, "Why?"

But she could not, would not answer my unfinished question. She merely shrugged. "I didn't think you would be interested."

Not interested in my own father's life? Maybe donating the papers to the University had been just her way of trying to forget; shut the door to the past and move beyond the pain.

And what had she been doing during the countless hours it had taken my father to write the millions of words after they met? What dreams had she had for the future? How had she spent the time? Sitting quietly in another room, urging him on with her silence?

That first year at UF, while other boys my age explored campus life in all the ways an eighteen year-old boy would, I spent every waking moment of my life, when I was not in class or doing the minimum amount of studying to get by, in that small quiet cubicle high above the campus, reading over in the chronological order in which they had been conceived, every word my father had ever written and saved. Some were just the barely decipherable, scribbled notes on thousands of scraps of folded paper; crumpled in a sweat-stained pocket and later retrieved.

There were notes written on a moving freight train; journal entries from the two months in 1939 he spent in Hollywood under studio contract, trying to translate his early mysteries into screenplays. He had hobo-ed back from Los Angeles on the railroad, crestfallen, wearing only the clothes on his back and carrying the small Royal typewriter, cradling it between his legs while he slept so no one would steal it. It was his "ticket" and he knew it.

There is an accounting of the labor strike and the first smashing of his knee by a pick-axe handle. A strike-breaker didn't like any outside agitators and singled out my father as an outsider. The account was apparently written from the hospital bed where he was taken. There is box upon box of paper fragments, novel notes and outlines, carbon copies of typed passages. It was all unsorted and un-catalogued, as if it had all been thrown into a cement mixer, or shuffled like a card deck. The neat labels on the boxes had been misleading window dressing.

When I was finished with every scrap, I went back to the beginning of his career and started all over again.

I became lost in the plotlines of any one of sixty magazine short stories and over thirty mystery novels. Several of the novels were elaborations on earlier magazine stories and I was able to trace the development of his work methods and abilities as he fleshed out his short-story characters, beefed up their plots, and rearranged his structures to accommodate the longer novel length.

It was almost as if the short-stories were a market survey, written for a test audience. Many of the characters he met as he hitchhiked around the state and wrote about in his journals and non-fiction reporting, he later reinvented as fictional characters in his short stories. Even later, they reappeared in novels. Several local Palm Beach characters, apparently based on real acquaintances, hold a permanent place in all of his stories.

Is it possible, for anyone but the author, to memorize an entire novel, verbatim? More than one novel? I did. I had once wondered how an actor in a Shakespearean Repertory Company could memorize the lines of a half-dozen plays and recite them in rotation, night after night, without confusion. What kind of mind could absorb and recite all those words written in iambic pentameter without rhyme? Well, I found out how it's done.

I can close my eyes right now and recite pages of my father's fluid prose, words that reflect an intimate knowledge of the land he wrote about: a land that's all but disappeared, buried beneath concrete and greed. His words do not flow in iambic pentameter, but there is no question it is a style worthy of being called poetic. An overflow of unrestrained emotions and images gathered on the road, recollected in more tranquil moments, and handwritten in mechanical pencil on yellow legal pads. His is the voice of a Florida songbird at the first light of daybreak.

My father's task was apparently an effortless one, and by reading his works chronologically as I did, from his first reflections in his notebook written in 1921, to the first report in his W.P.A. journal in the mid-1930's, to the final page of his last, unfinished novel in 1956, I was able to trace his development as a writer. His technique fascinated me, possessed my mind and imagination, as if suddenly his hidden life bloomed forth and offered me an entire, new existence to dwell in.

It was the world of Florida in the 1920's and the 1930's and the 1940's, and it was the place where I took up residence as a college student from 1971-1974.

"And let me tell you people: it was some kind of paradise ."

My father, the great undiscovered *noir* novelist who immortalized the Florida of the 1920's, 1930's, 1940's for anyone who cared to read his works, was born in Florida in 1900, the son of a man and woman who worked for Henry Morrison Flagler, Standard Oil Tycoon, Florida Railroad Builder, and Visionary. In the closing days of World War I, my father was able to attend Cornell University in Ithaca, New York, thanks to money given to his father by old man Flagler himself. When Flagler was building his Overseas Railroad to the Keys over a three year period ending in 1908, he used a labor force of 5,000 derelicts. He knew there was going to be a huge attrition rate from the heat, the working conditions, and the malaria. He hired labor agents to "recruit" workers off skid row in the Bowery and "Shanghai" them to South Florida. There, these workers, whose lives held little value, were held captive at their work assignments, with no way of getting off the Keys. In 1907, Flagler was indicted for violating an 1866 slave-kidnapping law, or *peonage.* My grandfather testified in his defense and eventually the charges were dropped by the Government. Flagler was forever grateful. In the personal note to my grandfather that accompanied the (bribery?) check, Flagler had written just before his death in 1912, *"for the education of the son of one of my most loyal workmen."*

In 1921, after graduation from Cornell, my father had put all the books he had bought in college in a steamer trunk and put it on a freight train back to West Palm Beach. Then he walked to the nearest highway, stuck out his right thumb, and hitchhiked home to Florida from Upstate New York, mostly on U.S. Highway 301. He had just the clothes on his back and a pad and a pencil in his hip pocket. For the next fifteen years, using his parent's house as a base, he thumbed his way across the state, crisscrossing North and South from Key West to Two Egg to Pensacola and back to Immokalee. He worked in turpentine camps in the Panhandle, cattle ranches along the Kissimmee.

He lived aboard a canal-dredging barge as it chewed its way through the jungle west of Fort Lauderdale creating a navigable waterway. The canal crew built a wooden barge on dry sand and loaded the dredging machinery onto it. The machinery, a cable-driven steam shovel, dug a hole in the ground. The hole filled with water and the whole operation was afloat. It ate its way through the jungle trees, sand and limestone bedrock, digging the canal and spewing spoil off to the side that would eventually be used as a roadbed for Alligator Alley.

In 1926 he helped put out the fire at the Breakers Hotel. There is a 16mm home movie someone shot. The cinematographer stood back as the others rushed toward the black smoke. One shot in the film shows my father in a crowd of men who had formed a bucket brigade. All the men wear a look of exhaustion and adventure on their soot-smudged faces. His look is one of sadness.

There are pictures he took in Coral Gables at the height of the Florida Land Boom. Busloads of people coming to the former swampland in Southwest Miami to listen to the fast-talking land speculators selling the new tropical paradise to eager, excited, wide-eyed northerners escaping from the frigid winters of the East Coast.

And then there are the pictures that ended the Gold Rush on Florida land in a matter of two hours. On September 26, 1928, a hurricane ripped through South Florida; swept across Lake Okeechobee creating a tidal wave that slopped over the south shore and drowned two thousand unsuspecting migrant workers while they slept. A few hours later a neighbor knocked on my father's door with the news: A man on horseback had made it through to the coast, delivering the horror story.

My father grabbed his notepad and camera and ran to the West Palm Beach dock where a sea-plane tourist concession had stood. He had hoped to persuade the pilot to fly him out, land the plane on the now becalmed Lake Okeechobee. But the plane had flown north, out of harm's way, just before the hurricane passed through. My father about-faced and hitched a ride on a truck out State Road 80, and was the first professional photographer on the scene to record the devastation; the ruined buildings chest-deep in water; the flattened shanty-towns. Later, as the water receded, the twisted, contorted ashen bodies of the drowned victims scattered in flattened muck-fields were covered in lime; the stacking of the coffins like cordwood; the bonfires of stacked bodies when the coffins ran out; the bewildered bleakness on the frightened survivors' faces as they wandered through town in a daze seeking answers, searching for lost loved ones, wondering if the storm was coming back. One day they're picking pole beans with their sons and daughters. That night they fall asleep on a pallet in their shanties. The next morning they walk into town carrying their drowned children in their arms wailing "Why didn't someone warn us?" In my father's journal from those days he describes a young Red Cross Volunteer who smiled at him with exhausted eyes. Did he speak to her? A few days later, he helped to load truckloads of the coffins for a convoy into West Palm Beach. The water table in the Glades was too high for any burials. There was no cemetery for black people in town then, certainly not for the hundreds who were swept away. They were buried in unmarked mass graves near Banyan Street in West Palm Beach.

In 1934, during the Depression, my father was able to land a job with the W.P.A. Florida Writer's Project, recording Florida's historic folklore for twenty-two dollars a week. He was one of an army of 200 young men and women who roamed like nomads conducting interviews and collecting folklore in an effort to preserve it before it disappeared forever. It was a job he had been doing on his own for thirteen years. While he traveled he absorbed the local color; facts and lore and rich dialogue, characters that would live on paper, unbeknownst to them, long after their deaths. He picked oranges, cut sugar cane with Jamaicans, sold baby alligators at tin-can tourist camps, lived with convict labor in the Panhandle.

He rode the rails with itinerant wanderlust, from that Panhandle to the docks of Key West, and then on a ferry to Cuba and back;

He wrote of croquet tournaments played at the Breakers by wealthy Wall Street sports in dazzling white costumes;

Once, during Christmas week, he was on the Alabama border. As the sun set in his face, he climbed the highest pine tree, fighting his way through the ever tightening web of branches as he approached the top. It was more than the view that brought him to this height, although the sun resting on the rolling hills to the west against a dark blue sky might have been enough for most. No, he was after something more. At the very top, he snatched a handful of mistletoe leaves encasing a cluster of tiny white berries. Climbing down, covered with pine needles, bark and the sticky pitch that turned black at his touch, he eased the cluster into his inside pocket and stuck his thumb out on the eastbound lane of US90. In two days, Christmas Eve, 1925, he hung the mistletoe from the living room archway in his parents' cottage and stole a peck on my grandmother's cheek as she walked underneath.

He waded chest-deep in an endless sea of sunflower fields in a late October sunset on Archer Road outside of Gainesville;

He photographed an army of young men with desperate faces in the Civilian Conservation Corps as they developed the rock-pool at Rainbow Springs;

All the time humming Duke Ellington's hypnotic *Mood Indigo.*

As he rode the endless miles of Florida rails with other frightened men, he lamented along with Jimmy Rodgers' *Hobo's Meditation,*

*"Will there be any freight trains
in Heaven?
Any boxcars in which we might hide?"*

He spent the night in tin-roofed lean-to's in the Panhandle pine forests;

He fished in tournaments with Ernest Hemingway;

Whistled down a dirt road as Monday morning, just-washed sheets blew listlessly in a blaze of sunlight and humidity;

He tramped past the strawberry fields that stretched forever near Arcadia;

Slept in abandoned cars rusting along the roadside and was awakened by the sounds of a Carolina Wren with a Mockingbird joining in on the chorus;

He ate boiled peanuts from a roadside shack, moist and salty mush, with any companion who happened by to join him for part of his journey;

Gazed across pine tops from a forest ranger's tower;

Mingled with road gangs as the nervous guards taunted him with racial slurs as they flaunted their twelve gauge shotguns;

Hiked the rolling red clay hills of the Panhandle;

Rolled cigars in Ybor City with aging first-generation Cubans as the *lector* read from the daily newspaper and Cervantes;

Inhaled the sweet oils of Cedar in the pencil factories of Cedar Key;

Shared olives and feta cheese with Greek sponge divers in Tarpon Springs who stank of sweat and dead fish;

He witnessed a ragtime knife fight while swilling moonshine at Cunningham's jook-joint in Alachua.

With the fiddle players in White Springs, he was present at the creation, when Ervin Rouse plucked the strings during the very first, improvised opening lick of the *Orange Blossom Special*.

He watched as a Jamaican sugar cane cutter bled to death after stepping too close to his partner and receiving a whack to his femoral artery. His partner wailed, helpless, as his friend died and was buried on an anonymous irrigation canal bank while the others were ordered back to work.

The pictures he took of people waving from front porches could fill an entire coffee table book. Another Florida phenomenon disappeared. No one waves to motorists from their front porches anymore.

He watched the first slapping stroke of dark green enamel painted onto a park bench in St. Pete.

He watched Conch boys riding on sea turtles; he dove the Breakers Reef; sat across the aisle from Jack Kennedy in the balcony of the Paramount Theater in Palm Beach during a winter matinee;

Watched the Washington Athletes play the grapefruit league where the Kravis Center now stands;

Walked the decks of steamboats and paddle wheelers as they splashed their way past the paper mills spewing poison into the St. John's River; chopping their way down through Big Lake Tohopekaliga and disappearing into the morning mists and serpentine twists of the Kissimmee River.

On the way up the Loxahatchee River to visit Trapper Nelson, he watched the filming of an early Tarzan movie; the director in monocle, beret and jodhpurs, cracking a riding crop on his thigh, while Tarzan's chimp sat in a canvas-backed chair and contemplated his choice of agents.

He caught a glimpse of Al Capone at his hideaway in Jupiter on the ranch later owned by Burt Reynolds; attended the funerals of Addison Mizner and Paris Singer; the last Barefoot Mailman; and the Ashley Gang after their massacre by the Palm Beach County and Martin County Sheriffs' deputies at the Sebastian bridge.

In many ways he was an imposter, Tom Joad in appearance and manner, with a college degree from Cornell University and money from home waiting for him at the next Post Office down the road. He lived the life of a hobo, without the pesky fear of a

penniless future or a wolf at the door. He traveled, groveling in the stimuli, while secure in the knowledge that his father would provide for him; that he would always have a home and a means of support beyond the twenty-two dollars a week from the Florida Writer's Project.

He rubbed shoulders with the great historians and photographers of the era who were showing the world how Floridians lived. A roll call: Dorothea Lange and Marion Post Wolcott....Stetson Kennedy and Charles C. Foster and Alan Lomax.... James Agee and Walker Evans. *Let us now Praise Famous .....Floridians.*

He had long talks with the three Marjories of Florida history: Marjorie Kinnan Rawlings on the nature of literature;

Marjorie Merriweather Post on the nature of money.

Marjory Stoneman Douglas on the nature of nature.

How strange it is to open a book on Florida history in the late 1980's and see a stranger described as your father...the man from whose loins you have sprung.

He is a part of history. I am a child of that history.

His thumb took him down dusty roads toward Armadillo Junction at the corners of Gopher Tortoise Highway and Raccoon Pass.

He spent the night huddled and hungry at Hobo Jungles along the rail tracks, swapping lies for a plate of beans on a flat board;

There are simple photographs of a Florida crossroad complete with a cracker house with a broken-spined, rusted tin roof in the background. A lone pecan tree stretches its limbs toward the winter sky.

He witnessed the pineapple harvest by the Japanese farmers of the Yamato Colony in Delray, and picked tomatoes in Immokalee to earn some bread and cheese.

And what do I like best about the photographs and the articles and the journal entries of his early travel throughout the state?

That answer is easy:

No one is there!
The place is almost almost empty.

Oh, and yeah, no out-of-state auto tags. No traffic gridlock. No one cutting in front of anyone on line. No pasty white skin, sunburned-to-lobster-red and smeared with thick gobs of Noxema and Aloe.

No bad attitudes. No lack of civility.

No "Worlds" for 44 million tourists to visit each year.

By reading my father's words and looking at his pictures I can simply reduce the population of the state from eighteen million to just one million.

Poof!
Happy days are here again.

Dense in detail and folklore, his journals provide a rich history of a *"disappeared* Florida." He interviewed residents of early migrant camps, rode every mile of passenger and freight rail, hitchhiked on baking shell-rock highways and watched the Florida Land Boom go belly-up as a prologue to the Depression.

He worked at ice houses in 1926 for the newly formed consortium of Florida Power & Light, and helped run the first electric cable through the Everglades. Wherever he went he carried his camera and his sweat-stained spiral notepad in his hip pocket and a pencil behind his ear.

That picture of him during his later years when he had a car, sitting on the running board of his Whippet close to his typewriter, tells the whole story at a glance.

His head was bloated with the images he had been collecting, bloated with the same sense of urgency as those hurricane survivors.

His travels throughout the state had put him in touch with thousands of tourists, crackers, surviving slaves, and the sons and daughters of slaves, Seminoles and carpetbaggers and a young black girl from Eatonville whose "eyes were watching God," as she made "dust tracks on a road," and who grew up to be Zora Neale Hurston. He had rubbed shoulders with wealthy politicians and down-and-out hoboes who had ridden the rails down to the last resort: Key West.

In 1935 he documented the rebuilding of Flagler's Overseas Railroad to Key West that had been nearly destroyed by the hurricane. Now, it would be known as The Overseas Highway. Less than thirty years old, one of the greatest engineering achievements ever constructed up to that time would not be rebuilt as a railroad, but as a roadbed for automobiles and trucks. Never one to avoid getting his hands dirty, he pitched right in with the laborers when a wooden form had started to collapse under a load of wet concrete. After helping to shore up the form, the structure had given way under the mass of the wet concrete. My father's already badly crippled knee was crushed once again, this time by a collapsed timber. They sent him home to his parent's house on the train. He would spend the rest of his days walking with a severe limp and with constant pain he once told my mother was excruciating.

That winter of 1936, after his recuperation, he remained in Palm Beach, got a job on another Flagler property where his father had connections: The Breakers Hotel. He worked as a groundsman, reminiscing and daydreaming as he cut grass on the golf course on a sit-down mower that allowed him to stretch out his bum leg in a cast. He wrote story ideas on crumpled, sweaty pieces of paper and stuffed them in his pockets.

After fifteen years of research on the road, writing and letting the material ferment, my father was ready to exploit his first-hand source material and mold it into the mystery genre, set in Florida. It was all here in 1936: greed, corruption, murder, and the best politicians money could buy. Why not put it to use?

Assimilation and Synthesis.

One night, when he could not wait another second, he sat down and tried his hand at writing detective fiction. In one month he completed his first novel. By the end of 1936 he had completed three more.

What Faulkner would create in Yoknopatawpha County, Mississippi; what Dashiell Hammett was doing in San Francisco; what Raymond Chandler and James M. Cain were doing in Los Angeles; what Earl Stanley Gardner was doing in legal-land; what John Dos Passos had done for Manhattan; what Carl Sandburg had done for Chicago; Elliott Phipps was planning to do in Palm Beach: *Create his own World.*

Not only did my father create that world, but he defined the genre set in that world. Elliott Phipps wrote his mysteries about Palm Beach before, during and after World War II for a largely unappreciative local audience. In New York he had a small following and a loyal publisher. His stories were picked up in The Black Mask Magazine and his novels were published by their affiliated, yet obscure publishing arm, Spade/Archer Press.

None of his work ever made more than a few dollars in his lifetime; none of them found their way through Hollywood for translation to the silver screen despite his frustrating three months out there. He went out there in a blaze of enthusiasm, with visions of the money finally making his life easier. In his journal he wrote:

> *"They say they love my stories and the evocative images of Florida. They just want to change a few things: the plot, the characters, the dialogue. I cannot abide it.*
>
> *I would rather return to mowing lawns at The Breakers and write in permanent obscurity than to suffer the indignity of what they propose."*

He was forced to work as a greens keeper on the same Breakers Hotel Golf Course on the island across the waterway from where he had grown up. At night he would come home, exhausted from working in the jungle heat, and write until he dropped off to sleep.

There may be other existing copies of his shorter published works somewhere, but the only known copies of any of his novels stand at patient attention on that Spartan bookshelf, near a dormer window, on the fourth floor of the old University of Florida Library. Waiting.

They are *waiting*.

Reading about my father and reading his work became my obsession. I spent endless nights in those stacks researching his life and work, trying to find some link, some clue, some secret that would allow me to know him better–to write like he did; some method to his thought process. In the later books, written after I was born, I hopelessly sought some veiled reference to a son he would eventually choose to leave behind.

I read every pulp novel in the order he wrote them:

PALM BEACH EXPRESS (1936)
    The entire action of this first novel takes place over a twenty-four hour period on a train from New York to Palm Beach. A murder occurs and is neatly solved by a private investigator named Leo Edwards. Tightly constructed and cleverly plotted, the murderer is caught as the train rolls into the West Palm Beach station.

MOONLIGHT PALMS (1936)
    A murderer strikes Palm Beach during each full moon for a year. Leo Edwards sets an ingenious trap to nab the killer on the beach on a brightly lit moonlit night. Lots of moody Palm Beach ambience.

GULFSTREAM GETAWAY (1936)

At a Polo Club in Gulf Stream, just south of Palm Beach, a married heiress falls in love with a swarthy polo player from Argentina. When his prized, champion horse is found dead, the Argentinian shoots the jealous husband in a fit of rage. At the end it is discovered the horse was killed by an enemy of the husband's, a former lover of the heiress.

UNDERTOW (1936)

A young, cocaine-addicted heiress' life spins out of control when she is blackmailed. Very dark for its day.

LIGHTNING ZONE (1937)

Two charter fishing boat captains, lifelong friends, become bitter enemies. Most of the action takes place out in the Gulf Stream.

PALM BEACH SUNSET (1937)

A murder is committed at dawn and the crime is solved in one fast-paced day ending at sunset.

TROPICAFFAIRE (1937)

Two society types from New York meet by coincidence while in Palm Beach for the Season. They fall into a torrid affair and take the opportunity to plot the murder of someone from back home that they both hate. They figure if they murder her down here, it could look just like another tourist murder. When both socialites are found dead instead, it's up to private eye Leo Edwards to find out whodunit.

SHARK BAIT (1937)

A charter fishing boat captain fallen on hard times steals artwork from Palm Beach mansions and smuggles it to the Bahamas for a European syndicate.

LITTLE CASINO (1937)

The first of three mystery novels featuring Colonel Jeremy Archer, owner of Palm Beach's most extravagant and exclusive gambling casino. The casino is obviously based on the infamous Bradley's Casino in Palm Beach. Archer is a suave, tuxedoed host who mixes high stakes poker with romancing the most beautiful of Palm Beach's women. In keeping with Archer's talent for entertaining his friends, a *séance* is held after closing one night as a treat for special guests. While the lights are off, a guest is murdered. Jeremy Archer finds the murderer in this classic of "The Closed Room" genre. Lots of white dinner jackets and red carnation boutonnieres; pomade and pencil-thin moustaches.

PALM BEACH HEATWAVE (1938)

Bordellos in West Palm Beach attract some high rollers from across the Intracoastal Waterway.

PALM BEACH/OFF SEASON (1938)

A Summer romance among the dunes turns to murder as a jealous Palm Beach husband plots to kill his wife's lover.

SOUTH DIXIE HIGHWAY (1938)

A "tin-can" trailer camp south of town is the site of a series of murders. The trailer park is sealed off as one by one, the list of suspects is narrowed down.

SEMINOLE SEDUCTION (1938)

Leo Edwards ventures to Big Cypress Reservation when a Palm Beach heiress falls in love with a reclusive Seminole Chief and disappears. Her father hires Leo to track her down.

TOURIST TRAP (1939)

Attractive, swarthy couple from Miami preys on winter guests in Palm Beach.

POINCIANA CAKEWALK (1939)

Set in 1920 and told in a flashback. All clues lead to a woman ballroom dance instructor at the Royal Poinciana Hotel being a murder suspect. Young private investigator, Leo Edwards, signs up for lessons and dances to the syncopated rhythms of the Beale Street Sheiks. After a torrid romance, Edwards reluctantly proves his lover is the murderess and turns her over to authorities.

LIGHTHOUSE LIAISON (1939)

Adultery, Palm Beach style, with a moonlit, speedboat chase in the Jupiter Inlet and an exciting climax at the Jupiter Lighthouse, built in the 1860's.

HOT JAZZ (1939)

A second Jeremy Archer Casino mystery. A clarinet player in the casino band blows hot jazz by night and sleeps with rich widows by day. After one rich widow cries foul, the clarinet player dies on the casino stage during a performance. Jeremy Archer solves the mystery against a background of Rhapsody in Blue.

PALM BEACH COVER-UP (1940)

A crooked politician and a political scandal leads private investigator Leo Edwards on the trail to Tallahassee to uncover a fraudulent land deal which ended in death.

FOREVERGLADES (1940)

(Also known as SEMINOLE SUNSET in some early reference work). Ten miles west of Boynton Beach there is an Indian mound in a hammock of Cypress, Live Oak, Sabal Palm and hardwoods. The sandy ground is raised above the wet season water line, and beneath the surface is a treasure of Indian artifacts buried in a mixture of beach sand and shucked oyster shells. The pre-Columbian inhabitants carried millions of clay pots-full of beach sand, ten miles overland, until the watery hiding place deep in the Everglades was filled up high enough for them to keep dry in even the rainiest of seasons. A *midden* they call it. Is that why they did it? Or were they seeking safety from other human predators through their inaccessibility? No one will ever know. How many dry seasons did it take them? The years can be counted like rings on a tree stump, separated from the last by another layer of sand. The last bucket of sand was carried on the same day that Columbus set sail into the great unknown. Maybe they sensed a stirring in the air; a fearful premonition they could not articulate, only respond to.

In 1920, a Seminole Indian is killed near the Indian mound, ostensibly during an argument over otter pelts. The real reason is that he was a material witness in another murder case and was killed by a contract killer hired by the murderer in the first case to cover his tracks. The hired killer does not know the real reason he was hired to kill. When he discovers the real reason, he turns to Leo Edwards, the only white man he can trust. Leo steps into a rampage of rumor and deception concerning a scam involving the secret discovery of oil in the Everglades.

23 STEPS TO HEAVEN (1941)

In this highly unusual novel, my father takes an incident from 1915 and re-tells it through voice of an eyewitness in 1990, seventy-five years after the central event. The remarkable facet of this story is that not only does the fictional story propel the reader into the future, but my father had to actually create a Florida-world-to-be, fifty years in his own future. He accomplishes this feat with remarkable agility and prescience.

In 1990, when the skeletal remains of twenty-three men are uncovered during construction of a highway bridge over part of Hungryland Slough near Jupiter, a newspaper reporter seeks out the only surviving witness to a ritual execution of a chain-gang from seventy five years earlier in 1915. The witness, Calvin Musselwhite, an elderly black man, reads from his own long-hidden, handwritten account of the events of that Christmas Day, 1915. He titled his diary: "*23 Steps to Heaven: The Incident at Hungryland Slough.* "

A morality play on capital punishment pushes the *noir* novel form to its limits in this gruesome tale even Jim Thompson couldn't match.

From Calvin's long-hidden journal, we discover that on Christmas day in 1915, twenty-two prisoners and the fifteen year-old Calvin are taken on a work detail by a deranged guard. The prisoners are the hardest of prison society: murderers, rapists, kidnappers, and child molesters. The guard chains young Calvin to a Cypress tree up to his neck in water.

Each of the twenty-two prisoners is then ordered to dig a shallow grave in front of himself. The first climbs in and is buried up to his neck by the second man on the chain. The second man climbs into his grave and is buried up to his neck by the third man in line.

By mid-morning, the heads of the twenty-two prisoners are the only things visible above the ground. Then as fifteen-year old Calvin looks on in horror, the Bible-thumping jail guard becomes each prisoner's judge, jury, and executioner.

PALM BEACH INSIDER (1941)

When the publisher of a Palm Beach Society Newspaper is found dead, private investigator Leo Edwards searches old issues to find a motive for the murder. What he finds shocks the entire town and the eventual suppression of the story makes Edwards realize that some people consider a public facade of decorum more important than private truths.

CONCHTOWN I: (1941)

The first in a trilogy set in Riviera Beach, or *"Conchtown."*

Based on true events that Elliott Phipps witnessed. A young woman, Veronica Huss, is sent from the Florida Writer's Project in Jacksonville to document a group of Bahamian fisherfolk who settled in Riviera Beach. An aspiring novelist, she was intrigued by the area and the subjects she met.

Scheduled to stay for just two weeks, she wound up staying for fourteen months, falling in love with the area and a mentor she encountered. Although not a mystery, my father would write in his journal that it was his favorite creation.

SLOAN'S CURVE (1942)

A valuable piece of property on the South end of Palm Beach is up for grabs when the owner, long known for his refusal to sell the property to even the highest bidder, is found dead on his yacht.

LOW SOCIETY (1942)

A sociological study of a dysfunctional Palm Beach family, circa 1936. A tyrant father is murdered. Was it his browbeaten wife or one of his six spoiled children? A highly cerebral novel for its time, it pre-dates by a decade anything close in its esoteric, psychological complexity and nuance.

DRIFTWOOD BEACH HOTEL (1942)

Within weeks after the bombing of Pearl Harbor, the United States was forced to mobilize thousands of troops. In the winter of 1942, almost 80,000 newly signed Army Air Corps flyers descended on one of the few places that was warm enough to train and had sufficient lodging: Miami Beach. Over 300 hotels were taken over to house the influx. Along with the soldiers came hundreds of camp followers; prostitutes looking for an easy buck. In this daring novel for the time, no fewer than five soldiers fall in love with hookers, while every wannabe Glenn Miller and Frank Sinatra provided the background music. Leo Edwards is called in to investigate the brutal murders of a ring of prostitutes.

CABANA CLUB (1944)

Romance and intrigue, poolside at the Breakers Beach Club in 1926. Leo Edwards discovers the Breakers' fire was started in order to destroy evidence of the rape of a maid. (This story was originally told to my mother at work one day. She then relayed it to my father. Because of the high profile of the rapist, it was hopeless to try to respond to the crime, even twenty years later, so my father included this thinly disguised story in this book. The trail leads to evidence of cocaine addiction of Flagler's second wife that had resurfaced years later).

DOLDRUMS (1944)

Summertime in Palm Beach and the livin' is lonely. Not much for the locals to do but get into trouble. When a local burglar is found dead in a Palm Beach mansion, Leo Edwards crosses Lake Worth to West Palm Beach and heads north to Hobe Sound to track down the killer at the military installation, Camp Murphy.

HURRICANE SEASON (1945)

A September hurricane in the early 1920's isolates the island of Palm Beach from the rest of civilization for forty-eight hours with no electricity, water, or telephones. In the aftermath of the storm, a house guest is drowned. Private investigator Leo Edwards proves it was no accident.

A-1-A (1946)

Just off a lonely stretch of beach road, a teenaged couple has been found murdered. Was it the work of a transient just passing through? Leo Edwards works his way through a labyrinth of horror to find the killer.

THE BOAT HOUSE (1947)

Set in 1926 during Prohibition, a Palm Beach boathouse is the perfect place for rum-runners to smuggle in their booze from the Bahamas. And the perfect place to leave a body and make it look like the work of smugglers. Private investigator Leo Edwards is called into the case when the true identity of the body is discovered.

LOW TIDE (1948)

The body of Palm Beach's most ostentatious party-giver washes up on shore near the Palm Beach Pier. Last seen completely intoxicated at his own party, did he simply fall off the pier? That's the consensus until the very next day, when the body of another prominent Palm Beacher washes up on shore at the same location.

JUNGLE QUEEN (1948)

Leo Edwards is called to a movie set in the Ocala National Forest where a film producer he befriended in Palm Beach has been accused of murder.

Juniper Springs is doubling for an African Jungle for the filming of a B-movie about a jungle safari. The producer's beautiful young protégé is killed with a prop spear and Leo must find the real murderer while filming continues.

On-location shenanigans by the cast and crew, including a trained orangutan and the director's affair with the macho male lead, demonstrate Elliott Phipps' astute sense of humor, while mocking the huge egos of mid-1930's Hollywood stereotypes. Some of the characters were obviously inspired by his brief stay in Los Angeles.

STINKTOWN (1948)

From the early 1900's through the end of WWII, an ocean-front shark processing plant in Melbourne, Florida, was the focal point of the town's economy. Sharks were caught offshore, brought here, slaughtered, and processed for their parts and oil. The unbearable smell permeated everything for miles around, and earned the area the name STINKTOWN.

In many ways it was a combination boomtown and slum, with the mentalities that accompany both. In the early days of the war, it only got worse.

A series of brutal rape/murders during the war years brings out the local constabulary to solve the crimes with much of the action and the climax taking place in the processing plant.

Racial tensions mount as a black plant worker is falsely accused of the series of crimes, with little or no evidence.

MANGROVE MURDER (1949)

A Palm Beach heiress arranges a rendezvous with her lover in the tangled mangroves up past "Burnt Bridge," at the north end of Lake Worth. When the lover arrives, he finds the woman's dead body floating, tangled hopelessly in the clutches of the Mangrove branches. After he's arrested and charged with murder, the lover calls his old friend, private investigator Leo Edwards, to find the real killer.

JUPITER PIER MURDERS (1949)

At dawn, a young boy hides in the sea oats near the recently completed Juno Pier, where he has been poaching Loggerhead Turtle eggs. He watches an old fisherman meander to the end of the pier and bait a hook. A passing speedboat slows and approaches the pier. Words are exchanged with the fisherman and he drops to the plank pier deck in a hail of Tommy-gun fire from the boat. When the boy steps forward as a witness to the murder, his life is threatened and he must go into hiding until Leo Edwards can track down the speedboat killers.

MYSTERY OF THE JUPITER LIGHT-HOUSE (1949)

Elliott Phipps' only foray into the field of adolescent literature, in an attempt to create a series of boys' mysteries 'ala "The Hardy Boys."

A group of five local boys meet an eccentric old man at the local train depot who claims to be the descendant of Jonathan Dickinson, the famous Quaker explorer who landed on these shores in 1696.

The old crackpot shows them a pirate's map and the boys are off on a treasure hunt filled with modern day pirates, escapes from alligators in the Loxahatchee swamp, rum-runners in the Jupiter Inlet, an encounter with a mysterious old Seminole shaman who claims to be the grandson of Billy Bowlegs, and a chase on the roof of the Jupiter Lighthouse as the clock strikes midnight. It is the only boys' adventure book in his planned series, despite a strong ensemble cast of characters and some great fun for young readers.

HYPOLUXO (1950)

In one of his few references to World War II, and a second of his novels that propels the reader forty years into the future, Elliott Phipps tells the tale of a young Jewish girl who is the daughter of a general store proprietor on Hypoluxo Beach, twenty miles south of Palm Beach. During the war, German submarines patrolled for southbound freighters right off shore. A landing party of four Nazi seamen arrives by rowboat one night in 1943 as the store proprietor is about to close. Shocked into near paralysis, the owner sells them the goods they seek. As they leave, the Nazi captain sees the beautiful daughter and vows to return for her. The next night he returns alone and they make love in the dunes. Her father discovers them, kills the Nazi Captain with a shovel, and buries the body in the dune after swearing his daughter to secrecy.

The story then jumps forty years into the future to 1983, when the Captain's skeleton and mutilated skull are found during excavation for a beach front condominium in Hypoluxo. The SS Medal, Maltese Cross and dog-tags found on the skeleton lead private investigator Leo Edwards to the Nazi archives in Berlin to find out who this Captain was and what happened to him. Is there anyone alive who knows what happened? To Leo's surprise, the trail leads back to South Florida.

A mother and daughter living in Palm Beach hold the key to this shocking novel that is the best example of my father's visionary powers and craft.

TANNER'S COURT/CONCHTOWN II (1951)
The second novel in the CONCHTOWN TRILOGY.

Another non-mystery, the story is an episodic, slice of life novel of the residents and snowbirds from up north who inhabit the tiny trailer park known as Tanner's Court in Riviera Beach. Several of the female lead characters are recent war widows from the Korean War who have come to Florida to rebuild their lives.

A GROUPER SERENADE/CONCHTOWN III (1952)
The final novel in the CONCHTOWN TRILOGY.

Set thirty years in the future from the time he wrote it, Elliott Phipps predicts what life will be life for hook-and-line fishermen who remain behind in Riviera Beach. They struggle to maintain their lifestyle, while fighting off corruption, greedy land developers, and marijuana smuggling. I'm not sure how he did it, but his portrait of a decaying town is accurate in its depiction.

MURDER AT CLUB COCONUT (1952)
In this final entry in the Colonel Jeremy Archer casino series, a flashy New York gambler expresses his desire to buy the casino, while simultaneously mounting up unpaid gambling debts. When the gambler is found murdered at the roulette wheel, owner Jeremy Archer himself is the prime suspect. Following a gentlemen's agreement with the town's Chief of Police, the suave Colonel Archer is given twenty-four hours to clear his name and find the real murderer.

MIDNIGHT/MOONLIGHT (1954)

Derivative of his own earlier work, MIDNIGHT/MOON-LIGHT is my father's weakest novel, but still not a bad read, taken in the context of its times.

During the Palm Beach Social Season, a serial killer is murdering wealthy widows in Palm Beach each Saturday night at the stroke of midnight. What's the connection? Private Investigator Leo Edwards solves this one with a surprise ending right out of a Charlie Chan movie.

It's an enormous body of work, especially in light of the fact that he worked an exhausting full-time job the entire time he wrote; in light of the fact that the slow, even non-existent sales might have paralyzed another writer. He could only have been obsessive about his work.

During the seven year period 1936–1942, he wrote over two dozen novels; as many as five per year. Somewhere between five–ten pages per day, every day for seven years, and that's not counting the numerous magazine fiction and articles he wrote.

In 1943, the year he and my mother married, he didn't write anything, and he wrote only about one or two novels per year after that. He must have been in love.

After I was born, it took him three years to get through one complete, and one *unfinished* novel. Was he spending all his time with me? Or was he just wearing out?

Or had he come to the stultifying conclusion so many writers deny because they cannot accept it: no one is really interested.

I saved his *unfinished* novel to describe last.

PALM BEACH CONFIDENTIAL

(1956–unfinished, never published)

Or at least the yellowing, delicate carbon copies of the novel's pages, the only record of the incomplete work known to exist.

The original had apparently been written on a legal pad in the tiny scrawled hand of the veteran reporter he was. He had placed a carbon sheet between the top page and the copy. For safety from theft or loss, and as insurance against having to recreate what he had already written, he had apparently kept the two copies separate. It's an old writer's trick from the days before electric typewriters, copy machines and word processors.

PALM BEACH CONFIDENTIAL was based on a story he had written first for BLACK MASK MAGAZINE, *"Double Effort."* In 1956, leading up to the time of his suicide, my father was re-cycling the short story; expanding the "Double Effort" storyline into what he hoped would be his next, full-length novel. He didn't know it at the time, but it was to be his last novel attempt. *Or did he?*

He was almost finished extending the form of the magazine story into the novel, when, by coincidence, the short story version was finally published and circulated to newsstands across the country in BLACK MASK MAGAZINE. According to a clipping of a Palm Beach Society column, the story had apparently made quite a sensation among certain circles when it hit the local newsstands. The island was abuzz with speculation as to the true identity of some of the lead characters.

He had only the final pages of the novel to complete, when for reasons he apparently didn't care to discuss, he decided to end his misery in this world. Was it his lack of success? Was it his inability to provide for his wife and child in a better way? Was he unable to cope with the chronic depression so many writers wrestle with? Was it the apparent pointlessness of his efforts through the passing years?

He walked down our street to where it dead-ended into the F.E.C. railroad tracks and put a bullet into the brain that had created this vast, detail-enriched, all but relatively unknown compendium of fiction and essays. It is a body of work unparalleled in Florida writing.

Not John D. MacDonald; not Marjorie Kinnan Rawlings; not MacKinlay Kantor; not Erskine Caldwell; not Harry Crews; not Zora Neale Hurston; not Carl Hiassen; not Marjory Stoneman Douglas; not Phillip Wylie; not Sidney Lanier; not Thomas McGuane; not Thomas Sanchez; not T.J. MacGregor; not Charles Willeford; not Theodore Pratt; not William Bartram; not Russell Banks; not Harriet Beecher Stowe; not Douglas Fairbairn; not Henry James; not Jonathan Dickinson; not John James Audobon; not Elmore Leonard; not John Muir; not James W. Hall; not Sam Harrison; not Ernest Hemingway; not Wallace Stevens; not Peter Matthiessen; not Padgett Powell; not Tim Dorsey; not Richard Powell; not Laurence Shames; not Bob Sacchochis; not Edna Buchanan; not Stetson Kennedy; not Isaac Beshevis Singer; not Tennessee Williams; not Cherokee Paul MacDonald; not James Leo Herlihy; not Paul Levine; not Sarah Orne Jewett; not Ring Lardner; not Jonathon King, not Les Standiford; not John Lutz; not Alice Hoffman; not Randy Wayne White; not Lawrence Sanders; not *any* Florida writer who ever wrote about this state can match the lyrical descriptions; can capture the cracker dialogue; the haunting beauty of his beloved state as well as he did. The night he died, all of his untold secrets spilled out onto the cinders by the railroad track and flowed into the ground. It was as if he was returning all those secrets to the Florida earth that had borne them and that he loved so much.

The novel PALM BEACH CONFIDENTIAL, like all his novels, is rich in historical lore and local color, as only an eyewitness and WPA reporter/photographer could have recreated it. I marveled over his prose style, his eye for detail, his turn of phrase, his memory of an era sometimes as early as fifty years prior to his writing; of his ability to look into the future of what Florida would become forty years after his death, and see a world turned upside down, almost as if he were a visionary.

Palm Beach during the Twenties and Thirties was quite a place, all right. Green and white is what I visualize whenever

I read what he described. Everything was green and white: The Palms and the Beach. The striped awnings. The lush vegetation and the mansions. The money and the people. Everything was green and white.

The central character in PALM BEACH CONFIDENTIAL is a worn out House Detective living in residence in a dilapidated hotel. This same House Dick, Leo Edwards, was the character my father had used in almost twenty other novels which preceded this one. After years of being a star private investigator, Leo is reduced to working as a night watchman.

First introduced twenty years earlier in PALM BEACH EXPRESS, Leo Edwards, by 1956, was almost sixty years old and down on his luck. He moves through the empty, off-season halls with the ache of a hopeless, dotty old man. Was this how my father felt himself, grasping at straws to make ends meet? In desperation, the aging private investigator decides to blackmail a former client.

The story flashes back more than thirty-six years to just after WW I. When The Royal Poinciana Hotel closed down during the off-season, the young, aspiring private investigator, Leo Edwards, was free to do extra work. At night, he became a solitary figure, patrolling the stifling, endless, empty hallways of the largest wooden structure ever built, checking for vagrants or signs of fire.

In 1920, a fictitious Palm Beach millionaire my father called Andrew Blake had hired Leo to follow his wife to determine if she is seeing another man. Leo, grateful for the moonlighting job, tails Blake's wife. He discovers that the wife has an identical twin sister, working in a whorehouse across Lake Worth on Clematis Street in downtown West Palm Beach, a whorehouse Leo himself had been known to frequent more than occasionally during his lonely off-hours.

Leo discovers the twins have conspired to steal Blake's money. What they start as a gruesome joke, a way to escape the dreary monotony of their lives, develops into an elaborate, but ill-conceived and poorly executed blackmail scam that crumbles apart. They are simply not bright enough to pull it off and greed gets in the way of whatever good judgment they may have had.

Part of the scam called for the twin sisters to switch places in life. The prostitute would live in the mansion, and Blake's wife would spend her nights "spreading her legs in a West Palm Beach whorehouse."

Over time, the prostitute bears Blake's second son.

One night, Blake's real wife, still posing as the whore, is killed by a John; a club-boxer from a gym down on Clematis Street beats her to death while still bloodthirsty and hyped up on a cocaine injection following his victory over an opponent in the ring.

When Blake discovers that it was his real wife who was the murder victim, he realizes that it is his sister-in-law, the whore, who is actually the mother of his second son. To save face in the community and avoid a scandal, he decides to keep his real wife's death quiet, and go on with life as if nothing has happened. He pays off the Chief of Police, the only cop who knows the true identity of the twin. He also pays off investigator, Leo Edwards, to keep it quiet. Blake's two sons, two years apart, grow up as full brothers in everyone's eyes but their own father and the two other men in-the-know. In a bizarre twist, even the surviving twin sister does not realize her "husband" is aware of her true identity.

By 1956, when *"Double Effort"* /PALM BEACH CONFIDENTIAL is set, thirty-six years have gone by. The once quick-witted sleuth has been reduced to wandering empty, off-season hotel corridors at night, keeping the vagrant population out and the rats as well.

Down-and-out, the house detective Leo Edwards, approaches the millionaire, Blake, for a loan. When Blake demands collateral, Edwards explodes. He threatens to shakedown Blake in exchange for keeping the old, long-hidden scandal a secret. He will tell "the wife," the two sons, and the entire community, unless he is justly compensated. Blake, not wishing to dredge up old disgraces, agrees to pay off Edwards. The next night, Edwards burns to death during a mysterious hotel fire that engulfs an entire wing of the old hotel where he works. Local police blame the fire on vagrants known to use the derelict, empty hotel for a place to sleep during the off-season.

Or at least that's what happens at the end of *"Double Effort,"* the BLACK MASK MAGAZINE short story version. The uncompleted handwritten original of the novel manuscript, presumed by all to be with my father the night he killed himself by the railroad track, was never found; the manuscript pages drifting northward on the Flagler Railroad right-of-way. No one knows how he would have finished the novel version of the story.

During the final stages of writing this novel, my father apparently committed suicide. Why? No one has ever been able to even venture a guess. No scholar has searched the record for clues, and my mother was more baffled than anyone who knew him.

After years of trying to draw the story out of my mother, she finally told me about my father's last night.

As he often did, he would walk down to the railroad track, and sit silently in the glow of a worklight mounted on a concrete switchbox. He would pore over what he had handwritten that night, smoking up to a half pack of Camel cigarettes in the two hours he was revising his work. Before he started composing the next night, he would type out the handwritten notes he had revised the night before.

It was a writer's typical routine. At midnight, he would walk home and slip into bed next to my mother, while I, then three years old, lay in my bed in the next room. Six hours later they would rise and prepare for work before hopping on their bicycles and riding across the bridge to The Breakers Hotel.

On the night he killed himself, my father had walked to where my mother was sitting in the living room, sewing. She distinctly remembers seeing his yellow legal pad folded in half under his arm. As usual, he was singing his favorite song.

"Pack up all your cares and woe,
Here I go, singing low,
Bye-bye, Blackbird.
Where somebody waits for me
Sugar's sweet, so is she,
Bye-bye, Blackbird."

He'd bent close to her, smiled and kissed her on the cheek. "See you in bed, sweetheart."

He stood, walked to the front porch. The screen door slammed behind him making the same sound it does thirty years later. He lit a cigarette she would not let him smoke in the house. There was pause as he inhaled, and then, as he walked down the sidewalk in the dark my mother heard the last words she ever heard my father speak:

"Make my bed and light the light,
I'll arrive late tonight, Blackbird, bye-bye."

His voice trailed off and he was gone.

When my mother woke up at three o'clock in the morning and he wasn't beside her, she dressed and ran down the street to the railroad track calling his name in panic. He was there, sprawled out and slumped up against the concrete power box, frozen in despair. His bum right leg which had caused him so much pain in life, was contorted below him as if he had collapsed on it. There was a small, semi-automatic pistol in his hand and a bullet hole in his right temple. She had never seen the gun before; didn't even know that he owned one. Many of his notes were scattered, blown away down the tracks in the draft created by a passing freight train. Covered in his blood, she never thought to pick up the pages. Her wails brought out the neighbors, and one of them ran to check on me. Just three years old, I slept through it all. By the time the police arrived, the remaining blood-stained pages were tossed into oblivion, blown up the track by another northbound train.

And so my father, the great Palm Beach *noir* mystery writer, was never to be discovered by the readers or the critics. He was never to earn enough money at his craft to be able to stop mowing lawns for idle golfers; unclogging hotel toilets for rich tourists on vacation.

He never achieved the fame of a Raymond Chandler or a Dashiell Hammett or a James M. Cain or a Jim Thompson. He was never to be rediscovered a generation later by readers, who having seen the Forties' film adaptations of his stories, subsequently devoured the novels and demanded delighted publishers to republish the long out-of-print books in retrospective editions complete with Art Deco covers and forewords by John D. MacDonald.

That his work went largely unappreciated used to bother me. But I think I like it better that way. Now, those secrets of old Palm Beach are forever safe with me and no one else can get to them. Those secrets which were revealed to me after climbing out the window and sitting on the ledge of the University of Florida library dormer, reading in the cool night air by the light that spilled across the campus to the slate roof tiles. I earned the right to learn and keep those secrets to myself during my Freshman year, digging into my father's personal vision of Palm Beach County history, while I was 260 miles away, perched on that Alachua rooftop.

The great undiscovered Palm Beach *noir* mystery novelist, Elliott Phipps, became the subject for my Master's Thesis. I catalogued over 500 separate characters he had invented or recreated, and I was able to trace many of them back to his earlier essays. As could be expected, many of the characters were composites of real people he had met and interviewed. Their lineage can be traced for all who spend the time searching.

One such character was the father of the character my father called "Andrew Blake," the Palm Beach millionaire with the twin wives from *"Double Effort"* /PALM BEACH CONFIDENTIAL. He was based on a real-life, but unnamed, turn of the century Palm Beach resident my father had encountered while researching a Palm Beach incident that came to be known by locals as *"The Carnival in Niggertown."*

Along North County Road, there was a swampy, low-lying area known as "The Styx." It's the area opposite the Paramount Theater and behind where St. Edward's Church and the Palm Beach Hotel now stand. Men who had built Flagler's grand hotels of Palm Beach and servant families lived in The Styx shantytown, in hovels not dissimilar to what their predecessors had lived in during their days of slavery. The Senior "Blake" wanted the property in question for development, but the black squatters living there in squalor presented a problem, even after he had purchased the property from an absentee owner.

"Blake" and his henchmen devised a plan. They brought a circus and sideshow into West Palm Beach that was on winter hiatus and set up a carnival for local residents to enjoy. The trains arrived on Flagler's Florida East Coast Railroad tracks and the little boys played hookey to enjoy the spectacle. Elephants were led up the hill from the railroad tracks in West Palm Beach to help erect the big top. Most residents had only seen pictures of circuses and could only imagine the thrill of exotic animals from all corners of the world. The bearded ladies and Uncle-Sams-on-stilts were a novelty. They had already seen enough freaks and snake oil salesmen.

On the last night of the circus, ostensibly as a special concession to local black residents who had been excluded from the fun because of Jim Crow laws, the real-life model for the fictitious "Blake's father" opened up the event and invited as his personal guests, the black residents of the Styx to come across the bridge and up the hill to enjoy the last night on the midway. There would be refreshments. Everything was free. Music, cotton candy, "fun for the pickaninnies," Blake told them all.

Many Styx residents dressed in their church clothes and at sunset walked across the wooden railroad trestle bridge, now the site of the Flagler Memorial Bridge, and up the hill. Their laughter filled the dusk air with anticipation. Their faces beamed as they told their children tales of white bearded men who walked on stilts with striped pants. They had seen pictures. Many of them clutched brightly colored flyers in their hands in anticipation.

Those reluctant ones who stayed behind, too tired from an exhausting days' work, were *re-invited* by a handful of men who came through the shantytown on horseback. It was "bad manners, disrespectful not to accept the invitation," they were told. The few who further demurred were then offered another incentive: they were forced off at gunpoint and led across the trestle like prisoners on a chain-gang.

When they were all gone and the riders on horseback had checked all the scrap-wood shacks, the real-life millionaire model for my father's "Andrew Blake Sr." nodded to "Andrew Jr.," who held a kerosene torch. Within minutes the only black settlement to ever be established on Palm Beach Island was burned to the ground.

Those Styx residents in attendance at the carnival were listening to a small brass band when screams from down the hill brought them outside the circus tent. They looked up to see the Eastern sky turning orange, and stood wondering what had happened, until the last few men who had been forced off at gunpoint finally arrived and breathlessly told their stories.

The drawbridge trestle to Palm Beach was closed off that night, the wooden planks untrodden in the still air, and Lake

Worth's waterway became a moat that isolated the castles of the
rich from the speechless black servants who watched the flames
of The Styx from afar. The suddenly homeless black families slept
shivering in fear on the sawdust floor of the circus tent. Early the
next morning, they were jostled from their sleep by the roust-
abouts when the circus prepared to leave town.
"The Carnival in Niggertown" was over.

My father's research had provided him with a prototypical
Palm Beach millionaire on which his most evil character was
based. For me, his research and writing provided a basis on
which to research my own Master's thesis. At that time, I was the
only graduate student at the University of Florida who was ever
allowed to write a dissertation on his own father.
Just when you think you know it all, you discover you don't
know anything at all. But what does an eighteen-year old freshman at UF really know about life?

CHAPTER 23

What does a thirty-three year old school teacher from West Palm Beach, who's never really left home, know about life?

Half asleep in my bunk, I heard the phone ringing.

I struggled to catch my breath, hoping it was Bobby with word about Joachim. "Hello?"

"Jimmy? Do you know who this is?" It was a woman's voice, subdued, muffled.

"I'm not sure."

"It's me, your buddy, Joachim." I recognized the voice now. It was Adrianne.

I was silent at first, not knowing what was going on, not realizing at first that she was toying with me.

"Did you hear me? It's Joachim, your boyhood friend. Don't you recognize my voice?"

"Adrianne? Is this you? What did you do with Joachim?"

"You're not listening, Jimmy. This isn't Adrianne. It's me, Joachim. Don't you want to know how I am?"

"Adrianne, let's cut the bullshit. What's going on here?"

"Let me hear you say, 'Hi, Joachim'." Her voice was taunting.

I was tired of playing the game, afraid for Joachim, so I went along with it.

"...Hi, Joachim...."

"That's it? That's all you can say? I'm putting my life on the line out here, and all you can say is 'hi'? What kind of friend are you, anyway?"

I suppose Adrianne thought she was being cute, and I wanted to strangle her, but I didn't want to jeopardize my friend anymore.

"Hi, Joachim, how are you?"

Her voice took on a new tone now. "I'm not doing so well, you motherfucker! I thought you were supposed to be my friend? If you don't have that cocaine that they want in another twenty-four hours, they're going to kill me."

I broke character. "Listen, Adrianne...."

She laughed out loud and hung up.

I put in a call to Bobby at home, waking his wife. She said he was at the office. I called him there, but no one had seen him in hours. He didn't answer his pager.

CHAPTER 24

That night I dreamt my father and I were sitting on that Library roof at the University of Florida, planning a fishing trip to Lake Okeechobee. The soft breeze was filled with the scent of decaying Live Oak.

A twelve year-old girl who looked just like the pictures I had seen of Nikki at that age, came and sat down between us. She looked at us both and smiled her smile.

On the horizon, a circus tent was burning and I could hear the screams of children.

CHAPTER 25

I awoke the next day asking myself a disturbing question. "If I were sixty-five years old and wanted to fuck a fifteen year old girl, where would I find one who was willing?"

I dressed and bicycled down the dock and across Flagler Drive to the bus station. Inside, it was empty except for the clerk behind the counter. Any minute, I knew, a busload of disenchanted young teenage girls would come; arrive by busload from Cleveland, Minneapolis, Alberta, Watkins Glen, or Springfield, Mass. Young girls, tired of living in trailer parks in the small, drab, dreary, economically depressed industrial towns where they grew up in the north; arriving by bus, knowing in their heart of hearts that they would find happiness somewhere in Florida. Where is the big money? Palm Beach, of course. Arrive in Palm Beach and become the favorite toy of some guy who drives a Porsche and who could take care of them in their time of need; who would show them fast times and shower them with excitement.

Did they realize when they first got on their bus back home in their small town that they were going to have to barter their bodies and souls for any excitement they might receive?

Did they know that they would have to spread their legs so some old guy could get his rocks off before he would even think about going one step further on their behalf? Did they have the foresight to think about that before they left home? Were they willing to make that sacrifice? Did they think, "What's a five minute piece of ass as long as it gets me to where I want to go? Who does it hurt? If that's what it takes, then, fine, I'll cooperate for the free ride. Come and get it, Mr. Palm Beach Porsche Driver." Dream on.

I walked up to the bus station ticket window. A listless clerk with transparent white skin was shuffling paper, wondering where his life went.

"I got a cousin coming in from New York today. When's the next bus due in?"

Without looking up or checking the schedule the clerk responded as if he'd been asked the question a million times before. "It was scheduled to come in at eight this morning, but it won't be in for another hour.

"Does it come in every day at that time?"

"It's scheduled to come in at eight, but it comes in a different time every day. Today it's ten. Tomorrow it might be nine or it might be five in the afternoon. Depends on the connections."

I rode my bike back to the marina and hung around by the phone until a few minutes before ten o'clock. I put on a khaki fishing captain's hat and pulled the brim down low. With my Ray-Bans on, I looked like any one of a hundred other guys from around here. I bicycled down the dock and across the street to the bus station.

A towering ficus tree dominates the parking lot next to the bus station, its car-sized tree trunk made up of dozens of root-like tendrils which hang down from the branches in search of nutrients. On the far side of the tree, I shinnied up one of the vein-like tendrils and climbed to the top. There, by stepping on a branch, I opened up an unobstructed view of the lot.

The bus was another half-hour late, and my leg was starting to cramp from holding down the branch. Finally it pulled in, a

'Miami' sign in the destination window scroll. A dozen people got off to stretch and get something to eat before the final leg into Miami. A sleepy teenaged boy in new jeans was met by his parents. An elderly, obese black woman hobbled toward a cab. A fifteen year old runaway, trying her best to pass for a sophisticated eighteen-er, stood in the baking sunlight, getting her bearings, waiting for her new life to begin as an attendant pulled a cheap, red plaid suitcase from the luggage compartment and handed it to her. She had arrived in Florida, the land where dreams come true. Especially bad dreams.

She fit the same profile as the three I had seen the night before at Fletcher's: young, broke, alone, desperate white trash running to Florida to start a new life away from her parents. Florida attracts kids like her like dead meat attracts maggots. "Things will be better down there." Sure. At least it's warm in the winter. She lit a cigarette and was headed for the shade of the tree I was hiding in when she was approached by a woman who appeared to be in her late twenties.

My timing was perfect if what I saw happening was what I thought it was. The woman wore a straw hat and sunglasses, but it was obvious who it was. She asked the girl a question I couldn't hear, and then in a halting, awkward manner, the two of them started a conversation. It continued for five minutes, the woman coming on to the girl and the girl trying to ignore the woman by looking around the parking lot, not sure of herself in this new environment, not wanting to talk to strangers no matter how friendly.

Finally, the girl acquiesced, nodded her head and followed the woman to her car. Her new life had begun. This is what she had run away from home for, wasn't it? It was that easy. Florida: truly the land of opportunity.

As they got closer to where I was perched, I confirmed the older woman's identity. It was Adrianne, of course. I wanted to tackle her in the parking lot; bring her to her knees; call Bobby to arrest her; force her to lead us to Joachim. But I didn't do any of that.

They headed out of the parking lot, and I was trembling so badly I almost fell out of the tree. Could it have been just some bizarre coincidence? When Consuelo had told me the girls were recruited by a woman, is Adrianne who she had meant? What else would Adrianne be doing picking up teenage girls at a bus station, if, in fact, that was what I had just witnessed?

I shinnied back down the tree so fast I scraped my thighs and chest. Adrianne's car was pulling out onto Flagler Drive as I hopped on my bike. Where was she taking this girl? How far could I possibly follow before I lost them?

The late morning traffic was working in my favor as they drove slowly north past the marina. I caught up to them at the First Street traffic light and then started losing them again when the light changed. I was pedaling as fast as I could, when Adrianne veered off onto the Flagler Memorial Bridge access ramp.

From there, I knew immediately where she was headed. Even if they hadn't been stopped by the bridge going up, I would've known where to find them. She was so obvious. But then, why would she think anyone was following her? Why should she be cautious? I leaned against the concrete railing, pretending I was fishing. Wasn't I fishing?

They turned north on Bradley Place, but instead of following them, I turned and headed toward the bike trail, riding parallel to them, separated by a block of trees, then the Biltmore Hotel. I rode as fast as anyone has ever ridden on the narrow trail to the intersection where the short bridge to Alligator Island crossed over it. There, under cover of a stand of Areca palms, I saw Adrianne's car pull over the tiny bridge and stop at the guard house. I was right. Where else could they be heading than toward Fletcher's private compound on Alligator Island?

Knowing I was right and knowing what it all meant were two different things. If Adrianne worked for the Fletchers, that meant that the Fletchers knew where Joachim was, knew I was somehow involved with the cocaine. Were they the ones who had imported the cocaine, or was there interest purely in the partying potential possible for whoever could wield it, like I had seen the night before?

I leaned against my bike, trying to catch my breath, trying to overcome the dizziness created by what I had just found out.

I coasted back to the boat, trying to put all the pieces together. What was I going to do? I had to contact Bobby again, let him know I knew where to find the connection: Adrianne.

CHAPTER 26

I stormed past Hal Burns, the reporter who was lurking outside Bobby's office and walked into the cubicle without knocking. Bobby was not pleased to see me. "Jimmy..."

"I tried to call you last night. No one knew where you were. That woman, Adrianne, called me last night, pretending to be Joachim. She was just busting my balls. They said I have twenty-four more hours or they're going to kill him. Have you found out anything?" It came out in a rush of words.

"Jimmy, take it easy. I'm doing what I can."

"It's not enough! What are you doing? For all we know he's dead already, and all you can think about is that you don't want it in the papers!"

Bobby exploded from behind his desk, papers scattering to the floor, angry for the first time in a long time. "No, Jimmy, *you* don't want it in the papers, remember?" We stood face to face, both of us angry at the other, like never before. "Jimmy," he was being firm, pointing his finger into my chest. "Keep-your-voice-down!" He walked to his glass door and looked outside. "That big-mouth asshole is standing right outside!"

"What do I care? What's more important here, saving Joachim's life or not getting our names in the papers?"

"Jimmy, you've got to trust me on this one. You've got to stay out of it. I've got my guys working on it. I swear to you. If we don't have something when they call in twenty-four hours, we'll help you fake a switch with stuff from the evidence locker, make sure no one gets hurt. No one but you and me and a couple of my guys know he is missing. Thank God Maria is out of town." He looked down to his desktop. "And you are still sure you don't know where the cocaine is?"

I looked him straight in the eye and once again, didn't lie to him. I even shrugged my shoulders and shook my head to make it all more convincing. "I'm telling you, it's not on my boat. I've looked. You can come down and look for yourself if you don't believe me."

There was something about Bobby's attitude that started to gnaw at me. I didn't quite know what it was, but all of a sudden, I decided to clam up. Now I didn't want to tell him where he could find Adrianne.

"We'll put a tracer on your phone. When they call again we'll know where to pick them up."

"Why didn't they put Joachim on the line? What do you think is going on with them?"

"She was just dicking with you, Jimmy. We're working on a couple of leads, so just be patient for another twenty four hours. Will you do that for me, please? Let's not make a case where there is no case.

"What about taking that cocaine out of the evidence locker for ransom, like you said?"

Bobby gasped a breath, as if to recover from what he had just offered me. "I swear to God, Jimmy, you ever tell anyone I said that, and we'll both rot in jail." He paced the floor. "Now get out of here and let me work on this."

As I pedaled back home, all I could think about was that something was not right. What did Bobby have up his sleeve? Why was he saying crazy things? I'd never known him to have a dishonest thought in his life.

It was time for me to find out more about what was going on at the Fletcher's estate besides some serious partying; what Hamilton and the good Senator knew about Joachim and the missing cocaine; where Adrianne fit in to it all.

How could they be tied to the cocaine? Were they responsible for Joachim's kidnapping? If they were, I was going to nail their balls to the wall, and I would do it without Bobby's help or blessing.

It was time for me to do something really stupid.

CHAPTER 27

I drove out to the Mall and headed toward "Country Churn Ice Cream Shoppe." When the blonde-haired clerk behind the counter saw me, she beamed.

"Wow, my favorite English Teacher! You've made my day."

Last winter, Suzanne Bishop had been failing my Senior English class and was destined to miss graduation if she didn't pass her midterm exam. She approached me after class and discreetly offered to fuck me senseless if I gave her a passing grade in return. I immediately became so frightened by her remark I had to sit down at my desk. I'd gathered my thoughts, made sure no one was in hearing distance, thanked her for her compliment, told her I'd found her offer very flattering, but declined and suggested I tutor her in the library after school every day in full view of the library staff.

Suzanne had been disappointed by my counter-offer, but she accepted it and managed to graduate with a "C-." Now she was scooping ice cream and making dry chicken-salad sandwiches on two day-old pita bread for minimum wage. It would probably be the best job she would ever have. She was tiny and was coy and waif-like almost to the degree of self-parody. She looked at least three years younger than the eighteen years indicated by her driver's license. But on her petite frame she had the body of a woman; proportioned perfectly.

I asked her to join me for coffee on her break, and we walked around the corner to a sidewalk cafe. I got right to the point. "You remember your offer last winter?"

She was surprised and smiled. "Hey, you're pretty smooth, Mr. Phipps. I like your style. I knew you'd come around to my way of thinking someday."

She was stoned. I recognized the symptoms. "I'm serious. Are you still interested?"

"With you? Any day of the week."

"What about if it wasn't with me?"

"Wow, Mr. Phipps! You surprise me." She smiled. "What, are you pimping on the side now?"

That made me stop, almost. But I was in too deep already. "No, but I need to get some real important information, and this is the fastest way I know how to get it."

She laughed out loud. "Wow. Intrigue. Sounds interesting. What's in it for me? I don't need to pass English anymore. I'm through with school. What can you offer me?"

"I'll pay you. A thousand dollars."

She looked around the mall to see if anyone was watching. *A month's salary* flashed in her eyes. "Who is it? What's involved?"

"A couple of older guys. A few other women your age. A sort of party."

"What else?"

"What do you mean?"

"I mean do they have any goodies? Any drugs? Coke? Quaaludes? Pop some heroin? Anything? That's what I call a party. I can get all the fucking I want anywhere and anytime."

I was starting to hate myself. "Lots of coke. Probably some bootleg Quaaludes." Her eyebrows raised. Jackpot.

"Now you're talking. You're on. Any chance of you joining us?" She smiled and reached across the table and covered my hand with hers.

"I've wanted a piece of your ass since the first day of school."

"No, I won't be joining you. As a matter of fact, you have to make believe you're from out of town."

She looked disappointed until she remembered the thousand bucks. "So what do you want me to find out?"

The next morning at six, Suzanne met me by the docks and we drove to the bus station in Jupiter. She had a small, cheap suitcase and was wearing a halter top and cut-offs, just as I had instructed.

"So tell me again what I should listen for."

"Get off at the West Palm Beach station across from where I just picked you up. When you get off, look around like you're a lost soul from Cleveland who just ran away from home. If a woman with long dark hair and sunglasses approaches you and tries to pick you up, play hard-to-get for a few minutes, but go with her. She'll probably take you to a house in Palm Beach for the party tonight. Just play dumb and find out what you can about the woman and anything else that goes on. Ask where they got the coke but be discreet about it. Be sure to ask where you can get some more coke for yourself. Get names if you can."

I hesitated here. I was hating myself more by the second. "They may ask you to do stuff you really don't want to do, and if they do, I'm sorry."

"Listen, if there's coke and Quaaludes involved like you say, I can't think of too many things I wouldn't do. Don't worry about it. I'll have a good time unless they're into 'pain' or some other weirdo shit."

"Try to get the woman to drive you back to the bus station when you wake up tomorrow morning. Tell her you're due in Miami, or something. Tell her you'll be back. If she hesitates, start acting frightened and panicky. When she leaves, give me a call and I'll come pick you up."

"Hey, man, this is pretty exciting. I feel like 'Police Woman'."

"Listen, Suzanne, I really feel awkward asking you to do this, but a lot is at stake here. It's important to me."

"No sweat, man. This is fun. Don't give it another thought."

She climbed out of my car and wandered toward the front of the building. She looked like a lost runaway from Cleveland. She turned just before she disappeared around the corner. "Hey Jimmy!"

"Yeah?"

"You're a lot cooler than all the kids think you are."

She was wrong.

Not only was I not cool, but at this point, I was probably subject to arrest. During the twenty mile trip south from Jupiter, I was overwhelmed with guilt. What right did I have to ask a former student of mine to do something like that?

I drove down through Juno Beach on Double Roads. Those same roads I had taken with Nikki our first night on the beach.

One of the earliest, most realistic dreams I had of my father was when I woke up in the middle of the night. Soft moonlight poured into the room and a gentle breeze off the lake blew the white, incandescent curtains softly inward in lazy gusts. He appeared at the foot of my bed, smiling a loving smile, looking at me for a moment before he sat on the edge of the mattress and put his hand over mine on top of the sheet. The only advice I ever got from him came in four words at the end of that dream. He smiled that smile as he squeezed my hand. He spoke barely above a whisper, so as not to awaken my mother.

"Be a good boy."

Those four words were all he spoke. My eyes moved from where he held my hand to his eyes and our eyes locked. A train whistle blew softly in the background and he cocked his head, following the whistle's beckoning call, as if to say, "Gotta go." He smiled at me before standing and walking toward my bedroom door. He turned back one more time.

"Be a good boy," he whispered, and was gone.

I awoke suddenly, with such a strong sense that he had really just been there that I raced into the hallway to catch a glimpse of his back. But the house was still except for my pounding chest. I collapsed back on the bed, sobbing as if my heart had been ripped out of my chest. Just those four words. Maybe the best advice a father can give to a son. Perhaps the only advice.

And now, I was not heeding his dream-state advice. I wasn't being "a good boy."

CHAPTER 28

An hour after dropping Suzanne off in Jupiter, I was back at my vantage point in the giant Ficus tree. She arrived an hour late, and stepped down from the bus looking appropriately groggy. Adrianne entered stage left, right on cue. From the tree I watched as Suzanne gave an award-winning performance trying to put off Adrianne's advances. She looked around nervously before consenting to let Adrianne lead her away in her car. At the last second, when Adrianne was already in the car and not looking, Suzanne turned to the tree-top and gave me a little smile and a thumbs-up wave before climbing into the car herself.

It never even got to the stage of self-debate. I had already subconsciously decided I was going to go back to the cabana. Before I could even begin to reason myself out of it, part of me was packing up my dive gear and getting ready for my journey back to Alligator Island. Part of me was telling myself that what I had asked Suzanne to do was wrong, and that by going back over there to watch her was immoral. But from somewhere down inside of me came an answer. I wasn't going to miss it for anything. I wouldn't even reconsider for a second.

One of the first safety rules of scuba diving is to breathe normally. But on my trip across to the boat house, my breathing

became rapid, shallow, in anticipation of what I was going to witness. I kept telling myself to turn back, knowing that I was fighting a losing battle with myself. Is this what an addiction feels like?

I repeated my efforts from the night before. This time, as I
walked across the lawn, I picked up two coconuts and silently
screwed one of them into the sod in front of the cabana porch.

On my hands and knees, in a position that resembled begging,
I slithered under the Bahama shutter to where I had knelt before.

The scene before me was a variation on all that had taken
place on my recent visit. This time there were new players. Lucky
was replaced by a man I didn't recognize, who was standing with
his cock in a girl's mouth. I couldn't see her face, but it looked like
one of the young girls from the previous night, thin, like Suzanne,
but with curly black hair. Hamilton sat on the couch, a new, young
girl sucking him off. His brother sat next to him, asleep like a
beached whale.

As I settled in, Adrianne and Suzanne walked in from the
bathroom on the far side of the cabana. They were both naked,
and I was stunned by the beauty of both of their bodies. It had
only been a matter of a few days since I had first seen Adrianne
with her nipples erect, wet, naked, shivering on my boat. If I had
known Suzanne looked like this with her clothes off, I never
would have been able to spend those hours with her in the high
school library. She would have driven me to distraction. It had
been fifteen years since I had seen a naked eighteen year-old, and
I had forgotten about the taut firmness of the skin, the forthright-
ness of the breasts. Her petite frame made me feel all the more
deviant, as if I were lusting after a twelve year old girl, rather than
someone of legal age.

They walked past the coffee table, and as casually as if passing a tray full of hors d'oeuvres, they stuck their fingernails into
the bowl of cocaine and snorted it up their noses. Adrianne led
Suzanne over to the bed in front of me and lay down with her

head toward the center of the room, her feet toward me. She made a quick off-hand gesture toward her muff. Suzanne murmured a soft, "Uhmmm," knelt in front of me and began eating Adrianne without hesitating, and with an enthusiasm that surprised me. Did she realize I was watching? Hoping? Was her performance for my benefit?

I couldn't believe my eyes. I couldn't believe what I had come all this way for, was happening inches from my face.

It went on in one form or another until after four in the morning. I postponed my departure time and time again, unwilling to miss someone waking up to start all over again. What had come over me? I didn't seem to be in control. I almost expected to drown on the swim back to my Zodiac.

CHAPTER 29

The next day was showdown day. Something had to happen. Bobby had to report some kind of progress if he expected to save face with me. Suzanne would call, and hopefully so would Adrianne.

I didn't know what to expect, but I decided to stay close to the phone.

Suzanne called at ten, like we had pre-arranged. It sounded like she was drugged. I felt like I was drugged from lack of sleep.

"Are you okay?"

"Sure. I'm just wiped out. I've been up all night fucking and sucking. I think they put me on the bonus plan."

I know that, I wanted to tell her.

I picked her up at the bus station ten minutes later and drove her to her apartment in Lake Worth. She looked haggard, like she'd been through the wringer.

"Jimmy, you wouldn't believe this party. I never thought I would get my fill of sex and drugs, but last night came pretty close. I'm so sore I can hardly walk."

I kept my eyes on the road as she continued.

"I got a chance to talk to one of the other girls. I got a phone number, you want to get in touch with her. She got picked up by this woman Adrianne a few days ago, just like I did yesterday. Adrianne took me on a tour and explained the ground rules. She was pissed when I said I had to leave this morning. Anyway, one of the other girls, she's been there ever since last week. If she doesn't kill herself from too much coke or fuck herself to death, she'll probably stick around until they throw her out or they get bored with her."

"Does this go on all the time?"

"She told me they go through a couple of girls a weekend that way. All the coke you want, all you gotta do is do whatever they want and hang around the pool naked all day, let the old guys cop feels, whatever."

"What about the coke?"

"Endless. They were chopping the stuff with a meat cleaver out of a soup bowl-full of the stuff. It was almost like a joke. I thought I was with Tony Montana in SCARFACE. Are you sure I couldn't go back there again?"

"No."

"Just as well. I'd probably overdo it anyway."

"Did you find out where the coke came from? Where it goes? Any names?"

"No. They didn't say anything specific and I didn't want to appear too nosy."

"Do you think you could pick this woman Adrianne out of a police line-up?"

Suzanne laughed out loud. "Are you kidding? We ate each other's pussies for two solid hours, I think I can identify her."

The scene from last night wouldn't leave my mind.

"I bet I know what you're thinking...."

I pulled up in front of her cottage.

"Why don't you come in for some coffee? I can give you some more details about what happened. A demonstration, maybe."

"No, I gotta go. I appreciate the offer."

"Maybe someday."

"Hey Suzanne, you okay?"

"Sure."

"I know this is a crazy situation. I don't know what, if anything will come of it. You may...you may have to testify in court someday."

"No problem. What's this all about, anyway? Never mind, I probably don't want to know. I had a great time." She was staring at me dreamily. She was crashing. I handed her fifty, twenty-dollar bills. She let out a short laugh and before I could stop her, she squeezed my crotch playfully and got out of the car. She turned and leaned in the window.

"You know, this is really strange."

"What?"

"Somehow I feel really peaceful."

"Too many Quaaludes."

"No. This is different...more peaceful somehow, *satiated*."

I looked at her.

"I learned that word in your vocabulary class."

"I figured."

"*Ironic*."

"That one, too."

"Yeah." She shook her head and walked toward her apartment.

I drove back to the boat. Suzanne seemed to have come through the ordeal without much damage–assuming she didn't catch AIDS. Should I have felt so guilty for setting her up with what was, to her, the best party she'd ever been to? For the best party I'd ever witnessed? I tried to force the images of the last few nights from my mind. That way lies madness.

CHAPTER 30

We had been married for two years when Nikki woke me in the middle of the night. She had gone into the kitchen of the main house for a glass of milk and while she was gone, I drifted off. When she returned she was crying, shaking. She looked like a little girl, lost, afraid, vulnerable.

"I want to go see my mother."

"What's wrong? Is everything okay?"

"Everything is fine. I just want to see my mother."

In an hour we were in Nikki's Mercedes on I-95, heading for North Carolina.

Once enroute, Nikki fell into a deep sleep.

North of Daytona, the weather started turning cool, and when we crossed into Georgia two hours later we had to stop to buy sweaters and winter coats. As we passed South of the Border Motel, it started to snow. We picked up Route 74 and headed west toward Shelby.

Nikki hadn't uttered two sentences in almost twelve hours. She was distracted, and when I tried to find out what was going on or offer words of comfort, she brushed them off. All she would say was that she had to talk to her mother.

Near Shelby, we headed northwest into the mountains, toward

Asheville and Great Smokey Mountain National Park, the snow
flurries turning pirhouettes in the Mercedes' headlight beams.

For the last two hours of the journey the snow stopped and we
followed a snowplow to a gas station and waited while they put
chains on our tires.

Nikki paced the hard concrete floor of the freezing cold garage
restlessly, lost in what appeared to be some form of emotional
pain she didn't wish to share with me.

By dusk we had arrived at Dove Cottage, the poetic euphemism given to the psychiatric hospital run by an order of nuns I
had never heard of. Covered by six inches of snow, the grounds
appeared immaculate, surrounding the large wooden structure
that was once a turn of the century spa. The Gilded Age lived on,
in these surroundings.

Inside, just three dozen patients, all from wealthy East Coast
families, were given round-the-clock, one-on-one attention. They
were never left alone. Their conditions ranged from drug addiction to dementia and all fun-stops in-between, and all involved
high degrees of embarrassing nuisance factor for their families.
What was important was to keep them ware-housed, as far away
from their families as possible.

Out of sight, out of mind. As long as you are out of *our* sight,
you may remain out of *your* mind, was the implied message left
for these patients by their families. Not that they had the mental
capacity to understand the message.

It was dark, almost 8 p.m. when we arrived after sixteen hours
of driving. The last of the patients had been ushered out of the
dining room and back to their rooms.

A sister, dressed in nun's habit, stepped quickly from behind
the desk when we walked through the front door and into the
lobby, leaving a wet trail of snow in our tracks. It was obvious

they were not used to seeing unexpected visitors.

She was polite, yet firm. "May I help you?"

Nikki hadn't spoken a word in over four hours. She cleared her throat. "I want to see my mother."

"Who would that be?"

"Nancy Fletcher."

"Yes, I see. Do you have an appointment?"

"I don't need an appointment to see my mother."

"Yes, ma'am. I'm afraid that you do."

"I want to speak to a higher authority. And I'm not in any mood for any of that 'God' stuff."

"I'll get Dr. Winslow. Won't you please have a seat?"

Nikki, clearly more agitated than I had ever seen her, took a seat near the door. I joined her. "Are you all right?"

"I will be after I see my mother." Her appearance and demeanor were starting to frighten me.

The first nun reappeared followed by another. She carried a file and walked with the confidence of someone sure of her authority. She smiled, but it was only a formality. "Hello, I'm Sister Kathleen. May I help you?"

Nikki stood up, and tried to take charge. It was a mode I had seen her slip into easily in the past whenever she felt it necessary.

"I want to speak to Dr. Winslow."

Sister Kathleen kept her firm smile. "I'm Dr. Kathleen Winslow, yes."

"You're a doctor?"

"Yes. A psychiatrist, more precisely. How may we help you?" She opened the folder in her hands.

"I want to see my mother."

"You're Miss….Fletcher?"

"Was. Mrs. Phipps, now."

"Mrs. Phipps, I'm sorry, but we require advance notice for such visits. You can understand that we can't have people stopping by when they're passing through the neighborhood."

"We weren't just passing through. We just drove sixteen straight hours through a snowstorm to get here."

"Mrs. Phipps, I'm sure your assertiveness carries great weight in the business world and in your Palm Beach social circle, but right now, you're on my turf. Your mother may be your mother, but she is my patient, and I will decide who she sees and when she sees them."

Without flinching, Nikki opened her purse and pulled out her checkbook. "I'll write the hospital a check right now for one hundred thousand dollars."

From the look on Nikki's face and her demeanor, I could tell she was not bluffing. She taunted the doctor. "Come on. Right now. One hundred thousand dollars. Just turn your back and let me speak to her for ten minutes and you get a hundred grand for your hospital." She started to write the check. "I'll make it out to you personally, if that's what it's going to take."

Dr. Winslow held up her hand in a stopping motion. "Just one moment, Mrs. Phipps." She turned and walked through swinging double doors behind the reception desk.

Nikki finished writing the check and with a flourish, tore it from her checkbook and extended it toward the first nun. The nun, arms folded across her breasts, remained immobile.

"Come on," Nikki taunted her, but the nun walked behind the desk.

In less than sixty seconds, Dr. Winslow returned accompanied by two orderlies. The larger of the two, easily three hundred pounds, could have played tackle for a professional football team. The smaller, black man, was muscular, ready to spring. Nikki, thinking they were about to escort her through the ward, was relieved. "Now we're getting somewhere."

Dr. Winslow stopped at where Nikki still held the check aloft. "Mrs. Phipps, I regret to inform you that your mother has expressed to me the desire to receive absolutely no visitors at this or any other time."

"I'm her daughter." Nikki's voice was raised in disbelief. I had never seen her this agitated. "Did you tell her it was her daughter?"

Dr. Winslow's composure started to waver. "Mrs. Phipps….." She hesitated before going on, unsure of whether to proceed. Would it be unprofessional?

Nikki screamed in the woman's face. "I'm her only daughter! I've got to see her. Now."

"Mrs. Phipps, her exact words were '*especially* my daughter'. I'm sorry to have to tell you that. Perhaps you and I can sit down and have a cup of coffee and discuss…"

But by this time Nikki had turned and run out the door.

When I arrived at the car, Nikki was slumped in the front seat. At first I thought she was asleep, but she was sobbing deeply. I put my hand on her shoulder to comfort her, but she brushed it off.

"There's a motel at the bottom of the hill. We passed it on the way up the mountain. I'll see if there's a room available."

"I want to go home. "

"Nikki, we've been awake for twenty hours. We need to get some sleep."

"So go to sleep. I'll drive home. "

Twenty hours later, after another snow storm and stopping only to remove the snow chains, buy coffee and go to the bathroom, we pulled into Palm Beach. Nikki hadn't said a word on the entire ride home. I hadn't slept in forty hours. As I unloaded the car and walked toward the cabana, Nikki started off across the lawn toward the main house.

"Are you all right?"

"I'm going to sleep in my room," was all she said, disappearing into the kitchen door at the rear of the house.

I didn't realize something then, or even if I had realized it, I

would have never understood it. Whatever it was that had precipi-
tated our marathon drive to Western North Carolina, I was never
able to determine. But whatever it was, it was the beginning of the
end of our marriage.

Three hours later I was teaching *SILAS MARNER* to tired,
hungry inner city students who couldn't wait to get out of there. I
knew how they felt.

CHAPTER 31

After I dropped off Suzanne at her Lake Worth Apartment, I waited until dark before the next call came. A hundred times I wanted to just call Bobby and tell him to forget the whole thing. Tell him I knew where to find Adrianne, where the coke was, that I was sure Hamilton and Danforth were behind the whole thing. Instead, I waited. Finally, the call came.

"Jimmy, honey, baby, sweetheart. Adrianne here."

"I want to know how Joachim is."

"Hah! And *I want* to drive a new Rolls Royce for the rest of my life. So what? You need to figure out the difference between *'wants'* and *'needs'*."

"How is he?"

"He's fine. But that's not why I'm calling. You ready to make the switch?"

I cut her off. "Adrianne, we need to talk. Are you alone?"

There was silence for a moment at her end of the line. My comment and tone were unexpected. She was used to having the upper hand and now that she could sense the tables were turning, she was trying to figure out how to deal with it.

"What are you talking about, man? The only thing we need to talk about is the coke. You deliver the coke, we deliver your fat boyfriend. Just like the note said."

"Is he alive?"

"I'm not sure he's ever been *alive*."

"IS HE ALIVE ! "

"Shit, yeah, he's alive. Alive and kicking. Or should I say 'kicking back'."

I took a deep breath and began what I had been rehearsing ever since I saw Adrianne pick up that first girl at the bus station, ever since I had watched her and Suzanne together.

"Adrianne, listen. I've got some bad news for you. I know who you are working for and I know what you do. I know what you do at the bus station–those girls– and I know what goes on at the Fletcher cabana. Unless you want to go to jail for contributing to the delinquency of minors, procuring minors, statutory rape, kidnapping, soliciting, conspiracy to distribute cocaine, and any other charges you and the Fletchers are tied up with, you should stop and think a minute. You're not calling the shots anymore."

"Well, aren't we being assertive. How did you get to the girls?"

"That's not important. Tell you what. Make some excuse to get away from wherever you are and come over here by yourself and we'll talk. I'm serious about this. I've got people willing to testify against you. Minors."

"Who?"

"You know the new girl you got yesterday afternoon? Said she was from Cleveland? She's ready to blow the whistle."

"I knew she was ready to blow......" She laughed, dismissively.

"There are the others." I described the three girls I had seen, but made it sound like the information had been passed to me by an eyewitness; *another* eyewitness.

"Do they sound familiar? You help me out on this and I'll help you stay out of trouble." I was whistling in the dark at this point, but there was no way she could know that.

Finally, there was a nervous sigh at the other end of the line. "I'll be there in ten minutes."

It took her twenty minutes to get there. This time she was

dressed in khaki shorts and a navy blue golf shirt. Very preppy. She walked around the cabin of the boat as if she had never been there. She was straight and very frightened. "Okay, man, what do you want?"

I stood up and looked around. A hundred–two hundred darkened windows in every direction. One shot from a high-powered rifle is all it would take.

"I want my friend.."

"I know, I know. And I want the coke."

"You mean you and the Fletchers want the coke."

"What makes you say that?"

"Come on. I know what's going on over there. I've talked to people who have been there. Like I said on the phone, I know about the girls at the bus station. That Cleveland girl has a big mouth. She's ready to I.D. you in a police line-up. I know the Fletchers want the missing cocaine for their parties. She told me there was enough around to use a shovel."

Adrianne looked at me for a moment, letting it all sink in, trying to find a way to manipulate her way out of the situation she was in.

"It's no use. You have no choice. You gotta let my friend go, or I'll see to it that you go to jail. You think the Fletchers are going to stand behind you? Pay for your attorney? You're on your own with those guys. They'll turn their back on you so fast you won't know what hit you."

She stared at me. She knew I was right. "What do you want me to do?"

"Go back to where Joachim is and let him go. Or take me with you."

"Don't be stupid. I can't do that. They'll kill us both if I do it."

"So make it look like he escaped. I really don't give a shit what you and the Fletchers do. I'd just as soon let the whole thing blow over. I just want my friend back, safe and sound . Just let him go and this will be all over. Do it right now or I call in the cavalry. I'm three steps from my phone and Bobby is on my speed dial."

"You want me to help him to escape? Do you know how risky that would be for me?"

I pulled out all the stops. "Would you rather go to jail? You don't help me, I'll see you in jail, even if it takes me every penny I own to bribe the State's Attorney's Office. Make your decision right now. I'm on my way to the phone. It's decision time."

Finally, she turned contrite. "So what do you want me to do?"

"You know where he is. Help him escape. Make it look like he overpowered you if you have to, anything. Just get him out of there and this will be all over for you."

"Will you try to protect me if I do?"

"I'll do what I can. Where is he, anyway?"

"What about the cocaine? I want some of that shit."

"I don't have the coke. I don't know where it is. Feel free to search the boat......again."

She buckled. "They got him stored in a warehouse out west of town. After you left that day he fell asleep watching the baseball game; too many beers. I clobbered him over the head with your portable television set. He was bleeding all over the place. I called in on your cell phone and they sent out a helicopter on pontoons a few minutes later. I had him tied up and ready for delivery by the time they got there. They landed within twenty feet of your boat. Such precision; it was beautiful."

"Lucky?"

"It wasn't 'lucky.' That guy is good."

"I mean Lucky, the pilot."

"Yeah, how did you know?"

"Who else would it be?" More confirmation. Hamilton's pilot was tied into Joachim's kidnapping, and therefore, Hamilton himself.

"So how is he now?"

"He's fine. Got a few bruises, maybe a broken arm in the

struggle."

"What do you mean, 'maybe a broken arm'?"

"He tried to put up a fight when he came to, even after I tied him up. Lucky had to rough him up a little.."

"What for? Joachim doesn't know where the shit is."

"He started coming on like a smart ass, just like he did when I first met him. So Lucky fucked him up a little....batting practice."

"Why did you come on my boat that night?"

"Hamilton wanted to get the boat away from the dock so they could search it. He figured he'd get you out in the ocean the next morning and make a complete search while there were no witnesses around."

"What was I supposed to be doing while they were searching my boat?"

She turned away from me and shrugged her shoulders. But I knew the answer. "What made Hamilton think the stuff was on my boat?"

"I told him it was. Before she died, Nikki told me she had stashed it on the boat and sailed it through customs. But I couldn't figure out how to get it all by myself, so I cut them in on the deal since they figured it was their coke anyway. Now, I think they're trying to squeeze me out."

"Do they sell any of it?"

"Sometimes for Danforth's campaign financing. But they don't need to make any money. They use it to get laid. You wouldn't believe what those girls will do for coke. It's 'fuck powder' for sure. They move a lot of girls through there in a year; over a hundred at least."

Another irony. Import coke, sell it to support your ultra-conservative, right-wing political ideas. How original.

"But mostly they get it just to fuck with."

"So there was no boat at the Brazilian Docks and you didn't escape from there without your clothes and swim over here."

Adrianne laughed out loud. "Hell, no. No party on the boat

and no drug dealers from Coconut Grove. We just made up that story because we knew you'd be gullible enough to fall for it. They figured you'd take one look at these beautiful tits of mine and sail to China if I asked you to. They dropped me off in the channel as they passed by. I only had to swim a couple hundred feet, and just like they predicted, you were off to rescue a 'damsel in distress'. What intrigue....what a sucker."

I thought about how naive I was. "But they couldn't find us."

"Right. They figured you'd go out in the Gulf Stream and stay there all night, or maybe go up the Intracoastal. They wanted to lure you away from the public eye; sea piracy on the high seas, and all that. They had someone on the jetty watching to see which direction we headed after we cleared the inlet."

I remembered the lone fisherman on the jetty who had turned away when I waved to him.

"They figured I'd call in on your radio at daybreak with a location, they'd fly around for a few minutes and they'd have you nailed. They didn't figure you'd sail out to Lake Okeechobee and tie me up. That was pretty swift. You really screwed them up when you took me out there. They hadn't counted on you being that clever and they didn't know what to do then. No contingency planning if they couldn't find us. Then when you conveniently provided us with a hostage in the form of 'Son of Blubber,' we thought we'd just save the trouble of searching any further ourselves, beyond a quick toss of your boat. Just hold onto Fatso until you came forward with the goods."

"What makes you think I know where the stuff is?"

"For some reason, Fletcher is convinced that you and Nikki were back on speaking terms and that she might have told you where it was, for insurance, or because you were in on it."

"In on what?"

"Oh, man, the whole scam we were running on her father and uncle. They had her stop in the Bahamas on her way back from South America to get the stuff and bring it back here. Then when she shows up here three days late, she told her old man that the stuff had been ripped off by some pirates off the coast on her way back. She had to have hidden it somewhere."

"Why did you two want to rip off her father?"

"I wanted in for the money and the coke. Who knows why she did it? She sure didn't need the money. Just something personal, I guess, between the two of them. Maybe she did it just to piss him off. She was real good at that toward the end. She lived for it."

"Did Nikki participate in those parties?"

"Participate? She was *the life of the party.* She was the one who used to bring the young girls there before I got suckered into that job. I mean, when I do coke, I like pussy as well as the next girl, but I'm not so sure about this *fifteen year-old* shit."

"You could have fooled me." I was thinking about what I had seen with Suzanne.

"What do you mean?"

"I mean, that's not what I heard."

She looked at me, not quite sure I was leveling with her. "But, anyway, she and her father must have had some sort of falling out. Right around the time Nikki gave you this boat. That's the reason she gave it to you. To piss him off."

So that was it. Nikki gave me the boat not out of love, but to annoy her father. I remember sensing that last day I was with her that her generous gesture had been quite uncharacteristic. But I had gone along with it, not asking questions: the dutiful ex-husband. I believed everything she had ever told me.

"She stopped coming to the parties and started fucking around town instead. Then one day a friend of Danforth's called to tell him that Nikki was drunk at *Chuck and Harold's* bar, talking about the Fletcher Brother's parties and the coke, blabbing all over town...that she was thinking about leaving the country. That really pissed them off."

I took a step toward her in the dim light of my cabin. "Can you help Joachim get out? Make it look like he escaped?"

"Maybe. I'll give it a try. They'll probably kill me when they find out he's gone. After we kidnapped Joachim, I think they realized we had gone too far. They're really out of control: Nuts. I'm not even sure they realize they're in way over their heads. Either that or they're just so arrogant they just think they're so fucking powerful they can get away with anything they want."

Or maybe, they're just stupid, I thought.

She reached out her hand and stroked my arm in sympathy. Tears began to well up in her eyes. Was she just playing me for a sucker again? I couldn't tell. "I really liked Nikki. I miss her too. Her father is just too weird for me, too violent, and his creepy brother turns my stomach. If I get your friend out, will you give me some of the coke?"

"What makes you think I know where it is?"

"Like I said, Nikki told me it was somewhere on the boat. You sure she didn't tell you where?"

"I've been over this boat with a fine-toothed comb. You're free to look if you want to." No lies there. I gave her my sincere, earnest look and she bought it.

"Shit, okay. I just thought I'd try. But you just gotta promise to keep the heat off me. That friend of yours can fix it up, can't he?

"What friend?"

"Your cop friend." A look passed over her face. A look trying to remember if she had revealed something she shouldn't have.

I looked at her. Had she realized she had said the wrong thing? Or was it an innocent remark?

She sensed my question and recovered quickly. "You know, that guy you were going to see when you left me on the boat with fat boy...You told me he was your friend... 'Mr. Speed Dial'."

She paused as if trying to come to a decision. She weighed the evidence and decided to proceed.

".....He seems to be real popular."

Before she even finished saying it, a sour taste formed in my mouth. I wanted her to convince me I had misunderstood her, that it was an innocent remark. "What do you mean?"

"You know him....Fletcher knows him...He's gotta be able to pull some kinda strings."

I searched her face for more answers. I'm not sure I wanted to know any more from her. I would get it straight from Bobby.

"I'll see what I can do. Just go back to wherever it is they have him and get him out of there. You sure you don't want my help?"

"No. Forget that. They see you out there and they'll panic and kill all of us. Let me take care of it, kinda low-key like."

I watched her disappear down the end of the dock, the fate of my best friend in her fucked-up hands.

CHAPTER 32

Contrary to what Bobby had said about me, Joachim had always been the best of us; the kindest, the most compassionate. When he had knocked his opponents unconscious on the football field that day in high school, he'd insisted we drive down to the Miami hospital that same night to visit them. He'd been moved to tears when he saw them and had begged their forgiveness.

In college, he'd asked Maria to marry him on their first date, scaring her off. Then, he pursued her for months around the UF campus, following her like a puppy dog. Anyone else and she probably would have thought he was a stalker. But Joachim was as harmless as that puppy dog and his intentions were strictly honorable. They had both waited until their wedding night to give up their virginity. Imagine. Since then, they'd become inseparable, loving one another like no other couple I had ever met. I feared for the safety of my friend. Had I made an irreversible mistake by allowing Bobby to handle this his way? Just to spare me more bad publicity? Keep me away from another assault charge and a restraining order on a snoopy reporter?

What had Adrianne meant about Bobby? What was his part in all this? I tried to visualize the worst-case scenario. It should have come as no surprise, but it did. I could sense he was behaving strangely from my very first day in his office. Had he known all

along what was happening? Was that why he wasn't more concerned about Joachim's well being? I had fallen for what now
seemed like transparent self-confidence. How could he do that to
Joachim? How could he do it to me?

There was nothing for me to do right then but wait to see what
happened. I tried calling Bobby, but no one knew where he was.

He wasn't at home, he wasn't at the office and he didn't answer
his beeper when his secretary tried to contact him. Unusual.
Unusual especially for a cop. Could he be having an affair, and
purposely staying out of contact during some afternoon frolic?

I fell asleep and dreamt about what I had seen in Fletcher's
cabana those two nights. Except in the dream I was there with
Nikki, Adrianne and Suzanne; watching, participating; taking
each one in turn, never finishing, an endless rotation acted out in
slow motion, as the others watched, a smile of dreams on each
face.

A loud thump on the deck woke me up. I was sweating profusely and had an erection that ached for relief from dreaming
about the party.

At the sound of the first moan, I knew it was Joachim and
I scrambled upstairs, my heart exploding out of my chest. He
was slumped on the deck, out of breath. His face was black from
bruises and the blood on his face was a dark red/brown. His nose
was probably broken. His left arm hung useless at his side, looking twice its normal size from a compound fracture. His shirt was
bloodied and the blood had turned to match his face. He squinted
at me through eyes swollen shut and smiled at me through swollen, blood encrusted lips.

"I made it Jimmy. I made it," as if here with me he was safe.
He was gasping hoarsely. His boastful manner belied the fact that
he was whistling in a graveyard. He was seriously injured.

The words formed involuntarily in the bottom of my throat

and came out as a cry, not an exclamation. "Holy Shit, Joco! Holy Shit!" I was afraid for him, he looked so hurt.

The sight of my friend in this condition sickened me, and I hated myself for allowing it to happen. All because of my hesitation and indecision–and my ex-wife.

"Adrianne just dumped me out of her car onto the dock." His lips were cracked and dry. "I made it back, Jimmy. I didn't let you down."

I cradled his head in my arms and let him sip slowly from a bottle of water.

He was pathetic looking, and I knew if I didn't get him to a hospital immediately he might lose his arm. How long had it been like that? He was at a point where he had ceased to be aware of any pain.

I helped him to his feet, trying not to show panic or become ill myself from looking at his injuries. "Jesus, Joco....what have they done to you?"

"I fell asleep on your boat, and when I came to, I was on my way to a helicopter with a cut head and a giant headache. I tried to get untied and clobbered this one guy. When we landed they took me to this warehouse and he worked me over with a baseball bat. He really knew what he was doing. They kept me blindfolded the whole time."

"Come on, we gotta get you some help." I looked up once again to my beloved West Palm Beach skyline. The buildings looked so benign, silhouetted against the sky. Were we being watched? Where was my police protection Bobby had promised?

Getting him into my Volkswagen wasn't easy, and by the way he reacted as I lifted his arms, I figured he had a few broken ribs. I kept my face turned away from him. I didn't want him to see the fear on my face or the fact that I was fighting back tears.

"Jimmy..."

"Don't try to talk. I'm taking you to Good Sam. We'll be there in two minutes."

"I gotta tell you what I know."

He leaned back against the closed window, and I thought he was going to pass out.

"I'm not sure, but I think someone saw me and Adrianne driving off. I was delirious when she came and got me. Listen, all that's not important now. You know that cocaine they want? Your ex-father-in-law sent Nikki out to The Bahamas to get it. He wanted her to bring it back and sell it to beef up his brother's campaign fund....maybe use a little of it themselves. Can you imagine? A political campaign funded by coke?"

Yeah, I can imagine it. But I didn't have the heart to tell him it was old news.

"But Nikki and her old man got into it over something, and she decided to keep it for herself. He's convinced you know where the shit is. Did you go visit him the other day, or something?"

"Listen, Joachim, just shut up and rest. I know all this from Adrianne already. Just try to rest."

We pulled into the Good Samaritan Hospital parking lot and I drove right to the emergency entrance. An ambulance was parked in my way.

An emergency room administrator stepped forward to meet us as automatic doors opened for us and we stepped into the freezing air conditioning. She looked at his arm and face. Joachim anticipated her question.

"I got mugged."

The nurse looked at us both skeptically and then to Joachim's arm. "And you waited two days to come in to be treated?"

"I can explain," he said sheepishly.

"Explain it to the police when they get here. You got insurance?"

Joachim and I exchanged looks.

"Insurance or you take him to St. Mary's."

"He works for the school board. He's a school teacher. He's insured."

The nurse looked at us both suspiciously, then turned and walked away on squeaky rubber soles to make the call and get help. I guided Joachim over to the row of plastic chairs against the wall. An elderly black man was sitting next to us, holding a white handkerchief around his hand. A khaki fishing hat was tilted back on his head. A fishing pole was at his side. A huge, treble fishing hook had passed all the way through the fleshy skin between his thumb and forefinger. He sat looking at his hand silently, waiting for a doctor. No more fishing tonight.

Joachim turned to me and whispered. "Get the hell out of here. I'll make up some bullshit to tell the cops. When I get out of here, those Fletcher boys are gonna wish they had been born poor."

"I'll stay here with you. We'll get Bobby to straighten it out."

Joachim looked at me with a look he usually reserved for opposing linemen. "Fuck Bobby. The cops aren't going to do anything to the Fletchers. This is something we gotta take care of by ourselves, on the street level. Jimmy, this gets really *complicated.*" He was losing consciousness. "We gotta talk about this as soon as we can."

I looked at him silently, surmising, yet not wanting to know what he meant, until he lifted his finger and pointed toward the exit door.

"Now," was all he said before he blacked out.

I turned my back on him. And walked out into the night.

In another four minutes I was back on my boat and on the phone trying to reach Bobby. He was still missing. I called all his other numbers again and was wondering what to do when my phone rang. It was Mrs. Escobar, my mother's next door neighbor who looked in on her every day.

"Jimmy? I think you need to come visit your Mom. I don't think she's feeling very well."

CHAPTER 33

Was Mrs. Escobar's understatement based on fear or misunderstanding?

My mother was sitting at the kitchen table when I arrived. If she knew that I came in and sat down next to her, she didn't indicate it. She sat there smiling in the golden light eking through the doorway from the living room floor lamp.

Spread out before her were pictures from an album I knew she kept. One of them was another pose from a familiar series, the one of my father that I had seen at the University library, sitting on the running board of his Whippet, dressed in a three piece suit, with the jacket and vest hanging from the rearview mirror. His forearms were resting on his bony knees, his straw fedora with the green visor was tilted back on his head. His smile was infectious. An orange-crate at his knees held his portable typewriter as he typed away. On the running board next to him, his Speed-Graphic camera: The tools of his trade which remain resting on a shelf in Gainesville. His finger tips are stained with nicotine, a Camel cigarette is dangling from his fingers as the types, the smoke swirling faceward, making him squint. I hadn't seen the picture since I had last left the University of Florida library, the day I turned in my Master's Thesis on him.

There was another picture of him next to it I remember seeing as a little boy. I had found it in the old album, years after he
died. My father was about ten years old when it was taken, about
the same age I had been when I had found it. He can be seen,
in faded shades of gray, standing in a crowd of twenty men, all
staring straight at the camera. In the foreground of the picture is
a black man, hanging from a Banyan tree, his snapped neck in a
noose, his swollen tongue protruding, his pants stained during his
final relief. My father is the only kid in the crowd, his face a blur
from having turned his head quickly, as if being called from afar,
during the long camera exposure. Standing next to him is his own
father, with his arm around my father's shoulders. My grandfather
is staring straight ahead at the camera with haunting eyes I recognize as my own. On the back of the photo, someone, probably
my grandfather, had scrawled in pencil, in the shaky, unpracticed
hand of the day, "Last nigger hung in Palm Beach."

What a different world my father lived in, similar only in the
boomtown, tourist-attraction mentality. His father brought him to
a public hanging and put his arm around him. My father barely
ever spoke to me, never touched me as I was growing up. Never
took me anywhere.

There is no one to talk to me about that day in the picture now,
to tell me what happened; what it was that caused the black man
to be hanged, what brought all those men together, why a young
boy was included in their gathering. Had my grandfather intended
to teach my father something from witnessing the spectacle? Is
this the day my father decided he would spend his life traveling
throughout Florida and committing his life to putting his observa-
tions on paper? On his dying day, did my father remember the
details from this object lesson of his youth?

Only my mother could tell me the unwritten stories she had
heard second-hand from my father; those stories-behind-the-sto-
ries that he never wrote down. But now I could see it was even
too late for that. She, herself, had now returned to those earlier

days, stuck forever in a happier time where the worries and lonely emptiness of the present couldn't get to her.

She held a postcard from the Whitehall Hotel in her hand, its Technicolor-like colors blaring vividly, unnaturally. Had these been the images that triggered the chain of chemical reactions in her brain that delivered her to wherever she dwelt now?

I sat there staring at the woman who had struggled to raise me by herself. A woman not much older than my despicable father-in-law. The woman who had given up her own dreams to provide for me; so I could have a life. Why do parents do that? The same protective instincts so easily demonstrated by a Momma cat and her kittens translates in human terms to scrubbing toilets so your son can go to college. An instinctive force, providing momentum for the great explosive evolutionary thrust of humanity. Was I ever going to do my part?

And now, having for years come home to a lonely son who didn't know any answers, and to a house devoid of a loving spouse, now it was over for her. Out to pasture, Mom.

Instead of being horrified or saddened for her, I was envious. She was where she wanted to be, reliving events of the past as real to her as my own empty, confused life now was to me. She could now be that young girl forever with the man she loved, sitting on the edge of that Palm Beach sea wall, slow dancing to the Big Band ballads that drifted across Lake Worth and that would now never stop playing. A one-way ticket on a Sentimental Journey filled with Moonlight Serenades, with a limping old man who charmed her with his visions and the cadence of his words, spoken in a rhythmic, poetic, Southern drawl.

I sat with her, the palm of my hand covering the back of hers, until the sun came up the following morning. I didn't want to be the one to break the spell. Joachim had escaped from his captors and was being cared for, probably even under police guard, and my long overdue confrontation with Bobby could wait a few hours.

My mother's facial expression never changed during the night. As the sun came up she was in the same position as when I had arrived. At six in the morning, as the room began to fill with soft morning light, she looked up at me with an absent look. I touched my fingers to her cheek and smoothed a lock of her hair away from her forehead, and I thought I saw a smile begin to form. Was it a smile of recognition or just a reaction to the gentle touch of a stranger?

I called her doctor. I called her sister in New York. They both agreed my aunt should come down and take my mother back home to the family homestead up on the shores of one of The Finger Lakes. Mrs. Escobar and I waited in the driveway for the ambulance service to arrive and take my mother to the nursing home. By nine o'clock that morning they had slid her between cool white sheets and her doctor had arrived. He told me to leave. She didn't know I was there anyway. In another two hours my aunt would fly in and prepare to take her home to New York on the late afternoon northbound train.

CHAPTER 34

It was eleven by the time I stopped at the Tulipan Bakery for some *cafe Cubano*. I needed to wake up, and a *colada* would do the trick.

Back at the docks I stepped onto my boat, trying to clear my mind of my mother and concentrate on what I was going to tell Bobby. By now, I was sure, he knew about Joachim at the hospital. Everyone on the force knew they were friends and it didn't matter what line of bull Joachim told any officer who had shown up to interrogate him. Word would get to Bobby that one of his buddies had had the ever-living dog shit kicked out of him like some red-headed step-child.

But whatever I was going to tell Bobby was quickly forgotten when I opened the hatch and saw Adrianne. Apparently, Joachim's hunch had been right. Someone had seen her helping him escape.

She was on the bunk, propped up in the corner, trussed up with nylon cord like a Thanksgiving turkey. Her face was raw meat and two of her teeth were stuck to her tee-shirt in a glob of coagulated blood where she had gasped them out sometime during the beating that had killed her. Her mouth was a black hole, stuffed with a red rubber ball. From the color and texture of the pool of blood she was in, she hadn't died very long ago; during the night or early morning, when I was at my mother's house. My guess would be they brought her here alive, peacefully, assuming that there might be a twenty-four hour watch on my boat. Once safely aboard, they then tied and bludgeoned her. It was a sickening sight. How could anyone be so inhumane?

The facial bones under her eyes had been smashed in, leaving her eyeballs protruding from the grotesque flatness of her face. She had not been fortunate enough to receive the very most a lot of people can only hope for and expect out of life: a quick, painless death. They obviously wanted Adrianne to suffer for as long as possible and from the looks of things, they had succeeded. Whoever had done this to her had probably practiced on Joachim: Lucky. Adrianne had been right. They were nuts. Very crazy. Very stupid.

In Adrianne's clenched fist was a bloodied piece of paper, as if she were holding it out for me. I pried it from her sticky fingers.

"You're next. We want that
stuff within 24 hours or
you're dead. Get it ready now."

I put in a call to Bobby. I didn't tell him why I was calling.

"What did Joachim tell you?"

His question sounded so innocent, so concerned. "Just get over here. We need to talk. Come now and come alone." I hung up before he could protest.

Bobby arrived within ten minutes.

The reaction on his face when he saw Adrianne was one of defeat. "Ahhh, no....." No wincing at the sight of blood or horror over her suffering. He had seen it all too many times before. Just a tired look on his face. Finally he turned to me in defeat.

"Why, Jimmy?"

"Because she helped Joachim escape."

"That's not what I mean."

"What do you mean?"

"Why is it that no matter how hard you work toward something, something else just keeps fucking up your life?"

I didn't know what he meant, so I didn't say anything. I just waited for him to finish.

When I looked at Bobby again, he was wiping tears away from his eyes.

"I just wish you hadn't gotten involved in this."

"Jesus Christ, Bobby! I didn't *ask* to get involved. They came after me. What was I supposed to do?"

"I mean with that whole family...years ago. They're all crackpots.....They're nuts! They have no conception of right and wrong. You just don't know how crazy those two brothers are. You don't know. You don't know."

"You seem to know, so why don't you tell me?"

He ignored my question and continued on his own train of thought. "How arrogant can you be leaving dead bodies around as warnings? Do they think no one is going to find out about this?" Bobby seemed to be talking to himself now, more than to me. A lament for his own future, it was now becoming apparent.

"Do they really think I'm not going to do something about this? That I'm going to turn my back on it and ignore it? Cover it up? How can they be that arrogant? Don't they have any respect for me at all?"

But he already had figured out the answer to that last question.

I looked at my boyhood friend and wanted to know the precise moment in history when we had started drifting apart. It was as if he were throwing his arms up in the air in a hopeless gesture of surrender.

"How are you involved in this, Bobby?"

He looked at me hopelessly. Instead of answering he changed the subject. "I always knew that Nikki was murdered."

"Who?"

He turned from me. He didn't have to answer. I knew. "Why didn't you do something?"

But Bobby couldn't answer that one. He stood facing Adrianne's body for a long time, not really seeing it. Finally he turned back to me. "I'm going to call the office. This has gone far enough."

While we were waiting for the police to arrive, I sat and stared at the grotesque remains of Adrianne's once near-perfect body. I had never seen a murder scene before, and for some reason the stillness that is there came as a surprise. It's not like you see in the movies. In Nikki's case, I didn't see her body until I was taken to the morgue. Adrianne wasn't going to wake up, stretch, stand and walk away, no matter what. My boyhood friend waited on deck. I decided I had to know something, and I knew there was only one way I would ever know the truth.

Within ten minutes the dock was flooded with a dozen policemen and as many newspaper and television reporters. My reporter pal, Hal Burns was at the forefront.

The cops forced them to stand behind their yellow plastic ribbon as they brought her body out and wheeled it down the dock on the gurney. I waited until everyone was gone before I made the phone call. I wanted to beat the television news at noon. I dialed Fletcher's number. Consuelo answered.

"Jimmy," she was pleading. "Please don't make any trouble. Hector and I.......we're struggling."

"Okay, Consuelo....Okay."

She forwarded the call.

"What do you want?" was the way Fletcher answered the phone.

"I have something for you. Why don't you meet me at my boat tomorrow night and pick it up?"

"What are you talking about?"

"The note you left."

"I don't know what you mean."

"Why don't you come by at nine tomorrow night? Come alone or the deal is off." I hung up before he could respond.

CHAPTER 35

The next morning's newspaper read:

WOMAN BLUDGEONED ON YACHT:
HEIRESS DEATH CASE TO RE-OPEN
by Tribune Reporter Hal Burns
(West Palm Beach)

A young woman found beaten to death on a yacht in the West Palm Beach Marina early yesterday may be linked to the death of a Palm Beach heiress two months ago.

The battered body of the unidentified woman, described by police as a transient, was found by the boat's owner, Jimmy Phipps, former husband of the late heiress Nikki Fletcher. The victim was tied up and bludgeoned on a small bunk in the forward hold of Phipps' sailboat. Police say Phipps is not considered a suspect in the murder.

Last April, authorities concluded the death of Nikki Fletcher, heiress to the huge Hamilton Fletcher lumber fortune and the niece of Florida Senator Danforth Fletcher, was due to a self-induced drug overdose. Her nude, cocaine-ridden body was found in a derelict apartment, surrounded by cocaine and heroin paraphernalia in a Riviera Beach waterfront area known to natives as Conchtown.

The death of the thirty-year old heiress two months ago, originally considered a drug over-dose, may now be reopened as a murder case, according to police sources.

Newly discovered evidence, linked to yes-terday morning's beating death indicates Nikki Fletcher may have actually been a victim of the same killer. The Fletcher heiress was the original owner of the yacht, *Ariel*, before she gave it to Phipps as part of their divorce settlement earlier this year.

A new probe into the drug overdose death has been started by West Palm Beach, Riviera Beach, and the Town of Palm Beach Officials.

I stood at the paper rack at the end of the dock, reading, the newspaper shaking in my hands. The shit had hit the fan.

"Mr. Phipps?"

I looked up to see Hal Burns, the goofball reporter from Bob-by's office and the author of the article I had just read. His shirts sleeves were rolled up, his tie askew.

"No comment."

"What about....?"

"Are you deaf? This is private property. You're in violation of your restraining order. I'll have the dock master throw you off if you don't leave immediately. I said, 'No comment'." I threw the sports section at him and walked toward my car. I had a lot of stops to make and it was time to move.

I drove up Flagler Drive, then cut over to US-1 through the ghetto area known as Pleasant City. I passed through Northwood. A once upscale neighborhood known for architecturally inter-esting buildings, Northwood had slipped into decay in the last decades. First the prostitutes on North Dixie Highway had chased the tourists away from the Ma and Pa motels. Then the burglary rate had skyrocketed when the B&E guys found out the neighborhood was filled with defenseless retirees. Easy pickin's. They could walk into a place and clean it out before the eighty year-old arthritic owner could manage to get herself out of her chair and call the police. A feeble attempt to gentrify the area had followed, but that was sabotaged by the crack epidemic, and so it was now only a matter of time before block after block of beautiful Spanish style homes would begin to look like Beirut.

I drove across the border into Riviera Beach. Just past the Port of Palm Beach I turned toward the waterfront: Conchtown. Bahamian fishermen had settled the area around the beginning of the 20th Century. For fifty years it was their own foreign enclave. Now it was just another crack alley.

I pulled up in front of the two-story apartment building where the police had found Nikki. I knew the address from the newspaper accounts. I had never been able to bring myself to drive by my wife's death scene. I guess at the time I just didn't have the stomach for it. Now, as I looked up to the facade I wondered what room it had been. The building looked abandoned, and the surroundings looked like news footage of Soweto; mud splattered buildings in green and pink and turquoise surrounded by yards filled with debris. No grass, just ruts and weeds and the remains of junked dreams of just making-do, left behind when hope ran out.

Cicadas screamed at me as I wandered up the sidewalk, stepping over a soggy mattress and box spring. I hadn't even reached the entryway when I was greeted by a black guy wearing greasy plaid double-knit, bell-bottom pants and a silk shirt that clashed; Haitian *Haute Couture*.

"Are you the guy who wants to buy this place?" His accent was thick with French patois.

I looked at him and decided, What the hell?

"Yeah, sure, what can you tell me about it?"

He led me through the portico to a central courtyard. It looked as if the tenants threw their garbage out the windows. How convenient. A feeling of fear was thick in the air, as if something unexpected, lethal, were about to happen. I could hear the monotonous drumbeat of distorted rap music coming from out of an open window, as if the entire apartment was a speaker. I tried to imagine Nikki spending her last hours here. How did she get here that night? How, *why* had it come down to this?

The tragedy of her life was all coming back to me. You live in an area all your life and suddenly you are transported to a nearby place where you would never think of going. A place you might have passed close by a million times but would never think of entering. Finally, you wind up there in the stink of the night. Then, in one out-of-control moment, your life is over. Contorted, naked, trying to scream but just choking for breath. No one to help; anyone within earshot ready to do you more harm than help; glad that you're dying. How did it happen?

That night, I had been at my mother's house, grading papers on *THE SCARLET LETTER*, when my friend, Lt. Baldwin "Bobby" Starke showed up at my front door. It was a night I'll spend the rest of my life trying to forget.

As soon as I saw the look on his face through the screen door that night I could surmise what happened. Like Victor had said to me earlier, it was really only a matter of time before a call like that one came.

Before Bobby could say anything, I said, "Nikki's dead. Right?"

He squeezed his eyes shut. "I'm sorry, Jimmy. I wanted to be the one to tell you."

I tried to be strong, but it didn't work. There were footsteps behind me and I turned to face my mother. She led me to a chair in the living room, sat down and I fell face down in her lap, sobbing. Her little boy needed comforting.

The screen door had creaked open and Bobby stepped in and knelt beside me. "I'm sorry," was all he had said, over and over.

"I'm sorry."

"We're cleaning it up, little by little," my Haitian guide said half-heartedly.

"Who owns this place?"

The man stopped abruptly and turned to look at me, suddenly suspicious. "What difference does that make?"

"Just curious."

"It's being handled by Melaleuca Properties."

Of course. I should have known. But then nowhere, in any account I had read of the investigation, or in any discussion I had had about the case with Bobby, had it been revealed that my ex-wife had been found on ghetto property owned by her own father: industrialist, lumber tycoon, slum-lord. Another convenient idea, like throwing your trash out the window

The Haitian man was staring at me as if I were crazy. "Hey, man, you wanna look at this or what?" His new-immigrant arrogance, as if to say, 'you *used* to be in charge,' annoyed me.

Instead of answering him, I did an abrupt about face and turned back to my car. I had seen enough. I suddenly decided I couldn't bear to go to the room where Nikki was found. I had lost the stomach for it; couldn't face it, no matter what morbid curiosity had led me here.

He followed after me. "Hey man, what's the matter? You not gonna tell anybody I chase you off, are you?"

At the curb, two young men in business suits had just stepped from a station wagon and were looking at the building. One held a briefcase. Attorneys, trying to spend some of that '80's windfall. New generation slum-lords. As I got to the curb the one with the briefcase spoke to me. "Excuse me, we've come to look at the property?" New-rich, out-of-town arrogance, as if to say, "we don't care if you are a third generation native, get out of our way." The long-time locals here get it from both directions.

The Haitian stopped abruptly. I didn't have to turn around to know what the expression on his face would look like. "What?

You guys are here to look at this place? Hey, then who are you?

I didn't answer.

"Hey, man, I'm talking to you!" He was angry, put-out.

"Not like that," I said. I spun around abruptly and faced him, confronting his arrogance.

"Hey, man, who do you think you messin' wit?"

I slowly lifted my left hand toward him and just slightly above his face.

"You see that scar on my palm?" I asked.

He lifted his face up to my hand hovering above his head and squinted. "What scar?"

With my right hand I backhanded his Adam's Apple. When he reached for his throat in pain I kicked in his left knee cap with my right foot. He fell to the ground with the pop of the cartilage. He was trying to scream in pain but only gurgling was coming out. The two suits stepped back.

"Hey, no problem here, man."

"He tried to steal something from me," I explained above the Haitian man's screams. They looked to one another and then to the man on the ground.

"We have another appointment," they said, turning to the street.

"Me, too."

I got in my car and drove south. I called my home phone for messages. I figured Fletcher had seen the news or read the paper by this time, and there would be an enraged call for me on my answering machine. There was another message, but it wasn't from Fletcher. It was from Hector, Consuelo's husband, asking to meet with me again. When he had recorded the message, she had been crying in the background. I could hear her imploring cries, begging "no."

It was on my way to my next destination anyway, so I decided to stop by.

CHAPTER 36

The front door was open when I arrived. Through the screen door I could hear Consuelo crying. She lifted her head.

"Come on in, Jimmy."

Inside, it was stifling, the air still.

Hector started immediately. The rage was written all over his face. "That bastard fired her today! You know why? Because you called over there last night and she put the call through to him! And then he spoke abusively to her. If I weren't in this wheelchair I would go over there and kill the bastard! But since I cannot, instead I will destroy him in the only way I know how...with the truth. I will tell you things that we couldn't tell you before because she was afraid of losing her job. But now it doesn't matter anymore. He will regret the day he fired her. Now I will tell you everything."

I looked over on the sofa. Consuelo had her face buried in one of the throw pillows, stifling her sobs. Hector wheeled his chair closer to where I stood.

"Consuelo used to see your wife at her father's house also doing those bad things."

I knew this from Adrianne, of course, but for some reason I wanted reaffirmation, or maybe something I didn't already know. "What kind of bad things?"

"What kind of bad things do you want? They got all kinds over there. I told you, they pack more shit up their noses in an hour than we could pay for in a month. All kinds of bad things were going on there....What do you think information like this might be worth to the cops? We don't have an income now. Now what are we supposed to do? She saw your wife there the night she died. The were all naked, snorting cocaine, when Consuelo walked in on them. Why should she have to see things like that? Those things are illegal and I want that bastard to pay!"

Hector stopped his tirade. He was out of breath and his face was red. Consuelo's crying had slowed to hoarse breathing. Hector watched me looking at her.

"And if that isn't enough to do him in, we'll tell all of it!"

Consuelo sat up with a look of fear on her face. Her eyes were red and her make-up was smeared all down her cheeks. "No, Hector! Please, you promised!"

Hector turned to me once again and Consuelo was on her feet. "Please, no!"

"When your wife was a young girl, fifteen, she would spend the night in her father's room!"

Now it was my turn for a beating. I felt as if someone had hit me in the chest with that baseball bat. I started to feel sick.

"No, Hector, you promised! Consuelo was hysterical now, and she threw herself at my feet. "I'm sorry, Jimmy, I'm sorry. He promised never to tell you." But I wasn't listening. I was running down the sidewalk, trying to block the sound from my ears as I ran toward the car. I wanted somehow to reverse time and never have that knowledge. I started to cry and I tried to keep myself from vomiting. My beloved Nikki, precious woman of my dreams. So vulnerable, defenseless. I was going to protect her from life's brambles.

I thought back to that first night Nikki and I had made love. The first thing I remember seeing in the cabana was the family portrait filled with people I didn't know then, but would eventually meet. Nikki at fifteen sitting on her father's knee. And then I remembered something I hadn't thought about in all the years and thousands of times I had looked at that picture. In the photograph everyone is posing for the camera, smiling toward the lens. Everyone except Hamilton. Hamilton is staring at his young daughter sitting perched innocently on his knee. The bemused look on his face now took on an entire new, more accurate meaning.

"I'm fucking her," his face now seemed to convey to whoever looked closely at the picture.

CHAPTER 37

There was nothing to do but head toward my original destination like I had planned earlier. I had wanted to talk to Victor about the newspaper article that he must have surely seen. Now, I just wanted him to deny what Hector had told me; give me some shred of memory to hang on to.

The motorcycle lot was empty and so was the shed, so I walked to the trailer. If I hadn't heard the shuffle of papers, I probably would have turned and left. But instead I let myself in. Inside, it was even stiller and hotter than Consuelo's house. I could hardly breathe. Victor sat propped in the corner, his eyes red, staring into some distance. Beside him was the morning edition of the newspaper and a note in what looked like Nikki's handwriting. He held a legal pad attached to a clipboard in his lap, and he held a pen poised as if waiting for some muse to strike him. He didn't seem to know or care that I was there.

"Victor?" My voice seemed inappropriately loud to me. I lowered the volume and extended my hand out to him in a calming gesture. "I need to talk to you again. I need to know some things."

He looked up at me, but now the hopelessness on his face had turned to determination. Uncharacteristic behavior. It should have been a warning to me.

"What do you want to know?"

I picked up Victor's newspaper and held it in front of him. "Victor, do you know what this is all about? Do you know what was going on with your sister? With your father? How she died?"

To my surprise, Victor stood and wiped his eyes and nose on his greasy shirt sleeve. He turned to me with a resigned look.

"I don't know for sure. I only know that for years he had these.....get-togethers."

He could tell by the look on my face that I knew about them already.

"When my mother found out about them, she....withdrew. We were about twenty-two when he finally had her taken to that private psychiatric hospital in North Carolina."

I had to know for sure. "What did Nikki do at those parties?"

Victor tried for a moment to maintain his composure, but the pain was too great. Instead of speaking, he extended the legal pad and clipboard toward me. In a moment of hesitant resignation I stepped forward slowly and took it from him. Before I could begin reading, Victor said something so softly, I had to ask him to repeat it.

"What?"

"I loved her."

I nodded. "I loved her too, Victor."

He shook his head and gave me a half-smile. It was one of those condescending, superior, no-you-don't-understand-smiles. "No. It was different with us."

He turned his head away and leaned back against the wall, and I took that as my cue to read what he had written on the pad. To my surprise, it was a letter addressed to me. Why had he written a letter to me?

Dear Jimmy,
    I have waited far too long to write this letter to you. I have been waiting for years to get this off my chest, and you are the only logical person to tell and the time now is apparently right.

Nikki was not a normal woman leading a normal lifestyle. I suppose that sounds like a gross understatement, considering what you have found out about her this past year. But in reality, you are only aware of the outward manifestation of a deeply troubled and disturbed woman.

What you don't know is the cause of her actions. When Nikki and I were growing up together, we were as inseparable as only twins can be. Outwardly, our relationship was typical of what you would expect of a pair of ten year-old twins. It was during that time, however, that Nikki and I discovered our almost psychic ability to communicate with one another. Schizophrenics, I've heard it said, are two people in the same body. Nikki and I were the same person in two bodies.

Our new discovery amused us for hours, an endless game that was never the same. It was during this exploration of our uncanny, almost frightening skills that we discovered, quite naturally, our unusual physical attraction for one another.

As ten year olds, not yet even adolescents, we were both confused and afraid of our feelings toward one another. At first it started simply with us masturbating together. We thought it was enormously funny. We even had contests.

But then, one afternoon during summer vacation, only hours away from erupting full blown into adolescence, we both suffered an outpouring of passion I can only liken to a nuclear explosion. We were thirteen years old and attacked one another with uncontrolled hysteria.

It was as if we were trying to kill one another with our lust, pummeling and tearing at our nakedness like rabid dogs. It was so close, so convenient, so fast and more intimate than anyone could possibly imagine. And all so natural and endless.

It was all so natural.

If my parents had been home that first day, if only we had been discovered, caught, punished, that would have been the end of it. But they weren't home, and we weren't caught, and for a solid year we had no control over our emotions or urges.

My cock was in her morning, noon and night, hardly ever out of her really, every day for an entire year. I know you are probably thinking how perverse this must have all been, but we were without control. Whenever we were out of my parents' sight, I was inside her. She wanted it more than I did; insisted on it.

We were possessed with one another, and I felt a love for her that I don't think would be possible with another.

I suppose we tried to rationalize our behavior like any single person would rationalize masturbation. Since we were truly the same person in two bodies, wasn't what we were doing simply the same thing as someone who masturbates?

After two years, my feelings for Nikki grew only stronger, while Nikki's seemed to wane. Perhaps for her, the novelty had worn off.

And finally, although she still loved me, she refused to make love with me anymore. I pleaded with her. I was heartbroken to the point of paralysis and physically ill for months. It was over and I could not accept the loss.

Just after we turned fifteen and just when I began to feel a little better about myself, I discovered that Nikki was sleeping with our father. At first I was outraged, then grief-stricken. I confronted her and she tried to comfort me, even offered herself to me, but by then I was too overwrought to do anything. There was no one to turn to. I had lost my one, true friend.

I begged her to stop, but she wouldn't. She

was *in love* with him. To ease my pain, she continued to offer herself to me, but I couldn't bring myself to do it any longer.

Another two years went by before I discovered something even worse. My father had begun to share his own daughter with his brother, our distinguished State Senator.

For almost ten years I lived with that knowledge, living in anguish and torment, watching my mother's mental state deteriorate because of what she must have surely seen, but refused to acknowledge.

I tried to convince Nikki to stop. I begged her to go away with me so we could live together away from the family. I wanted to care for her, help her heal what I recognize now was her profound mental illness. A mental illness created partially by myself and fueled by endless rationalization.

Finally, seven years ago, I couldn't take it anymore and I confronted my father and uncle. My father laughed at me. He gloated when I told him what I knew. I now know how people feel seconds before they kill in a moment of passion. It didn't matter what the consequences would be. I wanted to rip his throat out no matter what the cost. The only reason I didn't kill him on the spot was because Nikki stopped me. She told me if I killed him I would never be able to achieve my dream: To go away with her and start over.

And so I left home and moved in here. I waited for Nikki to join me since that first day away from home. Occasionally, she would come over and spend the night, just holding me. But that was all she could do, she would say. I was content to have it just be like that. I would have settled for that if only she would go away with me forever....

Victor's letter to me stopped there, and I looked up at him,

trying to catch my breath. I felt as if my entire being were cring-
ing, shriveling up. Everything in my life, every basic assumption
was being disproven. As if anticipating my questions, he handed
me the note by his side. It was dated the night Nikki died.

April 21, 1986

My Darling Victor,

I am so tired I think I am going crazy. Tired
of the incessant drugs and the endless nights of
constant, meaningless fucking.

I have finally decided to leave here forever
like we have always talked about and do nothing
but rest with you. I feel as if I could lie down and
sleep for weeks. I want it to be like it was back
then, with just the two of us, in each other's arms,
forever.

I know we will be able to find a place to be
quiet and alone. Perhaps deep in the jungle in
Brazil, like we used to talk about, we can get the
rest and peace we both need. We can learn to
speak Portuguese together and it will be just the
servants and each other for company.

We can lie in a hammock in the jungle and
read *Sonnets from the Portuguese* (ha-ha).

Several times I have tried to explain to Father
our need to get away, without him going crazy on
me, but he won't listen. He just doesn't want us to
be happy together. He says what you and I have
is sick. But we shall prevail.

I have made all the financial preparations on
my end. You need to do the same. Can we *please*
leave this weekend?

                              "N"

I would have recognized her handwriting anywhere. I looked
up to Victor. His shoulders heaved with silent sobbing. I crouched

next to him and put a hand on his shoulder. He didn't shrug it off. I wanted to hug him, somehow let him know that I shared his grief. But I just let my hand rest on his shoulder. Like the day of Nikki's funeral, I was too overwhelmed with my own grief. It took every ounce of restraint to keep from retching.

After awhile, he stopped. Without lifting his head from between his knees he spoke. "Leave me alone, will you? Give me some time to be by myself. Come back later . I'll tell you everything, I promise."

I wanted to say, "No, tell me today, now. Then I'll go with you to the police."

Instead, I respected his wishes and walked toward the door, leaving him alone once again. I glanced back over my shoulder as he was picking up the note in Nikki's handwriting.

I drove home along Flagler drive, trying to contain the feelings that were spinning through me. I had almost reached the point in my life when such introspection was at an end. What good did it do to analyze such things? No good at all. Even less good to over-analyze them. What can we learn about ourselves? About the human condition? Probably nothing. Or at least nothing that would make me feel positive about anything; feel good about myself. Why waste my time?

But then I couldn't stop thinking about the nights I had spent with Nikki, holding her in my arms, thinking pure, clean, All-American Boy thoughts about the sanctity of marriage and the special act of love. How exclusive it was between us, how private. How all consuming and beautiful. The moonlight on her face; her look; the eyes that bore through me; and the back of her hand that caressed my cheek.

Just when you think you know it all, you find out you don't know *anything* at all.

CHAPTER 38

Back at the boat there was a phone message from my aunt. She had arrived and taken a cab from the airport to my mother's house. There, she had packed a few things and was picking up my mother at the nursing home. Would I meet them at the Amtrak station at three o'clock? Sure. If I didn't, I knew I might never see my mother alive again.

I hadn't seen my aunt in ten years, but she looked as if she had aged twenty when I saw her standing alongside my mother at the railroad station down on the end of Clematis Street. She had that displaced look many northerners have when they first arrive here, as if they didn't belong here. Haggard, the wrong clothes, no tan, a visitor from another planet, or at least another time. A look of, 'what am I doing here'?

My mother sat in a wheelchair, staring off into space, waiting for the 3:10 Silver Meteor to take her home. A damp wisp of hair hung down over her forehead. Did she know she was leaving from the same railroad station, from the railroad tracks that had brought her here forty-four years earlier in the opening days of WWII? What was she thinking as she sat, waiting to return home, after a lifetime, to the house where she had grown up? She boarded a train one day in the bright promise of her youth and in the blink of an eye she was going home to sit in a rocking chair and stare out toward Seneca Lake through the lace curtains of her parlor window until she slipped off into an endless sleep. A lifetime neatly book-ended by train rides.

My aunt met me with a sad smile and opened her arms for a hug.

"Hi, Jimmy. You're all grown up."

"Hey Aunt Lucille." I broke from the hug and knelt to eye level with my mother. In exchange for a lifetime of love and hard work, her son comes to spend just a few minutes with her before she leaves town forever. I have since come to the brilliant realization that those who spend too much time thinking about themselves, spend far too little time thinking about others.

I didn't know what else I could do. I reached out and kissed her cheek and touched her hand, but there was no response. *Where had she gone?* I stood up to face my aunt.

"Thanks for coming down. I have a few things to take care of around here and then I'll be up at the end of the week."

"There's no hurry, Jimmy. It would only be to make you feel better about it. She won't even know you're there. You know about Alzheimer's. She's in and out real bad. Take your time and come up before school starts for a few days if you can. I'm gonna take her home and see that she's comfortable. The doctor said that's about all anyone can do at this point. Sixty-three years old. She's still a young woman"

I knelt beside my mother again and held my head to her breast. I looked into her eyes. Where was she now, riding the Orange Blossom Special, massaging my father's tired hands while he rested from his labors? Was she peering silently, patiently, through the crack in his office door to watch him peck out the imagery that exploded through his fingertips? I wanted to cry, but nothing was coming out. I was all cried out from the past few months, even the last few hours, I guess, and the well was dry.

The train pulled in from Miami to pick up its only two north-bound passengers. Two black porters lifted my mother's wheel-chair up the steps and the last I saw that day of the woman who bore me and spent her life caring for me was when she disappeared behind the hydraulic hiss of stainless steel doors.

Separation and Loss all over again.

Aunt Lucille turned at the top of the steps. "There's some stuff of your father's I found when I was packing up. I left it on the kitchen table. I thought you might want to have it."

I nodded. "I'll call you tomorrow." She waved and turned. The train started rolling before I could say thank you. How do you say thank you for what she was doing? I really didn't know how. It was a kind of thing that only sisters do for their sisters. I stood there, alone on the platform, and watched the train disappear around the bend past the City Water Department. My mother was actually redeeming her round-trip ticket purchased in 1942. She was leaving town by the same Seaboard Coastline railroad tracks she had arrived on, the same railroad tracks near where my father had departed from this life.

CHAPTER 39

With a few hours to kill before my appointment with Fletcher, I drove back down to the little house on Mango Promenade where I had spent most of the first twenty-five years of my life. In another few weeks, the house would be bull-dozed along with the rest of the block to make way for the new UPTOWN/DOWN-TOWN development. The little hideaway my parents had built as a love nest would be first reduced to a pile of rubble, then scooped into the back of a dump truck and hauled away for landfill. Gone forever. A clean slate. Nothing left for the archeological digs of future generations but the unfulfilled dreams of the owners.

On the kitchen table was my father's straw fedora and a legal size stationery box. I picked up the hat, touching it gingerly. I had never seen it except in photographs. Where had she kept it for the past thirty years? Inside, the band was stained from his sweat. I put it to my face, inhaling, trying to capture any essence he might have left behind. But all that remained was the mustiness of an old closet. I sat at the table and just stared at the box for a moment. Everything that had happened in the past few days had me in turmoil.

Inside the box was a cheap, nickel-covered pocket watch and

an old Zippo lighter. It smelled like Camel cigarettes. A gold high-school class ring from Palm Beach High, Class of 1916 rested in the corner. Engraved inside the band were the initials E.P. I slipped it on where my wedding band had been. It fit.

At the bottom of the box was a loose stack of papers from an old writing tablet. It looked like the stuff my father had used to draft his stories. I had seen plenty of it at the University library where I had spent my college days and nights. A day had not gone by when I didn't think of what I had seen during my stay, but it had been twelve years since I had made a pilgrimage to actually see it all again. Between the teaching and the marriage, there had been little time for exploring the source, or getting lost in my ancient daydreams. But the sight of the worn paper brought it all back to me. I recognized the paper and the handwriting. But what I didn't recognize was the ink or the subject matter. It wasn't written in #2 pencil like all his other original drafts. These were the carbon-paper copies, alternate pages, torn from underneath the handwritten originals on the writing pad and stored separately for safekeeping. I had read everything he had ever written, or so I thought. Yet these words before me were unfamiliar.

And as I read I was transported out of my parents' little bun-galow, back to a Palm Beach mansion in 1920. I had only to read a half-dozen sentences before I realized this was from PALM BEACH CONFIDENTIAL, the novel he was working on when he committed suicide. These were carbon copies he had left behind at the house when he had taken the originals down to the railroad track to revise his work in the dim switch-light, like he had done every night.

My whole life I had tried to imagine his state of mind leading up to his suicide. Maybe like poor old Willy Loman, he knew he was on the skids, and worth more dead than alive. Did he consider himself a gimp-legged, never-was, has-been writer with no audience; growing old and frightened, losing whatever dignity and self-respect he once possessed? He was the father of a three-year old, who had no money except what he could make trimming hedges, sweeping floors and mowing fairways while he day-dreamed his life away. Maybe the day-to-day struggle just became too overwhelming for him. It happens to some men.

> *"Make my bed and light the light,*
> *I'll arrive late tonight.*
> *Black-bird, bye-bye."*

The last words my mother had ever heard him speak.

The last words he ever *wrote*, jumped off the page at me.

It was only a synopsis, some cryptic notes, written in Elliott's own handwriting that mapped out the expansion of his short story on its way to being enlarged upon into the novel version.

Leo Edwards, hero of almost twenty of my father's novels, reminisces while sitting in the security office of the George Washington Hotel. Things have not gone good for him, and at the age of 56 he is still playing security guard at a hotel. His private detective business had deteriorated, and so now, here he was, at a time when most men his age were thinking about retiring and playing a little golf at the club, he was patrolling the hallways of yet another hotel. Except this time it wasn't the glamorous Royal Poinciana Hotel of the Roaring Twenties' Palm Beach. Now it was a run down hotel on the waterfront of West Palm Beach, frequented by salesmen and retirees from the Midwest during the season, nearly vacant in the summer. The indignity of it all. The exciting life he had led as a younger, dashing detective had slowed to a standstill. He yearns for the adventures of his younger days.

His bank account didn't have much to show for all the years he had put into his agency. What had all those years yielded? A couple of hundred divorce cases, chasing cheating spouses around Palm Beach, trying to snap their pictures as they came out of the Casa Juno motel way up in Juno Beach.

And so now, in 1956, he spent his evenings patrolling the lonely hallways of a hotel in a city without crime. There hadn't been anything but petty thefts and small time crimes for years in the area, except for maybe the disappearance of Judge Chilling-worth and his wife over in Palm Beach the summer before. But in '56, who knew where they were? After they disappeared from their beachfront home in Manalapan, their bodies had never been found. Maybe they had just taken off for South America. Their murders wouldn't be solved for another four years; Their bodies never found. The first murder trial in Florida without bodies.

I sat and read the rest of the carbon copy of the manuscript notes of the unfinished novel my father was working on when he died. It was a part I know the University of Florida never had. No one else had ever read these notes. Not until this moment in history.

From the very first sentences, the book took on an eerie famil-iarity. Was it because I knew the book premise from having read the short story, *Double Effort*? There was more to it than that, I just couldn't put my finger on it first. I was hovering like a tick-hound; circling a spot on the ground over and over, looking for a place to alight.

Knowing what I know about how my father's stories evolved, my mind started to backtrack. Weren't so many of them based on people he knew, cleverly disguised within the confines and stric-tures of a *nomme de guerre*?

After three hours of reading this version of the ending and combing the tightly scrawled marginalia, I have come to the con-clusion that the Palm Beach wags were right. The characters were based on real people and the plot was based on a true story, or at least a close variation on the truth. It had taken place in the mid-Twenties.

The ending of the novel is different from the magazine's *Double Effort*, and gave too strong a series of clues as to who the 'fictitious' Palm Beach Millionaire was.

He wrote in his notes that there really was a set of two boys who are half-brothers. In 1986 they would be in their early sixties.

What does it all mean? Was my father threatened, killed because the new ending he was writing was too close to real life, and some rich Palm Beach guys wanted him killed?

When I finished reading the final few handwritten pages of PALM BEACH CONFIDENTIAL, I sat, trying not to tremble, trying not to loose my breath. What did it all mean? I did what I had always done when reading my father's work. I turned back to the first page and started all over again. This time when I was finished I was trembling more, breathing more heavily. Every dread was confirmed.

I put the papers down on the kitchen table and looked again at the straw fedora that used to keep the sun off my father's head. That head I now suspected somebody had put a bullet hole through that night in 1956 while I slept in my crib a few hundred feet away.

I looked at the series of pictures of him sitting on the Whippet, his hands extending the typewriter and camera toward me. But now, he didn't seem to be bragging, "look what I can do." Now, the implications of the picture took on a new meaning. He held the tools of his trade aloft, imploring, "use these to help yourself, son."

I ran out the door and down to the railroad track. I had been there a thousand times as a boy. I even spent nights crying there on the spot where my father had died, wondering what had happened, why he did it.

This time was different. This time, I knew, someone had killed him for the words he had written on paper. This spot on the tracks had gone unchanged for probably fifty years. If I had been there a week earlier it would have looked the same as it had that night in 1956, or any night thirty years earlier.

But the bulldozers had come through, and now the surrounding area looked like Hiroshima after the bomb. Twisted, jagged metal protruded from blocks of concrete foundations, and solitary, steel-frame staircases stood silhouetted against the horizon; steps to nowhere but blue sky. The little silver switchbox on the railroad right-of-way was still there. I almost expected to see my father's blood on it. What had happened that night? I sat where he had sat.

A southbound freight train came rumbling by. I could have reached out and touched it. When we were kids, Joachim and Bobby and I would come down here at night when we knew the freight cars would be rolling through. In the darkness we would lie on our backs with our heads inches from the tracks, watching the underbelly of the train rush overhead.

To a very great degree, for a certain span of time, the history of Florida is the history of the railroads. Its arrival signaled the beginning of modern life here; it was through the railroad where Henry Plant on the West Coast and Henry Flagler on the East Coast opened up the state to outsiders; it was the railroads that brought civilization; established Palm Beach as a playground for the wealthy; it was the railroad that my father hobo-ed and where his life had ended; it was the railroad that book-ended my mother's Florida sojourn; and it was now where I lay, staring straight up into the steel giant that was whizzing over my head just inches away, steel wheels on steel rails muffling my screams, as I tried to figure out what I was going to do.

As the train disappeared, I decided the first person I had to contact was Victor. Did he know anything about what I had just read? As long as he was in a confessional frame of mind, would he help confirm what I thought I had found out from my father's notes?

CHAPTER 40

If I had only known to ask him these questions that morning when I was there, he might have answered me.

Instead, when I got to the trailer, Victor's long-awaited muse had finally arrived. He had been dead for several hours. He sat propped up in the same position I had left him sitting in this morning. A red smear spread from the left side of his chest. He had shot himself in the heart, the source of his pain. The body wouldn't last much longer in this heat. What I should have recognized this morning as the beginning of a suicide note, was now carefully completed, an occasional grease smudge or what could be a tear drop running the ink as it cascaded down on the legal pad. My hands trembled with Victor's paper the same way they had when I had read my father's final notes.

> Dear Jimmy,
>   In conclusion, as you will no doubt know by the time you read this, I have decided to put an end to my misery. I have tried for years to overcome the depression that keeps me distracted twenty-four hours a day. I have tried to determine what might cure me of this, but with Nikki gone, I know the only solution no longer exists. And so I'll

end my pain in the only way now possible.

I want you to know that I have never held any grudge against you or had any feelings of enmity. What might have seemed to be a rivalry between us was the product of an overwhelming sense of guilt I have felt since you first came into my sister's life.

A shrink once told me this guilt, a horribly destructive and debilitating force in my life, is the result of my rage and hatred turned inward. If that is true, then so be it. I know I am worthy of every ounce of the hatred I have for myself.

I started to put this down on paper earlier, and this morning you read the beginning of it. But maybe by revealing the remaining sources of my guilt, it can somehow alleviate what I recognize is a similar painfulness in your life, so that you might find peace and dwell there, as I have not been able to.

Nikki loved you as much as she could love anyone else, I suppose. However you may have blamed yourself for the breakup of your marriage, you really didn't have very much to do with it. For that matter, you didn't even have much to with 'the creation' of your marriage, either.

I paused in my reading. 'The creation of my marriage?' What did he mean? I read on.

Nikki's relationship with my father changed over the years. At first she was petrified, completely dominated by his power, so much in love with him was she. Then, as she got older and saw his fits of jealous rage every time she dated a boy, she learned that it was actually *she* who controlled *him*. And she began to abuse it, humiliating and tantalizing him at the same time reveling in his lust. She would cock-tease my father and uncle until they would become enraged, and then just as willingly satisfy both of them. Their power games escalated until Nikki discovered there was a way she could truly humiliate and intimidate both of them in a way that would punish them even more than if there were a full public disclosure of all of their activities. It was truly a malicious plan, but as you witnessed firsthand, that could be Nikki's nature.

Nikki knew that if she ever got married, it would infuriate my father and uncle. Further, she knew if she married someone that they didn't approve of, she could really manipulate them and they would be immeasurably destroyed. But for Nikki, even those two obvious tactics weren't enough. Nikki always had to go one step further; tighten the screw one extra twist, take it right over the top, like she always did.

And so she tracked you down to marry you. Not just any husband. Not just any husband she knew they would disprove of because you were 'beneath their class.' Something far more powerful than that. Something that would antagonize them incessantly, a constant burr under their saddles. It was her game.

I stopped reading and caught my breath. Was I really that despicable to these people? Because my grandparents and parents had served in their kitchens and cleaned their yards, would I never be accepted by them, no matter what I did? Was I to be held in contempt, for life, because mine were kind, giving, albeit poor parents, who loved me and taught me the difference between right and wrong?

I thought of the nurturing, the teaching, the loving my mother had provided me with. To be hated by these animals because I didn't have their money was more than I could comprehend or accept.

But no matter how angry, how perplexed I felt then, it did not prepare me for what I read next in Victor's note.

> Nikki tracked you down and singled you out;
> ambushed you at the bar where you worked,
> forced you to fall in love with her, manipulated
> you into marrying her despite your reservations
> caused by my father's displays of outrage. Why?
> For a very simple reason. It wasn't because you
> were just any husband to be jealous over. It wasn't
> because they considered you poor white trash
> and beneath Nikki's station. You only sensed they
> felt that way because it was so obvious and easy
> and convenient and because you couldn't possi-
> bly know any different; know the real reason. You
> couldn't possibly know the real reason.
>
> My father and uncle were outraged, morti-
> fied, almost psychopathically paranoid when Nikki
> brought you home, because you were Jimmy
> Phipps, surviving son of the late writer, Elliott
> Phipps.

It was the first time outside the walls of the University of Florida Library that I had ever seen my father's name in print.

I thought back to that day when Nikki presented me to her
father and uncle. Their displeasure was evident and I remember
them looking at Nikki like she was a lunatic.

"Have you lost your mind?"

I couldn't quite fathom the depth of their agitation and I passed
it off as just my being the "poor-boy at the party." But it seems
that wasn't it at all.

Just when you think you know everything.

> Jimmy, I don't really know how much you are
> aware of your family history. But surely you must
> know that your father was a short-story writer
> back during the War. I know quite a bit about my
> family's history, it was drilled into us since the first

day we could listen to stories about how the family fortune was made. I know all the accomplishments, all the career paths, all the diversifications of the family fortune, starting with the Confederate Army rip-offs during the Civil War, when the art of price-gouging the government reached new proportions.

I know things about my family tree that few people know and that make a difference to fewer. No, they hardly make a difference anymore, except maybe, to you.

Hamilton Fletcher III and Senator Danforth Fletcher are brothers to almost everyone who knows them. They look alike, they act alike, they have the same tastes. Their family portrait depicts them with their parents and the family dog, living a contented and successful 1930's Palm Beach lifestyle.

What the picture doesn't tell you is that although Hamilton Fletcher II is father to both the boys, the woman standing with her arm on Hamilton Fletcher III's shoulder is only Danforth's mother.

I stopped to catch my breath. I already knew the story, but the puzzle pieces once missing or inverted for the sake of fiction, were now falling into place.

Danforth is not my father's brother, he is my father's *half*-brother. Sure, Hamilton Fletcher II was the father of both of them, but baby Hamilton's mother was murdered when he was less than two years old.

Hamilton's mother and Danforth's mother were apparently twin sisters. Danforth's mother was a prostitute in some fancy whorehouse on Clematis Street.

I looked up a moment knowing what was coming next. Over in the squalid corner, Victor's blood was turning black.

You may be wondering what all this has to do with you. Why these facts, kept secret for sixty years should suddenly take on importance for you, would upset my father and uncle so much when they first met you.

Jimmy, your father was hired by my grandfather during the mid-Twenties to follow his first wife, Hamilton's mother. Hamilton II suspected his wife of cheating, and he did not feel suited to the role of cuckold. Your father found out that she was leading a double life, switching identities with her twin sister so both could take turns leading the good life my grandfather provided, alternating sex and wifely duties. He was duped, of course, not knowing of their ploy. They even had a blackmail scheme going.

He got a dose of gonorrhea. He thought it was from his wife. It turned out it was more likely he got it from her twin sister, but maybe not.

My father's mother was killed screwing some crazy boxer, and your father found out and told my grandfather. The local cops covered it up and no one ever knew about it. Instead of my grandfather being outraged by his wife and her twin, he was apparently intrigued with the idea enough to continue the hoax or maybe he just didn't want the scandal or to let other people know he was duped into being married to a whore.

Instead of him mourning the loss of his real wife, he took it out on your father and threatened to kill him if he ever told anyone. He continued living with his sister-in-law, allowing her to pose as his dead wife, as if nothing had ever happened. He saved face. She either didn't know he had found out, or just went along with the scheme for the lifestyle it afforded.

For another thirty years, or so, your father kept the secret. But my grandfather had followed Elliott Phipps' career as a writer of magazine stories and some pulp novels. He may have even been your father's most avid reader, but it made him nervous. He had a vault where he kept all the books and magazines he bought up that your father published. He didn't want them circulating in the area because he knew Elliott used real Palm Beach residents as models for his fiction. He would send out his chauffeur to all of the newsstands to buy up all the copies so your father couldn't develop a local following. There were never any available for sale so he couldn't even build a following in his home town, despite record sales figures in this area. My grandfather again warned your father to forget about it, and your father promised he would.

Apparently, your father was desperate for some good material for a story though, and what he knew about my grandfather was a perfect premise. In September of 1956, when you were three years old and I wasn't even born yet, a story appeared in some mystery magazine. Apparently, your father's fictional detective was down-and-out. No doubt, just as your own father was desperate for story material at that time, he made his detective, Leo Edwards, desperate for money. They both tried to capitalize on the thirty-year old blackmail schemes. Even though the events were disguised, my grandfather apparently felt betrayed and outraged by your father's rather transparent storyline.

The story so enraged my grandfather, that he ordered his two sons to murder the man who had not heeded his warning and was trying to expose them. My father was 33 at the time, my uncle, 30. "Make it look like a suicide, destroy the evidence," my grandfather told them, and they did.

> My uncle and my father met your father at the railroad track, where they knew he went for a smoke every night, stole the final, controversial pages of the manuscript and killed him. They threw a bunch of the more innocuous pages to the wind, so no one would question where his writing was.

Those were the last words Victor wrote. I put the letter down. Victor confirmed what I wanted to know. His final words on the paper were his last goodbye and I could pretty well figure out whatever else there was to know.

Nikki had married me to antagonize the man she loved, her father, the very same man who had killed my father. My days with her passed before me now in a stream of images. Like proofreading, I reviewed the hours, trying to recall a sign; a sudden look; a miscue that would have revealed her deception. But there were none. Her performance had been flawless.

Now Nikki and Victor were both resting peacefully, and I was numb with confusion.

I picked up the clipboard with everything I had read that day and left Victor where he lay in a pool of his own blood. He wasn't going anywhere and I didn't want any last minute discoveries to provide a distraction and interfere with tonight's meeting. I would tell the cops later.

Earlier, when I was planning what to do with Fletcher, how to catch him in a trap, somehow it had all seemed unjustified, part of my naive nature again. I had felt guilt-ridden. The plot that I had started to hatch to have my father-in-law charged with cocaine possession would now be a confrontation with much greater significance. Now, knowing what I knew, anything I did would be justified. In 1956, Hamilton and Danforth, a rich man and a man who grew up to be a State Senator, were about the same age I was right now when they killed my father. Simply on the direct orders of their father. I always wondered what would have to happen to be able to convince me to kill another human. Like Victor had written me earlier, now I knew what it would take to murder someone.

Tonight, I wanted Fletcher to come in and claim the coke that rested in a long white tube beneath my boat. As he left I wanted Bobby to come in like the cavalry and find Fletcher in possession of it all and arrest him. If Fletcher brought the Senator with him, all the better. If not, I had enough to go to the newspaper with the story. Hal Burns wanted a story? I had one now. Suzanne's testimony would confirm it. Would I ever be able to admit what I had witnessed? Witnessed twice? Would I ever be able to teach again if it was known what I had paid Suzanne to do?

Can someone be arrested for a murder committed more than thirty years ago? Where was my proof? The faded scribbles of some obsessed writer? A suicide note from the murderer's own disturbed, disinherited son?

CHAPTER 41

It was seven o'clock by the time I got back to my boat. I lay in the bunk opposite where I had found Adrianne yesterday. Bobby's people had taken the bedding and the mattress, but there was still blood splattered on the walls.

I was exhausted. What I had found out about my wife, my mother, my father, my late ex-brother-in-law in the last few hours was enough distressing news to last a lifetime. What else could possibly happen?

One hour to go. One hour before I could confront the man who beat up my friend; fucked my wife starting when she was just a little girl.

Killed my father.

What would I do when I saw him? How would he react when Bobby arrested him? Suppose he sent his goons over instead of coming himself?

I thought I'd had enough of introspection to last me a life-time, but as usual, I was wrong. What do you say to a man who deprived you of a normal childhood? What would my life have been like with my father alive as I grew up? Would he have taught me how to write like he did? Would his writing finally have paid off? There were simply too many questions to ask, too many hypotheses contrary to the fact that he wasn't alive, to waste time trying to play them all out.

I called Bobby to confirm he would be there a few minutes after nine. I would give him some new information I had for him, I told him. He was distant, sounding distracted, but he agreed.

The last half hour seemed to last all night. Joachim arrived a little after eight as we had previously arranged and he stumbled into the far corner. He'd spent the night before having his nose and arm set and had checked himself out of the hospital. They forced him to sign a "hold harmless" waiver before releasing him. His shoulder was in a sling, his ribs were taped, and his face was bruised and puffy. I brought him up to date. When I got to the part about my father, he could only shake his head. "Jesus, Jimmy. I hope you know what you're doing. Maybe you ought to think about this before you do anything."

I had to laugh at that one. "Why?" I had already spent a life-time of thinking. Now I had to do something.

Finally we heard Fletcher's footsteps on the dock and the moment of truth had arrived.

I stuck my head out of the hold as Hamilton Fletcher III came aboard. *The man who killed my father.* He was all business. "Let's make this quick. I have important things to do." He unrolled a gym bag large enough to hold two cubic feet of cocaine.

I looked around conspiratorially "Come on down." It convinced him. Or maybe he just had nothing to fear. Did he know I knew? Did he even care?

He stepped below decks and adjusted his eyes to the light. I watched his eyes pass over the bloody wall to where Joachim was sitting. He was unfazed, did not even acknowledge Joachim's presence. He looked at us condescendingly. I was ready to kill him then.

"Let's have it."

"Let's have what?"

"Don't play games with me, Phipps. You saw what happened

to Adrianne." He nodded over his shoulder toward the blood. You saw what happened to your grease-ball friend, here." Joachim ignored the insult.

"What about what happened to Nikki?"

He smirked. "What about it? She had a big mouth. She was starting to say things that weren't true."

"What could she possibly say about you that wasn't true? You fucked your own daughter, not to mention who knows how many other minors." He hardly reacted to the accusation at all.

"Did she tell you that?"

"No."

"Who then?"

"Your son."

"That weakling? He was just jealous."

Fletcher didn't even know his son was dead.

"Come on, Phipps, give me the stuff so I can get out of here."

"I want to know how you can stand there and rationalize fucking your own daughter."

"I don't have to rationalize it. We both wanted to do it, so we did it. She wanted to as much as I did, from the very first time. It was no one's business but ours. She was nothing but a loud mouthed nose-whore."

"What does that make you?"

"I like to indulge myself from time to time. It's no one's business"

"With fifteen year old girls and even with your own daughter?

"Nikki insisted on it. She was in love with me. I can't help it."

"What does a fifteen year old girl know?"

"She knew what she wanted to do."

"She was your *own* daughter."

"Not after that she wasn't. She was just another hungry, bothersome little cunt."

"What about those young girls?"

"Can I help it if I have what they want and they have what I want? That seems fair and equitable. Supply and demand, shit-head, supply and demand. Welcome to Free Enterprise Capital-ism. That's what makes the world go around. Not helpless, inef-fectual dreamers like you. I guess schoolteachers never have to deal with the real world. Anyway, what business is it of yours? Come on, let's go. You got that off your chest, now let's move."

The last was a command. Before I could react there was a foot-scrape on the dock and someone else came on board. I knew it was Bobby, a few minutes early, but we could take care of that. Pull the coke out of the water, give it to Fletcher, have Bobby call in the troops to arrest him. I knew Bobby would lie for me. Easy and simple like everything else in life.

Fletcher turned up at the sound of the footsteps, startled. Did he sense a trap? Then he looked over at me. Bobby descended the steps and then there were the four of us crowded into the small space. Bobby had a sick look on his face. Fletcher laughed out loud when he saw who it was. Bobby stared back at Fletcher.

Fletcher shook his head in disbelief, looking at us all. "What is this, The Three Musketeers?" Bobby didn't answer.

I had the same question now. "Yeah, what is this, Bobby?"

Bobby stared numbly at Fletcher's shit-eating grin. Finally, he turned to me. "You should have left it all alone, Jimmy. I kept telling you."

"Enough of this morbid sentimentality. Give me the goods, Phipps, so I can get out of here."

I looked to the friend of my youth. I tried to remain calm. "What does he mean, Bobby? How can he stand there and demand to have his cocaine in the presence of a police officer? Aren't you going to arrest him for possession? What's going on?"

Fletcher laughed out loud again. "Tell him Starke. Why not? What's he gonna do?"

Bobby was silent. He moved to the bunk and sat down.

"Tell me, Bobby? What does he mean? You know he killed Nikki?"

Bobby nodded and spoke matter-of-factly. "They killed her at the cabana. Then they took her over and dumped her up in that shit-hole in Conchtown and made it look like an overdose."

"You knew this all the time? What are you telling me?"

Fletcher was grinning at Bobby. "Go on, tell him. This has all the elements of a regular Greek tragedy...greed, ambition......real drama. He'll enjoy it."

Bobby's voice was so low I could hardly hear it. He stared down at the floor as he spoke.

"They killed her because she was becoming too difficult to control; too....frenetic. She was telling people about the parties, the drugs. Then she took their last shipment for herself, double-crossed them. She was basically blackmailing them. She was going to leave the country. If word got out about the Senator....."

"But why didn't you do something?"

Fletcher almost giggled. "This is getting good. Go on, tell him so I can get out of here."

But Bobby didn't move.

"Go on. Tell him. Tell him about your grand political ambitions. The big plans...the big move to Tallahassee....political attaché to Senator Danforth Fletcher....grooming for the House of Representatives.....finally, 'Governor Baldwin Bobby Starke'!" Go ahead, share your little dreams with your friend like you shared them with me. Pour your heart out. Except he won't be able to give you a million dollars to make it happen, will he?"

"You took money from them?"

Bobby dead-panned in protest.

"Of course he took money."

"It wasn't the money. They offered me a job. I was gonna go to Tallahassee to work with the Senator. They knew I had political ambitions. They said I could be in the State House within three years. They got to me..."

"He wants to be Governor! Where is a small time operator like him going to get enough money to be Governor? Come on,

enough. You two guys can kiss and make up later. I've got to get
going."

I knelt at Bobby's feet where he was sitting and looked into
his face. "Is this true, Bobby?" I thought he was going to cry. I
couldn't get him to move.

I grabbed his shoulders and looked into his eyes. "Bobby, listen to me. He and his brother killed my father. They shot him in
the head in cold blood because *their* father told them to do it. My
dad wrote something....."

"SO WHAT? WHAT ARE YOU GOING TO DO ABOUT
IT?" Fletcher was screaming as he pulled a .32mm from his
windbreaker. He pointed it at me. "This man here, your loyal boyhood friend, isn't going to do a damn thing about it. Your father
was nothing but a small time nosey snoop who couldn't keep his
mouth shut...A worthless daydreamer, just like you turned out
to be. This is yesterday's news, Phipps. He's known all that shit
since the day he started working for us years ago." Fletcher started
to laugh again.

I stood up and backed away from them. It was too much to
take in all at once. "You knew?"

Bobby didn't answer.

"Come on, officer. Get your friend here to give up the goods
so we can be on our way. We've got a party to go to. You have to
recharge your batteries before you plan your campaign strategy."
His laughter was becoming an ugly cackle as he waved the gun
in my face. The man who killed my father and made my life the
miserable existence that it was, was laughing about it all.

Bobby stood, defeated. In a motion so natural I didn't even
know what he was doing, he pulled a snub-nosed .38 police special from his waistband and put it against Fletcher's temple. "Give
me your gun."

From the look in his eyes I could tell Fletcher gave a moment's
thought to threatening me with his gun and I thought there might
be a Mexican stand-off with me in the middle. Fletcher started

to protest, but Bobby flicked his wrist and whipped Fletcher's temple with his gun barrel. The older man winced, defeated, and his hand dropped limply to his side to allow Bobby to pull the gun from his fingers.

Bobby grabbed Fletcher's hand abruptly and squeezed the man's fingers against the trigger of his own .32. It blew off the head of the man who had done the same thing to my father thirty years earlier.

I opened my mouth to scream, but nothing came out but a deep-throated guttural moan; the kind of primal noise that comes as you awake from a nightmare, trying to warn others around you of the danger in the dream. The bullet caught Fletcher in mid-laugh, but his eyes were open long enough to see what was coming before his brains splattered against the far wall. His body collapsed in a heap, as the deafening explosion rang in my ears and the smell of cordite filled my nose. Joachim cowered in the corner, splattered with blood. My eardrums were damaged with the sound of the gunshot and I couldn't really hear myself. "Jesus, Bobby! What the fuck are you doing?" Joachim was wiping blood splatters and brain matter from his face in disbelief.

Bobby sat, defeated. "It was the only way. He'd never stand trial. Never get convicted."

My heart was beating so fast, I started to hyperventilate. Bobby methodically lowered Fletcher's lifeless arm, making sure the man's fingers remained within the trigger guard. Bobby was ghostly white and his eyes welled up with tears as he continued to tamper with the evidence.

He spoke quickly. "I wish you had never met her, Jimmy. I wish you had never married her. If you had just let everything alone, just taken your boat and sailed around the Caribbean this summer....maybe everything would have been all right. I should have known better.

"I remember when we were up at school, how relentless you were, in search of whatever it was you were looking for up in the library all that time.. I should have known you wouldn't let this go, either."

He stood and then sank down on the bunk. He started crying, and I thought back almost thirty years to when I had last seen him crying on a playground in first grade. Joachim and I both leaned in toward him.

"Sometimes I wish we were still ten years old, Jimmy, fishing from Burnt Bridge.....camping out on Peanut Island....diving the Breakers Reef. Remember those days, Jimmy?"

Of course I remembered them. I relived them every day of my life.

"Remember our first night in Gainesville? How scared we all were about what was going to happen to us? If we would fit in?"

I remembered. Sitting on the bike racks outside Murphree Hall, listening to the music of a band playing at a Freshmen Welcome party on a blocked off street opposite Plaza of the Americas. Three small-town boys afraid we wouldn't fit in. Afraid we couldn't cut it. Afraid they would laugh at the three inseparable friends from West Palm Beach. "Yeah, I remember."

"I'm a lot more scared, now. I don't want to go to jail, Jimmy. You know what they do to cops in there?"

"Bobby...."

"And my family...I can't stand to see them in disgrace. I'm sorry Jimmy....I'm so ashamed of myself. You never did anything to hurt me."

Then he looked at Joachim and me and whispered something through his sobbing.

I couldn't hear it, or didn't think I had heard accurately what he said. "What?"

He said it again. Joachim and I exchanged glances.

At first I didn't understand what he meant. Then he put the gun in his mouth.

I looked at the best friend of my childhood in that split second. How does life happen so fast? One day we're putting shiny new pennies in our loafers in the fourth grade. The next day we're hometown football heroes and we're on the way to the University of Florida. The day after that is the end; the last official gathering of the entire membership of the *Secret Society of Coconuts.* It all happened that fast, in that split second before he pulled the trigger.

How is it that some people, linked so tightly together by so much more than just common roots and the passing of time, lead such divergent lives? We were just three average guys. One of us wanted to be a star football player and got fat and bald. One of us wanted to be a famous politician and got powerful, then corrupt. One of us wanted to escape the painful realities of a life marked by mediocrity, and just get lost in the novels of his father, but instead, through no effort of his own, without lifting a finger, he became a rich widower.

Joachim and I stood there and watched him do it, too slow, too *paralyzed*, to intervene in time. No sudden lunging would have been fast enough to save our friend. The time for heroics was long past.

The cops came after the second gunshot and questioned Joachim and me until dawn. We told them what almost happened: two suicides, back-to-back.

I told them about Victor, and as I did, it occurred to me somewhere in the middle of my story and subsequent questioning that Fletcher never got to find out his son had committed suicide. The Fletcher lineage had come to an end in a greasy, fetid trailer on the wrong side of the tracks; a dynasty built on the exploitation of Florida's natural resources and the insufferable conditions and misery of others' labor.

When we came to the part of the story about the cocaine, I gaffed the monofilament line looped around the piling and pulled it to where it was tied to the nylon rope. The officers shined their flashlights over the edge and watched patiently. Slowly, hand over hand, I pulled the twenty-feet long PVC tube toward the surface. But when they unscrewed the cap, the long white coke straw was empty. We stood in a circle on the dock gaping at one another with stupid looks on our faces. Had it been empty all the time? I had never had the PVC tube above water; never unscrewed the cap. Had Nikki removed whatever might have been in it when she first arrived home from Columbia? Had it been empty the whole time? Had someone seen me hiding it? I don't suppose we'll ever know.

It was another week before the police stopped coming by with more questions about what had happened the past few days.

CHAPTER 42

The cycle of seasons in South Florida is marked most dramatically by population, not weather.

Up north, the seasons change but the population remains the constant. There is no sense of a population loss during any one time of the year. Here, it's the seasons which seem to be constant. Thinking back on events of the past, it is difficult to remember the time of year they took place, since there is no weather-related touchstone to associate with them. No football game played against a palette of red and yellow leaves. No walk with a new love on the first snowfall of the season. No exhilaration on the afternoon of an approaching spring.

No ancient memory of mine coincided with the falling leaves. Nothing ever happened in my life on the first snowfall of the season. I never skipped school after coming down with incurable Spring Fever. A possible exception to this rule might be what occurred during a hurricane. The events linked to those weather changes can never be forgotten.

No, here in South Florida, the swelling of the population marks the time. It used to be a dramatic change. The roads were thick with congestion and the beaches would be full even on days too cold to attract the natives. Now, they are all just always overcrowded and congested. There was a time when Blowing Rocks

Beach was an isolated sanctuary. Now, in the lot they built to handle the parking, there are never any parking spaces, even in the slowest months. Florida's peninsula is engorged with the flow of tourists all year round.

But if you stand still long enough to notice, you will experience a faint, subtle weather cycle of seasons in South Florida. Long hot days, heavy with the humidity which brings afternoon thunderstorms, segue slowly to cooler autumns. If you look at the branches of the Bald Cypress, you'll see the only conifer that is not "evergreen." It sheds its greenery in the winter.

As the days race toward Thanksgiving, you will occasionally smell a hint in the air of a northern autumn if you know what to smell for. In time, dry, mild winter days bring cloudless blue skies and fire red sunsets.

Just northwest of Palm Beach, in a hidden part of a magic swamp, there is a tiny environmental range where two distinct types of flora co-exist. A small circle on this swamp's floor marks the southernmost extremity of certain deciduous hardwoods, and the northernmost existence of several tropical plant species. Just a few feet farther north and it is too cold for the tropical plants to survive any winter. Just a few feet farther south and climactic conditions will not sustain the deciduous trees. Each species is in its most extreme outpost of existence. It is but a tiny, distinct, overlapping spot, a few small square yards in size, and unique on the planet.

My father wrote about this small, overlapping circle where these two ordinarily mutually exclusive species coexist, and he described it as being in two separate climates at once, where a northern forest and a southern jungle converge and cohabitate in just a few, secret, shared, square-feet. Maybe he was referring to himself metaphorically. A Southern boy, educated in a northeastern, Ivy League college, returns home to write. Like some of the plants in this swamp, he couldn't thrive any farther north. And like the others, he couldn't thrive any farther south.

There, in that tiny spot, the monotonous sameness of South Florida can be seen in the same field of view as the more dramatic changes of the northern climates. As the dry winter season approaches, the deciduous trees burn with the splendor of a New England autumn alongside a prehistoric, rain-forest fern that will remain bright green regardless of month or temperature. These endless cycles of seasons in the swamp repeat themselves, in both forms, not far from view of the millions of unknowing inhabitants of South Florida.

It was in this tiny, overlapping circle, in the enchanted swamp near Indiantown, that I started my second journey in my father's footsteps.

With the police no longer knocking at my door, there was something I wanted to do. Something I had to do. I wanted to determine, once and for all, what it was about Florida my father loved so much. I wanted to see what had survived. I wanted to determine if he would be heartbroken to see it today, as he approached what would be his ninetieth birthday.

I wanted to find out what it must have been like, hitchhiking around the state on shell rock roads, recording the dying-off of native cultures; riding Flagler's triumphant Overseas Railroad to Key West; following the evolution of Adison Mizner's Moorish design schemes–Mizner's brother's crooked money schemes; witnessing the Ashley gang stealing the tomato and pineapple farmers' savings from a bank in Hobe Sound and Boynton Beach; looking the other way as Joe Kennedy smuggled in bootleg gin from the Bahamas; listening to the click of the roulette wheel during gambling sprees at Colonel Bradley's Casino; riding idly down Root Trail in the front wicker basket of an Afro-mobile; smoking Cuban cigars on the balmy veranda of the Royal Poinciana Hotel, dropping ashes into the terracotta pots of the fishtail palms. Would I have slicked my hair straight back with pomade and worn white duck pants like all the others?

What about that young Jewish girl from his novel HYPO-
LUXO? Is she, too, based on a real character? A real event? If so,
today, where is the child of her union with the Nazi submarine
captain?

As a way to escape the reality of what had happened to me
in the last few weeks and start the healing process and as a way
of purging myself one last time of his work's grip on me, I once
again became lost in his world. Just as every addict has promised, I told myself I would indulge myself, immerse myself in my
addiction just this one last time before going cold turkey. Except
this time, instead of taking the journey on paper in the UF stacks,
I would do it as he had, on foot.

I began my pilgrimage after making copies of his original
maps published and hand-marked sixty-five years before, and followed his scribbled itinerary. I wanted to see what he saw, smell
what he smelled, touch what he touched, and fill my soul with the
sensations he felt.

I started in what is now known as Barley Barber Swamp,
near Indiantown, where the two distinct foreign enclaves of flora
barely brush fingertips. With just a pack on my back, some pencils
and spiral notebooks, well-worn hiking boots, and a heavy heart,
his footsteps led the way.

Like him, I heard Florida singing her song.

CHAPTER 43

"ROAD SONG"
From Elliott Phipps' Journal

May, 1936:

> *Starting from an Indiantown swamp;*
> *Home to the dark, the mysterious; the bald eagle, the*
> *gallineul; the wood stork, the coot, the 800 year-old cypress tree,*
> *and the strangler fig, the Spider Lily and the gumbo-limbo.*

> *The butterflies gather to wave a wing-ed good-bye.*
> *The Zebra;*
> *The Monarch and the Buckeye;*
> *Viceroys and Skippers and Blue Morphoes and Fritillaries*
> *All wave their farewell.*

> *On foot, light-packed,*
> *I take to the open back roads of Florida.*
> *They take me wherever*
> *I wish, left or right, north or south.*
> *The choice makes no difference on the open road.*
> *They all lead to my discoveries.*

I ask not for fortune;
The road brings me riches.

Far from the tourist traps;
Far from the tourists;
Far from the crowded beaches and the postcard hawkers;

Aware only of my senses,
Of my footsteps,
Of the sights I see,
Of the perfumes I smell,
Of the dampness I feel,
Of the terrain I trod, as I walk with my cypress knee walking
stick,
Of the bumps and the shell rock on the road, the sand and
grit in my shoes, the sand spur in my socks pressing against my
ankle, the roasting of my soles.
All set to the music that I hear.
I hear Florida singing.
I sing a song to Florida, the origin of my lyric.

What are the thoughts and the dreams of the man who comes
and sees this land before him?
The land that Bartram described and drew and listed and
catalogued and wrote about to his father to describe his
awestruck wonder and its bounty;

What were his thoughts that he could not articulate; the
beauty, the quiet, the silence, the oppressive heat weighing him
down step after step. I follow in Bartram's footsteps.

With dedicated and committed steps numbering in the
hundreds, the thousands, the millions, I tramp across my Florida.

I stop to listen to
The Cracker
The Negro
The Cuban
The Indian
The Greek
The Finn
The Canadian
The New Yorker
The Conch
The Ohioan
The Spaniard

They all provide the words.
I hear their voices in a thick, rich patois gumbo;
living their lives; working their work; their faces down to the
job at hand.
Dark skinned shoulders laden with bananas and sponges;
Finger tips rolling cigars.

They chant as they work, some silently, some aloud, they
chant the songs of their families; the songs of their mothers and
fathers, their sons and daughters.

Join me, I say to them,
Follow me,
Be my companion for a moment or a day.

Come along with me on my tramp;
Embrace what I see;
What I feel;
What I smell and taste;
What I hear;
For Florida truly is the origin of my poems, the genesis

of my songs.

For the woman mending quilts;
For the bait caster mending cast nets;
For the mate mending sails;
The songs are second nature.
A part of lives from a time before they can remember.

Teach me your songs.

I greet them and they welcome me;
I extend my hand and they embrace me;
They join in my journey a few steps; a few yards; a few miles;
They share their songs and I share mine.

They lead me to the next crossroads,
And then, turn again to their labors,
A new bounce in their walk,
A new song in their heart.

I march on to meet others and invite them;
Kick up some dust with me and leave your mark on the trail.
Awaken your neighbor and tramp with me.
Inherit from me as I inherit from you.
Burn your feet as I have burned mine.
Wipe the sweat from your brow,
Drink from the springs
Rejoice at the cry of the meadowlark,
Let your soul free for a day and join me on my trek.

We will join in a chorus and raise our voices so that all might
hear our spiritual to our land, our Florida.

And if some should stand in our way,

We shall sing a song to charge their hearts,
So that they will put down their plowshares and join in our
march.
And we shall write poetry as we go,
Dipping our quills into tannen-stained streams
And the saps of a million slash pines and
Into the milk of coconuts.

With coconut ink we shall write our stories for the world to
read.

Let the waters of the Okeechobee, Tohopakaliga, and
Ichetucknee refresh our souls and quench our spirits.

And as we walk and as we talk, we shall share our stories
through song.
And our voices will echo through the orange groves
And what we see and what we hear shall be called out in a
responsive reading for our entire congregation.

Who will not follow?
Who will not sing of this land where milk and honey marks
just the beginning?

A student? Put down your books and learn true meaning.
See the bounty that our land provides.

It's endless, this road of mine, stretching from Atlantic to
Gulf;
From St. John's River to Florida Bay.
From the orange blossoms that nourish the world
From sugar cane to sweeten the taste;
From tomatoes and corn and peas and pole beans and
grapefruit and tangerine, and honeybell.

Enough bounty to fill the plates of everyone;
Beef cattle and cat fish;
Sheep and Sheepshead;
Hog and Snapper and Hog Snapper;
No Hog-Butcher-To-the-World can stand as tall.

I wave to the Farmer's Market that stretches across Florida.
I wave to the Strawberry pickers in Starke;
The celery pickers in Sanford;
The potato and bean pickers in Homestead;
The tomato pickers in Immokalee.
Cucumbers and peanuts and onions and watermelon;
Tobacco and sweet corn;
Pecans and peaches and pears and Tung Nuts.
Cotton and Tupelo Honey.

I sing the song of my homeland, my heartland,

I hear my Florida singing.
It sings for a balmy Keys breeze;

I stop to inhale the smell of the heavy musk of gladiolas/
The smell of the wet woods
The needles of pines
The swimmers and divers
The smell of sun and oil on a young girl's shoulders

The swimmers in Alexander Springs and Rainbow Springs
and Salt Springs and Silver Springs and Homosassa Springs
I swim with the swimmers.

I toil with the fathers and sons in the deep muck soil, a
thousand years of pond-apple peat squeezes up between my toes;
A child runs to embrace me

To learn the words of my songs.

I turn her shoulders toward the open road,
My arm on her shoulder;
And she, too, begins to sing.
I gesture toward the swamps and savannahs and beaches
and bays.
She breaks free and runs ahead, singing her own lyrics.

I sing of the Air; it blows against my face.
A glance above and I behold indigo blue skies.
And in the air above I hear the Carolina Wren and see
The Roseate Spoonbill.
I see the Flamingo and the Anhinga;
The Wood Duck and the Wood Stork and the Wood Ibis;
The Bald Eagle and the Pelican;
A Snowy Egret and an Everglades Kite;
A Barn Owl and a Burrowing Owl and a Cormorant;
They circle above with the Sea Gull, the Mockingbird and the
Blue Heron.

They circle above and teach me a new stanza.
The flapping of their wings serves as counterpoint.
I gaze toward Heaven as the music descends.
I sing of the Sea; the music of the sea reverberates in my
ears.
The ebb and flow of the ocean and estuary;
The plodding of my wading feet
The rocking of a moored boat
The rolling of the steam boat
The beating of my heart
Set the rhythms of my songs.

I sing of the Land; and the land sings to me.

Tramping, tramping, tramping,
Stepping over the rails;
Stepping on the tracks,
Hopping the freights
Sleeping in hobo jungles,
Sharing a can of beans,
Sharing a story for a safe place to spend the night, listening
to the peepers, while my other comrades, far away, listen to
the sounds of the pounding surf from their Breakers' seaside
cottages.

And I hear Florida singing back to me;
The black man plucks the banjo;
The Italian immigrant strums the mandolin;
The farm worker sings his gospel baritone;
The Miami Beach chanteuse;
The Conchtown lady singing a lullaby;
The folk songs of the cannery;
The opera of the cicadas;
The moonlight sonata on a gentle shore;
The symphony of a nighttime swamp;
Bull gator, wood duck, croakers, crickets, all singing first
chair, drowning one another in an endless, nightlong chorus.

The chug of the steam engine, the steamboat, the steam
locomotive, the steam bath;
The conductor and the tourist and the spinning roulette wheel
of Bradley's Casino;
The plop of the fishing bobber;
The motor hum of a small fishing boat;
The cranking of the reel;
The scraping of fish scales on a sheep's head as the angler's
knife sends them flying;
The squawk of the pelican as it bobs on the water waiting for

the entrails;
 The sounds of the night;
 The sounds of the day;
 The sounds of a late afternoon thunderstorm blowing across
the Everglades;
 The sound of the rain on a tin cracker roof;
 The sound of the rain on a Traveler Palm frond;
 The sound of the rain on open water;
 The sound of the rain on my bare head;
 The sound of the rain on a tourist's towel;
 The sound of the rain on the Hialeah Race Track turf;
 The sound of the rain on a green and white awning;
 The sound of the rain on a tourist's beach umbrella;
 The sound of rain on a cabana;
 The sound of rain on a straw boater;
 The sound of rain on a tuna tower canopy;
 The sound of rain on a picnic lunch on the first day of
Summer;
 The sound of rain on a student's umbrella on the last night of
Summer vacation;
 The sound of rain on barrel tile;
 The sound of rain on Micanopy rooftop;
 The sound of rain on a Silver Springs boil;
 The sound of rain on the planks above my head under
Rainbow Pier;
 The sound of rain on the tin roof of a Ybor City cigar factory;
 The sound of rain on an empty swimming pool;
 The sound of rain on a flattened cardboard box providing a
night's shelter;
 The sound of rain on the dried palmetto fronds of a chickee
hut in Big Cypress;
 The sounds provide the staccato drumbeat of my song.

 I stop and talk to the Red Man.

The Seminole Woman, a child of Osceola, threading rainbow
beads on a waxed string;
    Pulling the needle through the bowl of tiny beads, swooping
one up into colorful garb humming softly to herself;

    The Seminole Man chipping, chipping away at a cypress log
with an adze;
    Chip, chip, chipping away. A dugout canoe?
    Just a show for tourists?
    I hunt with the Seminole Brave:
    Quail and squirrel;
    Doves and jacksnipe and coots and raccoons;
    Muskrat and otter and wild turkey and geese and marsh hens.

    The Seminole child, her eyes full of wonder and mystery,
    disbelief, anger, hurt, bitterness, fear, regret,
    Standing straight,
    Standing tall,
    Standing unconquered in her abject poverty,
    Her voice the sound of the poet, the philosopher, the victim,
the seer, listening to the passing of her mother's and her mother's
mother's stories to another generation.
    They provide the chorus to my song.

    We hear the names of their forefathers as their voices are
carried on the Everglades' winds:
    Miccosukee
    Tequesta
    Hobe
    Caloosa
    Miami
    Temucuan

    And their voices echo in the lyrics they left behind:

Wekiva, Caloosahatchie, Loxahatchee, Okeechobee,
Tallahassee, Suwannee, Choctawhatchee, Wakulla, Ochlockonee,
Sopchoppy, Myakka, and Hypoluxo.

What was once "water eyes" is now Wewahitchka;
What was once "the fish where fish were eaten" or
Thlothlopopka has become Fisheating Creek.
What was once "head chief" is now Micanopy.
I stop and watch the alligator wrestling in the Miccosukke
Village.

I stop and talk to the Spanish man.
The spirits of the Spanish Conquistadors march through our
swamps and through our blood,
Their armor glistening in the morning mists as they explore
in search of youth and wealth like the multitude who have
followed:
Ponce de Leon,
San Ybel,
Sebastian.
And in their wake, the names they have left behind season
our tongues;
Boca Raton,
St. Augustine,
Castillo de San Marcos,
Captiva,
Fernandina,
Matanzas,
Marianna,
Panama City,
DeSoto City,

And I stop to talk to the African man.
And I see him, back broken from unending labor, building the

railroads, building the bridges, dredging the canals, building the
Breakers
 And I see their proud moments and their bleak;
 I see the terror of slavery and the joy of the freedman;
 I see the hope of new lives,
 And the end of despair;
 I see the father and the mother in the fields,
 Their children, drowsy, hiding from the midday sun
underneath the truck.

 I stop and talk to the newcomer.
 I see the frightened faces of immigrants,

 I stop and talk to the Tourist.
 Those who join us come in all shapes and sizes and colors
and smells and tastes.

 They arrive by automobile on Routes 301 and 17.
 They arrive by rail on The Florida East Coast and the
Seaboard.
 They arrive by air on Eastern and National.
 They arrive by foot in their Endicott and Johnson work
shoes;
 They arrive looking, searching, questioning, asking, begging,
pleading, hoping, wondering, not knowing what to expect; not
knowing what to fear.
 By bus they come:
 Florida Motor and Atlantic Greyhound;
 Pan American Bus Lines and Union;

 By steamship they come:
 Clyde-Mallory;
 The Merchants and Mines;
 The Mobile Ocean Line and

The Pan Atlantic.
The New Yorker, the Bostonian.
The Montrealers, the Chicagoan, the Clevelander.
Tired of the cold, tired of the filth, tired of the poverty of their lives,
Tired of the crowds they come here to make new crowds.

From Pennsylvania and New Jersey,
From Detroit and Baltimore,
From Michigan and Wisconsin.
They crossed the streets;
They crossed the Hudson;
They crossed the Delaware;
They crossed the prairie;
They crossed the Smokies and the Poconos and the Alleghenies.
They crossed their chests with the sign of the cross.
They arrive and stand on the shore of South Beach;
They wriggle their toes in Lake Worth Lagoon;
They splash up to their ankles on St. Pete Beach;
They wade up to their waists in Biscayne Bay.
They hop Hupmobiles and tool along Ormond Beach and Daytona Beach;
They cannonball into the Lido Pool in Palm Beach.

They play shell games at roadside stands;
Giant Alligators;
Baby Alligators;
Stuffed Alligators;
Alligator bags;
Alligator belts;
Pecan Clusters;
Fireworks;
Slot machines;

Post cards;
Thick milk shakes;
Fresh-squeezed orange juice;
Grapefruit-We Ship Daily!
Salt water taffy;
Trinkets;
Notions;
Souvenirs;
Carved coconut heads;
Knick-knacks and paddy-whacks.
Conch shells bleached and shiny pink;
Cypress knee ornaments, boiled and sanded;
Flower bouquets made from tiny seashells.

They buy swampland and bungalows on shotgun lots;
They buy their futures;
They buy Heaven's waiting rooms.

I stop to salute my old friends
I wave to the bean-pole pickers in the fields
I wave to the man behind the mule;
I wave to the man chopping cane;
I wave to the man collecting the drip of turpentine sap;
I wave to the woman in the do-rag sorting tomatoes;
I wave to the woman hanging clothes in the front yard
I wave to the mechanic up to his shoulders in the guts of his
truck;
I wave to the cane-pole fisherman on the canal bank not
trying to catch anything;
I wave to the policeman, unsmiling, telling me to move along;
I wave to the county commissioners at the barbecue;
The Governor at his mansion;
I wave to the mayor, the preacher.
I wave to the convicts on the roadside;

The convicts in their black and white stripes;
The convicts on contract labor;
The convicts in their sweatboxes;
The convicts sweltering in the turpentine camps;
Swinging their sledges, swinging their scythes,
Swinging their chains, swinging by their necks.
And even they have their own song of Florida;
Sung to the beat of the backbreaking work and the master's
whip;
Sung to the slurs and the spitting and the fear and the hatred;
Sung while they build the railroads and the hotels and
the roads and the skyscrapers in the unrelenting heat and
brightness;
Sung while they are weak from dehydration and exposure
and exhaustion;
They sing their song of Florida.

None can hide from my wave;
Rich and poor, I embrace them all and let them teach me
their song.

I see canal boats and sail boats and fishing boats and
pleasure boats;
I see canoes and steamships and rowboats and schooners
and johnboats;
I see paddleboats and dugouts and glass-bottom boats and
ferries and trawlers and shrimpers.

They all suit my purpose.
They take me over the waters that quench my spirit.

Bait the hook, tease the line, reel in the fish, big or small,
sport or feast.
Fight the tarpon in the low-lying flats off a Thousand

Islands;
Fight the catch
Off the pier;
Off the bridge;
Off the sandy beach while surf casting,
Off the spillway for snook.
Jigging for mullet;
Okeechobee Bass;
Okeechobee Catfish;
Appalachicola Oysters;
Sebastian Clams;
Crappie on a canal bank cane-pole;
The Shrimper in Key West pulling in his drag nets;
Kingfish and Spanish Mackerel and Sailfish and Swordfish;
Marlin and Whiting and Grouper and Barracuda and Jack.

I spend the night watch with the Shrimper in the Boynton Inlet.
I watch as he dips his light near the dark midnight water's surface and listen to the hiss of the swoop of his drop net as he scoops up the shrimp.
Jetties filled with fishermen, angling for their spot.
Barnacle encrusted mangrove, building islands for the future before our eyes.
And each body of water, each river, each estuary, each canal, each brook, each stream, each tide pool offers up a new discovery as I cup my hands and peer beneath the surface.
The tide pool yields the tiny crustacean
The riverbed yields the prehistoric fossil
The submerged midden yields the ancient clay pots and arrowheads
The fishermen rolling on the ocean at sunset, pulling in their lines with arms of sinew.
The ship joiners and the smell of their sweat

And as I wander on an early morning, my comrades join me:
Osceola and Billy Bowlegs;
The Barefoot Mailman and Trapper Nelson;
Henry Plant and Henry Flagler and Julia Tuttle;
The Kissimmee Cowboy and Carl Fischer;
The Cuban Cigar Roller and the Black Migrant Farmer;
The Greek Sponge Diver and the Swedish Immigrant by way
of Minnesota;
The Conch Fisherman by way of the Bahamas.

As darkness approaches, we seek shelter to pass the night.
We grille fish and fresh deer meat,
As the embers die out we sit in the glow and we share our
dreams of Florida.
Each in our own separate Dreamscape;
Each now singing our own separate song.

With the pluck of the banjo;
With the blow of the mouth harp;
With the stomp of the clod-hoppered boot;
With the clap of two hands;
With the strum of a Sears Roebuck guitar;
With the scrape of a fiddle bow;
With the buzz of a blow-fly.

Inspired by Jimmie Rodgers and Robert Johnson,
We stand at the Crossroads and wave to the hobo on the
northbound train.

We stand together as an act of faith
And wait until the lonesome train whistle gives its wail.
Not too close–down the road apiece.
Far enough away to haunt.
It has to be a distant, going, going, gone whistle.

At night while we sleep
A Florida Panther curls up on my lap and purrs;
A Black Bear cuddles up behind me, his hairy paw
Reaches around and pulls me into his embrace.
We lie like three spoons in a drawer.

My tramp takes me to the churches on Sunday mornings.
White clapboard and board and batten;
Tin roofs and tin belfries.
Inside, a handful sing of a Mighty Fortress; A bulwark never failing.
Outside, picket fences stand like tombstones, surrounding the gravesites of their mothers and fathers,
While sandstone and wooden grave markers stand like picket fences, at attention, fighting with the weeds for notice.
The names and dates catch my eye and raise a thousand questions.
Who were they?
How did they get here?
Why did they stay?
How did they marry?
What hardships did they face?
Why did their children die before them?
How did they die?
How? Why? When?
What kind of lives did they live?

I hop the freights of the Atlantic Coast Line and the Florida East Coast.
Run from bulls on the Georgia Southern & Florida;
Hide with hobos on the St. Louis and San Francisco.
See faces I'll never see again. Hear voices I'll never hear again. My time here is short.
Watch with wary eye as I drift off to sleep.

I take the tour and visit the big cities, teeming with my new friends.
I tread the overseas highway to Key West;
Built on the spine of Flagler's railroad,
Destroyed in the Hurricane of '35.
Conch houses steal style of the British and New England by way of the Bahamas.
I fill my plate with shark and turtle.
I stop at the Southernmost House in Key West;
Stop to see my friend Ernest and share a drink.

In Coral Gables, where lines of desperate land buyers rush the real estate offices. They celebrate their victory with a dip in the Venetian pool.
Drink cocktails at the stately Biltmore.

In St. Augustine where the old slave market stands in disgrace near Flagler's Ponce de Leon Hotel.

In Sarasota, the Ringling Brothers house their circus in the winter.
The freaks will not speak to me. I am an outcast.

With my right thumb extended, I panhandle for a ride.
Speeding down two-lane black-top at speeds up to 45 miles per hour.
The landscape blurs and I get out.
I tramp through Belle Glade and see the migrant camps.

I walk the shaded streets of Arcadia;
Climb the Devil's Millhopper in Gainesville;
Descend into caves outside an Ocala cattle ranch.
Visit the veterans' retirement homes of the Union Army soldiers in Zephyrhills;

I scoop up cedar shavings and inhale the fragrance in a
pencil factory in Cedar Key;
  The carillon from Bok Tower slows my melody;
  But the melody lingers on.

I walk through Frostproof and Christmas on the hottest days
of the summer.
  I follow the engineering expedition through the swamp and
jungles of the
  Everglades as they plot the Tamiami Trail;

And as I walk my land I am shaded by Live Oak and Spanish
Moss;
  Dade County Pine, scrub oak and palmetto and Gumbo
Limbo.

And on the islands of the river of grass;
  Hammocks and Highlands.

I'm in the studios of WQAM in Miami when they go on the
air in 1921;
  I'm with Sheriff Baker in Indian River County on that
November 1 night when he guns down the Notorious Ashley
Gang in 1924;
  I'm in Bayfront Park in 1933 when Guiseppe Zangara tries to
shoot F.D.R. and has to settle for Mayor Anton Cermak;
  I'm in Ocklawaha when Ma Barker is gunned down in 1935;
  I'm in Belle Glade in 1928 when 2,000 die in an hour; their
faces frozen in fear, their hands outstretched for air, their mouths
contorted in screams.
  Their eyes were watching God.
  I'm there again in 1930 to watch the Hoover Dike being
built around Lake Okeechobee so nothing like that ever happens
again.

I'm in Lakeland and Miami and St. Petersburg and Starke
for the public parades for the Ku Klux Klan.
I'm in Jacksonville for the ribbon-cutting of the new
Jacksonville Naval Yard. Do we really need a Navy this
powerful?
I'm in the jooks in Alachua drinking shine;
I'm in the turpentine camps in the Panhandle;

My quest takes me to Fort Pierce, Fort Myers, Fort Drum,
Fort Jefferson, Fort Walton, Fort White, Fort Jupiter and Fort
Dade and Fort Lauderdale.

From Two Egg to Cork Screw to Fruitland to Enterprise
To Harlem to Havana;
From Picnic to Climax to Lick Skillet to Lake-June-in-Winter.

I'm with the Conchs in Riviera listening to their cockney
English accent telling tales and folklore;
A Conch man tells me, "In the winters we live on
Yankees and in the summers we live on fish."

I'm with the Hartley Toots Orchestra in Miami;
I dance to the music of Ace Harris and his
Sunset Royal Orchestra in West Palm Beach.
I toss the Bolita sack; a dollar wager lost.

I'm there for you.

I tramp the steaming ground following a summer shower;
The dripping fronds release their wetness;

Facing East from Miami's shore I can see Africa;
Facing West from Tampa's shore I can see Mexico;
Facing South from Key West's shore I can see Cuba;

*Facing North from Jacksonville's shore I can see a horde of
frantic tourists.*
    Facing inward to myself I see another country.
    Trodding my paths, escaping from what?
    Running toward what?
    Looking, learning.

    I face my Florida and purvey all within my reach.
    Can I inhale her sweet soul into my breast?
    Can I possess her?
    Can I take on her life?

    Walking near Tomoka I saw a live oak growing,
    Standing alone, the largest tree in Florida.
    *Entwined in Spanish Moss, ever stretching, ever standing,
ever shading through storm and sun and wind and rain; through
drought and neglect it stands.*
    Standing year after year, never giving, never weakening.
    *Like the tallest cypress, The Senator, near Longwood
standing sentinel for 3,500 years.*

    *I jump off the bridge at Palm Beach and let myself drift with
the current.*
    Out the inlet I go, pulled by an outgoing tide.
    I hitch-hike a ride on a loggerhead;
    In and out, up and down,
    My sea-road's swift current carries me out to sea with the tide.
    Out to the shipping lanes
    Out to the shrimp nets
    Out to the channel
    Out to the Gulf Stream
    Northward toward Bermuda I am swept.
    I see Spanish galleons sink beneath my feet;
    I see Stephen Crane's OPEN BOAT off the Daytona Coast;

I see gun runners and rum runners;
I see slave ships.
The trawlers, the ferries, the barks,
They all pass me by and wave as I swim on my Sea-road.
And when day is done,
It lifts me up and places me on shore to walk again.

My friends, my comrades,
We all share the songs of the open road.
A road without end;
A road indifferent to washouts and brambles and gullies;
A road indifferent to the dung of horses and cows;
A road never ending for a song never ending.
A road indifferent to weather.
A road empty, yet rich with rewards;
Forever awake, forever alive, forever moving and changing.
A road forever speaking, whispering, nudging.

What is the best time of day for my walking?

The Mornings are the best time of day
The smell of the morning;
With a waking of life.

The Sunsets are the best time of day;
The smell of the sunsets;
With a cooling of the air.

The Evenings are the best time of day;
The smell of the evenings
With a taste of brine blowing off the inlets and bays.
So what do you hear now, Barefoot Mailman?
Do you recognize your home? Your beaches?
Do you hear the farmers sing to their mules?

Do you hear the crowing of the cock at the break of day?
Do you hear the Spanish guitar and the noise and din of
boats?
    I hear the buzz of mosquitoes and the buzz of crop dusters.
    I hear the buzz of traffic;
    I hear the hum of rail commerce;
    I hear the Baptist wailing his hymns;
    I hear the Catholic whisper her rosary;
    I hear the Jew murmur his Psalms;
    And to me they all sing the song of my Florida.
    The Greek tradesman;
    The Cuban shopkeeper;
    The Japanese pineapple farmers at Yamato Colony;
    All sing my song.

And I dream'd in a dream
That one day all mankind
Would walk backward from whence they came
And there would be a great migration North and South
And East and West
And once again, my Florida would be my Florida.
Alone, silent, empty of loud voices and brawling men;
Empty of cars and trucks and trains;
Empty of house trailers and tourists;
Empty of migrant shanties;

And then my Florida shall be my Florida once again.

I yield this promise:
To sing your songs;
To tell your tales;
To spread your wisdom and your gospel;
To preach your sermons;
To wail your sadness;

To brag your expanse;
To dance on your beaches and embrace your Royal Palms.

And in my songs
You will see the trails disappearing into the piney wood hills;
You will see my footprints in the sand;
You will see my dust tracks on a road;
You will see my signature on a tree-trunk;
You will hear my song in the air.

I leave behind the smile on my face;
I leave behind the love of my heart;
I leave behind the stink of my sweat;
I leave behind the sparkle in my eyes
I leave behind the words to my music for any who wish to
listen and sing along.

One entry was written after my father had stopped his regular hiking around the state. He still took weekend trips, mostly in his Whippet that can be seen in his photos. He would use these short trips for brief vacations, for periodic inspiration and to validate descriptions of specific locations he was including in his novels. Authenticity was important.

He even spent a few days showing Marion Post Wolcott around, the photographer from the Farm Securities Administration. He lead her through western Palm Beach County when she took some of her famous pictures.

This later journal entry was written just before WWII. His bitterness in what he sees is readily apparent in what he writes.

ELLIOTT PHIPPS' Journal
April, 1940

Florida: I rejoice at her beauty and mourn at her loss.

She is the fresh bloom of youth you fall in love with as a boy;
She is the old whore of desperation.
She turns her back on you;
Giving up her innocence for any rich man who beckons.
While he has his way with her, she glances over her shoulder
to see if you still watch.
Money changes hands and now satiated, he moves on.
"Next in line," she demands.
How many times can she give herself before her smile no
longer glows?
How many times can she give herself before her shoulders no
longer stand straight?
Her eyes avert as you try to ask her why?
And as you ask her, the Little Flower of your youth pretends
to listen, spreading her legs once again.
For money she turns you over.
For money she drops her guard.
For the money she levels her forests and befouls her water.
She strips bare her beauty and starves the birds above and
the beasts of her earth.

For the money she turns her back on you who loved her and
sells her soul, her beauty, her future.
And yet you can't stop loving her, can't stop looking at her.
So you search in vain for anything that remains behind to
Remind you of what once was;
Remind you of the pink Hibiscus she placed in her hair;
Remind you of the fragrance of her breathing life in your ear;
Remind you of the solace she once gave.
Instead you find a befouled old whore, trying to find out her
own answer to the question you've asked her over and over:
"Why?"
But the line of takers stretches out past the horizon while
you stand by helpless and watch, empty of pocket, full of ideas,

powerless to move; full of hope and desperation.

Again, she turns her back to you and waves the next one forward. Time marches on.
A parking lot;
An office building;
A new road;
Ditch and drain;
Fill in the swamp;
Wipe out the Snowy Egret and the alligator and the Crocodile and the Everglades Kite.
We don't need them anymore.
We need to build.
We need to destroy.
We need to sell.
Sell it while you're young and can still get your price.
Why wait?
What are you holding out for?
Why say no?
Let them buy it.
Let them have their way with you while Mr. Helpless stands by and watches it all happen.

So much in love.
So broken hearted.

The final journal entry from Elliott Phipps' days of walking were written when his wandering days were just about over.
In his handwriting we read a direct quote from Walt Whitman.

Do Whitman's words reflect the thoughts of my father? What was he searching for?

ELLIOTT PHIPPS' Journal,
November, 1941

> *Long having wander'd since, round the earth having*
> *wander'd,*
>> *Now I face home again, very pleas'd and joyous,*
>> *(But where is what I started for so long ago?*
>> *And why is it yet unfound?)*

Walt Whitman
1860, 1867

Did my father ever find what he was looking for? Maybe he found it on the floor of the living room, bouncing me on his knee.

And from what I learned on the open road during my own trek, what would my father probably sing today, in mid-year in 1986?

It would be *a farewell song; a lament.* It might go something like this.

> *Farewell to the beauty;*
> *Farewell to the quiet;*
> *Farewell to the serenity of the swamp.*
> *Farewell to the fishes of the water and the beasts on the land.*
> *Farewell to the clean waters of Lake Apopka and Lake*
> *Okeechobee.*
> *Say good-bye to the Everglades and to Florida Bay;*
> *Say good-bye to the land you loved and the waters you fished*
> *and swam.*
> *Say good-bye to the Kite and the wood stork and the bobcat*
> *and panther and deer.*

> *Say good-bye to the people who marched in chorus and sang*
> *your song.*

*Say Adios to Biscayne Bay and the Lake Worth Lagoon with
"water as crystal as gin," and Tampa Bay and the St. Lucie
River.
Say good-bye to the Indian River Lagoon;
Say good-bye to Fisheating Creek.
Say good-bye, Florida,
Say Goodbye.
You really blew it,
You greedy, blind, mindless fucks.*

CHAPTER 44

It was during the thirty-second day of my walking tour when I began to hallucinate from dehydration. You've never really sweat until you've spent a summer in Central Florida. The sun reflects off the white pavement beneath your feet, baking them, blistering your soles; blistering your soul. With every step your raw feet bleed into your white socks. With every step your heart bleeds empty. My face was sunburned and my chapped lips were cracked.

White Springs wasn't intended to be the last stop on my journey, but it was.

From White Springs I had planned to go to the Tomoka River near Ormond Beach and find that largest Live Oak in Florida, and from there, zig-zag on over to Gainesville.

But I never made it.

After sleeping under the stars one last night, I showed up at the Stephen Foster Folk Culture Center, way down upon the Suwannee River. That was where the Florida State Historical Museum had stored some things I was looking for. I had come with a purpose.

The curators looked at my appearance and hesitated, but

finally I convinced them of my credentials and the importance of my mission. It was here in White Springs where the priceless voice recordings made by Alan Lomax and Zora Neale Hurston and Stetson Kennedy during their Florida Writer's Project years are available for the public to hear. During the late 1930's they traveled Florida's back roads with an acetate recorder, preserving the precious oral folklore of Florida's elderly-and-soon-to-be-forgotten. They hooked the bulky, 100 pound recorder to their car battery and recorded a bygone world through a steel stylus that etched this now-lost world into the acetate disks. Similar in appearance to an LP record album, the disks were a primitive form of recording, filling the technology gaps between Edison's wax cylinders and the wire recorders of the Forties and early Fifties, before audio tape came into widespread use.

Along with the millions of documents, photographs and artifacts painstakingly collected by the 200 writers of the Florida Writer's Project, many of these acetate recordings were systematically destroyed when the Works Progress Administration was disbanded at the outbreak of WWII. There was simply no money left for storage, so the material was burned. Florida's precious heritage, up in smoke for lack of storage space.

In reading over the mountains of computerized transcriptions of the acetate recordings that did survive the mass destruction of the archives, I came across a sheet of paper where my father's name leapt off the page at me.

He had scheduled a recording rendezvous with Alan Lomax, Zora Neale Hurston, and Stetson Kennedy, somewhere west of Gainesville in June of 1935. The transcription reads:

ALAN LOMAX: "Just move that microphone a little bit closer to Mrs. Rogers please, Elliott."

STETSON KENNEDY: "Elliott, we're recording. Are you ready to begin?"

ELLIOTT PHIPPS: "Yes, I think so. Zora, why don't you ask Mrs. Rogers to talk to us? Tell Mr. Kennedy and Mr. Lomax the stories you told me yesterday about what it was like being born into slavery? And sing us some of the songs your grandmother taught you to sing when you were a young girl, the ones she said her grandmother had passed down to her."

I bought an audio cassette tape copy of the original acetate recording and rushed out to play it on the Walkman in my back-pack.

Outside White Springs I crawled down to the base of the Spring House and finished off the last of my Gatorade while soaking my bleeding feet in the shallow trickle that bubbled up through the sluiceway. I lay back on the bank and stared up at the canopy of Live Oak, Cypress, and Spanish Moss. Exhaustion and heat stroke from the last few days, coupled with the memory of my recent discoveries and losses, brought on a sadness that overwhelmed me. But now, I was about to step over the threshold and into my father's domain. I was now about to hear his voice for the first time that I could ever remember.

I put on the headset and inserted the tape. Suddenly, in the stifling, oven-heat, I felt a chill run through me.

The audio quality was terrible, with scratches, clicks, pops and surface noise inherent in the primitive, acetate recording technology.

But the miracle was there, my father's voice finally speaking to me from over fifty years earlier. It is the sad, sweet voice of a man obsessed with a love for his work. It is a voice filled with compassion, raspy from too many cigarettes, yet exactly as my mother described it: a trace of Florida Cracker accent, tempered by an Ivy League education. Confident, lilting, a practiced orator, a born storyteller.

At one time during the old slave woman's tales of her childhood she tells a funny story, the ninety-five year old woman proudly delivering her first-person account of her days in slavery. First Zora, then my father can be heard laughing out loud at the woman's anecdote, as if surprised that she possessed a sense of humor at all, after what she had lived through. It is a sound I have been waiting to hear my entire life. My father's laughter. I tried to match it to the broad smile and sparkling eyes I knew from old photographs of him.

I rewound the tape and drank in the sound of his laughter over and over again.

Can a laugh be happy and sad all at once? He must have known there would never be enough time to tell all the stories he had heard; everything he wanted to say. How could anyone ever have enough time for what he had witnessed?

At the end of the fourth acetate recorded on that date, he graciously thanks the old slave woman again and their easy laughter mixes together and then stops in mid-sentence. Like his life, there was no slow fade to black, just an abrupt stop without warning.

Like that first night in the University of Florida library when I was eighteen, I began to sob uncontrollably and in my weakened physical condition, I eventually rolled into the streambed.

In my semi-coherent state, a realization swept over me. I could never live up to what he did, no matter how hard I tried; no matter how many miles I walked. As I lay in the cooling waters, choking back tears of inconsolable remorse, I became delirious and finally passed out from exhaustion and exposure. The long days in the sunshine (in the son-shine) had finally caught up with me.

Two girls from the University of Florida who were out kayaking on the Suwannee found me and called the police. From my appearance and condition, the officers assumed I was homeless, and paramedics took me to Alachua General in their ambulance. I woke up with tubes in both arms. Another two hours in the heat and I would have died from dehydration and exposure, if I hadn't first rolled over in the four inches of water and drowned.

A few days later, after checking out of the hospital and hiring a rental car, I stopped in at the University of Florida in Gainesville to see Mrs. Todd at the Library, but she was gone. She and her brother had retired to North Carolina five years earlier. As I walked outside, I took a last glance over my shoulder to the dormer roof where I had perched during my college years, safe and distant from all that went on below. I'd half expected to see my father squatting up there, smiling, offering me a wave. But he wasn't there as he had been in so many dreams before.

CHAPTER 45

When I got back to West Palm Beach, I tracked down two of the cops who worked the scene at the railroad tracks the night my father was killed. They both said it looked like a suicide to them. They were surprised and skeptical to hear the real story.

The reporter who covered the story for the PALM BEACH TRIBUNE was harder to find. He was retired and living in Cherokee, North Carolina. He vaguely remembered the incident, but said he was only at the scene for five minutes and couldn't provide any further details.

CHAPTER 46

On the last day in August, when the air is heavy with the threat of Caribbean thunderstorms and African Hurricanes, I hopped on my bicycle and pedaled through West Palm Beach down to Mango Promenade to the little house where I had grown up. The skyline I had watched change as I grew older was no longer mine. Would my father even recognize it?

Making that journey I felt so alone. In the eight weeks or so since the shootings on my boat I'd done more than retrace my father's footsteps. I'd flown north to spend some time with my mother. But after three days, when I realized she really didn't know whether or not I was there, or even who I was, I came home with my aunt's blessing. "Go live your life," Aunt Lucille told me, as she whispered goodbye at Elmira Airport.

I worked in the little love nest my parents had built, cleaning out the lifetime of junk that remained behind. There were a few more pictures.

I had signed the necessary papers with the development people. I called the demolition company and they had given me the approximate time of the execution, which was what had brought me here at this particular time, on this particular morning.

In the corner of my back yard was a large Banyan tree. Is it possible for someone to have a close friendship with a tree?

It is for a small boy. Alone as a child, I formed a lifelong bond with this tree. As a boy, the tree took me into its arms, welcomed and accepted me, no questions asked. Unnecessary to explain for someone who has experienced this. Impossible to understand for someone who hasn't. Later, with my two new friends we had spent hours in the branches as kids; branches that invited the building of a tree house, had a father been around to help with the design and construction. In my case, there was no father around, and so no tree house.

I hadn't climbed the Banyan in over twenty years. I remember the specific day of the last climb. It was the last day of summer vacation before the start of the Seventh Grade, when you try to squeeze in all the things on that last day that you had planned to do on your summer vacation, but never got around to doing. The last day of my childhood. After then, it was Junior High School, and our priorities would suddenly change.

Above, these tree branches, too, were still my old friends, growing larger, stretching out to seek their own destinies, yet still rooted to a common trunk. I knew every twist of their woody arms from memories of their embraces, and even though I hadn't seen them since that last day of my boyhood, every gnarl and scar on the bark was familiar to my searching touch while I climbed upward.

As I pulled myself up through the branches, I was startled by an object I had not seen nor thought about in those twenty-odd years. Yet as soon as I saw it, I remembered with sparkling clarity the day and circumstances when I had propped it up there.

It was a toy soldier, made of lead, left behind in a tight crook, still on guard duty in my treetop retreat, aiming his bent rifle in my face as I climbed higher. He had been standing guard all this time, night after night, waiting for my return. He had been there while I played football in high school; when I got lost in the stacks at Gainesville; my night on the magic mountain with Nikki; the night she died. I left the lead soldier there standing guard, to watch over the childhood of another boy who would discover it and fill his heart with dreams. I climbed higher and higher.

In the past, the tree had served as a pirate-ship's crow's nest and a medieval castle turret. From that perch I had defended the castle and preserved the honor of Guinevere. The tree where I had spent summer nights suspended from a hammock, now had a polyethylene, day-glo pink ribbon wrapped around its trunk. It would be spared. The only landmark that would survive the bulldozer; my own personal touchstone to my past would live on in a downtown green space. The stories it could tell to anyone who cared to listen.

My parents' little stucco house had no such day-glo pink ribbon wrapped around it to preserve it. No more time for stories.

Hidden in the leafy canopy of that Banyan, twenty feet in the air, I watched an ebony-skinned man at the controls of a bulldozer as he drove across the back lawn, leaving his hatch marks in the sod. Had his great-grandfather witnessed the burning of The Styx?

Then, without hesitation, without a moment of respectful silence for the little dreams in life that never come true, he lifted the dozer blade up above the back porch roof, and without further ceremony, collapsed my parents' honeymoon handiwork into a pile of rubble. Where does the love go? I half expected to see the spirits of my young newlywed parents rising from the Dade Pine splinters.

It took him only a few minutes to destroy the dream house they built. How could he know what his few idle hand movements on the bulldozer's controls were destroying? Then, like a kid in some giant sandbox, the bulldozer operator went on to the next house. He never knew I was there, watching.

I climbed to the highest point in the tree, until the branch could no longer support my weight. Hanging on, I threw my feet out. The branch dipped slowly, delivering me safely to the ground.

("*And so I, too, dream of becoming a swinger of....*"*..Banyans.*)

My mother will spend her remaining days in the home of her sister. The real tragedy of that part of my story is that her doctor says she could live another thirty years like this. Adrift in time and place, knowing she is alive, not knowing who she really is. She never found out that her husband was loyal to the end, did not, in fact, abandon her and their son. I tried to tell her, but she was too far gone.

Joachim is coaching football with an arm in a cast this season. The players wonder what actually happened to his arm and, during team huddles, they whisper stories extrapolated from newspaper reports.

It hasn't been decided what will happen with Bobby's pension, and as far as the million dollars he got from the Fletchers, maybe his wife knows where it is. If she does, she isn't saying.

As for the vault at the Fletcher residence that allegedly contains duplicates and the only other copies of the collected works of Elliott Phipps? I don't suppose I'll ever know. I can't expect that the Senator would be forthcoming if I inquired.

There was no hard evidence linking Senator Danforth Fletcher to anything, and the State's Attorney's Office won't be pressing any charges. I really can't say that I was surprised the Senator would get away with it all. He will be allowed to rip-off his district as long as his constituency from Palm Beach continues to support him. No doubt, more teen-aged transients and the little girls from Cleveland will have their big Florida dreams disappear like Pat Boone's "Love Letters in the Sand." Lucky and his friends will probably continue beating the shit out of people when they aren't flying Danforth around in his helicopter.

"Forget it, Jake. It's Chinatown."

As for Mr. Phipps, Nikki's "Little Professor," he would not return to teaching English that fall at Palm Beach High. He has too many personal problems to attend to. Things like deciding: Who or what to mourn first? What emotional suffering will take precedence? My mother's lapse into Alzheimer's Disease and the murky netherworld of senility while she is still a relatively young woman? The loss of my childhood friend? The loss of my wife?

The discovery after thirty years that my father never committed suicide? That he probably really loved me and really wanted to be a successful writer so that he could live his dream; we all could have more fulfilling lives; he could play catch with his son in the back yard; go on fishing trips; poke holes in the brass tops of mason jar lids while watching his wide-eyed son catch fireflies at twilight? I now know what his laughter would actually sound like during moments like that; In my mind I can see his face in golden shadows as the sun sets over his shoulder to mark the end of another summer day.

One of the last dreams I had of my father takes place during such a summer twilight. Everything is a burnt orange and the sweat on his face glows brightly. There are just the two of us, and we are unaware of the presence of any other person on earth.

He is standing in silhouette, his back to the sun, flipping a shiny silver dollar up into the air. The only sounds are the pressing of his thumb against his forefinger and his thumbnail hitting the thick, heavy edge of the silver dollar.

The silver dollar is tinted gold as it flips end-over-end, as if in slow motion, disappearing into the blue-black sky near the top of its arc. The spinning slows as it runs out of momentum, as if it is sneaking up on its destiny. And as the heavy coin reaches the top of its arc, it stands still for one perfect moment frozen in eternity. At that precise split-second in time, when the silver dollar is neither rising nor falling, my father looks down directly into my eight-year old boy's face, as I stand before him in idol-worship. He smiles and says just one word.

"*Apocheir.*"

Then, the silver dollar, lulled from its one tiny fraction of a second of inertia, begins falling, gaining momentum, until it crashes heavily into the sandspurs at our feet.

He picks up the silver dollar, blows off the dirt, repeats each preliminary motion, and flips it up again and again and again, each time looking at me as it reaches the apex of its ascent and stops in a freeze-frame painted gold by the setting sun, before plummeting back to earth.

"Apocheir."

"Apocheir."

"Apocheir,"

he says each time; the last time, but a whisper.

I had no earlier recollection of ever hearing that word prior to my dream, and it wasn't until I came across it in a Physics textbook that I understood its meaning.

For a physicist, *apocheir* is the precise moment when an ascending object stops absolutely still for a pico-second, before descending.

For the father in my dream, who lived and thought in metaphors, he apparently enlarged upon the concept to mean a brief moment of perfection in the evolutionary cycle of one's life.

All things in nature experience *apocheir*; all life forms; all civilizations; all societies; all relationships.

Life cycles have an *apocheir*, some lasting just split seconds, others perhaps days, weeks, even years.

Perhaps our society, our civilization, has reached its *apocheir* in the last few decades of the 20th Century. Although twenty years is a long time, in the billion year scheme of things it's but a nano-second. And now, as we have arrived at the millennium, as it must be with all phenomenon, our society, having achieved *apocheir*, is poised to plunge into darkness and chaos with gathering speed.

Perhaps Bobby was thinking about his own life's *apocheir*, but was unable to articulate his thoughts with anything more profound than his last few words on earth, *"The Belle Glade Game."*

For, of course, that's what he had said to Joachim and me the moment before he had pulled the trigger on himself. Perhaps it was his way of pleading with us to forgive him and to please remember him in a happier time, during his few minutes of personal triumph.

As for me, my own personal *apocheir* was attained during the few hours on the magic mountain and in the long, hot, endless summer days that followed when I was falling in love with Nikki. In retrospect, although my days of perfect grace lasted but a few weeks, it was the proverbial wink of an eye. Since then, my plummet back to earth has been rapidly gaining momentum. There's no fighting this type of gravity.

I paid a University of Florida graduate student top dollar to work up in the Library stacks with Mrs. Todd's replacement. The student, yet another poor literature junky, leased her own Xerox machine and had it moved to that corner on the fourth floor in Gainesville where I had become lost during my entire college career, wandering, metaphorically speaking, around Florida's dusty back roads during the 1920's with my father. In my mind, in these walks that never took place, he always had his arm around my shoulders while we kicked up dust tracks on a shell rock road, and he told me of his travels. It was that image that had comforted me on my own walk.

The graduate student carefully photocopied and collated every piece of paper in my father's collection, torn snippets and all, and bound it all between carefully labeled report covers; compulsively neat and orderly. She even duplicated the tiny scrawled notes written in his faded pencil scratch on the backside of a Camel cigarette label, diner receipts, butcher paper, and hand-tinted postcards.

Twenty cartons of material arrived at my boat via UPS, and it was just a matter of selecting what I wanted to read during my long voyage. Should I re-read the works in the order that he wrote

ıould I read them in the chronological order in which
t? There is a difference, you know.

__ were still so many unanswered questions I need to find
answers to. Was my father just a burned-out writer, shaking down
a rich guy because he knew the ugly past of his wife? Had he run
out of ideas and used a story too close to the truth, as Victor had
written in his letter? Maybe he had just given up trying to be a
writer and, thinking he was destined to be third-rate anyway, in
a moment of desperation, simply tried to blackmail Fletcher for
a few bucks with some information he had acquired years before.
What difference did it all make now anyway? Over thirty years
had slipped away. A lifetime for some people.

It used to bother me that my father's books went largely
unread. But now I'm glad. Most readers would probably miss the
point of what his books are really all about. Beneath the text, far
within the sub-text, is his insatiable, abiding love for the Florida-
that-once-was. The storylines, the mysteries, the characters are all
just so much window dressing for what they were really about.

Except for a few months during his brief encounter with Hollywood, except for three years as a student of literature at Cornell University in upstate New York, he never left the state. He
couldn't bring himself to leave.

In his journal entry dated the week he decided to return to
Florida from Hollywood, he asked,

*"Can a piece of 35mm celluloid capture my emotions, capture
the beauty I see? Can the sun that strikes my eyes and changes
the physical composition of the chemicals in my brain–can that
same sun cause a more effective image on that film, than what
I composed with my #2 pencil and yellow legal pad and an old
Royal typewriter?"*

For me, this is not a rhetorical question. I know the answer and the answer is "no." Nothing but his raw words on paper can begin to match his love for the beauty and his emotions for his home country.

I decided to start at the beginning of his career and work my way through the journals and magazine articles first, then the short stories and then the novels, all the way to the end, just as I had discovered them before as an eighteen-year-old boy. Maybe by going through the same process, in the same way, I would be able to *re-discover* some of the emotions I had felt back then.

But this time the ending would be different.

In looking back over the chronology of the books my father wrote, it again occurred to me that the first three years of my life were fallow times for him as a writer.

Maybe my crying as an infant had prevented him from working. Maybe the demands of a baby in the house had distracted him. Was he just losing his powers with age?

But then again, maybe he had stopped being a writer to start being a father to a long-awaited child. Maybe he spent his evenings with me on his hands and tired old knees, limping around the carpet playing goochy-goochy; finding on the floor of the home he had built, a happiness equal to or greater than what he had once found treading Florida's back roads. Maybe being a writer took a back seat to being a father. People do change.

One of the last pictures I found of him provides the only hard physical evidence I have that I ever even met the man. It was one of the pictures Aunt Lucille uncovered. My father is seated on the front steps of the little bungalow he and my mother built on Mango Promenade. The shadow of my mother, holding a camera, can be seen encroaching in the bottom of the frame, cast by the late afternoon sun. He is holding me on his knee, in much the same way he held his Speed Graphic in the earlier picture. His cigarette is in place, the smile is there as he looks down at me.

Does his smile mean he loved me? It's enough evidence to

convince me.

I can never thank him for the legacy he gave me: my mother's love; my own love of my home and state; a love of words far beyond my own ability to use those precious words to describe that love. The fact that he was a hopeless dreamer gave me permission to dream, a privilege few people in this world are fortunate enough to have. Some people have the imagination, but no time. Some people have the time, but no imagination. Few have the permission. My father bestowed upon me all three.

And so I spend my life dreaming. *To sleep, perchance to dream* of him once again. To discover what secrets he had seen, but had no time to write about. To share some secret with me that will end my unhappiness. Maybe he would give me the advice, *"Pain and suffering are an unavoidable part of life. Misery is a choice."*

My life, a mystery to me for so long, was no longer a mystery. And this story? It was a love story. As I said at the beginning, three love stories.

"A love story between a man and a woman?" Easy; my mother and father, a love that began in joy and hesitancy and ended in lingering despair, dissipating in the morning mists.

"A love story between two people who hardly ever knew one another?" That's an easy one, too. My love for my father, forever unrequited, and yet, somehow now I'm starting to feel an occasional moment of peace with it.

"A love story that should never have happened?" Another easy one. What *kind* of person would do to someone what Nikki did to me? A person like Nikki, that's who. Didn't she love me just a little? Did my love for her hold any value whatsoever? Or had she built an immunity to anything involving emotions?

Still looking for a mystery? You might say this story is the "long-awaited-by-no-one," completed version of Elliott Phipps' unfinished mystery novel, PALM BEACH CONFIDENTIAL. For this is how the story really ends that my father started telling so long ago. Like most of his other novels, nobody lives happily ever after in this one, either.

Maybe that's why he didn't become famous. Everyone is looking for a happy ending.

How about this one? Nikki's estate took away the "hopeless" part of my description. I'll never have to worry about earning money. Victor also left me in his will. Now I have *two* trust funds assigned to me, twice as much money to salve my unhappiness. My mother and aunt will never have to worry about finances as long as they live. Nor will Consuelo and Hector. A call to the Senator got their house signed over to them.

"Blackmail," you say? Yes. I put them both on salaries with generous pension plans and medical care: benefits without deductibles. When they asked me what their duties were, I told them I would try to think of something while I was out at sea. In the meantime, just hang loose and cash the paychecks. Live a little. Buy central air-conditioning for the house. Hire a yardman. Go to Disney World. Visit long-lost relatives in Cuba. *"Live a little,"* that was their job description.

Perhaps the ultimate irony? When Senator Danforth Fletcher dies, the house on Alligator Island goes to me. I'm the only heir, since Nikki and Victor's grandfather willed it to them before he died. Will I be able to live in a house filled with ghosts? Climb the magic mountain with all that it represents? I haven't decided.

A guy I went to high school with is a yacht broker here in town. He took *The ARIEL* in trade, and with a little extra incentive I bought myself a *55 foot Frer.* It's nicer than the old one, and it doesn't have some of *The ARIEL'S* accoutrements: a hollow mast, ghosts of a failed marriage, the blood of my childhood friend, the splattered brains of the man who murdered my father. Too much excess emotional baggage for one little boat to carry.

My yacht broker friend will sell *The ARIEL* to an unsuspect-

ourist next season. They'll never know three people died on board.

As for me, I plan to spend the rest of the hurricane season sailing the Bermuda Triangle trying to live with myself. I have an overwhelming desire to be alone; to not speak to anyone for a long time. I need to find out how I can stop living my father's life and begin to live my own. Or if I really do want to live his life instead of my own. Could a child of mine live my life if I asked her to, like I have tried to live my father's?

In a few days, I'll set sail on an outgoing tide and following the freighters, let the Gulf Stream carry me northward like it did that first night with Adrianne, while twenty miles away, lightning bolts against pitch black skies light up my horizons.

I plan to spend a lot of time lying topside, smiling enigmatically over things that might have been. Dozing off from the sun and the monotonous rocking of the boat, forcing myself to dream.

I'll gaze to the skyline, imprisoned in my father's novels, serving a life sentence with no chance of parole, and resigned to the knowledge that there is no chance of ever escaping.

I'll remember happier times: my boyhood days camping on Peanut Island with the Secret Society of Coconuts, fishing with Joachim and Bobby on Burnt Bridge, surfing off the Pump House.

I'll remember my later boyhood nights, waltzing in dreamtime with my poor Nikki, on a mysterious Magic Mountain in Palm Beach, as ocean breezes roar through her brine-soaked blonde hair and she stares at me–through me– with her sky blue eyes; eyes that hid secrets I cannot even pretend to comprehend. I was so sure she was in love with me. Couldn't Victor have been wrong about *just that one thing?* And that first night with my beloved Nikki: my own private *apocheir*. But, by definition, an *apocheir* can only occur once in a lifetime.

As I drift aimlessly northward on my raft of self-discovery,

I'll try, somehow, to slow down that final sunset long enough to find relief from a torment that never seems to let up.

I'll keep my promise to my father to "be a good boy."

Maybe I'll bump into Huck and Jim.

AUTHOR'S AFTERWARD:

In the early 1980's I was a Field Producer for PM MAGAZINE on Miami's Channel 4. When Katrina Daniel, the program's co-host, and I discovered our mutual admiration for Florida mystery writer John D. MacDonald, we arranged for an interview with him through his literary agency.

MacDonald was living on Siesta Key, on Florida's West Coast. He agreed to do the interview, but for reasons of privacy, would not allow it to take place at his home.

Katrina and I offered to fly him in and interview him at the Bahia Mar Marina in Ft. Lauderdale, a suitable site, since that's where his most famous creation, Travis McGee, docked his fictitious houseboat, "The Busted Flush."

Just hours before his plane was to depart for Miami, MacDonald made the discovery that PM MAGAZINE was not a printed magazine, but a *television* magazine. I don't think he was a big fan of television. He wanted to renege on his promise, but luckily for us, he honored his commitment.

On December 3, 1982, we spent the day with MacDonald, his wife, and our friend, producer/cameraman Jim Duffy and television engineer, George Butch. MacDonald was at once gracious, self-effacing and surprised to find out television producers not only knew how to read, but were in fact, loyal fans of his works.

We conducted over two hours of on-camera interviews for our seven-minute feature story.

MacDonald talked about the creation of McGee and his character's eventual, inevitable death in the series; of Victor Nuñez' filmed adaptation of his 1959 novel, A FLASH OF GREEN, and his latest novel in progress, about a television evangelist, ONE MORE SUNDAY.

I am embarrassed to relate that all videotapes, with the exception of the finished story, were re-cycled by the station management. The bulk-erasure of an historical moment. Our interview may have been the only time he appeared before a television camera. The only other record of what MacDonald said that day is on several audio cassettes I used to transcribe his interview to hard copy.

During the course of my MacDonald quest, I had encountered some amazing statistics. When he was first discharged from the service after World War II, he was determined to earn his living as a writer. Instead of finding a job right away, he conducted an experiment to see if he had whatever it takes to be a novelist. He sat down at his typewriter and began to work. Over the next four months–120 days–he wrote the equivalent of *ten* novels. That's a novel every twelve days, ten times in a row, without stopping. I'm exhausted just thinking about it.

What kind of mind is capable of doing that?

By 1983, his seventy novels and story collections had sold over 90 million copies. Over twenty of those novels feature Travis McGee.

MacDonald died in 1986 in his seventieth year, taking his love of Florida and his unique point of view with him. His most recent brush with fame came with the Martin Scorcese remake of CAPE FEAR, based on MacDonald's novel, THE EXECUTIONERS.

As I write this, Leonardo DiCaprio has just turned down the film role of Travis McGee, and directors Oliver Stone and Paul Greengrass have both walked away from a new screenplay adaptation of MacDonald's THE DEEP BLUE GOODBYE, by Dennis Lehane.

Determined to find out if I could match MacDonald's early prolific output in my own crude way, I planned out the opening pages of this novel. On June 21, 1983, I sat down and wrote the first sixty pages of what was then entitled, *"DEATH UNDER SAIL."* Then, life got in the way. It would be another six years before I picked up my early efforts and wrote "page 61."

In between 1983-1989 I wrote six screenplays, and one, based on *STREET 8* by Coconut Grove author Douglas Fairbairn, a true visionary, was under option to a Hollywood producer. Two years in development and sixteen drafts later, I returned to Florida from California, determined never to deal with "those Hollywood people" again.

I sat down and wrote the next 200 pages of what I then called *"ensueño."*

Life got in the way again. For the next two and a half years, I wrote and directed dozens more television programs, documentaries and commercials. My travels took me literally all over the world. All over, that is, except to the work closest to my heart.

Another *ensueño* hiatus occurred when I spent several years developing a film project called *CONCHTOWN*, inspired by Charles C. Foster's landmark Florida non-fiction work, *CONCH-TOWN, USA.*, published by University Press of Florida. I conducted extensive video interviews with Foster and Stetson Kennedy. Foster based it on his travels as a W.P.A. photographer. Like the other 200 folklorists mentioned in my novel, Charles C. Foster traveled the state, gathering data and taking photographs. Most of the photographs and documents were destroyed when World War II started; burned for lack of funding for storage space. The negatives he used for his book survived because he took them home for safe storage. *CONCHTOWN, USA* tells of the Bahamian immigrant fisher-folk who settled what is now Riviera Beach in the early 1900's. The central character is a real person, a young woman writer who wrote for the Florida Writer's Project in 1939, Veronica Huss. It is a wonderful, true story for what it depicts about an earlier time in Florida as the Conchs struggled to survive the Depression.

After three years of agony trying to raise money for the *CONCHTOWN* film, I came to the conclusion that no one wants to make an inspiring film about a fact-based episode in the life of a young woman who wants to become a novelist, yet fails.

In my fictionalized account of a year in the life of the real person, Veronica Huss, I have her meet and fall in love with Elliott Phipps, the fictionalized writer I had previously invented for this novel. Their brief affair, if it had really happened, would have occurred two years before Elliott was to meet his wife in *ensueño*. In the world of my fiction, he was to become the father of Jimmy Phipps, the protagonist of *ensueño*.

Finally, in 2002, twenty years from the time I was first inspired by John D. MacDonald, I was able to finish the *first* draft of this book you now hold in your hands. Again, life got in the way. After 100 Florida PBS documentaries and writing and directing the feature film TURKLES, I finally finished subsequent drafts and this final version thirty-one years after I started it.

To all the forgotten mystery writers who have spent their days and nights hunched over a typewriter in order to purge themselves of whatever it is that forces its way out of their guts; to Charles C. Foster, Veronica Huss, Stetson Kennedy, Zora Neale Hurston, Alan Lomax, and the 200 other men and women of the WPA / Florida Writer's Project who roamed Florida in the 1930's to preserve the riches others have since been so successful in destroying; to my parents and grandparents who bestowed upon me the priceless gift of a love of reading; to my wife and twenty-one year-old son, Frank IV; and to John D. MacDonald; this book is humbly dedicated.

Frank Eberling, Jupiter, Florida
Summer, 2014

Also by Frank Eberling, soon to be published on Amazon.com, CreateSpace.com and other retail outlets for both e-books and Print-on-Demand.

NOVELS:

THE SHOOTER

SWEET CITY BLUES (aka GOODTIME CHARLIE'S GOT THE BLUES)

CONCHTOWN *(from screenplay)*

THE DEMAREST KILL

DRIFTWOOD BEACH HOTEL

SOUTH DIXIE HIGHWAY

FEATURE-LENGTH SCREENPLAYS:

TURKLES, *produced/distributed, 2014.*

BUT HE WASN'T WEARING A WEDDING RING WHEN I FIRST MET HIM

WALK INTO THE WOODS

DEADLY SURRENDER (aka SWEET SURRENDER), *produced/distributed, 1994.*

GOODTIME CHARLIE'S GOT THE BLUES (winner, first Florida Governor's Screenplay Competition, 1985).

STREET 8 / *CALLE OCHO* (from Douglas Fairbairn novel)

STARRY NOTIONS

SNOW BIRDS

CONCHTOWN

A.E.R.O. (Air Emergency Rescue Operations) (Television action/adventure series pilot)

FLIGHTS OF DESTINY (from Katherine Harris novel)

BOX OFFICE (with Michael Wells)

THE FIRST RESORT

HEART SPRINGS/HEART STRINGS

STAGEPLAYS:

WINTER STORM: Performed on PBCC stage, 1991

CONCHTOWN: Performed on FLORIDA STAGE, 1991

A LITTLE TRAVELIN' MUSIC

A THOUSAND STARS

B-7

BAKER'S DOZEN

BLINDED

DANCE CARD (aka LEFTOVERS)

DROWNING IN THE GENE POOL

FOXHOLE REFLECTIONS

GETTIN' ROWDY

HI, MY NAME IS BOB

INDIGO DAWN

JUST SHUT UP

LILY OF THE VALLEY

MYSTERY MEAT

NECESSARY

OFF-KEY

PEAVINE

POPCORN BREATH

SHEBA

THAT'S NOT WHAT SHE SAID

THE ROAD TAKEN

WE ACCEPT CREDIT CARDS

WE'LL CALL YOU

ZORA GETS FIRED

FEATURE LENGTH TELEVISION DOCUMENTARIES:

PUDDLE JUMPERS OF LANTANA: CAP's COASTAL PATROL 3
DURING WWII, 2006.
Sixty minutes, for Historical Society of Palm Beach County.

JONES HIGH SCHOOL:
The Lives of Students, 2005, sixty minutes, Florida PBS.

A CONVERSATION WITH SENATOR BOB GRAHAM, 2005,
sixty minutes, Florida PBS.

WHITE SPRINGS JUBILEE:
Florida Folk Festival, 2004-2005, ninety minutes, Florida PBS.

MIAMI BEACH WALKING TOUR:
With Hunter Reno and Historian, Paul George, Ph.D. Sixty minutes, for
WPBT-CHANNEL 2 Miami's Public Television Station.

SENATE RACE 2000: *Bill McCollum vs. Bill Nelson*
Sixty minutes for Florida PBS.

GOODNIGHT, SWEET PRINCE:
A Tribute to Watson B. Duncan, III
(starring Monte Markham and Burt Reynolds)
Winner: Ft. Lauderdale Film Festival/Best Broadcast Documentary, 1992.

ROCK-ED.ORG DOCUMENTARIES:

ROGER MCGUINN, founder of THE BYRDS

BILL PINKNEY, one of the founding members of the original DRIFTERS

MIKE PINERA, founder,lyricist of THE BLUES IMAGE ("Ride Captain,
Ride"), Guitarist, ALICE COOPER,IRON BUTTERFLY.

WAYNE COCHRAN, legendary "Blue-Eyed Soul" performer and inspiration
for the Dan Ackroyd, John Belushi act, THE BLUES BROTHERS.

PETER GURALNIK, author of critically acclaimed biographies
of ELVIS PRESLEY and SAM COOKE.

ABOUT THE AUTHOR

Frank Eberling is a native of New City, New York. He made his first film in 1962 at the age of fifteen.

Since then he has made 3,000 films and video programs, mostly for broadcast television. He has made 100 documentaries for Florida PBS Stations and 100 programs for The Armed Forces Radio and Television Service.

Along the way he has earned an EMMY®, a CINE GOLDEN EAGLE, five TELLYS, and numerous other awards for writing, directing, and cinematography. His two feature-length films, DEADLY SURRENDER and TURKLES, have been screened at film festivals throughout Florida, have won several awards, and have been distributed internationally.

His stage plays have been performed at THE FLORIDA STAGE, STAGE WEST at PALM BEACH STATE COLLEGE, and THE BURT REYNOLDS' INSTITUTE FOR FILM & THEATRE.

Originally a high school teacher, he has taught at PALM BEACH STATE COLLEGE for twenty years and THE BURT REYNOLDS' INSTITUTE FOR FILM & THEATRE for ten years.

He is currently developing a slate of micro-budget indie films to be made in Florida.

Check www.amazon.com, CreateSpace.com, and other retail outlets for Print-on-Demand and e-books for additional novels, screenplays, and non-fiction work by Frank Eberling.

To contact Frank, go to www.frankeberling.com.

KEEP READING
for the opening chapter of
Frank Eberling's
classsic Country & Western comic novel,

SWEET CITY BLUES

Available Summer, 2014

SWEET CITY BLUES

a novel for film
by
Frank Eberling

© 1982, 2004, 2013 by Frank Eberling

For
LARRY McMURTRY
IRVING RAVETCH
HARRIET FRANK, Jr.

and for
MARTIN RITT
and
PAUL NEWMAN

for bringing to life their brilliant film collaboration,
HUD

CHAPTER 1:

SWEET CITY, FLORIDA, 1979
"And it's not even Monday"

Coming out of the turn at Twenty-Mile Bend, Goodtime Charlie McGill pushed his foot to the floor and leaned back against the cracked leather upholstered seat.

It was a straight drive into Sweet City from the bridge, and if the suspension in his '59 Caddy convertible held up on him, he would make it to work just in time. Lately the shocks had felt like they had been filled with warm Jello, and he had to grip the steering wheel extra tight whenever he took a turn or went onto the shoulder to avoid an armadillo or a pothole, to keep the car from swerving over the center line and into the path of an eastbound semi. At this time of year there were a lot of the big trucks, it being the cane harvesting season, and he didn't want a load of somebody's sugar futures forcing him off the road into the canal.

If that happened, "Night Train" would *really* get angry, because then, instead of being *almost* late for his on-air shift for the third time in a week, he'd be a "no-show," and Night Train's workday would be extended four more hours; keeping the housewives company via their A.M. radios after they sent their kids off to school and sat, drinking their third cup of coffee, while trying

ien, if ever, to take the rollers down out of their hair
e their bathrobes for a housedress, at least.

..., ...ght Train would definitely be pissed, and not only
would Charlie be dead from drowning in the canal, but he would
also get fired for being "almost late" again; which at this point in
time would be worse than being dead.

So he held on to the wheel for dear life and kept his bloodshot
and mirror-shaded eyeballs on the road in front of him, only glancing once into the rearview to see the sun make its first appearance
over West Palm Beach, thirty miles behind him.

The cardboard carton of Coca-Cola on the seat next to him
was already getting warm as he reached over without looking and
grabbed a bottle. In one motion, he grabbed his third tall-boy of
the day, popped its top on the dashboard-installed bottle opener,
took three long quick pulls, and heaved the empty bottle over his
shoulder where it caromed twice off the rear seat and landed with
a tinkling sound against the growing pile of other bottles on the
floor.

He turned up the volume on the radio, drowning out the first
word or two of Night Train's voice with his own liquid belch that
almost landed on the front of his cowboy shirt.

"And in just a few moments the old Night Train is going to be
saying *'Hasta Mañana'* for another day to make room for Goodtime Charlie McGill to come on in and help you wake up and get
the kids and husband off for the day."

Shit, Charlie thought, *if* I make it on time. He swerved out
into the passing lane to pass a blue migrant-filled school bus and
dodged back in front of it just in time to miss scraping his tail light
off on the bus' front fender. "The *time*, Night Train, the *time*,"
Charlie said aloud as the commercial ended and Night Train came
back on the air.

"And right now it's eighteen minutes before the hour, so if
you have to get up at six o'clock like I know a lot of you out there
do, you have time to roll over one more time and listen to a little

more good country music before you get up and get ready to face the world."

Eighteen minutes, Charlie thought, looking at his surroundings. On either side of the road a heavy low-lying mist was beginning to dissipate on the horizons, and in the foregrounds the sugar cane fields stretched as far as the eye could see before the green stalks disappeared into the fog. And there, just ahead, was Clifton, cutting cane right down off the edge of the highway with two dozen other cutters. Charlie beeped his horn, and the Jamaican lifted his broad-bladed machete. Showing off his big white teeth, Clifton waved to him. "Hey Mon."

Another fifteen miles, Charlie thought. No sweat if I don't run into any heavy traffic or deputies. He shifted his foot around in his gila-hide boot and put more pressure on the gas pedal. Behind him in the east the sun was rising quickly, getting itself ready to scorch the pool-table-flat-muck-farmlands another long November day.

A half mile ahead a small frame house sat down the embankment on the far side of a wooden bridge that crossed the canal. On the front porch stood a slim, attractive woman, wearing an apron and double-checking the contents of a brown paper lunch bag of the boy who stood in front of her. She handed the bag to the boy and knelt down to straighten his collar.

Out on the highway, a yellow school bus slowed and put on its flashers and a small "stop" sign swung out from near the driver's window.

Shit, Lulu, don't do this to me, Charlie thought, looking down at the mom as he lifted his foot off the gas and started pumping the brakes of the Caddy. It felt like he was trying to stomp all the water out of a wet sponge. For a split second he thought about running the stop sign on the bus. No one was getting off, and Lulu's kid was too far away from the road. *No one will get hurt*, he thought. But then he saw the front end of the deputy's patrol car squeaking out from behind the rear end of the bus and he just knew Boggs would be waiting for him to make such a stupid move.

Shit, Lulu, you're going to see the kid again at three o'clock, he thought as the woman ruffled her son's hair and hugged him one more time. Kids had been sent off to an entire summer-full of overnight camp with less of a good-bye than that.

He was out of the car and down the embankment in a flash, breathing heavily before he even got close to the porch. "Running late, Lulu" he smiled to the woman, jerking her son's hand out of her grasp, spinning him around and reaching over his own shoulder to plant a kiss on the face of the surprised woman. "Talk to you later."

The kid's feet were churning up the dust, trying to keep up with Charlie's quick strides as he was dragged across the wooden bridge, up the hill and across the highway. The bus door swung open, and Charlie heaved the boy up the stairs by the belt loops.

He was burning rubber before the kid had a seat and before the stop sign swung back with a slap against the side of the bus. As the hood of the big pink Caddy ran even with the deputy's open window, Charlie leaned on the horn and flashed Boggs a smile. Maybe next time Boggs, he thought to himself, as he settled in and popped another Coca-Cola for the final stretch into Sweet City. Somewhere deep within, the sugar and caffeine mixture was beginning to do its job. Charlie felt a surge bubbling from inside.

Ahead he could see the stacks of two sugar mills punctuating the horizon, emerging from the mist as sunlight warmed the black earth. He took off his hat and stuck his head out the window, inhaling deeply the moist muck musk. And for a moment, however brief, he forgot his troubles.

I can't stand any more of this. Either Caroline's husband is going to have to stop going on the road selling Kerby's, or she's gonna have to visit me out here in Sweet City, he thought to himself.

In the eight months since he had met her, Caroline's husband,

Harlan, had been out pushing vacuum cleaners and attending motivational lectures all over the state for long stretches at a time. His billing as top salesman in a twenty-three county area kept Harlan on the road a lot, en-route, no doubt, to some vacuum cleaner sales coup of the century. That star-studded billing thrust Charlie into his bed with his wife Caroline as soon as Harlan's car, packed with demo-models, left the city limits of West Palm Beach. The fact that Harlan was out hustling sucking devices all over creation when he had one of the very best models Charlie had ever met sitting at home by the pool every day knocking off cartons of Russell Stover chocolate turtles, was an irony that Charlie had not overlooked.

But the fifty mile drive from Sweet City to West Palm Beach every night, and then back again to Sweet City for his six a.m. radio shift was beginning to take its toll, not only on his car and his friendship with Night Train, but on Charlie, as well. Sleeping, correction, being in a strange bed every night, and then getting up at four-thirty to go to work had put small, black satchel-like protuberances under Charlie's eyes that were bad for his public image. Not to mention the fact that he was starting to have to wear his underwear inside-out since he hadn't had time to visit the laundro-mat in almost three weeks. The last time Harlan had returned from an extended sales trip, providing Charlie with a reprieve from Caroline, Charlie had filled every available washing machine at the same time at the Dixie-Wash by the time he finally had a chance to do his laundry. The last few days before that, he had spent without socks.

He felt the weariness in every muscle, and he finally understood what they meant by "bone tired." *It's time to get my shit together,* he kept telling himself. *But, first I have to get to work on time.*

He glanced down at his watch, but then remembered the battery was dead. "The time, Night Train, the time," he said aloud. He plucked off his mirror shades and rubbed his swollen eyes again. *I can't go on like this,* he thought.

"Six minutes before six o'clock. Six minutes before Goodtime Charlie McGill comes along to give you all the latest music and chatter to start off your day on what looks to be another beautiful Sweet City morning. Six minutes before six." Charlie understood that Night Train was talking directly to him over the public airwaves.

And, then, like every other day for the past nine years, Night Train played the closing song of his show as a reminder for the audience to stick around for Charlie's program. A few plucks of the pedal-steel guitar before the plaintiff voice of Danny O'Keefe started it off.

(*)Author's note: I'd love to quote Danny Okeefe's lyrics here, but copyright laws prohibit me from doing that. Please go to YOUTUBE and listen to GOODTIME CHARLIE'S GOT THE BLUES by Danny O'Keefe. Let them worry about the copyright issues.

Over Danny's whistle that ended the song Night Train finished his sign-off.

"And our own Goodtime Charlie will be along in just another minute, right after the latest news and weather, so stay tuned, and we'll be back again tonight at midnight for another night of music with yours truly, Night Train, and The All Night, Train Ride Show. Until then, have a nice day."

The outskirts of town were fast approaching as Night Train punched a commercial for Hardy Grain and Feed, and Charlie slowed down. *Shit, it's gonna be tight.* First, thirty seconds for a commercial, and then two minutes of headlines and weather, and then there would be another thirty seconds for a commercial and Charlie would have to be on the job. He tried to remember where he was on the highway the first time he was as late as he was now. It was going to be very tight.

"WELCOME TO SWEET CITY, WINTER VEGETABLE & SUGAR CANE CAPITAL OF THE WORLD: The Sweetest Little Town in Florida," read the sign that Charlie whizzed past as Night Train's friendly voice on the radio lowered an octave and became serious while he read the Morning News and Weather.

Just beyond the sign, the big Caddy slowed, and Charlie turned through a gap in the guard rail and drove across the gravel driveway of the station. The building was a converted white clap-board house with a big picture window in the living room for the jock to sit in front of while on the air. Behind the building was a rusted tower, 140 feet tall, with "W-G-A-H COUNTRY RADIO" stretching down its length in white, plywood letters.

Charlie screeched to a halt and his front tires bounced off the white painted telephone pole that lay on its side to mark the edge of the shell-rock parking lot. He hesitated for a second to let the dust catch up to him and pass the car before he opened the door and hauled his ass inside, just as Night Train ended the news and punched up the last spot. As the audio cart started, he jumped out of his seat and ran out of the booth as Charlie came bursting through the door.

"Goddammit Charlie, this is the third time in a week. This last-minute-arrival-shit is gonna have to stop." Night Train followed him around the reception area while Charlie peeled off his shirt, grabbed another from a collection heaped on the floor of the front closet, picked up the station programming print-out from Maria's desk, and poured himself a cup of Mr. Coffee.

"Sorry, Phil. I got stuck in traffic again. You know how slow those sugar-semis move when they're coming back from the Port."

"Well, I don't know how much longer my nerves can take it, you coming in just before air-time like you've been doing. I never know when, or even *if* you're gonna make it."

"I'll always make it, Phil, you know that," Charlie said, that faraway look in his eye that he got whenever his professionalism was put into question. Charlie stepped into the booth, and dumped the ashtray full of cigarette butts and crumpled coffee cups into the trash bucket next to his console. He reached under the turntable cabinet and pulled a warm Coke from a carton. He popped the top on the counter's edge, gargled with a swig, and then spit it out into the bucket. Slowly, he craned his neck, rotating his head on every axis, and as the commercial ended, not even a hint of his current mood could be detected.

He opened his microphone. "And a good morning to all you wonderful Sweet City folks. Well, it looks like we've got another nice winter day here in town. I'm Goodtime Charlie McGill, and we're here to keep you company until ten o'clock this morning right here on Sweet City Country Radio, W-G-A-H."

As he spoke into the mike suspended from the gooseneck device in front of the console, he reached up and pulled an audio cartridge from the rack in front of him, glancing down at the title. "And now let's get this morning started with a little music from nearby Pahokee's own favorite native son, Mel Tillis."

He poked the start button on the cartridge machine, potted down the microphone, and collapsed into the swivel chair. Night Train opened his fifth pack of Camels for the day and lit a new one off an old one. "You ought to seriously reconsider your lifestyle, old buddy. Otherwise I might suffer from a nervous breakdown or fatigue before my time, just worrying about you."

Charlie ignored him, and sat with his head in his hands only long enough to hear the first verse of Mel's new song. Then, in one slow sweeping motion he pushed Night Train's paperwork onto the floor and spread his own program log in front of him. It was all there: anecdotes, jokes, promotions, commercials, playlist, and school lunch menus ("It looks like mystery meat and powdered potatoes again today, kids. And what's this, no Jello? Rice pudding for dessert? I guess nobody liked yesterday's Chinese menu.") All Charlie had to do was rip-and-read wire-copy for the headlines, check the weather updates when necessary, and pour on the charm between the records.

How many songs in a row can I play without talking and still get away with it, he wondered? Maybe this would be the time to introduce some new album sides instead of just playing one song at a time and being personable between each song. Better not, he thought. Frank would get mad at him for jacking around with his precious programming concept which was designed to squeeze in as many commercials as possible without alienating too much of the audience.

Night Train broke his concentration. "And don't fall asleep too soon after you get off the air, because there's a big staff meeting at ten-thirty, and everyone is required to attend."

Charlie looked up at him through swollen eyes. "Why, what's so important?"

"Beats me. Frank just told Maria to spread the word to everyone here and to call everyone who works on the late shift to come in early." This was no mean feat, since Maria spoke only about four words of English: "Hello," "Please Hold, and "Goodbye." She spent her days answering the phone and then putting the caller on hold while she tracked down anyone available to handle the call in discernible English. That and practicing her typing. At last estimate she had just broken into the early teens in the words-per-minute department, and rumor had it that Frank was going to double her salary as soon as she broke into the low twenties.

Charlie remained immobilized until Mel was finished singing, and then slid a commercial into the slot for 'Hiway 27 Unlimited, Used Cars and Trucks City', providing himself with another thirty seconds to get himself psyched-up for the rest of the show.

Finally he spoke. "Okay Phil, I'll be there. Something real important, no doubt, like delinquent coffee dues. By the way, are there any of those stale doughnuts left over from yesterday?"

SWEET CITY BLUES
by Frank Eberling

AUTHOR'S NOTE:

I wanted the title of this novel to be, GOODTIME CHAR-LIE'S GOT THE BLUES.

Although the story content was not in any way inspired by Danny O'Keefe's wonderful, classic song, I felt the after writing the novel that the tone of the song happened to match the bitter-sweet tone of the story.

However, when I checked with Warner/Chappell about licensing the name they wanted huge amounts of money. So I thought I'd better change the name back to the working title, SWEET CITY BLUES.

If the novel is ever made into a film, I hope they use O'Keefe's song and the title. Maybe he'll get a little dough out of the deal.

The name of the town in the book was originally GLADES, since it takes place in Western Palm Beach County, but I didn't want it to be confused with the recent cable television series of that name.

The town of Sweet City, Florida, exists only in the imagination of the author, however, Palm Beach County, the other towns mentioned, and the State of Florida are believed to actually exist.

Although specific references to recording artists and movie stars refer to real people, all other characters and events in this novel are imaginary, and any resemblance to events or to any other persons, living or dead, is purely coincidental.

Most of the events in this work of fiction take place in the 1970's.

The incidents, attitudes, and situations depicted reflect those of that more irresponsible, carefree, bygone era.

You know, when sex was good, clean fun.

49467541R00235

Made in the USA
Lexington, KY
06 February 2016